Praise for *Night* [barcode: D0388097]

"Authentic and fast-paced, *Night Terrors* is a thrilling plunge into the mind of an obsessed killer. Palumbo draws on his vast knowledge as a licensed psychotherapist to bring his characters into focus, and his success as a Hollywood screen-writer to bring his story to a satisfying, climactic end. This is something you don't want to miss!"
—Stephen Jay Schwartz
LA Times bestselling author of *Boulevard* and *Beat*

"In *Night Terrors*, Dennis Palumbo takes a brilliant premise and turns it into the kind of thriller most of us wish we could write. Thrills, surprises, and memorable characters. A terrific book."
—Timothy Hallinan, Edgar-nominated author
of the Poke Rafferty and Junior Bender thrillers

"*Night Terrors* sends forensic psychologist Daniel Rinaldi on another thrilling, risky ride through the Pittsburgh area's crazies and-not-so-crazies. A brilliant, gripping emotional journey, full of the great characters and satisfying, unexpected turns we've come to expect from author/shrink Dennis Palumbo."
—Thomas B. Sawyer, author of the bestselling thrillers
The Sixteenth Man and *No Place To Run*

"Dennis Palumbo is a master of character, psychology, and setting; and *Night Terrors* showcases these skills to great effect. Highly recommended!"
—John Lescroart, *NYT* best-selling author of *The Ophelia Cut*

"Another terrific ride from Dennis Palumbo's Daniel Rinaldi series. A page-turner of the first order. I'm looking forward to the next one."
—Bobby Moresco, Oscar-winning writer/producer
of *Crash* and *Million Dollar Baby*

Night Terrors

Books by Dennis Palumbo

The Daniel Rinaldi Mysteries
Mirror Image
Fever Dream
Night Terrors

Other Fiction
From Crime to Crime
(Short Story Collection)
City Wars

Nonfiction
Writing From the Inside Out

Night Terrors

A Daniel Rinaldi Mystery

Dennis Palumbo

Poisoned Pen Press

Poisoned Pen Press
6962 E. First Ave., Ste. 103
Scottsdale, AZ 85251
www.poisonedpenpress.com
info@poisonedpenpress.com

Printed in the United States of America

Once again, for Lynne and Daniel

Acknowledgments

The author thanks the following people for their continued help and support:

Ken Atchity, friend and literary manager;

Annette Rogers, my editor at Poisoned Pen Press and an ongoing source of guidance, perspective, and good humor;

Robert Rosenwald and Barbara Peters, founders of Poisoned Pen Press, for both their editorial insights and zeal in promoting mysteries;

Jessica Tribble, publisher extraordinaire, who is defined in Webster's Dictionary under "Indispensable";

Nan Beams, Elizabeth Weld, and Suzan Baroni, also at Poisoned Pen, for their enthusiasm and unswerving attention to detail;

And, as always, my long-suffering friends and colleagues, too numerous to mention, but with special appreciation to Hoyt Hilsman, Bobby Moresco, Norm Stephens, Richard Stayton, Rick Setlowe, Bob Masello, Garry Shandling, Jim Denova, Michael Harbadin, Claudia Sloan, Dave Congalton, Charlotte Alexander, Mark Evanier, Bob Corn-Revere, Lolita Sapriel, Mark Baker, Mark Schorr, Bill Shick, Thomas B. Sawyer, Fred Golan, Dick Lochte, Al Abramson, Rich Simon, Bill O'Hanlon, Sandy Tolan, Stephen Jay Schwartz, and Dr. Robert Stolorow.

I came into the Unknown, beyond all science.

—St. John of the Cross

Chapter One

The killer and I sat together in the back seat of the late-model Range Rover, our shoulders just touching.

Wesley Currim, early twenties, in jeans and a faded "Beer Me" sweatshirt, shifted uneasily next to me, rubbing his cuffed hands between his knees. His face, profiled in the half-light glazing the snow-encrusted windows, was narrow, acne-pitted. Hard-planed as though etched with acid. His bony frame—so slender he seemed swallowed up by the threadbare County parka—practically vibrated with banked anger.

I turned away from him to stare out my own side window, out at the grey blur of blowing snow beating sideways against the car, as though propelled by a rage of its own. Beyond that relentless swirl of dirty white flakes clinging wetly to the window glass, stretched the darkly-forested, isolated landscape of rural West Virgina. Far from the interstate and highways, from the lights of the beleaguered small towns and gasping, dying farms.

I shivered in my own fleece-lined parka and gloves. My hurried summons down here from Pittsburgh—the desperate phone call from Detective Chief Avery Block, the nerve-twisting drive through a rattling storm to Wheeling PD headquarters, then over just-plowed county roads to the main lock-up to meet Wes Currim himself—all this urgent, headlong momentum had left me little time to think about what it was I'd actually agreed to. And why.

I glanced then at the two officers in the front seat. Or, to be more precise, at the backs of their heads. Though the temperature was just above freezing outside, the dashboard heater was pumping waves of thick, airless heat into the cramped forward area, and both men were sweating. Dark drops beaded the clean lines of their regulation haircuts along the backs of their necks.

The older of the two, in the passenger seat, was Chief Avery Block, far past middle-aged, balding, thick-waisted. Furiously chewing his ever-present nicotine gum. When he spoke, which was rarely, it was more like a grunt. The labored effort of a beaten, disillusioned small town cop for whom things hadn't exactly worked out as planned. And who no longer cared who knew it.

In the driver's seat sat Detective Sergeant Harve Randall, barely thirty, lean and wiry, gloved hands tapping anxiously on the wheel as he peered through the storm-blurred windshield. Dark sleeves of snow were pushed to the side by noisy wipers, only to be replaced by fresh clumps.

"This your first visit to West Virginia, Doc?"

Randall asked me this without taking his gaze from the windshield. His boss, with an obvious cough, turned to look at him through weary, rheumy eyes. Chewing slower now.

"Yes it is, Sergeant." I was their guest, so I went with polite. "Too bad about the storm, though. Looks like nice, wide-open country. Wish I could see more of it."

I watched the back of his head bob.

"Almost Heaven. Like the song says."

Chief Block pulled the exhausted wad of gum from his teeth, pinched it between gloved fingers. Stuck it up on the window visor, with its gooey brethren.

"You just keep your eyes peeled for that turnoff, Sergeant. Okay?"

Another head bob. "Yes, sir."

It was then that Wes Currim spoke. For the first time since we'd all climbed into the Range Rover back in Wheeling, shoulders hunched against the punishing storm, and then to head south through the back woods.

For the first time in an hour.

"Turnoff should be just ahead, up on your right there, Harve."

I could see Randall's hands tighten on the wheel.

"That's *Sergeant Randall* to you, douche bag."

Currim gave a low, dark chuckle. As if in response to some private joke in his mind.

I looked over at him again, and he swiveled his head to meet my gaze. A slow, deliberate movement. Like a clockwork person in a dream.

Yet his eyes were moist, bright, agitated. As though straining to convey either assured bemusement or callous disregard. A ploy betrayed by his thin, twitching fingers.

Of course, I knew this could just be my own mind, telling stories. A product of the numbing cold, the snow, the wind-whipped moonscape outside. Of the strange, sad journey we were on.

I'd no sooner had that thought than the Range Rover tipped and tilted over a hard snow rut, as Sgt. Randall wheeled to the right onto a barely-visible back road.

The vehicle's engine roared in protest, and, as we lumbered down the winding road, crisscrossed with deep furrows, whatever remained of the shocks noisily gave up the ghost.

Randall struggled to maintain control of the wheel.

"Just metal on metal under us now, Chief. And that transmission's about to go, too."

"You just get us there, Harve. In one fuckin' piece, if you don't mind." Chief Block pushed another stick of nicotine gum into his jowled, reddened cheeks.

Wes Currim stirred again, straining to look past the chief's shoulder at the road up ahead. All I could see when I did the same was more goddam snow. Flying out of the gloom to be illuminated for a fleeting moment by the car's powerful headlights, only to disappear again.

"Almost there, gentlemen." Currim grinned with serene satisfaction. "End o' the road."

"For *you* it is, Currim." Chief Block turned then, eyes black as the coal they pull from the unforgiving earth all around us. "No matter what, it's the end of the road for *your* sorry ass."

Currim shrugged. "Don't see why you gotta be so nasty all the time, Chief. I swear, you oughtta give up on that gum and go back to the smokes."

Block just stared at him, chewing deliberately, and said not a word. Then he turned and faced front again.

With another shrug, Wes leaned back in his seat.

"Nice havin' *you* along, though, Doc. Elevates the company, if ya know what I mean."

"It's not like I had any choice."

My voice was flat. I could feel the fatigue, the strain of the past hours. The loss of a full night's sleep.

"Price o' fame, Doctor Rinaldi. You oughtta be used to it by now."

Sergeant Randall spoke up. "You keep your mouth shut, Wes, or I'll shut it for you. Now how much farther, you worthless piece o' shit?"

"Figure another mile or so, Harve." Currim clucked his tongue. "Though I ain't exactly thrilled with the treatment I'm gettin' here from the department. Especially since I'm cooperatin' an' all." Another glance at me. "Ain't I, Doc?"

I didn't answer. I knew what my job was at the moment: shut up and let Wesley be Wesley, whatever the hell that was. No pressing him about the crime, no attempts at connection or clinical intimacy to ferret out the gruesome details.

There was no need. He was going to tell us. *Show* us. As long as we went along with his little game.

Not twenty-four hours before, in a small interrogation room at police headquarters in Wheeling, Wes Currim had confessed—after declining legal counsel—to the murder of Edward Meachem, a businessman whose family had reported him missing the week before.

Following the confession, Currim asked to meet with the city's interim district attorney. He told her he'd be willing to take the police to where Meachem's body was.

"As a gesture to his family," Wes had reportedly said, "so they can have that...dammit, whatja call it?...that *closure* thing."

But Currim had one condition, one request that had to be honored before he'd show the authorities where he'd left the body.

"I want that shrink that was on the news last year to come with me. Works with the Pittsburgh cops. I need him to help keep me from wiggin' out, from the shock or whatever."

Apparently, the DA knew who he was talking about.

"You mean Daniel Rinaldi? The psychologist?"

"Yeah, that's him. I want Rinaldi to come with me when I show you where I left the poor bastard. And you better get him to do it. Or else I don't show you shit."

Chapter Two

An hour before Chief Block called me, before I'd ever even heard of Wes Currim, I was in my therapy office on Forbes Avenue in Oakland, overlooking the Pitt campus. My last patient gone for the day, I was standing at my window, peering down through the gloom of early evening. Through the glistening white veil of the latest storm.

New snow lay thick as frosting over the parked cars, the roofs of restaurants, the bare-branched tops of trees. It piled in deep ruts, in exhaust-blackened furrows carved by the tires of salt-pitted trucks and delivery vans. By buses full of seniors and students and civil servants. By taxis gamely heading for the airport, and car-pooling SUVs carrying weary commuters home from work.

And as swiftly and relentlessly as the snow fell, that's how slowly and torturously the traffic moved.

Watching from my window five floors above, I felt the residual emotions from my last patient's difficult session ease out of my body, to be replaced by a sobering image of myself in my reconditioned '65 Mustang, joining the slow-moving parade of traffic below. Making the long crawl across the Fort Pitt Bridge, and then up the recently-plowed roads to Mt. Washington. And home.

I sat down at my marble-topped desk. What I needed was a drink. Jack Daniels, preferably. Instead, what I had in my bottom desk drawer was two plastic bottles of Arrowhead water, a jar of instant coffee, a Snickers bar, and some aspirin.

Despite myself, I couldn't get that last session out of my mind. The patient was a young woman, Sophie Teasdale, a sophomore at Carlow College who'd been viciously raped behind a bar on the newly-gentrified South Side.

The assault had happened six months ago, but she'd only recently had the courage to report it to the police. An arrest was made, a court date for the perpetrator was on the books. After which, the wheels of law enforcement turned, the old gears clicked, and the machinery of justice moved on to the next crime, the next victim.

Except this particular victim was still traumatized by her brutal experience, showing the classic symptoms of post-traumatic stress disorder. Anxiety, depression, and frequent recurrent nightmares, as well as a heightened sensitivity to the possibility of future dangers.

So, as is part of my arrangement with the Pittsburgh Police, Angela Villanova, their chief community liaison officer, sent the young woman to me.

People like Sophie Teasdale are my specialty. I'm a clinical psychologist, specializing in treating the victims of violent crime. People who may have survived physically, but whose psyches were so damaged as a result of their horrific experience that they needed help.

Help coping with their fears, nightmares, profound feelings of powerlessness; even, for some, their shame, the belief that they perhaps deserved what happened to them. Or that they could've done something to prevent it.

Now, sitting at my desk, making some quick notes about Sophie's case, I couldn't help but think about my own experience with life-changing trauma. And about how so many of the symptoms that Sophie, and others like her, suffered, were those with which I was intimately familiar myself.

Especially tonight. January 6th. The Feast of the Epiphany. Like many another lapsed Catholic, though I'd fallen away from the faith and no longer attended Mass, the dates of the Holy Days are indelibly etched in my mind.

Historically, the Feast of the Epiphany marked the final day of the Christmas celebration, though most stores and homes had long since taken down the holiday lights and ornaments, the yuletide trees and the mistletoe.

January 6th. The same date, many years ago, when my wife Barbara and I had come out of a restaurant down at the Point, only to be mugged by some armed thug in a hoodie.

I'd been an amateur boxer in my youth—Golden Gloves, Pan Am games—so when the thief started to manhandle my wife, I tried to intercede. The gun, a 9 mm Glock, went off. Three quick shots.

The one that entered my skull kept me in the hospital for months. The two that entered Barbara's heart killed her.

For two long years after that, I felt like *my* life was over, too. Then, with help, I managed to move through the layers of remorse and shame—the paralysis of survivor guilt—to come out on the other side with a renewed sense of purpose. Something I'd rarely known before, having been wrapped up solely in my career, my ambition, my own needs and wants.

This coincided with the arrest and conviction of a notorious serial killer named Troy David Dowd. Dubbed "the Handyman" by the media, he'd killed and dismembered twelve people with pliers, screwdrivers, and other tools before his eventual capture.

One of his two surviving victims, a middle-aged single mother, had been so traumatized by her ordeal that the police were concerned about her welfare. Particularly Angie Villanova, who, in addition to her position in the department, was a distant cousin of mine. It was she who referred the woman to me, and it was this experience that led to my signing on as a consultant to the Pittsburgh Police.

I sat back in my swivel chair, bracing myself with a knee against the edge of the desk. I didn't have to turn my head to to hear—even feel—the push of the wind against the window glass. The storm was increasing in intensity, as though gathering strength from the approaching darkness of night.

What, I wondered, should I do? Go down to the parking garage, pull out onto the snow-draped streets, and fight my way through the log-jam of cars for home?

There was every good reason not to. The weather, the traffic, the potentially treacherous climb up the steep winding road to Grandview Avenue, my street.

But there was also one very good reason to make the trip: which was so that I could do what I always did on the night of January 6th. Go home, turn off all the lights, put on Gerry Mulligan's recording of "The Lonely Night"—a song he wrote with his wife, the actress Judy Holliday, shortly before her death—and then, quietly and without any fuss, get sincerely drunk. My annual ritual. For Barbara.

Though with every passing year, it was a ritual that seemed more and more pro forma. Mere habit. Having less to do with the person Barbara was, and more to do with some image of myself as loyal. Steadfast in my memory of her loss. The grieving widower.

I pushed away from my desk and stood. Stretched. Feeling suddenly exposed. Discovered.

After all, it wasn't as though I hadn't been involved with women since Barbara's death. Obsessively involved, in one particular case.

And even as I contemplated the journey home to honor Barbara's memory with booze and self-pity, wasn't I now attracted to another woman? Someone with whom I'd worked closely on a police investigation last summer?

These conflicting thoughts were still swirling around in my mind when the office phone rang, jolting me out of my reverie. It was a Detective Chief Avery Block, phoning from West Virginia, who said that he'd gotten my number from the Pittsburgh Police Department.

And that his call was urgent.

Chapter Three

The house loomed up out of the wash of the storm like a ship emerging from a North Atlantic fog.

"That's it," Wes Currim said, gesturing with both cuffed hands toward the isolated structure. "Just pull up on the lawn there, Harve. Won't have so far to walk."

Randall growled under his breath, but didn't reply.

Under Chief Block's baleful gaze, the sergeant manuevered the Range Rover across the uneven, snow-layered yard. I heard the tire chains crunch and pop as they struggled for purchase on the slick new snow.

"Stop right here, Harve," Block said, the nose of our vehicle about a dozen feet from the sagging, mesh-enclosed porch. Randall cut the engine, but left the headlights on.

The house was low, wood-framed, its ranch-style contours blurred by the hurtling snow. Windows glistened dully with frost. Roof gutters sagged under the weight of packed old snow and the accumulation of fresh.

Then, unsure that I was seeing correctly, I leaned up and squinted through the windshield. Given the purpose of our journey, what I saw was as tragic as it was surreal.

The house was strung along its eaves and around its front windows with multi-colored Christmas lights, twinkling forlornly in the blur of the storm. There was even a lopsided snowman on the front lawn, three lumpy balls of dirty rolled snow, with sticks for arms and a wind-battered hat jammed on top.

Randall leaned forward in his seat as well, using the palm of his gloved hand to clear fog from the windshield.

"Are those Christmas lights? Damn!"

Beside me, Currim ducked his head between his thin shoulders and giggled.

"Okay, then." Block sniffed once, which Randall somehow interpreted as his cue to get out from behind the wheel. Which he did, coming around to open the rear door for Currim.

A blast of frigid air hit me square in the face as that door opened. Grunting from the effort, Currim pulled himself out into the storm, helped to his feet by Randall's firm hand on his elbow.

I got out on my side, meeting Chief Block at the front of the Range Rover. Within moments, I could feel the cold wetness of the cascading snow on my coat. The bite of the wind on my cheeks.

Randall and Currim joined us, indistinct figures trudging up into the light of the twin highbeams.

I nodded at the house. "This your place?"

"Nah," Currim said. "Belonged to my uncle, died a couple years back. Me an' my brothers use it all the time, though. For huntin', fishin' in the Shenandoah."

"We don't give a shit 'bout your life story, asshole." Randall's shoulders hunched as he shoved his gloved hands in his coat pockets. "Right, Chief?"

Block didn't answer, just stepped a few feet away, boots crunching on the snow. Shivering, our breath coming in crystallized clouds, the three of us stood looking at him. Waiting.

Finally, Block turned to Currim.

"You do all this? The lights and everything?"

"It's Christmas, Chief. I always decorate the place for the holidays. In case my brothers and their wives wanna come up. Bring the kids."

"Any o' the family come up here this year?"

Currim shook his head sadly. "Nah. Had the place to myself. No reason not to make it look nice, though. Right?"

Randall tugged on Currim's elbow again. Hard.

"Enough o' this shit. Where'd you bury Meachem? Out back somewheres?"

Currim pulled himself from the sergeant's grasp. "In *this* weather? You got any idea how hard the ground is, Harve? Hell, I'd break my back tryin' to put shovel to earth this time o' year."

I stepped between Randall and Currim.

"Look, Wes, you brought us all this way. You said you wanted to give Meachem's family the opportunity to bring him home. Give him a proper burial."

"And I meant it."

Chief Block raised his head, like a bull roused from a deep slumber. His small eyes burned.

"Then show us where he is, Currim! *Now.* Or maybe *you* don't get to come back from here, either."

Currim pivoted toward me. "You hear that shit? See why I wanted you along, Doc? To protect me. Make sure these fuckers don't do somethin' awful to me, just for the hell of it."

"Nobody's going to hurt you, Wes." I stared at Block. "Kinda defeats the purpose, right, Chief?"

I turned back to Currim. "Now why don't you show us where Ed Meachem is, okay?"

The prisoner shook some snow from his sleeves and straightened his shoulders.

"Sure," he said casually. "Why the fuck not?"

I saw Randall's hands ball into fists, but he kept himself in check. Currim indicated the porch, and then led the way up the three wide, snow-carpeted steps.

The front door was unlocked, and though the interior was dark and cold, it was a relief to be out of the storm. No lights were on, so Randall pulled his departmental flashlight from his belt and clicked it on.

Meanwhile, Chief Block reached for a wall switch and flipped it up and down. Still no lights.

"Sorry, Chief." Currim smiled. "Most o' the bulbs went out a while back. Never got around to replacin' 'em."

Block's only response was a thick grunt, a throaty sound threaded with as much weariness as disgust.

Guided by the flashlight beam bouncing jerkily down the darkened, wallpapered hallway, the four of us headed into the bowels of the old house. The air thick, heavy as a shroud. Stale smells. Muffled sounds. Barely discernable shapes—a wicker chair, a ceramic-bowled table lamp—emerging from the shadows, as if summoned from some bleak, distant past.

"Holy shit…" Randall's voice was barely a whisper. The sergeant was clearly spooked. And, I thought, with damned good reason.

The old wood floor creaked beneath our feet as we moved forward. Carefully, more hesitently now. Beyond the beam of the flashlight, there were only shadows.

I felt my chest tighten. The hairs on my forearms were standing up inside the sleeves of the parka.

"Let's go through here, okay, guys?" Currim leaned against an opened door at the end of the hall. "I think you'll find what you're lookin' for in here."

Randall spoke again under his breath. "Prick."

Ignoring him, Currim grinned and stepped into what appeared to be the living room. The three of us followed.

Randall's light swept the room, revealing the shapes of old stuffed chairs, a coffee table, and a cold, long-unused fireplace. A broad, stained area rug, bunched at the corners. Brass floor lamps, with fake Tiffany shades. All straight out of the fifties.

Beyond the single, wide picture window, the storm raged on. Rattling the dust-coated blinds tied to opposite sides. Through the ice-encrusted glass, I could just make out the uneven yard, scalloped with snow. Some spindly trees, pencil-stroke branches bending in the wind.

"What's the idea, Currim?" Block planted his feet, bristling. "I don't see nothin'."

Currim frowned. "Must be the wrong room. My bad."

Randall lifted his flashlight like a cudgel, its light flaring off the ceiling. I thought he was going to bash Currim's head in. God knows, I wanted to do it myself.

"You better not be jerkin' us around here, Wes!" Randall took a menacing step toward the prisoner. "I mean it, asswipe, I'll just—"

"I have half a mind to *let* ya, Sergeant." Chief Block sighed heavily, eyes narrowing. "I'm done playin' games, Currim. Where the fuck's Meachem?"

Currim snapped his fingers. "Damn, *now* I remember! Okay, fellas…to the kitchen!"

Before anyone else could move, Currim strode from the living room and back out the door we'd come in. The rest of us were right on his heels, Randall training his flashlight on Currim's back.

The prisoner made an abrupt turn, momentarily vanishing into the darkness. Then, with equal suddenness, a room light flickered on, to our left.

With Randall in the lead, Block and I went through this second room's opened doorway. The uneven light was coming from twin ceiling fluorescent bulbs, only one of which was working. Sputtering, flickering on and off.

Like an eerie, slow-motion strobe. One moment, everything was cast in an ash gray, sepulchral light. Objects appeared, were given outline. Then, just as suddenly, they disappeared, swallowed up by a cold, hungry darkness.

Things seen, then unseen. There, then not there.

It was the kitchen, as Currim had said. Even in the blinking, uncertain light, I could tell that every appliance was old, long-used. The small formica table in one corner, with its twin lattice-backed chairs, another 50s relic. As was the patterned tile floor.

Where our eyes were drawn. Riveted. Straining to make sense of what we were seeing. Images out of a nightmare, bathed in a sickly light for a single, frozen moment. Then veiled once more by darkness.

Currim, standing in a far corner, folded his arms.

"Told ya," was all he said.

What was left of Ed Meachem was revealed to us in flickering patches of light. Scattered about the kitchen floor, like pieces of a blood-soaked jigsaw puzzle.

A spray of body parts, in no particular pattern. An arm, curled like a dried leaf. The jagged stump of a leg. Hands severed at the wrists. Feet at the ankles.

"Dear God in heaven," Block muttered.

Suddenly, the sole working fluorescent went out, with a loud, sizzling pop. Darkness enveloped us again.

"Holy shit!" Randall cried out.

I whirled, trying to gauge his position from the sound of his voice. Then I saw his flashlight beam plume up, flitting wildly against the dark.

"Steady, Harve," I heard the Chief say.

Breath coming in short, staccato bursts, Randall brought the light down and directed it shakily around the room. Poking into shadowy, stubborn corners. Searching, as though compelled against his will, for yet more horror.

He found it.

In the center of the room, a naked male torso lay marinating in a dark pool of old blood, blackening at the edges. Nearby, strands of human entrails were curled around chair legs, or looped like coils of garden hose.

Jesus Christ, I thought.

Randall started to retch then, struggling not to vomit. As I felt the gorge rising in my own throat.

But it was Chief Block who spoke, voice a rasp.

"Wes, you sick bastard, why'd the fuck you do this?"

"That's for me to know and you to find out."

Randall, still gasping, swung his light back and forth across the tile floor. "But his *head*…Where the hell's Meachem's head?"

The same question had occurred to me, at almost the exact same moment the answer did.

Without a word, I turned and raced out of the room. Slamming once against a table in the dark, but never breaking stride. Chief Block calling after me, voice raised in surprise, anger.

I ignored him as I ran down the darkened hallways and through the opened front door. Pounding off the groaning, wood-planked porch, out onto the yard. Slipping and stumbling over the slick, dead-white earth. Unmindful of the bitter cold, the hurtling snow.

Until I stood, breathing hard, eyes stinging from the storm, staring at the snowman in the middle of the yard. The three balls of snow, piled awkwardly into the form of a man. The small snowball at the top, wearing the floppy hat.

Except it wasn't a snowball.

It was a head.

Ed Meachem's severed head.

Chapter Four

"Hey, Danny, I saw you on CNN!"

It was Noah Frye, bellowing from behind the wall-length bar as I entered his saloon on Second Avenue. Called Noah's Ark, it was a refurbished coal barge permanently moored at the edge of the Monongahela River.

I came in out of the night and closed the door behind me. As I stood in the threshold, stamping my feet to loosen the snow from my boots, I could feel the musty warmth of the softly-lit room begin to chase the chill from my bones.

Over the years, Noah's Ark had become almost a second home to me. A convivial refuge after a particularly hard day. Or two.

Though boasting a gleaming, brass-trimmed bar, cozy café tables, and a small raised stage where jazz musicians performed nightly, the saloon's interior couldn't disguise its nautical heritage. Tar paper hanging from the ceiling. Port holes looking out on the black, ice-choked waters. That unmistakeable riverfront smell.

As I took a stool at the bar, just filling now with early evening customers, Noah sauntered over and put his beefy hands on the counter. He was a big, burly man in stained overalls, with a thatch of unruly hair and a lunatic's glint in his eyes.

Which only made sense, since Noah was—technically speaking—crazy. A paranoid schizophrenic, his grotesque delusions were kept barely in check by psychotropic meds and the devotion of his girlfriend—and the bar's sole waitress—Charlene.

I'd known Noah Frye since my days at a private psychiatric clinic, years before, when I was an intern therapist and he was a patient. Now we were friends.

"This must be old hat for you by now." Noah had turned to fill a schooner with draft Iron City from the beer keg behind him. "I mean, talkin' about whacko killers on the national news."

"It's not as much fun as you'd think."

He brought me my beer with a commiserating look.

"Hey, don't feel bad, Danny. Remember, the camera adds ten pounds."

I smiled at his open, generous face. "Thanks. I feel better already."

"Cool. Maybe I oughtta give up the bar and go hang out a shingle somewhere. I mean, hell, except for you and Dr. Mendors, every shrink I ever met was crazier than I am."

"You get no argument from me."

I sipped my beer. Nancy Mendors was an old friend of mine from Ten Oaks, that same clinic where we both met Noah. In the years since Noah was discharged, after his insurance had run out, she'd privately monitored his treatment, including prescribing his meds. Though I went into private practice after leaving Ten Oaks, Nancy stayed on, and was just last year promoted to clinic director.

The fact that Noah could survive—and thrive—as an outpatient, given his diagnosis, was due primarily to her efforts. Plus the daily love and support he got from Charlene, an equally-big, frizzy-haired ex-hippie from somewhere on the west coast. It also didn't hurt that the bar's owner, a retired businessman who'd bought and refitted the old coal barge, had taken such a liking to Noah that he named the place after him.

I finished my beer as Noah shuffled down the other end of the bar and clicked on the wide-screen TV. CNN. Doing another follow-up story to the one they'd been airing for the past two days. About Wes Currim. And me.

◇◇◇

It was a Monday night, and I was back from my weekend in West Virginia. Glad to be back in my therapy office this morning, seeing patients. Though nearly every one of them, having seen the news on Sunday, spent a good portion of our session asking me about the Currim case. In fact, as I locked up after work and drove over to Noah's, I began wondering if my "fifteen minutes of fame" was beginning to adversely affect my ability to work with patients.

After all, it had been the huge media hype concerning my involvement in the Wingfield investigation a year or so back, not to mention the bank hostage crisis this past summer, that brought my work with the Pittsburgh police to Wes Currim's attention. That prompted him to single me out, and ask that I accompany him when he led the Wheeling police to where he'd left Meachem's body.

I looked at the sliver of brown liquid at the bottom of my glass. Maybe I'd be better off declining the news media's requests for interviews. No big loss, I thought, for me *or* the profession. In fact, I'd often been alarmed when mental health professionals spoke glibly on TV about the emotional states of criminal suspects or Hollywood celebrities whom they'd never even met, let alone treated. Yet there I was yesterday, sitting in a makeup chair at a local TV studio in Oakland, about to do a remote interview with the lead anchor at CNN. Being asked by the makeup person if I wanted some highlights added to my beard.

Wincing now at the memory, I tapped the bar counter with my glass, drawing Noah's attention. Instead of a refill, he favored me with the wave of an impatient hand and pointed up at the TV. As if for emphasis, he aimed the remote control at the screen and raised the volume.

Over the now-familiar video of Currim being taken into custody in Wheeling by Chief Block and Sergeant Randall, the announcer repeated the facts of the case.

According to the suspect himself, he needed money and was lurking in the parking lot outside a local supermarket. His intent was to find an obviously well-off customer, and Ed Meachem, coming home from work in his Armani suit and pushing a cart loaded with groceries to his waiting Lexus, fit the bill perfectly. Though Currim didn't know it at the time, he was about to assault the vice president of one of West Virginia's largest coal mining companies.

Given the lateness of the hour, and the inclement weather, the lot was nearly empty. Under cover of darkness, Currim came up behind Meachem, knocked him out, and dragged him to his Toyota pickup three spaces over. Then he drove his victim out to his late uncle's backwoods house, apparently with vague plans to hold Meachem for ransom.

Currim told the police he was so stressed and agitated, he wasn't even clear in his own mind what exactly he intended to do. He figured he'd just get Meachem to the house, tie him up or something, then think things over.

He never had the chance. According to Currim, once he'd dragged Meachem into the house, the businessman roused himself and struggled to get away. That's when Currim killed him, striking him repeatedly on the head, though he couldn't now remember what he'd used as a weapon.

Then, Currim reported, he got the idea to dismember Meachem's body. He'd known about Troy David Dowd, of course. *Everyone* knew about the Handyman. Currim claimed he'd spent years watching news specials about him, perusing every newspaper and Internet feature he could find. He'd even read that bestselling book about Dowd, written by a *Post-Gazette* reporter.

So, inspired by the serial killer, Currim used a butcher knife from the kitchen to hack the body to pieces.

Here, the announcer's voice took on an even graver tone: "When asked why he used Meachem's severed head as the head for the snowman, Currim allegedly replied, 'I figgered it'd be funny. Besides, that's something even the Handyman never thought of.'"

Under a just-released mug shot of the suspect, the announcer said: "According to the Wheeling, West Virginia, District Attorney's office, Wesley Currim's family have retained legal counsel.

And a psychological evaluation will likely be ordered, to determine Currim's mental state."

The news report ended there. *Fine with me*, I thought.

By now, a few new customers, chilled from the cold outside and wanting drinks, had come into the bar, calling out to Noah. Men and women done with work for the day, gratefully undoing coats and removing scarves, leaning expectantly forward on their stools. With an aggrieved scowl, Noah muted the TV volume and began taking their orders.

Soon enough he got around to me, refilling my beer. Though the tense smile on his face, barely hiding his disgust, revealed how upset he'd been by the news report.

It also reminded me of something he'd told me once, regarding the Handyman's brutal crimes. "I don't mind the crazies," he'd said. "It's the evil fucks I hate."

Seeing the distress in his eyes, I thought it wise to try to refocus his attention elsewhere. To a topic near and dear to his heart, and one about which we'd long held differing views.

"By the way," I said casually, "you ever get around to listening to *A Kind of Blue*? I mean that new, remastered CD I gave you?"

He frowned. "Don't need to. Heard the original tracks years ago. You can't re-master music, Danny, just clean up the sound. And I still say, everything Miles Davis did *after* 1965 was better than anything he did before."

"And I still say you're full of shit."

It was a classic argument, especially among gifted musicians like Noah himself. Even among mere fans like me.

Which was the better Miles, pre- or post-1965?

There was a pretty clear distinction. The early Miles Davis, though obviously a genius, still worked in the classical harmonics of jazz. Then, starting around 1965, as far as I and many others were concerned, Davis turned his back on his audience. Not only figuratively, in terms of the postmodernist, anti-melodic quality of his playing. But even *literally*, in that he began playing concerts with his back to the audience, facing the stage's rear curtain.

Not that I'd ever convince Noah Frye of that. A skilled jazz pianist who often sat in with the musicians who appeared at his bar, Noah was definitely the more progressive of the two of us. At least where music was concerned.

"Here's what I don't get, Danny," Noah was saying now, brow furrowed. "You're not *that* old. How come you gotta be such an old fart when it comes to music?"

Before I could muster up a snappy comeback, a voice boomed behind me. Accompanied by a blast of frigid air as the front door opened wide.

"Ahoy, barkeep! Desperate man on the bridge!"

The words were loud and imperious enough to stop Noah in his tracks behind the bar, and cause me to swivel in my seat. Though, from its thick Brooklyn accent and belligerent tone, I knew who it was before I saw him.

Chapter Five

Assistant District Attorney Dave Parnelli, his portly frame swathed in a snow-flecked overcoat, sat heavily on the stool next to mine. Motioned to Noah.

"Jack Daniels, pal." He rapped his knuckles on the counter. "I've been doing battle with the elements and need reinforcements. Pronto."

Noah gave me a dark look before going off to get Parnelli's drink. I doubt he'd ever forgiven me for introducing the arrogant ADA to his bar a few months ago. To my surprise, Parnelli had become a more or less regular customer.

I'd met Dave Parnelli last summer, during that bank robbery investigation, and we'd bumped into each other a half-dozen times since then. Formerly a public defender in New York, he'd traded sides and cities to come to work for the district attorney here in Pittsburgh. Had racked up a pretty impressive record for convictions, too, given his short tenure in office.

Parnelli was a couple years older than me, with a broad drinker's face and thinning hair that he wore in a comb-over. As I'd come to learn, he played the cynical, seen-it-all lawyer stereotype to the hilt.

He'd also somehow formed the impression that he and I were *paisans*. Buddies. Brothers under the skin. Probably for no other reason than that we both drank Jack Daniels.

"You've been watching the news about Currim?" I asked.

"Sure, who hasn't?" He nodded to Noah as the whiskey glass was placed in front of him.

I glanced up. "I could use a refill myself, Noah."

"No shit? Well, I could use a three-way with Charlene and Angelina Jolie, but that don't mean I'm gonna get it."

But he snatched up my glass anyway and refilled it.

Then, grunting something unintelligible, he shuffled away to attend to other customers.

"Speakin' of Currim," Parnelli went on, "ya know how he said he was inspired by the Handyman? Well, jailhouse gossip says that Dowd didn't exactly take that as a compliment. In Mr. Dowd's considered opinion, the Meachem dismemberment was sloppy, and the whole snowman thing was just juvenile theatrics."

I shrugged. "I guess I get it. To a seasoned pro like Dowd, Currim's amateurism is offensive."

"Whatever you say, Doc. Though I wouldn't mind if the next severed head we find belonged to Dowd himself."

"You and most registered voters in the state."

Out of the corner of my eye, I saw Charlene, carrying trays laden with burgers and fries, push open the hinged kitchen doors with her wide hips and move out into the dining area. As she sauntered expertly past the bar, she gave me a friendly wink.

Meanwhile, Parnelli was holding his glass aloft, waiting for me to raise my own. We touched rims.

"To better days." He swallowed his drink in a single gulp. "By the way, Danny, I gotta get the name of your PR guy. You're gettin' more exposure than a porn star on YouTube."

He gave a short laugh, then motioned again for Noah.

Over the next twenty minutes, I nursed my beer and watched Parnelli go through four whiskeys. When it came to drinking, I thought, Parnelli had one thing in common with Dowd: they were both seasoned pros.

By now, happy hour had ended and the serious drinkers were streaming into the place. The bar quickly filled, as did most of the tables. Noah, sweating profusely in the close confines of the barge's interior, hurried to fill drink orders. Meanwhile,

Charlene moved about with surprising dexterity. Like a graceful mama bear, smiling and chatting with customers as she placed full plates on some tables and removed empty ones from others.

I got up and threw some bills on the bar. Before I could say good-bye to my hosts, as well as to Parnelli, the ADA took hold of my elbow.

"Hey, Danny, I forgot to tell ya." Voice slurred. Pale eyes blinking in the dim, stinging haze of cigarette smoke. No longer on his way to getting drunk. All the way there now. "Your name came up the other day. I was talkin' to that female detective, Lowrey…"

"Eleanor?"

"Yeah, some lame-ass case we're doin'. Doesn't matter. Anyway, like I say, your name came up."

"Cool." I easily but firmly removed his hand from my elbow. "But, listen, Dave, I've gotta—"

"Fine lookin' woman, that Lowrey. Totally buffed. Epic tits."

"Funny, that's the same thing she says about you."

"Bite me. But I mean it. I *envy* you, Rinaldi."

"Afraid there's nothing to envy. We're just friends."

"Uh-huh." A bleary-eyed, conspiratorial look. "Just make sure you tell your ol' buddy Dave all about it when you close the deal."

"Right. You'll be the first one I call."

I was getting pissed off now. It wasn't just the boozy familiarity. It was the casual way he spoke about Eleanor Lowrey. Though we'd only seen each other for drinks a few times since the summer—busy schedules, some family issues on her part, the usual contemporary approach-avoidance dance—I felt a pang of disloyalty allowing Parnelli to speak crudely about her.

Even drunk, this notion managed to penetrate his thick Italian skull. He tried to get to his feet.

"Hey, Danny, c'mon…Don't get your shorts in a twist. I *like* Lowrey. Really. Great cop. Helluva girl."

He wobbled a bit on the stool, and I reached with both hands to steady him. Which he acknowledged with a rueful smile, and then swiveled back to face the bar.

I turned quickly and headed for the door, nodding to a flustered Noah who was struggling to unlock the mysteries of the bar cash register.

I also bumped into Charlene, wiping off the table nearest the front door. Red-faced. Breathing labored.

"Do me a favor, will ya, Charlene? Make sure Parnelli takes a cab home."

"Sure, Doc. Since I'm just sittin' around, eatin' bon-bons, with nothin' better to do."

"I'd ask Noah, but—"

"But he's got the attention span of a goldfish. Okay, Danny, I'll pour the son-of-a-bitch into a taxi later."

"You're the best, Char. I think I see a tasteful gift basket in your future."

"Great. When you see a winning lottery ticket, get back to me."

I gave her a brief, goodbye hug and stepped outside into a bitter, angry wind. It was about eight by now, and while the snow had been slowing all day, pockets of flurries still rose up and veiled the night.

Nevertheless, except for the plowed streets, the continuing cold kept the snow layered in thick drifts as far as the eye could see. Endless sheetings of shadowed white, like bedcovers shrouding the nearby cars and low-slung river buildings, the spires of the fast-growing downtown commercial district, the rounded shoulders of the far-off Allegeny mountains. The Monongahela River to my left, a blackened ice slurpy moving like slow-flowing oil toward the Point, there to join an equally sluggish Allegheny and form the massive Ohio.

I turned then, chin buried deep in the collar of my coat. The temperature out here must've dropped fifteen degrees in the short time I'd been in the bar. Shivering, I hurried down the sliver of sidewalk toward where I'd parked the Mustang.

I never made it.

Two men in dark overcoats and hats, hands in their pockets, were moving like wraiths toward me. Emerging from the shadows between the parked cars. Footsteps silent on the blue-white carpet of snow.

I was still deciding my move—or even if there *was* one—when I saw the guy on the right shift his hand in his coat pocket. Saw the imprint of a squared bulge push against the fabric. A gun.

His partner got to me first, though. An even smile.

"Got someone who wants to say hello, Doc. An old acquaintance of yours."

"This old acquaintance own a telephone?"

"Why don'tcha ask him yourself? In person?"

Whatever menace he was trying to convey with his clipped, hard-ass voice was undercut somewhat by the puffs of frost coming from his mouth. Regardless, now that he was joined by his gun-toting partner, I figured I had little choice but to accept their invitation.

With me positioned between them, the two men walked me half a block down the sidewalk, in the opposite direction from where I'd parked. At the corner, with its engine idling, lights on, and wipers slowly grazing its icy windshield, a black Lincoln towncar waited.

The guy on my left reached past me, opening the rear passenger door.

"There ya go." Again, that professional smile.

I swung into the spacious rear passenger seat. Plush, dark leather. Feeble overhead light.

But enough illumination for me to see—and recognize—my fellow passenger.

I held out my hand.

"Well, I'll be damned. Agent Alcott. Was it something I said?"

Special Agent Neal Alcott, FBI, ignored me and lifted a cell phone to his ear.

"Package has arrived. We're on our way."

Chapter Six

"Shouldn't I be wearing a blindfold? Or a hood or something?"

Alcott favored me with a pained smile.

"Hell, if I had my way, Rinaldi, you'd be bound and gagged. *And* tranked to the gills. But I need you conscious, so I can get you up to speed. Besides, there's no mystery to where we're going. Beautiful downtown Braddock."

Well, that cleared one thing up. I glanced out my side window. We'd crossed the South Tenth Street Bridge, moved smoothly through the construction sites around the Point, and were heading east along the Penn Lincoln Parkway.

Though there were only scant flurries now, our driver—some junior G-man in a thick camelhair coat—drove slowly and deliberately through the unceasing gloom of night.

When I turned back, I saw the chiseled lines of Alcott's profile as he punched buttons on his iPad. The local FBI agent hadn't changed much since we'd met last summer. Same blond hair, with its military-style buzzcut. Broad, linebacker shoulders straining the threads of his tailored gray suit. The knowing, confident squint in his hooded blue eyes.

When the FBI was brought in to assist the police in that bank robbery, Alcott had made no effort to hide his disapproval of my involvement. Not only was I a civilian, I was a head-shrinker. Two strikes against me already, or so it seemed at the time.

So what was I doing in the back seat of a federal vehicle, with an FBI section manager? Being followed by another car, a somber black sedan, probably carrying the two field agents who'd collared me?

Good questions, I thought. So I asked them.

"Give me a minute." He didn't look up from his work.

I let out a long breath, and turned my attention back to the buildings rapidly receding behind us. Snow-veiled yet glittering, the skyline was dotted with the lights of a twenty-first century Steel City. No longer an industrial powerhouse, most of its workers had long since exchanged blue collars for white ones. The "new" Pittsburgh—with its world-class museums, universities, and hospitals—was an urban work-in-progress, continuing to grow amidst the brown bricks and cobblestone streets of its fabled past.

Its story was, to borrow a phrase, a tale of two cities: one, a faded patchwork of ethnic neighborhoods, steel mills, and coal barges gliding down its Three Rivers; the other, a modern engine of high finance and well-funded research, the nation's pioneer in nanotechnology.

I myself bridged those two realities. The son of an Italian-American beat cop who drank himself to death, and an Irish homemaker who died when I was three, I was the first in my family to go to college, become a professional. Yet I could still clearly remember the Pittsburgh of my childhood, when the skies were choked with the smoke of blast furnaces. When trolley cars rumbled down the old city streets, people sat out on their back porches listening to Pirates games on the radio, and everyone in the neighborhood knew your name.

Alcott jolted me out of my reverie by matter-of-factly dropping a heavy folder on my lap.

"What's this?" I flipped through the sheaf of papers. Police reports, crime scene photos, Xeroxed newspaper articles. Three stapled documents with the Quantico letterhead, from the FBI's Behavioral Science Unit.

"You can study up once we get there. To fill in all the details." Alcott shifted in his seat to face me. "But for now, let me give you the bullet points."

I closed the file on my knee. All this cloak-and-dagger stuff was fueling a rising anger.

"What if I don't want to play?"

"You don't have a choice, Rinaldi." He massaged his chin. "You haven't had a choice about it since six thirty this morning."

"Why? What happened at six thirty this morning?"

"You became, against my better judgment, a necessity. Comes straight from the top of the food chain. The director wants you brought in to help us. Which means, that's exactly what you're gonna do."

I met his confident gaze. "Sure thing, Alcott. As long as this magic pumpkin gets me home from the ball by midnight. I have a day full of patients tomorrow."

"Not to worry. We've cleared your schedule."

I have to admit, this threw me.

"What the hell? What do you mean? How—?"

"We hacked your computer, Doc. We got tech geeks who can do that nowadays. From any remote location. Not that your passwords were that hard to crack."

"I don't fucking *believe* this. You can't just—"

"Believe it. We got into your patient files, got their phone numbers, made some calls. My secretary did a great job as your answering service operator, informing your patients that you've taken ill. Nothing serious, probably the flu. But you'll be out for a few days."

"But those patient names are confidential. As are my case notes, and—"

"Listen, nobody gives a shit about a bunch of whiners and head cases. Soon as we made the calls, we deleted all the data." He raised his hand, palm out. "Scout's honor."

"Like that's supposed to make it okay? Like I even *believe* you? Go fuck yourself, Alcott!"

I made a mental note to copy and delete my patient files, ASAP. Reinforce security. Change the passwords.

"Easy, Doc. Besides, we cleared it with Pittsburgh PD. The director had a nice chat with your assistant chief. He agreed to loan you temporarily to the bureau. In the name of inter-agency cooperation."

"Too bad nobody had a nice chat with *me*. I work *with* the cops, not *for* them." I gripped the door handle. "Now let me outta this fucking car."

Alcott's jaw tightened. "You're not goin' anywhere."

From the front seat, the driver's voice. A rookie, all right, spoiling for trouble. "Is there a problem, sir?"

"Not at all, Billy." Alcott gave me a placid look.

I just stared at him in the car's pale light. Frozen by a mixture of anger and disbelief.

Which he thoroughly enjoyed. "By the way, if it helps, your patients felt really bad about you being sick. One lady even offered to bring you some chicken soup."

My hand tightened impotently on the door handle. Rage creating a burning sun in the middle of my chest.

"Listen, asshole, you have any idea what kind of a breach this is? The damage this could do to my patients if they find out their confidentiality has been violated?"

Especially, I thought, given the type of people I see. Crime victims whose lives had already been shattered. For whom trust in the emotional safety of our work together was as fragile as a soap bubble.

"No reason they should ever find out," Alcott said smoothly. "I mean, shit, *we're* not gonna tell them. Far as they know, it never even happened. No harm, no foul."

I didn't reply.

"Look, Rinaldi, the truth is, I think you're an arrogant prick who's more trouble than he's worth. But like it or not, the powers-that-be want you involved. So it's no good bitching about it."

"That's a damn shame, since I'm just getting started." Alcott failed to see the humor.

On the other hand, I thought, maybe he was right. Maybe the best course of action, at the moment, was to find out what was going on. With a long breath, I let my anger, my righteous indignation at what they'd done, drain away.

"Okay." I sat back in my seat, noticing at the same time that our vigilant driver's wide shoulders had relaxed now, too. For the first time in the past minute.

I turned to Alcott. "I guess that means you're going to tell me what happened at six thirty this morning?"

"Nope." He took back the thick file folder. "That's the *end* of the story. We've got to start at the beginning."

Chapter Seven

"You ever hear of a man called John Jessup?"

"No," I said.

"I'm not surprised. He's not exactly a household name, like Ted Bundy, or the Zodiac Killer, or the Handyman. Not even close to being in their league."

"Is Jessup some kind of serial killer?"

"*Was* some kind of serial killer. The sloppy kind, turns out. Anyway, he's dead. But even when he was alive, he pretty much did his thing below the radar."

"Do I want to know what his 'thing' was?"

"Nothing fancy. Raped and strangled four prostitutes. Two in Ohio, one in Kentucky, one in Indiana. Over an eight month period."

"Guy traveled a lot."

"Sales rep for a pharmaceutical company. On the road all the time. Classic profile for a serial killer. White, middle-aged, kept to himself. No friends to speak of."

"You said he was sloppy. Meaning what?"

"Meaning he left some DNA under the fingernails of the girl he did in Cleveland, Ohio. She must've scratched him during the assault. I mean, the guy wasn't a total idiot. Wore gloves. But he didn't consider the scratch. What it might've left under her nail."

"That's sloppy, all right. A smart predator would've done something about it. Like cut off her finger. Just in case." I'd once read about such an incident.

"Uh-huh. Anyway, the DNA was a match for some unknown perp who'd been busted years before for beating up a hooker in some fleabag hotel outside Detroit. So we got him."

"Nice story. How come I never heard of it?"

"No reason you should. For one thing, hookers get killed all the time, all over the country. Unless there's something sensational about the crimes, they rarely make it to the front page. Or the evening news." He paused. "You know what most cops say about a hooker's murder, right? I mean, wasn't your old man a cop?"

I nodded. "Yeah. He used to refer to cases like that as an NHI. 'No Human Involved.'"

"Right. As in, who gives a shit? Just another dead hooker. Plus, these murders happened in three different states, over a period of months. For a while, nobody even saw a connection."

"What's the second thing?"

A dark smile. "Truth is, most serial killers got a signature. Maybe they leave something behind at the crime scene. Like a calling card, or a taunt to the cops. Sometimes they send messages to the local paper. Or else they take a specific item from the victim. A lock of hair, her shoes. Something that identifies the crime as their work."

"But not Jessup?"

"No, the guy's got the imagination of a stuffed cat. Just gets his rocks off, puts his gloved hands around the vic's throat, and chokes the life out of her."

"More likely, he did both at the same time."

"That's what the M.E. thought, too. And Barnes. But it's just conjecture. Forensics were inconclusive, and Jessup clammed up after his arrest. Didn't say shit throughout his trial, either."

"Who's Barnes?"

"Special Agent Lyle Barnes. One of the bureau's top profilers. Been working out of the Behavioral Science Unit at Quantico for twenty years. Only retired a couple months ago, in fact. John Jessup was his last case."

"Was Barnes good at his job?"

"The best, some people say. Unrelenting when he caught the scent, if you know what I mean. Plus he was a data nut. Spent every free hour at Quantico compiling stats, poring over the records of past serial killers. Know how he spent his vacation time?"

"No idea."

"He went around to maximum security prisons, interviewing the monsters still alive. Spent hours talkin' with guys like Ted Bundy, John Wayne Gacy, the Green River Killer. Real fun group. Imagine living inside *their* fucking heads for the past twenty years."

I couldn't even begin to imagine. I said so.

"Damn straight. On the plus side, Barnes has a gut like nobody's business. When the DNA on the Ohio vic came in, the Cleveland cops asked for the Bureau's help with the lab stuff. Somehow Barnes got wind of it. Then, when there was a match to an earlier assault on a hooker, he got into the data base and—"

"Found the other cases, the other prositutes who'd been raped and strangled."

"Then all he had to do was contact Jessup's company, get the info on where their rep was working on any given date, and match up the locations to the scenes of each girl's death. Barnes himself led the FBI team to pick up Jessup at the Cleveland county jail."

"What happened at the trial?"

"Open and shut. So no media circus. Another reason the story stayed regional. A couple news cycles in Ohio, not even that in Kentucky and Indiana. Plus the timing was bad. One or two blogs about it from the crime junkies, and then it was back to March Madness. They take their basketball pretty seriously in that part of the country."

"And Jessup never said anything? About his motives, his fantasies? Did they do a psych eval?"

"Sure, his defense attorney insisted, and Jessup was declared legally fit to stand trial. Which was all the prosecutor needed. Some hotshot female in the Cleveland DA's office, making her bones with the Jessup conviction. Judge must've felt the same way, since he sentenced the guy to four consecutive life terms."

"But what's all this have to do with me?"

Alcott unhurriedly flipped to another page in the file. Bringing me into this may not have been his idea, but he was still determined to stay in charge.

"Relax, will ya, Doc? Like I said, none of this stuff is particularly unique. Multiple murderers are a dime a dozen. Got a lot of 'em locked up in SuperMax prisons. Bottom-feeder serials like Jessup. Gang shooters. Mob hit men. The crap floating in the sewers under society."

I had to smile. "Nice one, Alcott. A good soundbite for your next media shot."

"Yeah, I like it, too." A broad, unconvincing wink. "Anyway, John Jessup gets sent up to Markham Maximum Correctional in Ohio, nobody gives him another thought. Until he starts getting the letters."

"What letters?"

"Fan letters. Again, nothing new. You oughtta see the fan letters Charlie Manson still gets. Hell, Ted Bundy got marriage proposals. All these whack jobs have groupies, people sendin' them pictures, lockets, whatever. Lotta strange folks out there in the heartland, Doc. But I guess I don't have to tell *you* that."

"But you said Jessup wasn't a celebrity in that way."

"He wasn't. Maybe if he'd killed a dozen women. Or carved his initials on their tits or something. But I'm telling you, the jails are full of guys like him. Maybe they're nuts, maybe they're just evil pricks. But as far as I can tell, there wasn't anything special about Jessup."

"Were all these letters from the same person?"

"Looks like it. Though all with different postmarks. All typed on some kind of electric typewriter. A Sears Coronamatic, circa 1970. I mean, who even *uses* a typewriter anymore?"

"What were in the letters?"

"In a nutshell? How much the writer admired Jessup, thought he was brave, a maverick in a soulless society. How the people who put him in jail were the real criminals, part of the oppressive establishment. The usual conspiracy bullshit, with some groupie ass licking thrown in."

"Was the writer ever identified?"

"No. But he always signed the letters the same way. Well, typed them, I mean. Always ended them with the words 'Sincerely, Your Biggest Fan.'" Alcott laughed. "'Course, he was Jessup's *only* fan. A fan club of one."

"You said 'he.' You sure the letter-writer was male?"

"Our people in Behavorial Science believe it's a man. Barnes included. Most letters from females to inmates like Jessup are more...well, romantic, I guess you'd say. Lots of sexual innuendo. Flirting. More like love letters. These were the work of a fan, not a potential bride-to-be."

I nodded. "Jessup never received any other mail?"

"Just once. A package, right after the trial, from his widowed sister. His only living relative. In it was a Bible and a note saying she hoped he'd burn in hell."

"Did you follow up with her? Maybe she'd know who her brother's secret admirer might be."

"We would've, sure. Except the poor woman died the day after sending Jessup the package. Drove her car off a bridge into the Ohio River. Suicide."

"Any suspicion of foul play?"

"None. She took herself out, no question."

I gave this some thought. A deeply devout woman, perhaps fanatically so. Widowed, alone. Her only remaining family member a convicted rapist and murderer. Not much left for her to live for, other than the daily acid bath of shame. No wonder she—

Alcott cleared his throat. "You wanna stay with me here, Doc? We're only five minutes from Braddock."

"Sorry. Just thinking." My glance fell to the folder on his lap. "Was Jessup ever questioned about the letters? About whether he knew who was sending them?"

"Of course. But he claimed to have no idea who they were from. Didn't seem that interested, either. Not even flattered or whatever. Says here in the report that Jessup exhibited his 'customary flat affect.'"

I didn't reply. Because suddenly, some notion in the back of my mind, some vague memory, was starting to take shape.

"What prison was Jessup being held in again?"

"Markham Maximum Correctional. Bingham, Ohio." A slow smile. "I get the feeling you're starting to remember."

"Maybe. Wasn't there a news story a few months ago about some kind of riot there? Prisoners attacking the guards. Turned violent, bloody."

"That's right. To this day, nobody knows how it started. But somehow, John Jessup got caught up in the middle of it. Classic case of wrong place, wrong time. And he paid for it with his life."

"So that's how Jessup died. He was killed."

"Yeah. A guard named Earl Cranshaw did it. Beat Jessup to death with his baton. Caused a big controversy when Cranshaw wasn't charged with manslaughter. Just sent packing, stripped of his pension."

Alcott paused, aware of its dramatic effect. Then, almost delicately, he held a single plastic-wrapped piece of paper between his thumb and forefinger.

"You ready for this? Couple days after Cranshaw left the prison staff, this letter arrived. Addressed to the late John Jessup. The last letter sent by his Biggest Fan."

"What does it say?"

He squinted at the words through the thin plastic. "'I'm sad you're gone, but don't worry. Those that have wronged you will be punished. Your cruel mistreatment will be avenged. Because I know that then, and only then, can you truly rest in peace. Sincerely, Your Biggest Fan.'"

Alcott looked at me, jaw tightening.

"A week later, two days before Christmas, Earl Cranshaw—the prison guard who'd killed Jessup—was shot dead outside his home."

Chapter Eight

"ETA, five minutes, sir."

It was our driver, his voice breaking the sudden silence that had settled between Alcott and me.

"Thanks, Billy." Alcott leaned up, peering at the rear view mirror. "Simon and Garfunkel still with us?"

Billy's laugh was short, respectful. "Agents Green and Zarnicki are right on our tails. I made sure we didn't lose 'em on the highway."

"Good man." Alcott swiveled in his seat, gathering up the files. Almost as though I wasn't there.

"You gonna tell me the rest, Alcott, or do I have to wait till we get there? Wherever the hell *that* is."

Alcott shrugged. I could tell he was glad our journey was near its end. He was the kind of man whose ambition literally radiated from his body, which made him seem constrained if trapped too long in one place. Especially a small place, with a guy he didn't have much use for.

As though indulging me, he flipped open the folder once more.

"Sure, we have time to wrap this up. Earl Cranshaw lived in Steubenville, Ohio, in a split-level with his wife. No kids. He was 47, a drinker, member of the Elks Club. Had a temper, which is no surprise, given what he did to Jessup at the prison. Had received a couple prior reprimands from the warden, for using excessive force."

"Any leads as to his killer? Possible motive?"

"Nothing the local cops could find. The marriage seemed solid, if not exactly a love match. Cranshaw had a few buddies he played pool with. Though he cut off all contact with his former colleagues at the prison as soon as he left the place. Bad memories, I guess."

"Gambling debts? Some jealous husband?"

"No evidence of anything like that. Still, him getting whacked so soon after that last letter arrived...I mean, sure, it *might've* been a coincidence, but—"

I regarded him cooly. "C'mon, nobody believes that..."

"Well, if they did, they don't anymore. Which brings us to this very morning, Doc. Like I promised."

I waited.

"It's been kept outta the news because we can't find the sole next-of-kin. Apparently she's on a hiking trip with her boyfriend. Naturally, we don't want her hearing about it before we can contact her."

"Who are we talking about?"

"Helen Loftus. Mother dead, no sibs. She's a junior at Carnegie Mellon, and her father was visiting her for the weekend. She lives with a roommate in a dorm, so her old man stayed at a Hilton in Oakland."

"What happened?" Though I'd already guessed.

"Her father was shot in the hotel parking lot at six thirty this morning. Getting into his rental for the drive back home. One of the hotel valets heard the shots, came running, called 911. The vic died in the ambulance on the way to Pittsburgh Memorial."

"So...who was he?"

"Ralph Loftus. Judge Ralph Loftus of Cleveland, Ohio. The judge who sentenced John Jessup to life in prison."

◇◇◇

The streets of Braddock, Pennsylvania, were narrow and poorly-lit. Even along the main business strip. Probably due to the overwhelming number of closed and boarded up shops and restaurants.

We drove in silence through the no-longer-pumping heart of the small town. Like so many other coal and steel towns in western Pennsylvania, Braddock was a victim of a changing economy. A changing world.

Once a thriving, growing community, the steel mills that provided jobs to its multi-ethnic population had slowly closed down over the years. Which meant that, to add to the area's distress, strip mining for coal in the nearby hills no longer provided employment for families who'd toiled at the task for generations.

"The motel's up here on the left, sir."

Billy again, dutifully reporting our progress to his boss. His voice drew my attention past his shoulder to the windshield, the defroster spreading rivulets of spindly ice across its expanse.

No doubt it had grown colder, but thankfully the snow, at long last, no longer fell. What was left was the cold, vacant night. An arch of heavy clouds blotting the stars.

I glanced over at Neal Alcott, who sat tapping his fingers on the armrest between us.

"First, two weeks ago, the guard who killed John Jessup is shot," I said at last. "Then, this morning, the judge who sentenced Jessup to prison. So the Bureau figures it's the work of the same man, carrying out the promise he made in that last letter."

"That's the way we see it."

"A serial killer avenging the death of another serial killer?"

His fingers stopped tapping. "The guy who shot Cranshaw and Judge Loftus is no serial. Just some garden variety murderer, with a hit list. It's personal."

"Fine distinction. The point is, I assume you're worried that he hasn't finished his mission."

"Probably not. That's why we've contacted the ADA who prosecuted Jessup, the jury foreman, the Cleveland cops who bagged him…"

"What about Jessup's defense attorney? The killer might blame him for providing an inadequate defense."

"Maybe." A sardonic smile. "We could end up with a helluva long list…"

We came to a stop at a deserted intersection, then turned down a side street. Like nearby Allentown—whose economic collapse was memorialized in a pop song by Billy Joel—Braddock reminded me of nothing so much as a frontier ghost town. Foreclosed homes, shuttered family businesses. Streets needing repaired. Only the bars, neon lights buzzing against the hollow night, showed signs of life.

Then, just past the city limits, I caught sight of a low, brooding building off to my right. Easily twice the length of a football field, its knobby, uneven black shape stretched like a fallen giant against the foothills.

It was a steel mill. Or once had been. Abandoned now. Unworked, from the look of it, for many years. Smokestacks rose from its angled roof, no longer pumping clouds of soot into the sky. The blast furnaces that once burned like suns long since gone cold, dead.

Unlike Pittsburgh, whose seventeen miles of steel works had been torn down, victims of the economic cataclysm that ultimately revitalized the city, towns like Braddock had no reason to dismantle their dying mills and factories. Nothing was going to take their place.

By now I could see the blurred contours of a Motel 6 loom up out of the patchwork night. It was a squat, two-storied building half-buried under the past three days' snowfall. As we pulled into the lot, I noticed there were only a few other vehicles parked there, noses angled toward the lights of the motel, as though for warmth.

Alcott and I got out of the car, stepping into a bitter cold that seemed to cling, unyielding, like a carapace. Billy shut off the engine and joined us.

Moments later, the lights of the trailing black sedan swept the lot. The two field agents parked, then crunched across the snow to meet up with their boss.

"You three wait in the lobby a while, okay?" Alcott's gloved hand indicated Billy and the two agents. "Probably got a vending machine in there. Maybe get some coffee."

"Fine with me," Billy said. "Long as it's warm, I don't care where we go."

One of the other agents nodded gravely. Then, without another word, the three men went into the lobby, a small, well-lit room under a snow-draped canopy.

Agent Alcott turned to me. "Let's go, Doc." Breath coming in frosted puffs.

I followed him up an exterior staircase to the second floor, through a heavy access door, and down the corridor. The air in here was warm, close, prickling on the skin after the brutal chill outside.

Walking briskly down the corridor, our footsteps muffled by the stiff green carpet, we passed closed doors on either side of us. Old, worn, paint-flecked. Somehow I sensed—*knew*—that the rooms within were all empty.

Then, approaching the end of the hall, I heard—

"What the hell?" I froze, turned to Alcott.

It was coming from the last door on the right. The harsh, penetrating sound of raw terror. Choked, gasping screams. The keening of someone in intolerable anguish.

"Jesus Christ!" Heart pounding, I ran to the door. Grabbed the doorknob. It was locked.

Alcott was at my heels. I whirled, only to be met by his curiously flat stare.

"Who's in there, Alcott? Who the hell is it?"

"Agent Lyle Barnes, Doc. Your new patient."

Chapter Nine

I slammed my shoulder against the thin wooden door, twice, before it buckled. Swung free on its hinges.

I quickly stepped inside, Alcott right behind.

The room was small, with cinder block walls and heavy drapes cloaking the windows. Matching lamps glowed faintly on either side of the king-sized bed. The smell of damp wool, old cigarette smoke. Sweat.

On the floor near the bed, a young man in long sleeves and a tie was on his back, winded. Flustered. Struggling to get up on his elbows.

But it was the man on the bed who drew my gaze. In a t-shirt, trousers, and black socks, he sat upright, kicking free from a tangle of rumpled sheets. He was tallish, with long ropey arms and thin, sweat-matted hair. Wide, haunted eyes stared out at the room as though into the maw of hell.

It was his screams we'd heard, now silenced. Replaced by desperate, labored gasps. Mouth chewing empty air.

No one spoke for half a minute. Until the younger man managed to scramble up from the floor. Turning to Alcott with a sheepish look.

"Sorry, sir. He started yelling and crying out in his sleep, and when I went to calm him—"

The man in the bed interrupted him. "I woke up, and shoved Agent Stoltz off me. Like a wild man."

Breathing more calmly now, he shook his head. "It was my fault entirely, Neal. Stoltz was just trying to help."

The man ran his fingers through his thatch of hair.

"Man, I fucking *hate* this shit."

Agent Stoltz warily approached the man's bedside.

"On the other hand, sir, you *did* get some sleep. I checked the clock. About three hours."

Alcott spoke up then. "How long had Agent Barnes been awake before that, Stoltz?"

"Almost thirty hours. Frankly, sir, I don't know how the hell he does it."

Lyle Barnes, stirring in the bedcovers that cocooned him, gave a short, hard laugh.

"That's easy. Gallons of coffee, and a stubborn streak a mile long." His voice went flat. "Besides, anything's better than what comes when I'm asleep. What I *see...*"

He averted his eyes. I could tell that the admission—of his fear, of his unquestioned dread—was not easy for him. It suggested weakness, vulnerability.

Not the qualities, I guessed, that most people usually associated with him. As he gathered himself, straightening his hair and clothes, I got a better picture of the veteran agent his colleagues at the FBI knew. Saw the intelligence in his face. Its intimation of relentless focus.

Lyle Barnes looked to be in his mid-sixties, lean and spare. As if his body were as no-nonsense as his personality. At least under normal circumstances.

I hadn't said a word since entering the room. But suddenly Barnes glanced over at me, perhaps registering me for the first time.

"And who are you? Another suit from Quantico sent up to see how the crazy guy is doing?"

Alcott spoke again. "This is Dr. Daniel Rinaldi, Lyle. The trauma specialist they told you about."

I took a measured step closer to Barnes.

"That's right. Though it doesn't take a psychologist to see how the crazy guy is doing. Not too goddam well, looks like."

Barnes wiped his mouth with the back of his hand, then grunted suspiciously at Alcott.

"*This* is the guy that's supposed to help me? Keep me from losing my shit every time I shut my eyes?"

"The director has a lot of faith in the doc here." Alcott tried on a confident smile. "I worked with him myself, last summer. He didn't embarrass himself."

Barnes squinted at me. "Hell, that's high praise from Agent Alcott. The brown-nosing prick rarely likes anyone."

Standing beside him, I could see Alcott flush with anger out of the corner of my eye. But he kept his cool.

Meanwhile, Lyle Barnes had climbed out of the bed. He stood at the side table, sifting through a collection of over-the-counter medicine bottles until he found some Excedrin. Without looking up, he waved an impatient hand at his young caretaker.

"Okay, Stoltz, you're off the clock. Go get some shuteye, or a drink. Go get laid, I don't care. Apparently, me and Dr. Rinaldi have an appointment."

With a quick nod, Stoltz took a jacket from the back of a chair and slipped it on. This was followed by a huge black overcoat, a fuzzy scarf and tan gloves. Finally, he grabbed up a box of Ricola Throat Lozenges from the room's sole dresser bureau.

"You all set, Stoltz?" Alcott's voice was a growl. "We wouldn't want you to get the sniffles."

Shame-faced, Stoltz quickly buttoned up and strode from the room. As he scurried out, he bumped into the door, barely hanging from its frame, sending it swinging.

Barnes straightened, swallowed two Excedrin tablets with water from a tumbler.

"That goes for you, too, Neal. Last thing I need is for anything I say to the doc to get back to the director."

Alcott stiffened momentarily, about to respond. I cut him off.

"Agent Barnes is right. If he's to be my patient, then he's entitled to the confidentiality afforded anyone I treat. Now I know you tend to play fast and loose with that concept, but—"

He raised a hand in mock surrender.

"Hey, I get it. None of my business, anyway. I was just supposed to put you two together in a room. Which I did. Far as I'm concerned, it's Miller Time."

Barnes regarded him wryly. "Thanks, Agent Alcott. Though it occurs to me that Dr. Rinaldi and I might be more comfortable in a different room. One with a door, maybe?"

I smiled. "To be fair, that's on me. Sometimes I just go on impulse."

"Not a bad trait," Barnes replied. "When appropriate."

The retired profiler and I exchanged careful looks. I realized our relationship—such as it was, or would turn out to be—had already begun.

Oblivious, Alcott looked at both of us with a pained expression. It was clear he wanted to be anywhere but here.

"C'mon, let's use one of the other empty rooms. We bought out the whole floor, anyway. Might as well make use of it."

Chapter Ten

Lyle Barnes stood in front of the oval wall mirror, straightening his tie.

"I guess you've already figured out why the director reached out to you."

"You're suffering from night terrors, and he wants me to treat you. To help you manage the symptoms."

Barnes peered curiously at his own reflection in the dusty mirror. Squared his shoulders. Then turned back into the room, facing me.

I was on the corner sofa, in a room that was an exact replica of the one we'd just left. Though Barnes and I were the only occupants, I knew there was an agent stationed outside the door. Probably Green or Zarnicki.

In his smartly-done tie and pressed suit jacket, Lyle Barnes looked every inch the veteran FBI agent. Freshly showered and shaved, hair carefully combed. He came over to sit opposite me on the corner of the still-made bed.

"What do you know about night terrors?" I asked.

"Probably as much as you, Dr. Rinaldi. If not more."

I didn't doubt it. FBI profilers usually held at least a master's in psychology, with the added benefit of years of practical experience. Particularly with the more extreme forms of pathology, expressed primarily in homicidal—or at the very least, criminal—behavior. The kind of on-the-job training that most conventional mental health professionals never received.

With that kind of knowledge and experience, wedded to a cop's mentality, a veteran profiler like Barnes made a formidable agent. However, unlike how they're often portrayed in TV and film, most bureau profilers put in more hours doing research, building potential suspect protocols, and conducting post-conviction interviews than chasing serial killers down deserted alleys at midnight.

Although, given the steely glint in his eyes as he sat forward on the bed, it wouldn't have surprised me if Barnes had done his fair share of the latter. Back in the day.

"Just to fill you in, Doctor," he began, kneading his knuckles, "I've got the classic symptoms of night terrors. Wild, inchoate dreams filled with horrific images. Though not always distinct images. Shapes, sounds. Pervasive feelings of dread or imminent danger. Until I wake up screaming. Heart and breathing rates elevated. Adrenaline, too, which means cortisol levels off the charts."

He'd done his homework all right. Unfortunately. I'm always concerned when a patient feels too comfortable with the clinical lingo. It creates in him or her a false sense of control, of mastery over the situation. Which only means a greater sense of shame and disillusionment when the next episode occurs. As it almost inevitably does.

"How long have you had these symptoms?"

"About six months, on and off. Started about a week or two after I retired from the bureau. Though they've been worse in the past month."

"Since the murder of Earl Cranshaw, the prison guard who killed John Jessup?"

A grim smile. "I knew you'd go there first, Doctor. Too obvious, if you ask me. And remember, I said they started months *before* Jessup's death."

"So you see the symptoms being keyed more to your retirement than to Jessup's murder." I paused. "But he *was* your last case. The last serial killer you put away."

"Hey, I'm not ruling anything out. Your interpretation makes sense. But let's not put it in concrete, okay?"

"I never do."

A cool silence grew between us. Probably the first of many, I thought.

There's a lot of truth to the saying, "Doctors make the worst patients." From my own experience in therapy, I can attest that this is especially true for therapists. Now I was beginning to think the adage probably applied equally well to FBI profilers.

"The thing is," Barnes went on, finally, "for years, the night terrors diagnosis was reserved almost exclusively for young children. Pediatric psychiatrists have done studies and written papers on the subject since the middle of the last century. But now—"

"I know, I've seen the current data. Part of my research on trauma-related symptoms. In the past two decades, more and more adults are receiving the diagnosis.

"According to the Night Terrors Support Network, clinicians are blaming the unusual rise in adult symptoms to the uncertainty of contemporary life. The economy, terrorism. Even the recent natural disasters. Tsunamis. Earthquakes. The daily anxiety suppressed by adults during waking life, later invading their sleep."

He nodded gravely.

"Though this is just conjecture," I went on. "The cause may very well be organic, a brain disorder. Nobody knows why night terrors occur. And why they occur during stage four of the sleep cycle, the deepest, most tranquil stage, is even more of a mystery."

I nearly smiled. I rarely spoke in such a technical, almost pedantic fashion to a patient. But my read of Barnes was that this kind of collegial discourse was a good way to bond with him. To meet him, at least initially, at the level at which he felt comfortable. Intellectual, seemingly objective. Creating a sense of connection.

Barnes stirred. "Yeah, but from what I could find, most studies still favor stress or emotional upset as the cause. And in this crazy world, we got that in spades."

"True. But my guess is you're smart enough to see that such general anxieties probably have little to do with your own symptoms. After all, you've just retired from a long career in which you regularly engaged with the most heinous of predators."

"You got that right."

"Whether interviewing serial killers, building suspect profiles, or reading thousands of case files and police reports, you've been inside the heads of homicidal psychopaths. Daily. Hourly."

"*Deep* inside." Barnes raised an eyebrow. "Now aren't you going to ask how that makes me *feel?*"

I bristled. And let him see it.

"Cut the crap. I'm treating your intellect with respect. Do the same for mine."

Another strained silence. Then, unexpectedly, Barnes favored me with a broad grin.

"You know, Doc, this could work out after all. I mean, it might not be a total waste of time."

I nodded. "On *both* our parts. And why don't you call me 'Dan,' okay?"

"Sure. And you can call me Agent Barnes."

"Lotsa luck with that one. Lyle."

He just looked at me, massaging his firm jaw.

"There's something else," I said quietly. "What happened in the past few weeks to Earl Cranshaw and Judge Loftus. There's a killer out there, looking to punish those whom he feels are responsible for Jessup's conviction. And thus his death."

"Yeah, I know. That's why the bureau has me holed up here in a makeshift safehouse. They figure I'm one of the targets on his hitlist."

"That reminds me, why'd they put you *here?* I mean, in Braddock? You live somewhere near?"

"Close enough. I lived in Virginia when I was at Quantico, of course. But I moved here to Pennsylvania, to Franklin Park, after I retired. That's why Neal Alcott caught the baby-sitting detail, at least when it came to me. He works out of the bureau's

Pittsburgh office. I don't know where they're stashing the other possible targets."

"Why Franklin Park? You have family there?"

"I did. Had a wife. Died of cancer years ago." He looked off. "'Still, for that little while, we visited our possible life.'"

He smiled at my puzzled look. "From a poem by Jack Gilbert. Pittsburgh boy. I'm surprised you don't know him."

"I don't know much about poetry."

"Man's greatest achievement, far as I'm concerned."

I took this in. "You have any children, Lyle?"

"One. A son. But we don't exactly…" A long, leaden pause. "I guess you could say we're estranged. He lives in Chicago. Married, I think. With kids."

I let another, longer pause hang in the air. Let him sift through whatever thoughts now filled his mind. As his face changed, becoming a grey, unreadable mask…

I decided it was too soon in our work to pursue the more personal details of his life history. There was a good chance I'd lose him. So I brought us back to the present, to the situation at hand.

"You said the Bureau believes you're a likely target on the killer's hitlist. Do you?"

He roused himself. "Seems logical. I'd have to have a look at those letters Jessup received."

"You mean, you haven't seen them?"

He shook his head. "Since I'm officially retired, I can't get those bastards to let me have eyes-on. Yet without that, I can't work up any kind of profile of the letter writer. Even a general operating theory."

"What a stupid waste of your talents. *And* your experience."

"Tell me about it. Meanwhile, I gotta sit in this goddam motel, eating fast food take-out. Like I haven't done enough of *that* in my life." A rueful smile. "Once I retired, I hoped I'd regularly be able to have a good drink and a decent meal. At a real table. Like a civilian."

"God knows, you've earned it."

He folded his arms, gave me a reproachful look. "One more positive, supportive comment outta you, and I'm gonna have to reevaluate our relationship. I did some clinical interview training, too. I know all the tricks."

"So? Maybe I meant what I said."

"I'll consider that possibility. Once I've gotten to know you better. It's a two-way street, Doc."

I stood then, stretched. The sofa was backed against the poorly-insulated exterior wall, so I was near enough to feel the deepening chill just outside. Another night with the temperature below freezing.

I turned to Barnes again. Tried another tack.

"You really gonna be such a pain in the ass about this? If so, you're not as smart as I thought you were."

"I'm crushed."

"I mean, it's not like you don't have enough to deal with. Your psyche kicking the shit outta you every time you fall asleep, and some killer with a personal grudge out there looking to put you to sleep *permanently*."

"And your point is…?"

"For a guy in your situation, your attitude sucks."

"That's your clinical opinion?"

"*And* my personal one. In your case, it comes down to the same thing."

Barnes got to his feet as well. Body tensed, eyes hard. Wary. And then, with an abruptness that again took me by surprise, his gaze softened.

And he held out his hand.

"Here's the deal," he said. "I'll try not to be a shitty patient, and you try to keep me from losing my fuckin' marbles."

"I'll do my best. But what you're talking about is a kind of psychological triage. I mean, the bureau asked me to help you, and I want to help. They even took the trouble to free up my schedule to work with you. But only for a few days. And, frankly, that's not gonna cut it."

"What do you mean?"

"To get at the root of your symptoms could take weeks, maybe months. Plus the probable use of medication. There've been some good results from using antidepressants like Klonopin and Tofranil."

"Not gonna happen. I like my brain chemistry just the way it is."

"So we'll try other modalities. Relaxation techniques. Hypnotherapy. Prescribed sleep medications."

"Not until I research their efficacy. Possible side effects."

I didn't blink.

"You do what you have to, Lyle. And I'll do the same."

He'd long since let his his extended hand fall once more to his side. His voice grew an edge.

"*Now* who's being a pain in the ass, Doc?"

Before I could reply, there was a sudden loud pounding on the door. Impatient, insistent. Then Alcott's voice.

"You two decent? Another package just showed up."

Barnes and I exchanged puzzled looks.

Without waiting for an answer, Neal Alcott opened the door and stepped inside. His eyes found mine.

"Session's over, Rinaldi. We're moving."

"What's going on?"

"Remember that hotshot ADA I told you about? The one who prosecuted Jessup?"

"Yeah?"

"They just brought her in. Got her sequestered in the city."

Barnes stepped in front of me to face the other agent.

"Because she's probably on the killer's list, right?"

Alcott gave a gruff laugh. "Because she almost got crossed *off* the list. By the killer. He took a shot at her tonight, right outside her office."

Chapter Eleven

It was midnight by the time we got back to the city.

The sky was clear and Arctic cold, emptied of snow. Not a flurry had hit the Lincoln's windshield as we drove back the way we'd come. With most of the streets plowed, snow piled in lumpy drifts on either side, it took Billy, again our driver, just half the time to make the trip.

Still, it was plenty of time for Neal Alcott to fill us in. He sat in the front passenger seat, body twisted awkwardly around to peer in the dim light at Barnes and me in the rear.

"Her name is Claire Cobb, twenty-nine. Native of Dayton, Ohio. Went to work for the Cleveland DA's office right after law school. On the fast track, like I said. The Jessup case was her biggest plum yet. And she nailed it."

Barnes grumbled. "Wasn't hard. The evidence was overwhelming. Once he passed the psych eval, Jessup was toast."

"Whatever." Alcott took a breath. "Anyway, we'd just sent a team to Cleveland this afternoon, following the judge's murder. To convince her to accept FBI protection, stay in a safe house outside town till we got the prick."

"So what happened?"

"The goddam weather is what happened. Our two agents got stranded on the interstate heading there to meet her. Some kinda car trouble. By the time they got hold of another vehicle, it was too late. They show up at the Cleveland DA's office, only to find the whole block cordoned off. Black-and-whites. City ambulance. Turns out, Claire Cobb was shot going to her car in the parking garage. After work."

"How bad was she injured?" Barnes asked.

"Minor. Shoulder wound. The bullet went in and out. She was damned lucky, that's for sure. She told the cops the shooter was in some kind of blue or black van. Came barreling out of a darkened corner of the garage, leaning out the driver's side window with a gun. He fired two shots, only one of which hit her, and kept driving."

Barnes whistled. "She was lucky, all right."

"Where is Claire now?" I asked.

Alcott said, "Here. In Greentree, across the river. We have her stashed in a Marriott there."

I knew the place. I'd attended a clinical conference there once. Just east of the city.

"She didn't need hospitalization?"

"They took her to some ER in Cleveland, of course. But they patched her up and said she was good to go. At first, she just wanted to go home, but our agents talked her out of it. Told her the guy might try again. Scared the shit out of her. She caved."

"But why bring her here?" I was having a hard time understanding the bureau's approach to these shootings.

"I can probably answer that," Barnes said. "If I were Neal here, I'd want to run the whole show from one place. Easier to control intel, coordinate field agents. *Much* easier to keep potential victims safely tucked away."

Alcott nodded. "That's right. Besides, the Pittsburgh office runs FBI operations for the whole tri-state area. So the bureau can interface with the Steubenville cops on the Cranshaw killing, the Pittsburgh cops on Judge Loftus—"

"I thought he was from Cleveland, too," I said. "Where Claire Cobb lives and works."

"He is, but he was killed here in the city. So in terms of jurisdiction, it's Pittsburgh PD's case."

"Speaking of Loftus, has his daughter Helen been located? Informed what happened?"

"Uh-huh. Soon as she got back from her hiking trip, she got the next-of-kin notification. Took it pretty hard, according to the cops."

"No surprise there."

"Thankfully, her boyfriend was with her. Plus her dorm mate at Carnegie Mellon."

All the family she had left, I reflected. I hoped they'd be enough. I also made a mental note to follow up with her through Angie Villanova. To make sure Helen was getting the support she'd need.

Barnes cleared his throat. "So the Bureau is working the shootings jointly with the Pittsburgh PD?"

"Yeah." Alcott's frowned. "Not exactly a brain trust, but some competent people. If nothing else, it gives us more boots on the ground. To follow up on leads. Interview tangential witnesses. Background stuff."

Lyle Barnes mumbled something I didn't quite catch. But it was clear he shared Alcott's view of the local police department. The typical FBI condescension toward any law enforcement agency that wasn't the bureau. Including cops, the CIA, ATF, and, especially, Homeland Security.

Fuck 'em, I thought sourly. If Neal Alcott was the bureau's idea of a rising star, they had no business looking down on anyone.

"After the Cobb shooting," Alcott continued, "we've stepped up making contact with some of the other probables on the killer's list. So our people are getting in touch with them as we speak. The Cleveland cops who brought Jessup in, his defense attorney, the jury foreman…"

"That's a lot of manpower," Barnes said.

"Not to mention the overtime, but the director feels it's necessary."

Barnes pursed his lips, but didn't comment.

Having finished his report, Alcott swiveled face-front again in his seat. I turned to look at Barnes' chiseled profile, outlined in the faint light, like a medieval woodcut against the night-shadowed window. Before we'd left the motel, he'd downed two cups of black coffee from the lobby vending machine. Yet I could see the strain in his eyes, their ongoing battle with fatigue.

I sat back in my seat. It was strange. A veteran FBI agent. With a long and distinguished career.

A fearless man, afraid to fall asleep.

We drove the rest of the way to Greentree in silence.

◇◇◇

Assistant District Attorney Claire Cobb didn't fit the picture I had in my mind of an ambitious, "hotshot" prosecutor. Maybe because the last career-driven, whip-smart female ADA I knew *did*—in her stunning looks, take-no-prisoners attitude, and undoubted courage.

What Claire Cobb had, instead, was the steady manner and personal gravitas that made you believe in her utterly. In her competence. In her sincerity. At least, that was the initial impression I had as we shook hands. If it was all show, a practiced pose, she was a remarkable actress.

She was a heavy-set woman, quite stout, with short cropped brown hair. A smooth, oval face, with serious dark eyes behind Armani glasses. Her white blouse, black jacket and slacks, and medium heels—the contemporary working woman's uniform—seemed made to order for the persona she projected. Business-like, yet approachable.

The only glaring note was provided by the bandaged shoulder visible under her blouse, and the way her forearm was bent across her ample chest, held in a hospital sling.

"Sorry to meet you under these circumstances," I said, as she resumed her seat on the three-sectioned couch. I sat next to her. "Does it hurt?"

She managed a smile. "Only when somebody asks me that. And people seem determined to do so."

Behind me, Neal Alcott stifled a low chuckle.

We were in a suite on the top floor of the Greentree Marriott, on whose exterior double doors was a sign stating that the room was closed for remodeling.

The suite itself was modestly-appointed, yet spacious. Including the main sitting area—where we were now—and two good-sized bedrooms.

The larger of the two boasted a wide-screen TV whose volume was loud enough for us to hear it. The local CNN affiliate, covering the shooting death that morning of Judge Ralph Loftus. Lyle Barnes had gone in and turned it on as soon as we arrived, not five minutes ago.

Agents Green and Zarnicki, having dutifully followed us in from Braddock, were out in the corridor.

I'd noticed Alcott's posture and manner had grown more relaxed from the moment Lyle Barnes left the room. Though Alcott was the agent in charge, the now-retired Barnes' status and reputation obligated the younger man to keep him in the loop. And with Barnes making little effort to hide his disrespect for Alcott, it couldn't have been easy.

Which was probably why, when the TV volume from the master bedroom rose even higher, Alcott was only too happy to stride briskly to the door and close it. The news anchor's voice fell to an urgent muffle.

"Now we can hear ourselves think," the agent said to no one in particular. And received no reply.

Claire Cobb broke the sudden silence by turning to me.

Her smile was cordial, but wary.

"I understand you work with the Pittsburgh police."

"As a consultant, yes. I'm a psychologist, and I specialize in treating crime victims."

"Then remind me to get your card when this is all over. I'll probably need it."

She looked past me to where Alcott now stood, his back to the wide picture window. His reflection in the glass mingled with the diffused glow of the city's lights.

"Speaking of which, Agent Alcott, how long do you plan on keeping me here? And my fellow captive, Agent Barnes?"

He stirred. "As long as it takes, Ms. Cobb. Unless you think that's a bad idea…"

She shivered involuntarily, and I could see the naked fear she was containing under her placid demeanor.

"No, not at all. Just curious. Being shot at is enough to make a believer out of me."

"Don't worry." Alcott grinned. "We'll get the bastard. Catching bad guys is kind of a hobby of mine."

"Really?" She considered this. "Mine are needlepoint and Tantric sex."

I enjoyed watching the startled look on Alcott's face. And realized how much I was growing to like Claire Cobb.

"One last question." Claire turned her head, sweeping the room with her glance. "Where are the two detectives who brought me here from the airport?"

"Detectives?" I looked over at Alcott. "I thought *your* people brought Ms. Cobb in."

"They put her on the plane in Cleveland. Pittsburgh PD assigned two dicks to pick her up. Bring her in."

"Was I that dreadful a passenger?" Claire said wryly. "Did I offend them in some way?"

His smile was indulgent.

"No, ma'am. They're probably working the Loftus killing. Part of an investigation the bureau's running jointly with the Pittsburgh police."

Suddenly, Alcott's cell phone rang in his jacket pocket. He pulled it out, squinted at the display.

"Excuse me." He took the call, listened a moment. "Yes. Okay, send them up."

He clicked off and favored Claire with another easy smile. "Speak of the devil. They're on the way up. Looks like we caught a break."

Chapter Twelve

In response to the brisk knock at the door, Alcott strode across the room and answered it.

I stood up when, to my pleasant surprise, Sergeant Harry Polk and Detective Eleanor Lowrey entered. I felt the smile spread on my face as I approached them.

Polk's reaction, I must admit, was slightly less enthusiastic.

"Jesus Fucking Christ." His florid face turned three shades darker. "How'd I know *you'd* be up to your ass in this mess?"

"Maybe you're psychic, Harry."

"Or else goddam unlucky." He gave a gale-like sigh. "Anybody take a shot at *you* yet, Rinaldi?"

"Nope. Sorry to disappoint you."

"Yeah, well, a guy can dream."

Though I hadn't seen Harry Polk since last summer, we'd known each other since my involvement in the Wingfield investigation a few years back. Never a fan of my work with the department, he'd grudgingly acknowledged on more than one occasion that he didn't completely hate my guts. Disliked them, maybe. Found them irritating, absolutely.

The fact is, though he'd learned to tolerate me, as far as Polk was concerned I'd always be an acquired taste.

Luckily, Eleanor Lowrey felt differently

"*I'm* happy to see you, Danny."

She gave Polk a not-so-gentle nudge as she came over to me. As a black woman, and the junior detective in their partnership, she'd learned over the years how to handle Polk. From what I'd gleaned, it was the combination of her wry humor, steely competence, and steadfast loyalty that had earned his grudging respect. Plus, deep down, they actually liked each other.

"Glad to see you, too, Detective."

Though we'd shared drinks—and one powerfully intense kiss—in the recent past, under the circumstances it made sense that she'd merely taken my hand. Colleagues greeting each other at the start of a case.

"Looks like you and Harry caught a real red-ball here," I said. "Multiple murders."

"Be still my heart."

Only then did she allow a warmth to enter her violet eyes. As she slipped her hand from mine.

Eleanor Lowrey did, admittedly, fit the description Dave Parnelli had rhapsodized about at Noah's bar. Tall, with striking good looks, she had the strong, sculpted body of an athlete. Her rich blue-black hair, swept back from her face and up, contrasted with the burnt red gloss on her lips and fingernails.

Just as her scoop-necked fitted sweater and jeans, half hidden beneath her tan overcoat, contrasted with the fashion-challenged Harry Polk. Wearing his usual wrinkled blue suit, he'd already removed his Army surplus overcoat and tossed it over a chair.

By this point, Claire Cobb had herself risen from the couch and come over to greet them.

"Hello again, Detectives." The typical criminal attorney's collegial, though unmistakably superior, tone of voice.

"Counselor." Polk's reply was more grunt than speech.

"I understand from Agent Alcott that you've caught a break. On the Loftus shooting, I assume?"

Eleanor spoke. "No, Ms. Cobb. On yours."

She turned to Alcott. "We got word from Cleveland PD. An hour ago, Ohio Highway Patrol found the shooter's van. The one Ms. Cobb described. It was left in a ditch off the interstate, about twenty miles from the city. No plates, but the VIN number confirmed it as stolen. The owner had reported the theft earlier today."

"Not much of a break," Alcott said stiffly.

"Depends on how ya look at it."

It was Polk, collapsing onto a cushioned wingback chair with a weary sigh. As if breaking some kind of spell, this allowed the rest of us to find seats as well.

"We're just startin' to put things together," he went on, pulling a dog-eared notebook from his jacket pocket. "Steubenville PD emailed everything they have on the Cranshaw shooting, and we've had uniforms canvassing the Oakland area where the judge got whacked this morning. Biegler and the Assistant Chief want to meet tomorrow at nine a.m., to lay everything out. See where we are."

"Christ." Alcott shook his head. "Biegler."

I knew Lieutenant Stu Biegler as well, and pretty much shared Alcott's low opinion. Biegler was Polk's and Lowrey's boss at robbery/homicide, a high-handed stickler for procedure who spent most of his career making sure his ass was covered. Not that it mattered, but he was even less a fan of mine than Harry Polk.

Eleanor said, "I'll collate the data from the three participating departments, so we'll have what we need for the meeting."

Her eyes caught Alcott's. "Truth is, from what I've seen already, there might be more to work with than you'd think. Apparently, somebody saw the guy who shot Earl Cranshaw leave the scene in a Chevy sedan. Which was later found abandoned in a parking lot nearby."

"Had it been reported stolen, too?" Claire asked.

Eleanor nodded. "Yes. Again, plates gone, but traced through the VIN number."

"What about the judge?" Alcott said. "Anybody see the shooter? His car?"

"There we don't got shit," Polk replied. "So far. But we just started workin' the case. It's too soon to cry in our beer about it."

"The thing is," Eleanor said, "even with what little we know, we can build a map of the killer's movements. From Steubenville, where he shot Earl Cranshaw, to here in town to kill the judge, then back to Ohio—Cleveland, this time—for the attempt on Ms. Cobb. Apparently using a different stolen vehicle for each hit."

"Assuming he kept to the pattern when it comes to Judge Loftus," I said.

"Big assumption," Polk said. "Especially since our canvas hasn't turned up a single witness to the judge's murder. The killer coulda been drivin' the fuckin' Batmobile, for all we know. But it was so early in the morning, there weren't any other people in the hotel lot."

Alcott scratched his nose thoughtfully.

"Ohio, then western Pennsylvania, then back to Ohio. Not the most efficient route to take."

"Maybe he's not interested in efficiency," I offered. "Maybe he's crossing his victims off the list in a specific order. For some specific reason."

"Which presents another problem," Eleanor said. "Since we don't know for sure who's on the list...I mean, the number of people...how will we know when he's done?"

"Well," Claire Cobb said quietly. "One thing for sure. He won't be completely done until he tries again to kill me. And succeeds."

"Let's hope we nail him before he gets the chance."

"Yeah." Polk growled, climbing slowly to his feet. "Which we can't do if we're just sittin' around here."

As Eleanor and I rose as well, Polk tilted his head in the direction of the master bedroom.

"Who's watchin' the tube in there?"

"Special Agent Lyle Barnes," Alcott said. "Retired," he added meaningfully. "Since he worked the Jessup case for the Bureau, we figure he's probably on the killer's hitlist. So we're babysitting him, too."

"Well, he must be goin' deaf. Got the goddam TV up loud enough."

For some reason, Polk's words sent off an alarm bell in the back of my mind. Inexplicable, yet there it was.

Agent Alcott must have felt something similar, for his brow suddenly tightened, and then he was heading for the door to the bedroom. I followed him.

He turned the handle. It was locked from the inside.

Shit, I thought. Another locked door. With my shoulder still aching from breaking down the one at the motel in Braddock. At least, this time we had more manpower on hand for the job.

By now, Polk, Lowrey, and Claire Cobb had joined us at the door. We could hear the throbbing music of some inane TV commercial coming from inside the room.

Alcott impotently rattled the door handle.

"You're *kiddin'* me," Polk said angrily, unholstering his service weapon. "Everybody stay the fuck back."

Everybody did.

Polk cut Alcott a wry look. "Just make sure the Marriott sends *you* the goddam bill."

Then he fired, once, at the handle. Like a cannon going off. A spray of metal shards, smoke.

The door, dotted with gunpowder residue, swayed open.

We all ran in, Alcott and myself in the lead.

The volume from the flat-screen was deafening. The bed was still made, though I could see the imprint on the covers where Barnes had sat. Next to it lay the TV remote. Eleanor scooped it up and hit the mute button.

Meanwhile, Alcott, Polk, and I entered the large, strangely cold master bathroom. Frigidly cold.

Empty, too. Except for a spray of glass fragments on the gleaming tile floor. From the bathroom window, whose jagged, gaping hole was the source of the freezing air.

The broken window was small, but not so small a determined, agile man couldn't get through it.

A man like Lyle Barnes.

Polk went to the window, carefully leaned out. Looking up at the black, cold sky. Up and to his left.

"Son-of-a-bitch." Shaking off the chill of night, he poked his head back in. "Service ladder bolted to the wall. Goes all the way up to the roof."

Alcott and I exchanged stunned looks.

The FBI profiler was gone.

Chapter Thirteen

Alcott instantly clutched Polk's arm. "Get up that ladder after him! He could still be on the roof!"

"You shittin' me? We're thirty stories up!"

The two men glared at each other.

"Listen, Sergeant..."

I spoke sharply. "No, Alcott, *you* listen!"

He turned, obviously stunned at my tone.

"For one thing, none of us are thin enough to get through that window. Besides, if there's no way off the roof, Barnes isn't going anywhere. Not without a parachute. So there's no rush."

"But—"

"Let me finish. Odds are, there's a way down from the roof, and Barnes is already using it. Emergency stairs. Service elevator. Some damned thing."

Polk nodded vigorously. "Which means we're wastin' time standin' around here."

Without another word, Harry bolted out of the room, Alcott and me right on his heels. By the time we'd returned to the suite's front room, the agent was barking orders into his two-way, while Polk explained to Eleanor and Claire what was going on.

"Bet *I* can make it through that window." Eleanor quickly peeled off her overcoat.

"Bad idea." I turned to Polk. "Harry, don't let—"

But she'd already headed for the bedroom, her partner keeping pace with her, muttering his disapproval. Trying to pull rank, without much success.

Alcott turned and pointed a stern finger at Claire.

"I've got people stationed right outside in the hall. So just stay here, okay?"

"You don't have to tell me twice."

As Alcott strode toward the suite's door, I followed.

"I'm going with you, Alcott. I can talk to Barnes."

He almost laughed. "Yeah, I can see what a great job you've done so far."

We went out to the hallway, where Agents Green and Zarnicki lounged against the far wall.

"Green," Alcott said, "take the elevator down to the lobby and keep your eyes peeled for Agent Barnes. The son-of-a-bitch gave us the slip. Zarnicki, stay put."

Zarnicki dutifully drew himself up to his full height, the picture of protective zeal, while Green repeatedly pushed the elevator button.

I indicated the door at the other end of the hall.

"Service door, Alcott. The stairs."

I ran down the carpeted hall and pushed open the door, onto a landing with stairs going in both directions. Alcott came to stand behind me.

Above us, the stairs led to a metal door marked "Roof Access." Below us, they angled down into pockets of darkness interlaced with pale halos of light.

Alcott merely grunted. "Let's go."

With the agent in the lead, we hurried down the stairs, taking them two at a time. Until Alcott stopped so abruptly, I nearly ran into him.

"Listen!" he whispered.

Now I heard it, too. Footsteps, echoing dully on the concrete steps. The sound dopplering up from below.

"Gotta be him."

We quickened our pace down the stairs, landing after landing, floor after floor. But always with those other footsteps ahead of us, descending faster and faster.

Finally, Alcott and I arrived at ground level, just in time to see the door to the lobby sighing closed.

We pushed it open again and found ourselves facing a lobby full of people. Some lined up at reception, others clustered in small groups, or chatting on their cells. Still others following bellmen pulling luggage carts toward the main elevators.

Suddenly, I spotted a couple of tourist types, looking angrily behind them. As though someone had brusquely pushed his way past.

"C'mon!" I tapped Alcott's shoulder and took off, not bothering to wait for his response.

The tourist couple had just recovered their composure when I awkwardly side-stepped them, drawing another pair of angry stares. Up ahead, I saw a set of double doors marked "Employees Only."

I was about to shoulder my way through when Agent Green appeared at my side. Having probably seen the same thing I had when he'd exited the elevator.

By now, Alcott had caught up, and all three of us barreled through the double doors. This led to a service corridor, lined with wheeled tables, boxes of supplies, stacks of serving trays. An employee time clock hung from the wall just inside the doors.

Running now, we reached the end of the corridor, which led to another service door. I shoved it open, and suddenly we found ourselves in the hotel's kitchen. Dozens of workers in aprons and chef's hats. Room service personnel in smart-looking vests. All in a frenzy of activity, appliances buzzing and pinging, dishes clattering.

Adding to the din was the cascade of shocked, outraged voices as Lyle Barnes, visible between racks of plates and rows of ovens, zig-zagged his way across the room.

"There he is!" It was Agent Green, shouting and pointing, and then racing ahead of Alcott and me.

"Agent Barnes!" Alcott cried. "Stop! That's an order!"

Yeah, I thought. *Like that's gonna happen.*

Meanwhile, Agent Green, pushing aside the startled kitchen staff, knocking over a stack of trays, had closed the distance between himself and Barnes.

Suddenly, the older agent whirled, some kind of big cooking pot in hand, and threw it at Green. The younger man ducked, using his forearm to bat aside the pot. But when he stood again, Barnes had vanished. Through another door.

Alcott and I caught up with Green, then I jostled past them and pushed on the door. It didn't budge.

The two other men joined me. At a nod from Alcott, we all put our shoulders to the door. Pushed as hard as we could. It gave some, but not enough.

Green rubbed his arm. "He's blocked it somehow."

"No shit," Alcott growled.

It took roughly three minutes to retrace our steps back to the lobby, and then through the hotel's entrance doors out to the street. Due to the icy cold and lateness of the hour, there were few pedestrians, and only a sparse parade of cars, trucks, and taxis. But no Barnes.

"Goddammit!" Alcott swiveled his head back and forth, fists at his hips. Breathing hard.

"Looks like we lost him," Green said, demonstrating once more his ability to state the obvious.

◇◇◇

A short time later, we were all assembled back in the hotel suite, Eleanor's sweater still snow-damp from her brief survey of the roof. Polk stood grimly beside her.

"Well?" Neal Alcott's voice had lost a great deal of its officious command.

"I made it up to the roof and saw Agent Barnes' footprints," said Eleanor. "Luckily, the snow's untouched up there, like a carpet. Only one set of tracks."

"Yeah, luckily…" Alcott sniffed. "*And..?*"

"There's a small access shed up there, unlocked from the outside. Leads to those emergency stairs you followed him down."

I nodded. "Yeah, we saw the roof access. From the landing below."

Then Agent Green, who'd been standing at a discreet distance, cell phone to his ear, spoke up.

"Sir, that door Barnes went out leads to a back alley. He pushed a trash dumpster up against it to block it."

A seething Alcott rubbed his cheeks with both hands. Then, as though just realizing that Green was still there, waiting attentively, he gave him a brisk, dismissive nod. The young agent was only too happy to pick up his cue and hurry out the door.

"Jesus, what a screw-up." Alcott looked off for a long moment, neck muscles like steel rods.

Then, with a weary sigh, he turned to face the rest of us. Polk leaned sullenly against the sofa back, Lowrey standing a few feet away, arms folded. Claire Cobb, eyes blinking rapidly, was seated. Her palpable anxiety fed the tension already growing in the room.

I stood by the picture window, looking out at the thin coating of silver a pale moon had spread over the silent, snow-bound city. It was one a.m.

"I mean, we'll *find* Agent Barnes," Alcott suddenly added. "He can't have gotten far, and we have the manpower to do the search. Especially when you add in the police."

Polk shook his head. "Maybe you didn't get the memo, Agent Alcott. Keepin' the killer's next potential victims under wraps is the Bureau's job. *You're* the ones who let Barnes off his leash, not us. So you're the ones who have to bring him in."

"I don't care much for your tone, Sergeant." Alcott sniffed again. Maybe he was coming down with a cold. "In case *you* didn't get the memo, I'm running this joint FBI-police operation. And your chief promised the bureau total cooperation. Which means if I want to detail some local cops to help search for Agent Barnes, that's exactly what's gonna happen. Are we clear?"

Eleanor answered for her partner. "Crystal, sir."

Polk gave her a dour look, but remained silent. Which Alcott noted. Suddenly, I saw the concern on the agent's face that he'd overstepped. That he'd risked alienating the very people whose assistance he needed. Especially now, having to deal with the embarrassment of Barnes taking off.

"Of course, Detectives," Alcott said, reasonably, "I wouldn't waste *your* talents on some broad-based search. I realize your primary task is working these murders, and apprehending the killer before he finds his next victim."

Eleanor added, "And we *do* have a lot of work to do before this morning's meeting with Lt. Biegler and the assistant chief. We have to collate police reports from the various jurisdictions involved, get the ballistics test results, interview that witness to the prison guard's murder who's just come forward—"

Polk stirred. "Not to mention reaching out to the highway patrol to get some help finding the car the killer was driving when he shot Judge Loftus. It's the only one that hasn't turned up yet."

"It probably will, Harry," Eleanor said calmly. "Stolen, like the others. If the pattern holds."

Polk barely registered her.

"And another thing." He squinted at Alcott. "We don't even have the FBI's list of potential victims. Plus whatever you got on those fan letters our killer sent to John Jessup in prison. Fingerprints, forensics. Stuff like that. I mean, I hope we'll be seein' some of that interagency cooperation you were talkin' about sometime soon."

"You will, Sergeant. I'll assign Agent Green to assist you. Get you whatever we have. ASAP."

"You can't give us somebody else? Hell, I got a sport coat older than he is."

"Nobody else I can spare. Live with it."

Polk looked like he was chewing the inside of his mouth. But he finally nodded.

I cleared my throat. "Now that we're all best friends again, I'd like to bring something up. Anybody but me wondering why the hell Agent Barnes gave us the slip?"

Alcott frowned. "No idea. We're providing protection against a possible attempt on his life. Doesn't make sense. He's much more vulnerable to the killer on the outside, away from the Bureau's sphere of influence."

I took a measured step toward him.

"Maybe, maybe not. At least from his point of view. I've only known Lyle Barnes a short time, but I'd guess he was feeling pretty constrained and useless, sequestered in some FBI safe house while a killer's on the loose. Especially a killer who probably has him in his sights."

"But Barnes is FBI to his bones, Rinaldi. Been on the team his whole adult life. Lives and breathes procedure. Which means he'd know a search for him is an unnecessary strain on the bureau's resources, a dangerous squandering of manpower during a critical investigation."

"I'd tend to agree…*if* he were still on the team. But he's not. He's retired. Not only that, he wasn't even asked to consult on the case. Nor allowed to see the letters that John Jessup received in prison. The last guy he put away, for Christ's sake. My read on Barnes is that he sees this as an insult."

"Bullshit."

"Think about it. Barnes is the guy who nailed Jessup. The one most responsible for Jessup ending up behind bars, where he was later killed by a guard who just got a slap on the wrist. Now, Jessup's one and only fan—who sent him letters in prison—is on the loose, gunning down those he feels are responsible for Jessup's fate."

I took a breath. "You see my meaning? *This is as personal for Barnes as it is for the killer.* And there's no way a man like Lyle Barnes is going to sit it out. Especially if he feels he's been shunted aside by his own people. Hell, he was your best profiler, and he wasn't given access to the letters. Allowed to build a profile. Even asked to offer his opinion. Instead, he was treated like any of the other potential victims."

Alcott considered this. "So you think Barnes is out there flying solo, trying to track down the killer?"

"I don't know. Maybe he just wants some time to think. Figure out where he stands, what his next move should be."

Nobody spoke for a moment. Then, to my surprise, ADA Claire Cobb broke the silence.

"I guess *I* understand him, too. Even here, with FBI protection, some part of me feels unsafe. Vulnerable."

She glanced down at the sling draped from her shoulder.

"The killer tried to take me down once already. This guy, this avenging angel working through his goddam list…I don't know, I get the feeling he's pretty determined."

She looked over at me, eyes searching my face as if for confirmation. For support.

I tried to give it to her. "I understand, Ms. Cobb. Believe me, I know what it's like to know that somebody's out there, hunting you."

Alcott snorted. "You two wanna share your feelings or whatever, use the other room. We've gotta get things in gear. The detectives have their work to do, and I have to coordinate the search for Barnes. Crazy son-of-a-bitch."

He no longer even pretended to hide his frustration, his barely contained rage.

"Arrogant prick. I don't care why the hell he snuck out on his own people. But I *do* know this: If he gets his ass killed on my watch, I'll be buried so deep in shit I'll never see daylight again."

"Tough break, all right," Polk murmured, with a half-smile. Then he turned to me.

"Well, Doc, looks like your new patient's terminated therapy. I guess you can go home and get in your jammies."

Ignoring him, I looked over at Alcott.

"It's your call, but since the bureau's cleared my schedule anyway, maybe I should stick around. If you *do* find Barnes, I'm still willing to try to help him. God knows, he needs it."

"What Agent Barnes needs is a pair of ankle irons and a keeper." Alcott sighed heavily. "But you're probably right. I just don't want you underfoot, messing with my investigation. Do what Sergeant Polk here said. Go home, get some sleep, but keep your cell on. At all times."

"Maybe I'm not sleepy."

"Maybe that wasn't a suggestion."

I regarded him cooly. "Really looking forward to working with you, Neal."

Claire Cobb rose from her seat. Her eyes were pale and moist behind her glasses as she regarded Alcott.

"What about me? Do I just stay here?"

Alcott scratched his chin. "In the hotel, yes. But I'll get a female agent to bunk with you in another room. Here on the same floor, where we have teams patrolling the halls." He tried to sound reassuring. "You'll be quite safe, Ms. Cobb. I guarantee it."

Claire smiled grimly. "I've been around long enough to know there *are* no guarantees. Not in this life, anyway."

There wasn't much Agent Alcott could say in response to that. So he didn't say anything at all.

Chapter Fourteen

What the hell did I know about Agent Lyle Barnes?

This thought occurred to me as Billy, our driver from earlier that night, drove me back down to Noah's Ark so I could pick up my car. I could tell when I'd slid into the back seat in the Marriott parking lot that the young agent wasn't too thrilled with this assignment, but we both knew there also wasn't much he could do about it. Not as a junior G-man far down on the Bureau's food chain.

It took less than twenty minutes to drive through the empty, snow-plowed streets and arrive at Second Avenue. The bar had long since closed, and I imagined Noah snoring peacefully in his bed, spooning Charlene in the rooms they shared behind the kitchen. Yawning myself, I peered through the passenger side window at the unlit, low-slung saloon. Moored to thick railroad ties embedded at the embankment, the converted coal barge rolled and dipped silently on the black, sluggish waters of the Monogahela.

Billy pulled the Lincoln to a stop where my Mustang—the sole car on the street—was parked, covered in a silken layer of frost. I thanked him as I got out, and received a "Hey" in reply.

As I absently turned the key and let the engine warm up, I returned to my thoughts about Lyle Barnes. Though I'd been truthful with Neal Alcott about my interpretation of Barnes' actions, I also realized—even as I explained my reasoning—that everything I said was mere conjecture. Not only had I just met the retired profiler, I hadn't had the opportunity to fully explore his symptoms, or address the meaning his own diagnosis of night terrors meant to him.

In other words, did he see his horrifying night visions as evidence of a weakness in his character, the beginning of a downward slide into emotional vulnerability? I certainly suspected as much. For a man as formerly vigorous in mind and body as Lyle Barnes, the fear of such a psychological collapse would be intolerable. Shameful.

Utterly unacceptable.

Which, I suddenly saw, might have also prompted his impulse to escape the FBI's protection. His needing the help of a therapist for his night terrors was bad enough. Now, being guarded day and night by Alcott's team, Barnes was reduced to victim status. Lumped in with retired prison guards and elderly trial judges and trembling female lawyers. Lumped in with the weak, the defenseless. Those whom he'd formerly fought to protect.

I revved the Mustang's engine a few times, watching in my rear view mirror while exhaust smoke billowed against the starless winter sky. As I pulled out into the street, I mused on what the combination of Barnes' stern, self-reliant nature and his sleep-deprived, traumatized state might have created in his mind.

Men like Lyle Barnes were doers. Whether motivated by reason, madness, patriotism, guilt, or merely some sudden impulse, such men—once triggered to act—*acted.*

I drove across the Fort Pitt Bridge and then made the ascent up Mt. Washington, and home. But I barely registered the middle-last-century houses huddled between snow drifts along Grandview Avenue. Didn't even see the barren trees, stark as giant stick figures against the saffron, downy slope of low hills. Didn't even recognize, at first, my own house at the far end of the street, its feeble porch light glowing a soft, diffused yellow.

My mind was elsewhere as I pulled into my driveway, wheels bumping against the twin furrows of banked, salt-pitted snow.

Regardless of what had triggered Lyle Barnes, he'd followed the dictates of a lifetime's impulse to act, and had acted. He was out there somewhere, I hoped sheltered from the night and the cold. Thinking, perhaps rationally, perhaps not. Maybe driven half-mad by lack of sleep and countless nights of horrifying, demonic visions and twenty years spent living in the minds of the most evil of men.

What I *did* know—or at least believed—was this: Barnes was plotting a strategy, creating a scenario. Formulating a plan of action.

Just as, somewhere else in this same night, the killer was also thinking, plotting. Formulating a plan of action.

I shut off the engine and sat back in my seat.

What, I wondered, would happen if the two should meet?

Which one would survive?

◇◇◇

I showered, dressed in sweats and a long-sleeved Pitt t-shirt, and climbed under the covers.

When I'd entered my house, I didn't even stop to pick up the mail that had been shoved through the door slot and now littered the hardwood floor. Nor did I detour into the kitchen to make coffee for the following morning.

The only thing I did was use my landline phone at the rolltop desk in the front room to check my voice mail messages. No patient calls, though this was to be expected.

Thanks to Special Agent Neal Alcott, my patients were under the impression I was sick with the flu. Not that this would normally stop the most vulnerable of patients from trying to reach me, or at least leave a message. Which I'd always encouraged them to do. As I'd learned many years ago, being a therapist is a full-time job, regardless of one's stated office hours.

But, thankfully, things were quiet on that front. The only message was from Angela Villanova, my distant cousin and the department's community liaison officer. Since she hadn't called my cell or my home line, it was likely she was making a clinical referral. All she asked was that I call her in the morning.

Angie Villanova was a brusque, bawdy, no-nonsense woman caught halfway between a traditional Italian upbringing and the urgent demands of feminism. Ten years my senior, she still often treated me as she did when my dad used to pay her to tutor me in high school math.

The only downside to my relationship with Angie was the occasional Sunday meals I was forced to endure at her house. Though she was an excellent cook, not even her mother's special "Tuscany recipe" sauce, ladled onto perfectly *al dente* rigatoni, was enough to make dinner with her bitter, bigoted husband Sonny tolerable.

I put down the land line, hastily pushed thoughts of Sonny and his racist tirades out of my mind, and headed for the bedroom.

◇◇◇

An hour later, still awake and troubled by the long night's events, I got out of bed.

Stumbling into the kitchen, tiled walls bathed now in pre-dawn light, I managed to make coffee. Then I went into the front room and watched the early local TV news.

The shooting death of Ohio judge Ralph Loftus was the lead story, with the breaking news that the car his killer apparently drove had been found. It was a blue SUV, stolen, with its plates removed. The car had been discovered, abandoned in a ditch in Mt. Lebanon by a Pitt grad student driving home from a party just after midnight last night. Police had investigated at the scene, after which the suspect vehicle was towed to the department impound, where it was turned over to the crime scene unit. According to a police spokesperson, the detectives involved proclaimed the discovery of the SUV a significant break in the case.

I considered this. Regardless of how "significant" it might turn out to be, there was no doubt that Polk and Lowrey would be thrilled with the discovery. It meant that the shooter was sticking to his M.O., stealing vehicles to use in his murder attempts, then abandoning them.

I'd learned from watching both detectives work that the more consistent and repetitive a pattern, the better the chances that the police could anticipate a criminal's next move. Or, conversely, the more likely that they'd take note of a variation in the pattern.

Patterns. And their variations. Part of the contours of a therapist's world as well, I thought.

While watching the rest of the broadcast, I realized that the authorities had so far managed to portray Judge Loftus' murder as an isolated incident. There'd been no mention of the shooting of Earl Cranshaw in Steubenville, nor of the attempt on Claire Cobb's life in Cleveland. And no reason there should have been, even though Ohio is just one state over from Pennsylvania. By definition, local news is concerned primarily with local matters.

Just as well, I thought, sipping my cooling coffee. If it became known that the two out-of-state shootings were related to the Loftus murder, and that in each case the assailant used a different stolen vehicle, the notion of a planned, multistate killing spree would be irrisistable to the media. The story would break nationally, the Internet crime junkies would light up cyberspace, and the cops would be fielding hundreds of useless and distracting tips.

More importantly, it might well drive the killer underground. Maybe to wait until the furor died down and the story went away. Until the police and FBI were preoccupied with fresh killers, fresher crimes.

Only to begin once more his methodical checking off of the victims on his list…

The thought just added to my restlessness. Exhausted, but still too wired to sleep, I went down to my basement gym to turn my unease into healthy sweat.

Calling the pine-paneled, windowless room a gym was a bit of a stretch. It was a typical low-ceilinged, East Coast basement, lit by track lights, with a heavy bag, a weathered workout bench, and some free weights sharing space with storage boxes and old tools. But it had the grace of the familiar, the unchanging.

And it suited me.

At the far end of the room stood the door to the small, enclosed furnace room. Thick heat poured from the ceiling vents. I peeled off my long-sleeved t-shirt and attacked the bag, throwing combinations until my arms ached. Though usually I put something loud and propulsive on the CD player when I worked out, this time all I wanted to hear was the rasp of my own breathing and the slap of my taped, gloved hands against leather.

Pounding the bag, again and again.

Sometimes, I thought, *you just have to hit something.*

◇◇◇

At six thirty, after a second shower and another cup of black coffee, I padded over to the landline and called Angie at home. She answered after the fifth ring.

"I got your message," I said.

"I figured that. But I didn't expect to hear back from you so soon. Aren't you on loan to the FBI?"

"Boy, security's tight as a drum at the department, isn't it?"

"Look, Danny, I have breakfast with the assistant chief at least once a week. He told me the FBI Director himself called and asked for you. Some retired profiler's wigging out or something, right? And since Dr. Phil is busy, the bureau called you in."

"Jesus, Angie."

"Don't get all indignant on me, okay? I haven't even had my coffee yet. Besides, the assistant chief tells me everything. Maybe he has a thing for middle-aged Italian women with big asses. Anyway, thanks to him, I always hear the best gossip. Speaking of which, you wanna know how Stu Biegler and his wife's marriage counseling sessions are going? From what I hear, they don't need a therapist, they need a Fight Club referee."

Last summer, Lieutenant Biegler's wife discovered he'd secretly fallen off the fidelity wagon. The couple had been warring about it ever since.

"Fascinating, but you still haven't told me why you called. In fact, I get the feeling you're stalling."

"You have a suspicious mind, Danny. It's not your most attractive quality."

"Uh-huh. So talk. Are you making a referral?"

Her voice grew sober. "Yes I am. A woman about my age, who's in a really bad way. She knew about you and called the department switchboard downtown, who routed her to me."

"Local woman?"

"Not exactly." Her tone shifted. Hedging again. "But close enough. I spoke with her yesterday, for almost an hour, and I think she needs serious help. She can't eat, can't sleep. Severe panic attacks. The works. Right up your alley, God help you."

"What happened to her?"

"Well, it didn't exactly happen to *her*. It happened to a member of her family. In fact, it's still happening. And she's having a helluva time coping with it. You've gotta help her, Danny. Especially since it sounds like you're not working with the FBI anymore."

"Not at the moment, no. I'm sorta on call."

"Fine. Let me phone the woman back and tell her you'll see her today. She just got into town last night, staying in a motel not far from your office in Oakland. Just give me a time when you can see her and I'll make sure she gets there."

"Wait a minute, Angie. I still don't get it. She needs help because of something that's happening with a family member?"

"That's right."

"Who's the family member? What's happening?"

She hesitated again. "It's her son. He's in jail. Under arrest for murder. And I don't think this poor woman can cope with the stress anymore. I mean, she's really on the edge."

"Damn it, Angie, who is she? What's this all about?"

"Her name's Maggie Currim. Wesley Currim's mother."

Chapter Fifteen

I don't know why I said yes.

Especially since there were so many reasons to say no. For one thing, I'd agreed to keep my schedule clear, so that I could respond at a moment's notice if the FBI found Lyle Barnes. For another, I'd accompanied Wesley Currim and the Wheeling, West Virginia, police when he led them to the body of his victim. I'd stood right next to Wes as he casually, almost jokingly, displayed his gruesome handiwork, the mutilated remains of local businessman Ed Meachem. While this hardly constituted a clinical relationship, it did blur the boundaries a bit when it came to considering treating his mother.

Not to mention my own personal feelings of revulsion and outrage at Wes Currim's brutal actions. Could I keep these feelings in check enough to tend appropriately to his mother's distress? To help her manage her own undoubtedly tortured, tumultuous emotions? At least this was what I imagined she was going through. I certainly couldn't imagine anything else. Maggie Currim's son was a monster.

Which, in retrospect, was finally why I consented to seeing her. Like any parent would be, she was probably traumatized by the reality of what her son had done, as well as by terror at what presumably lay ahead for him. Life in prison, probably without hope of parole.

Was it right, then, for me to turn my back on the woman because of the sins of her offspring?

Though I did have one question left for Angie.

"What makes *you* so interested in Mrs. Currim?" I asked her. "You work for the city. For the Pittsburgh police. The Meachem murder is Wheeling PD's case. I assume that's where she lives, right? There are plenty of therapists down there you could have put her in touch with."

"But not any that do what *you* do, Danny. Besides, it's not my fault you've been all over the news for the past couple years. You want the fame, you take the blame."

"You know that's never what I wanted."

"Sure, *I* know that. But it's what you got." Her tone softened again. "Truth is, I kept puttin' myself in Maggie's shoes the whole time we talked on the phone. How I'd feel if one of *my* kids did something like hers did."

We went back and forth a few more times, but we both knew I was going to see Maggie Currim. Our phone call ended with my agreement to meet her at my office at eleven.

◇◇◇

I'd just finished dressing when my cell rang. To my surprise, it was Special Agent Neal Alcott.

"You awake, Rinaldi?"

"More or less. I'm standing in my bedroom, adjusting my tie in the mirror. So I'm upright. Beyond that, it's anybody's guess. What time is it, anyway?"

"Almost eight. So you got a couple hours' sleep. Which is more than I can say."

"Any luck finding your runaway agent?"

"None so far. I have my people—plus every uniform Pittsburgh PD can spare—checking the airport, bus terminals, and train station. We're also combing through cab company records for the past twelve hours."

"Hotels, motels?"

"What do *you* think? Though it's unclear how much cash he has on him. We've frozen his credit cards, and have a GPS on his cell. No signal, so he probably tossed it."

Alcott suddenly sneezed, loudly. Definitely getting a cold. I waited while he discreetly blew his nose.

"What about hospitals?" I said at last. "Free clinics, homeless shelters? Places that might take him in."

"Yeah, we thought of those, too." A healthy sniff. "But there are so many just within city limits, let alone the county, it'll take a while to check them all out."

I paused. "Funny, you're talking about Barnes as though he were a suspect on the run. Correct me if I'm wrong, but he's under no obligation to stay under FBI protection. I mean, as a free citizen, he can go anywhere he wants, right?"

It was Alcott's turn to pause.

"Sure, officially speaking he's a free man."

"And *un*officially?"

"He's an uncooperative former government employee with a connection to an ongoing investigation."

"Plus, as you pointed out, if he *does* get killed while on your watch…"

"Screw you, Rinaldi. Ya know, my personal take on all this is that it was *you* who spooked him. If the director hadn't insisted on bringing you in, making Barnes feel even *more* like some kinda nutcase than he already did, he might still be eating room service at the Marriott."

"Nice try, Neal. Now you wanna tell me why you called before I forget how to tie a Windsor?"

Again, a pause. Longer this time. I could sense his annoyance, even embarrassment. Alcott needed something from me, and I could tell this was not a position the agent enjoyed finding himself in. Finally, he spoke.

"We've got the rest of the other potential victims under wraps. At least we think so. The two cops who arrested John Jessup in Cleveland and held him until Barnes and his team picked him up. The jury foreman from the trial itself. And Jessup's public defender."

"Makes sense."

"Yeah. Like you, we figure if the killer is blaming everyone he thinks is responsible for what happened to Jessup, the lawyer who failed to keep him out of jail is probably high on the list."

"So what's the problem?"

"It's Claire Cobb. The Cleveland ADA who has the crush on you."

"Yeah, right. What about her?"

"She's scared shitless, that's what. Plus, she doesn't trust us. Doesn't believe we'll keep her safe. She wants to get a flight out of the country."

"Can't say I blame her."

"Well, *I* can. I was told she's a rising star in the Cleveland DA's office. Does a bang-up job sending bad guys to jail. So all of a sudden she's fallin' apart?"

"It happens, Neal. To the best of us. I remember the first time somebody took a shot at me. Takes a lot of air out of your tires, believe me."

"I don't care. We need all the potential victims in one place. Or at least in safe houses within the tri-state area. So we can co-ordinate their protection. Keep the killer's sphere of operation contained. You get me?"

I nodded, then realized he couldn't see it over the phone. "I get you, Neal. So what do you want me to do?"

"Talk to her. You two made a connection, even *I* could see that. She'll listen to you."

"You want me to convince her to stay in town?"

"It's crucial to the investigation. The director wants this case wrapped up fast, as in *now*. Before the story leaks—and it will, trust me. Thing is, we're getting new forensics on the letters our guy sent to Jessup in prison. You know what those lab geeks can do nowadays. Plus there's that witness from the Cranshaw shooting. With any luck, we can nail this crazy bastard in a couple more days."

"What if I can't convince Claire to stay put?"

A hollow laugh, tinny and mirthless coming through the cell's speaker.

"Then Ms. Cobb flies off to parts unknown, and we pray to God the killer doesn't hack into the airline's computer for her travel plans. This guy's no dummy, Rinaldi."

"At least there we can agree." I took a breath. "Okay, I'll talk with her. Is she still at the Marriott?"

"No. She insisted we move her to a Hilton downtown. I guess she figures it's better to be a moving target. Who the hell knows with this one?"

"Text me the Hilton address and I'll be there around one thirty."

"Hey, you're on call to us, Rinaldi. What if I needed you to come down now?"

"Then you'd be shit outta luck."

I hung up.

◇◇◇

Two hours later, I drove down to the city from Mt. Washington into a clear, almost sparkling morning. The sun was a suffused blur, offering light without warmth. No new snow had fallen, though what had already piled up along the streets and lay in sheets upon the hills still remained. Frozen into place by an unrelenting, windless cold.

I'd felt its greedy bite on my skin even on the short walk from my front door to my car. Once behind the wheel, it took a full five minutes for the Mustang's engine to come to life. And even now, as I wove in and out of downtown traffic on my way to Oakland, the dashboard heater proved no match for what one weather forecaster called "a typical midwinter chill."

Chill, my ass. The Steel City was shivering under a cloak of icy, unrepentant cold, and her poor citizens were going to spend the day blowing warm breath into their chafed, cupped hands. As it had been during most Pittsburgh winters since I was a boy. As it would probably always be.

I'd just put a Sonny Rollins CD into my dashboard deck when my cell rang again. It was Eleanor Lowrey, calling from the Old County Building. Police headquarters.

"How'd the briefing go with Biegler and the assistant chief?" I remembered the meeting they'd set for nine.

"Woulda gone better if Alcott hadn't invited himself. And pretty much taken over." Her voice was thick with fatigue. "Hell, we're not even finished yet. Alcott called a seventh-inning stretch to take a call from the director. At least it gives me time to grab another coffee."

"I'm guessing you never got to go home last night."

"Nope. Which means Luthor's probably looking for a new roommate by now."

Luthor was her Doberman.

"You do sound beat to shit."

"Thanks. You sure know how to charm a lady. But at least I'm doing better than Harry. He almost nodded off right in the middle of the meeting."

"Feel up to giving me the broad strokes?"

"Maybe I'm just sleepy, but that sounds kinda dirty."

"I was talking about the meeting, but I'm open to whatever you have in mind."

Somehow her chuckle was both wary and warm.

"Just keep your mind on the road, and I'll fill you in on what we have. In fact, maybe you oughtta pull over."

"Good idea."

It was. Though the roads were plowed, some of the older cobblestone streets were still slick enough to require more focus than I was giving them. Not to mention navigating the traffic on Liberty Avenue, a stop-and-start phalanx of angry commuters, hulking semis, and city buses.

At the first available intersection, I made a right onto a side street and pulled to the curb. My wheels locked and I felt a slight shudder as the Mustang's front fender made an impression on a low-slung wall of plowed snow.

I cut the engine and put the cell to my ear.

"Next time you talk to the mayor, tell him to make sure they salt the side roads, too."

"Sure. I'll mention it at one of our weekly sleepovers. Now you want to hear what we have or not?"

"*You* called *me*, Detective. Remember?"

"True. But I'm so wiped out I can't remember why."

"Maybe you missed the sound of my voice."

"Nah, that isn't it. But don't worry, it'll come to me." I could hear her stifling a yawn. "Anyway, stuff is just starting to trickle in, but we're making progress. The hardest thing about the whole investigation is coordinating evidence from three different police departments. Which means dealing with the egos of murder dicks in Cleveland and Steubenville PD, as well as our own."

"Sounds like fun. So what do you have so far?"

"Ballistics, for one thing. The bullets that killed Earl Cranshaw and Judge Loftus, and wounded Claire Cobb, all came from the same gun. A revolver, the Taurus 44M Tracker. Which Biegler insists means that we're looking at just one shooter."

"Probably, but not necessarily."

"Agreed. But it's the most likely scenario. Especially when you add in the M.O. of using a stolen vehicle for each hit. Indicates a consistent approach, a pattern."

"Makes sense. Psychologically, a guy working down a list would probably be invested in consistency, in sticking to a method. Particularly one that's working."

I heard Eleanor rustling some papers. "Then there's the eyewitness to the Cranshaw shooting. Some delivery guy named Vincent Beck. He was unloading groceries at a house three doors down when he saw the prison guard get shot. Saw the perp take off in his vehicle, too. Chevy sedan."

"Took Beck long enough to come forward."

"He claims he was afraid to get involved. But he felt so guilty about it, he told his story to his parish priest in confession. It was the priest who insisted that Beck call the Steubenville PD." She paused. "We have Beck's statement from the detective who took it down, but nobody here's too happy with it. Biegler's sending Harry to Ohio this afternoon to have another talk with the guy."

"Speaking of which, how's Harry been lately? I mean, the divorce...the drinking..."

"Still divorced, so still drinking." A heavy sigh. "You know Harry. Though he doesn't even mention Maddie anymore...so maybe that's progress."

I took a measured pause.

"How about *you*, Eleanor? We haven't talked in a while, so I was wondering about your brother..."

I heard the hesitation in her voice. Then:

"Teddy's okay. Back in rehab, but doing better, I think. I've been helping out on the weekends. With his kids. So it doesn't all land on our mom."

Her brother's addiction was one of a number of sudden and unexpected family-related problems she'd been dealing with since last summer. Though I had only a superficial knowledge of what she'd been going through. Whenever I broached the subject the few times we'd spoken since then, she politely but firmly backed me off.

Which was why that one intense, passionate kiss we'd shared all those months ago had never led to anything more.

And perhaps never would.

"Look, Eleanor..."

She quickly cut me off. "Not a good time, Danny. Besides, Biegler just stuck his head out of the conference room door. Looks like we're resuming the briefing."

"Okay. Thanks for keeping me in the loop."

It wasn't until after we hung up that I realized she never did tell me why she'd called.

Chapter Sixteen

I got to my office about a half hour before Maggie Currim was scheduled to arrive. Unoccupied for two days, both my consulting room and waiting room were cold enough to hang meat. I turned the wall dial to the warmest setting, but had enough experience with the building's erratic heating system to stay bundled in my coat.

With some time to kill, I booted up my laptop and reviewed the latest information about the Meachem murder case. I watched again the video of Police Chief Block and Detective Sergeant Randall perp-walking Wes Currim into custody. Though a new video had since gone up, from a press conference given by the Wheeling, West Virginia, District Attorney, with Block and Randall positioned prominently behind her. It was hard to tell which of the two cops was more uncomfortable on camera. I turned up the volume.

Given the horrific nature of the crime, and the public outcry that followed, the DA explained she'd pushed to get Currim arraigned as soon as possible. However, the confessed killer's defense counsel, a local attorney hired by the family, objected, claiming he'd barely had time to interview his client. The matter was still being argued.

Intrigued, I did a quick Google search on Currim's attorney, a trial veteran named Willard Hansen, and gleaned enough to know that he was smart, had an impressive record on behalf of his clients, and wasn't known for taking charity cases. Which made me wonder where the family had come up with his pricey retainer.

A few more clicks, a few more links, and I got my answer. Wes Currim's two older brothers, both married with children, had come to the rescue. One had taken out a second line of credit on his home, another had secured a sizeable bank loan. The brothers co-owned a successful chain of auto parts stores, and apparently had had little difficulty raising the money to hire a good lawyer for their youngest brother.

I sipped from the Starbucks I'd picked up across the street. Still hot, thank God. And by now, the central heating had chased away most of the room's chill. I pulled off my coat.

Switching my focus, I read a few follow-up stories about the victim, Ed Meachem. His obit from the Wheeling daily paper was online, as were a couple articles detailing his rise to vice-president of a major coal mining company. On the personal front, he seemed your average, conventional business executive: family man, weekly church-goer, avid golfer. He'd just turned sixty-four a month before his murder. A sidebar article included a recent photo of a fit-looking Meachem standing with his two teenage daughters at a soccer field.

From here, I trawled over to the latest on the investigation itself. The coroner's office reported that the remains found in the old house's kitchen were indeed those of Ed Meachem, and that the DNA matched that of the severed head found on top of the snowman. The cause of death was blunt force trauma to the back of the skull, weapon unknown. No bodily fluids or blood traces that did not belong to the victim were found on or near the body, nor anywhere else in the house.

Other than confessing to the kidnapping and murder, Wes Currim was refusing to reveal any further details of the crime. As he'd said when first arrested, he chose Meachem in that parking lot because the businessman looked rich and Currim needed money. Probably for drugs. According to local police records, he had a long history of drug use, dealing, and petty theft. Plus a couple of DUI's.

I glanced at the clock. Almost eleven, when I expected Maggie Currim. But before I logged off, one particular item caught my eye. I leaned forward, staring at the screen, having a hard time believing what I was seeing.

Apparently, soon after news of what Currim had done with Meachem's head hit the media, grotesque parodies of the crime started appearing online. YouTube had a number of videos showing snowmen with dummy heads on top, some with fake blood painted on the face. Also circulating was a cell phone photo taken by a medical student in the midwest, who'd used a cadaver skull from his anatomy class as the head of a snowman. By the time succeeding links led me to a crudely-animated dancing snowman, with a human head CGI'd on top, over which played a song called "The Ballad of Ed's Head," I'd had enough.

I closed the laptop and finished my coffee. Maybe I was getting old, but some of the places the Internet took us nowadays didn't offer much balm to the difficult, often sorrowful state of the human condition. If anything, it often reinforced the impression that things were swirling out of control, tilting toward chaos. Madness.

Unless, as has been suggested many times—starting with Freud himself—such barbaric levity in the face of tragedy was an inborn defense mechanism, a way for us to keep the horror at bay. I recalled how quickly similar cold, unfeeling jokes flew around the country after the Challenger space shuttle disaster.

Regardless, that last online image left me with a bitter, melancholy aftertaste that I had to struggle to dispel. Seeing the signal light go on over my office door helped. It meant someone had entered the waiting room and flipped the call switch.

My eleven a.m. patient. Maggie Currim.

◇◇◇

I guess my prejudice was showing, because the woman I ushered into my consulting room was not what I'd pictured. Given Wes Currim's flippant, surly manner, I admit I'd expected an older, female version of the stereotypical rural redneck he embodied. Or else a simple, terrified woman overwhelmed by the machinery of a justice system about to eviscerate her son.

Maggie Currim was neither of these, but a seemingly poised, well-dressed woman in her early sixties. She was tall and slender, and wore a blue blouse and black slacks under a heavy winter coat. Her raven-black hair was tied up in a bun. Her face, though handsome, was drawn and haggard, obviously drained by stress.

However, as we shook hands before she took her seat opposite me, her eyes shone clear and steady, gazing into mine. Proud. Determined.

As she busted me with her very first words.

"I suppose you were expecting some grizzled old Appalachian woman in a shawl, Dr. Rinaldi."

Great start to the therapy, I thought. So I did something about it.

"You're right, Mrs. Currim." I shifted in my chair. "I did have a different image in mind of what you might be like. It was unfair and I apologize."

She paused, then offered me a stern smile.

"At least you're honest. And you can say you're sorry. Most men I've known can't seem to manage that."

She took a long breath, exhaling slowly, letting herself settle into her seat. Then that steady gaze again.

I took the hint.

"Angela Villanova told me why you'd contacted her. I understand you're having difficulty dealing with what's happened with your son Wesley. The crime, the arrest."

She waited a moment before replying. Struggling to quell the agitation spreading on her face.

"I…" Maggie Currim looked off, toward my office window. At the bright coldness beyond its frosted glass.

I leaned in, but just slightly. "Yes..?"

"I don't want to talk about myself. My feelings. I mean, everything I told Mrs. Villanova is true. I can't sleep, can't eat. But—"

"And the panic attacks?"

"Oh, I have them, all right. Any time of the day. I just start shaking, and I can't catch my breath…I keep thinking I'm having a heart attack."

I nodded. "Most people who suffer a panic attack feel that way, Mrs. Currim. And there *are* things we can do to help alleviate them. Including, if appropriate, medication. But we can discuss that later. First, however—"

"*First*, don't call me Mrs. Currim. Maggie will do." She cleared her throat. "And I already said I'm not here to talk about my feelings, or get help with my jitters."

"I think they're more than jitters, Maggie."

"Think whatever you want, Dr. Rinaldi. I'm here to get help for my son. For Wesley."

"I'm not sure I know what you mean."

"I mean, he needs *help*. And he trusted you, right? He asked you to come with him when he showed those policemen the dead man's body."

I hesitated. "But he didn't really *know* me. He'd seen me on the news, that's all. Formed some kind of impression of me that prompted him to reach out to me."

"I don't care why he asked for you." Maggie was firm. "I just know he did. And that's good enough for me."

I let a silence build between us. Discussing the thoughts and motives of a person who wasn't in the room rarely made for effective treatment. In this case, it was also a way for Maggie Currim to deflect the conversation away from herself and her own needs.

I tried again. "Before we go any further, Maggie, I'll need to know a bit about you and your family."

Her mouth turned down. "Therapy stuff, eh, Doc? Just what I didn't want. I want to talk about Wesley."

"Okay, I'm willing to start there. Tell me about Wes."

For the first time since entering the room, her face softened. Eyes growing moist.

"Poor Wesley…" Her voice had lost its wary edge as well. "He's my youngest, you know. His two older brothers are both smart, hard-working. Did well in school. But Wesley…well, as my own folks used to say, Wesley was sorta the runt of the litter. And not just because he turned out skinny and frail."

"How so?"

"It was the way he acted. At school, at home. Lazy, always mouthing off. Skipping classes, cursing at his teachers. Like he was...I don't know...resentful, I guess you'd say. Mad at the world." A pained swallow. "By the time he was a teenager, he was already getting in trouble. Drinking, smoking marijuana. Shoplifting."

"That must've been hard for you."

She gave me a strange, quizzical look. "Do you have children, Dr. Rinaldi?"

"No I don't."

"Then you can't know. A mother who loves her son, who loves the way *I* loved Wes...Lord, you can't know what that means. His two older brothers were fine, and I loved them, but they didn't need me. They were more their father's sons. They even went to work for him at the auto parts store when they were teens. Heck, they *run* the business now. Built it up into a chain of stores..."

Her voice trailed off.

"But Wesley needed me. And *I* needed *him*. I'm not ashamed to say I doted on that boy, no matter what he did. No matter what kind of trouble he got himself into. And he felt the same about me. Wesley loved me. Doted on *me*. Told me everything. His fears, his hopes. Believe me, he could be the worst kind of devil out there in the world—a world that had no use for *him*, either, I might add—but he was always an angel to me. Never hurt me, never lied to me."

"What about his father? How was their relationship?"

"What relationship? Jack gave whatever love he was capable of giving to the two older boys. He *hated* Wes, and the feeling was mutual."

"Where's your husband now?"

"Who knows?"

I waited. A sheen of embarrassment colored her cheeks, and then she visibly recovered herself.

"Jack ran off with his secretary." A bitter smile. "Real original, eh? Some young thing he hired, after the business started growing. *I* offered to work the desk, but he wouldn't hear of it. I could've really helped out, too. I have a college education, for one thing, which was more than Jack could say. But he wouldn't budge. Then I found out they were sleeping together."

"Did you confront him about it."

"Yes I did. Next thing I know, he and this bitch take off together. Haven't seen or heard from either of them since." A deep sigh. "No loss there, believe me. For Wes *or* for me. The little slut can have Jack."

By now, Maggie was blinking back tears, though her expression was resolute. She noted the box of Kleenex on the table beside her chair and, as though impatient with herself, quickly snapped up a few sheets.

"Sorry, Doctor." As she dabbed her eyes. "I don't normally use such language."

"Nothing to be sorry about."

She shook her head. "I just don't want to get sidetracked. I'm here because of Wesley. I can deal with my own troubles my own way."

"I understand, but—"

She bolted upright in her chair, bristling.

"You don't understand a thing!" Voice quivering with anguish. "I'm a mother whose son is charged with murder! A horrible, sickening murder!"

Clearly mortified by her sudden outburst, she put a trembling hand over her mouth. Face ashen.

I said, "It's okay…Really…"

"No it *isn't!* I—I'm so sorry, I shouldn't have—"

"Look, Maggie, I can't begin to imagine what you're going through, and—"

"No you can't!" Another long breath. "But it doesn't matter. What I *feel* doesn't matter."

"Then what *does?*"

"The truth. The truth matters!"

I watched as she struggled again to compose herself. Bring her tumult of emotions under control.

Finally, I said, "I'm listening, Maggie."

Her voice now calm. Measured. "I know that Wesley confessed, Dr. Rinaldi. I know he led the police to where Ed Meachem's body was. But I also know something else."

Her eyes found mine. "I know that my son didn't kill that poor man. And I can prove it."

Chapter Seventeen

"You can *prove* it? How, Maggie?"

"On the night Mr. Meachem was killed, Wesley was with me. At my house."

I chose my next words carefully.

"Are you sure about that? You've been under a great deal of stress. You might have the nights wrong."

"No, it was definitely the night of the twenty-ninth, because I asked him to help me clean out the attic. My church was collecting old clothes to give to charity, and they wanted all the donations ready and boxed-up by the thirtieth. They'd rented some U-Hauls to come by our houses, pick up the boxes, and deliver them to Goodwill."

Maggie frowned. "Truth is, I'd been asking Wesley all week to come help me, but he kept putting me off. He knows full well I hate leaving things to the last minute, but it's practically a way of life for him."

"So Wes showed up at your house that night? Do you remember when?"

"Around six thirty. I made him dinner and then we went up to the attic. I had stuff in there that went back years, decades. You wouldn't believe the dust, the cobwebs."

"How long did Wes stay that night?"

"Till past midnight. Packing things in boxes and bringing them downstairs. We didn't even get halfway through everything, but by then we were both tired and thirsty. I remember he had a beer for the road before he left for his place. His apartment over on Eighth Street."

I leaned back in my seat, trying not to let Maggie see the doubt in my eyes.

"Did anybody else know Wes was with you? Maybe some neighbor saw him drive up to your place."

"I already thought of that. There're only three other houses on my street, and I asked about it at every one of them. Nobody saw anything."

"Not even his pickup in your driveway? It must've been there for almost six hours."

"No it wasn't. He always pulls around to the back when he comes to visit me. That's where I keep the trash bins. He picks up any cans or bottles and puts them in the truck. There's a recycling place a couple blocks away, and Wesley turns them in for cigarette money."

I considered this.

"So it's only your word that Wes was with you that night. With no other corroboration, you're his only alibi."

"That's right. So I don't have to tell you what the district attorney and the police think."

"They don't believe you. They think you're lying to protect your son."

She nodded slowly. "I even showed them the receipt the church gave me for the boxes when the U-Hauls came the next day. Do they really think I could've brought all those boxes down from the attic myself?"

"The point is, Maggie, you can't prove you *didn't*. Still, I'm surprised they haven't at least investigated the possibility—"

Here she slumped, for the first time since she'd entered my office. Hands clasped tightly on her lap.

"Why should they?" she said quietly. "After all, even Wesley says I'm lying."

"What?"

"He told the police he never came over to the house that night. He swears he *did* kill Ed Meachem. And that I'd probably say anything to save him."

Neither of us spoke for a full minute.

Beyond my office window, the sun had risen to its noon height, glazing the cold glass. The whole room suffused with a cheerless, hazy light.

When Maggie spoke again, her voice was equally muted. Bewildered.

"I…I don't understand it. Why would he insist that he's guilty? I'm not crazy, Dr. Rinaldi. Wesley *was* with me that night. Why does he deny it?"

"I don't know. I can't understand it either." I let out a breath. "I assume you've also talked with your son's attorney? Told him what you told the police."

"Of course. But Mr. Hansen is as puzzled as I am."

"Regardless, he'd be smart to put you on the stand. You make a more than credible witness."

"He said the same thing. But he also said that even if the jury sympathized with me, there's still Wesley's confession to deal with."

I nodded. "Plus his knowledge of the location of Ed Meachem's remains. Strong arguments for the prosecution."

Only then did Maggie look back up at me. Her gaze as frank as it was solemn.

"I have to ask you, Dr. Rinaldi. Do *you* believe me?"

I took a long moment before replying.

"Truthfully, Maggie, I don't know what I believe. Your story seems as credible to me as I suspect it would seem to a jury. But I was there when Wes showed us Meachem's body. And his confession was uncoerced. According to what the Wheeling police told me, Wesley seemed almost eager to confess to the crime."

Her jaw had almost imperceptibly tightened as I answered her question. Whatever our initial connection had been, I could see it dissolving. As though my doubt—no matter how carefully I tried to express it—was undoing what little hope she had.

I must have been right, for without another word she rose to her feet. That stern smile once more in place.

I stood as well. "Maggie, please don't go yet. We should still talk—"

"About what? I came to ask for your help and it looks like I'm not going to get it."

"But even if I knew for a fact that what you say is true, that Wes was with you the night of the murder, how could I help you?"

"By going to see Wesley. By convincing him that he should tell the truth."

"I have no reason to believe he'd listen to me."

"Maybe not. But you're the only hope I have left. My son *didn't* kill that man. I've prayed and prayed on it, and I can't for the life of me understand why he keeps saying he did, but I swear before Almighty God that Wesley was with me that whole night."

I hesitated, not sure what to say next. Suddenly, to my surprise, her hand was on my arm.

"I'm a proud woman, Dr. Rinaldi. It's not easy for me to ask for help. But I need it…my *son* needs it…whether he wants it or not. Would you at least *see* Wesley? Talk to him?"

For the second time that morning, I was being asked to convince someone to do something they were unwilling to do. Neal Alcott wanted me to talk Claire Cobb into staying in town, and now Wes Currim's mother wanted me to talk her son into recanting his murder confession.

I realized, as I stood looking into Maggie Currim's stricken eyes, that both she and Alcott had a faith in my persuasive powers that I didn't quite share.

Her grip tightened. "Would you at least think about it? Please? At least promise me that."

◇◇◇

I kept replaying those last moments with Maggie Currim in my mind as I drove across town to the Hilton where Claire Cobb was now sequestered. Traffic was knotted and sluggish, despite the snow-plowed roads, as though the unceasing cold had slowed the city's usual urban rhythm. As though everybody and every-thing was succumbing to a wintry slumber, a sunlit hibernation.

I found the hotel whose address Alcott had texted me and pulled into the self-parking lot. I shut off the Mustang's engine, listening to its muffled ticking as I slowly rebuttoned my coat.

Would I really consider talking to Wes Currim, a man I believed committed an unspeakable crime? And even if I did, how could I persuade him to recant his confession—if, as Maggie insisted, it wasn't true—when he clearly didn't want to? When he'd gone so far as to accuse his own mother of lying to protect him?

Besides, he could very well be right. Perhaps Maggie *was* lying. It was obvious she loved him dearly, fiercely. I had no trouble imagining the lengths to which she'd go to help him. To rescue him, even from the consequences of his own actions.

I rested my hand on the door handle, but didn't turn it. Moth-ers and their sons. A powerful, intricate, often difficult bond, as every therapist understood. Even me, though my own mother had died when I was three. And she'd been bedridden for most of those short years. Leaving me with no memory of being held in her arms, of her smell and touch, of a smiling, loving face looking down at mine. An absence in my life that was in some ways as crucial, as life-altering, as any presence.

Christ! I pushed those thoughts away. Not a place I wanted to go then. Rarely did, and never without a stab of self-pity that, despite myself, filled me with shame. As though somehow the longing, the loss, should have been dealt with—extinguished— long ago…

With more force than was necessary, I grasped the handle and shouldered open the car door, stepping out into a sharp, implacable cold.

Chapter Eighteen

As soon as Agent Green ushered me into the top-floor suite of the downtown Hilton, those assembled in the spacious main room stopped what they were doing to gape.

Neal Alcott, standing, cell in hand. Harry Polk and Eleanor Lowrey on a sofa, poring over files spread before them on a glass coffee table. Claire Cobb and a young woman I presumed to be her FBI protector sitting at a table laden with cups, sodas, and plates of sandwiches.

I heard Agent Green quickly close the door behind me, as though he couldn't wait to make his exit. Not that I blamed him. Every face in the room held the same look of angry, barely-contained frustration.

I smiled. "Isn't this the part where you all jump up and yell 'Surprise!'?"

"Funny as ever, Rinaldi." Alcott clicked off his cell, then used it to point at an armchair near me. "Sit."

I sat. But not without shooting a questioning glance at Eleanor Lowrey, whose returning look was unreadable.

Her partner was less circumspect.

"In case you're wonderin', Doc, we all look shell-shocked 'cause we're fucked." Polk stroked his chin. "The whole story about the shootings leaked a couple hours ago."

"It leaked?"

"Somebody broke it on a crime blog," Alcott explained. "It all went viral in a heartbeat. The letters John Jessup received in jail.

The sender now working his way down a list of people he blames for Jessup's death. The joint FBI-Pittsburgh PD Task Force."

I struggled to take this in. "What about the killer's M.O.? Using stolen cars? Do they know that?"

Lowrey answered. "Not so far. But they *do* know that all the bullets fired came from the same gun. Biegler said the chief is getting hammered with questions from the mainstream media. Requests for confirmation."

Alcott took out a monogrammed handkerchief to blow his nose. "Our office here is getting the same requests."

I had a sudden thought.

"What about Vincent Beck? The eyewitness in the prison guard's shooting?"

"So far he's under the radar, too," Eleanor said.

Polk grunted. "Wanna bet how long he *stays* under it?"

"Now that the media's connected the dots," Eleanor went on, "everything's up for grabs. Suddenly the local press in Steubenville is taking a second look at the Cranshaw shooting. Re-interviewing the cops involved, fact-checking Cranshaw's background. Harrassing his widow. Because what seemed a random unsolved murder is now part of something bigger."

"It gets worse," Polk added. "Some police groupie's website got hold of the M.E.'s report on Cranshaw, listing the cause of death as two gunshot wounds to the chest. Steubenville PD had managed to keep that detail out of the press the first time around."

"What about Ralph Loftus?" I asked. "How did *he* die?"

"Single shot to the head. But, hey, you don't gotta ask me. Just ask the judge's daughter. She wrote about it in her blog. She found out at the morgue when she ID'd her father's body. She's also posted photos taken of the makeshift memorial to him at the spot where he died. Flowers and Bible verses at the Hilton parking lot in Oakland." A sour laugh. "Bet *that's* great for business."

"The point is," Eleanor said, "now we're in the media spotlight. Which means political pressure, calls for a quick arrest. And that means sloppy police work, mistakes."

I turned to Alcott. "Jesus, this isn't a leak, it's a flood. How could this happen?"

"How it usually happens." Shoving his handkerchief back in his pocket. "Somebody talked to somebody. We've got dozens of our people working with cops from three different jurisdictions. Think about it. Combined, you're looking at detectives, uniforms, field agents, transportation, lab rats, communications. Intel flying back and forth throughout the tri-state area. Emails, cell calls, faxes, texts. Hell, maybe some rookie churning out Xeroxes for his precinct captain bragged to his girlfriend about something he read on one of them."

He sighed. "Given the size of this operation, I'm surprised it took this long to leak."

Another somber silence settled on the room. Broken suddenly by the sharp rattle of a coffee cup.

It was Claire Cobb, trembling hand still holding the cup as it rested in its saucer. As though unable to let go.

"This means the killer knows that *we* know what he's doing," she said quietly. "He'll be more cautious, more on his guard. More dangerous."

"Or just the opposite." Alcott's placid tone didn't disguise his impatience with her. "Knowing there's a major task force mobilized to track him down, he might get smart and call it a day. Maybe he'll figure he got enough of what he wanted."

Her smile was rueful. "Somehow, Agent Alcott, I'm not getting that vibe."

"Me, either," I offered.

"Well, luckily, law enforcement doesn't operate based on vibes." Alcott tilted his head at Claire. "And I understand that other matter's resolved, Ms. Cobb?"

She nodded, unhappy.

I looked from her to Alcott. "*Now* what the hell are we talking about? Claire wanting to get out of town?"

The agent actually grinned. "Oh, yeah, Doc. In all the excitement, I forgot to tell you. You didn't need to come down and have a chat with her after all. The director called the Cleveland

DA, who then called us here about two minutes later. Isn't that right, Ms. Cobb?"

Claire directed her answer at me, not Alcott.

"My boss read me the riot act. Said I had to cooperate fully with the operation, or risk getting fired. If the FBI wants me to sit in the hotel bathtub till next Christmas, I damn well better do it. And that's a direct quote."

"Sounds like he needs a little work on his people skills," I said.

She scowled. "What he needs is a new set of balls and an IQ upgrade. But you can't choose your boss—until you *are* the boss. I just hope I live long enough to take the damn job away from him."

Alcott folded his arms. "You sit tight and let us do *our* jobs, Ms. Cobb, and you'll be fine. As I've been saying all along." A glance at me. "In fact, a little attitude adjustment on *all* our parts wouldn't be a bad idea."

Claire got up slowly from the table, favoring her bandaged wound, and came over to face him.

"Well, don't expect it from me. Besides, I still have a job to do. So if you'll all excuse me, I have to check in with my office in Cleveland. There're cases pending, calls and emails to return."

She turned to look back at the female agent—to whom I'd never been introduced, I realized—and motioned for her to rise as well. She was young, sturdy-looking. But wary.

"C'mon, Gloria," Claire said. "Let's find us a room in this suite where I can have some privacy."

The agent glanced nervously at Alcott, who jerked his thumb toward a hallway leading off from the main room.

"Go ahead, Reese. Take Ms. Cobb to the master bedroom. There's a separate phone line, laptop, wireless access. Whatever she needs."

Gloria Reese gave a brisk nod and hurried to catch up with Claire, who'd already headed out of the room.

Alcott looked like he wanted to say something more, but must've thought better of it. Instead, he reached for his handkerchief again and wiped his reddening nose.

Just then, Lowrey's cell rang. The rest of us stared dumbly as she took it. She listened intently, offered a few "Uh-huh's," and then said good-bye.

"That was Lieutenant Biegler again." Looking up at Alcott. "They've worked up a new set of protocols for disseminating case evidence. To try to prevent any more leaks. The brass even has tech guys beefing up security to the tri-state online interface. We've got Pennsylvania up and running, almost done with Ohio and West Virginia."

"Good idea," Alcott said, officiously. "If every Barney Fife in every Podunk precinct has access to task force intel, we might as well just invite the goddam media to sit in on case reviews."

For the first time in a while, Harry Polk stirred. And gave Alcott his trademark squint.

"Yeah, well, on behalf of all the Barney Fifes in all the Podunk precincts, this case needs every pair o' eyes and ears we can get. Every boot on the ground, every cop on a beat."

He swiveled in his seat, taking in the rest of us.

"'Cause the real problem ain't that the story leaked, boys and girls. It's that we don't got squat on the killer. No prints from the abandoned cars the perp drove. No way to trace the gun. No ID, unless this Vincent Beck mook can give us something more than he told the Steubenville cops. No idea if or when the killer's gonna strike again. And no real reason to think that we've rounded up everyone on his target list."

He let out an exaggerated breath. "So maybe *I* need that attitude adjustment, Agent Alcott, 'cause from where I sit, we're lookin' like a pack o' fools here. Hell, maybe your old profiler Lyle Barnes was smarter than all of us. He had the good sense to just get the fuck outta Dodge."

Neal Alcott had stood motionless, arms still folded, during Polk's entire rant. Now he lowered his hooded eyes.

"I appreciate candor as much as the next man, Sergeant Polk. But I *don't* appreciate defeatist attitudes. Besides, historically, that's not the bureau's way. Not how we've gotten things done for the past hundred years."

I didn't even try to suppress a laugh.

"Give it a rest, will ya, Neal? Save the speeches for the next FBI pep rally."

Alcott favored me with a disdainful look.

"You know, Rinaldi, now that Ms. Cobb's decided to stay here as the bureau's guest, there's no reason you need to be here anymore. So consider yourself excused."

"What about Agent Barnes?"

"My guess is, Lyle Barnes will be picked up any time now. When that happens, you'll be the first one I call."

As if to emphasize the point, he held up his cell.

Which was why he was caught off guard when it suddenly rang. Startled for a moment, he clicked it on.

"Yes? Okay, good. Send him up."

He hung up, with a satisfied smile.

"Looks like Ms. Cobb's going to have some company. Another member of the bar. Agent Zarnicki just arrived with John Jessup's defense attorney. He's escorting him up right now."

I said nothing, but inwardly was relieved. For some reason, I'd felt all along that these two specific people—the ADA who prosecuted Jessup, and the defense lawyer who failed to keep him out of prison—were among those most likely to be held responsible for his fate by the killer.

Meanwhile, Polk had climbed to his feet.

"Look, I figure it's about time me an' Lowrey—"

Suddenly, Alcott's cell rang again. Seconds after answering it, his face tightened with irritation.

"Right, got it." Snapping into the phone. "You just make goddam sure he stays put! Be right down."

He practically jammed the cell into his pants pocket.

I raised an eyebrow. "Problem?"

"Jessup's lawyer took a detour to the hotel bar. Says he won't come up. So now I have to go downstairs and tear him a new one. Like I don't have enough grief…"

Alcott aimed a skeptical look at me.

"He wants *you* to come down, too. Says he knows you."

"Me?" I shrugged, at a loss. "I don't know this guy."

"He says you do. So you're coming with me." He shook his head, miserable. "Damn, Rinaldi, I can't seem to get rid of you."

Polk gave a dry laugh. "Welcome to *my* world."

◇◇◇

The dimly-lit, wood-paneled bar was located in a back corner of the ground floor, just off the lobby. Though not yet five in the afternoon, the dark, cloistered feel of the place—not to mention the haggard, red-faced bartender, the bored middle-aged waitress, and the scattering of weary businessmen staring into their drinks—made it seem like every corner bar in every chain hotel in every city in the world. Where it's always two a.m.

Agent Alcott strode in ahead of me, making straight for the end of the *faux* mahogany bar at which sat the field agent I recognized as Zarnicki. The younger man swiveled on his stool and beamed at us with a combination of chagrin and relief. Reinforcements had arrived.

Next to him, with his back toward us, was an older man in a tailored, though well-worn, Italian suit. Something about the way his shoulders sagged as he bent over his drink looked familiar to me.

I soon learned why.

After throwing back his whiskey, Assistant District Attorney Dave Parnelli turned and patted the stool next to him.

"Park it here, Doc. I saved ya the seat."

Chapter Nineteen

I stayed on my feet and stared at him.

"*You* were John Jessup's defense attorney?"

A hoarse, rheumy laugh. "Guilty as charged."

I wondered how many drinks he'd had before we arrived. His gaze already had that bleary, unfocused sheen.

Neal Alcott leaned in on Parnelli's other side, head swiveling back and forth between the ADA and me.

"So you *do* know this guy, Rinaldi?"

I nodded. "Though it looks like there's a lot I *don't* know." Eyes riveted on Parnelli. "Care to fill me in?"

"Happy to. Interestin' story." Parnelli motioned for the bartender. "For which I'll need fortifications."

He ordered another Jack Daniels for himself, but Alcott and I declined. Parnelli smiled at Zarnicki.

"Anything for you, Junior? Apple juice? Kool Aid?"

"I'm good, sir."

Parnelli laughed again. "That's somethin' you gotta admire about G-men. Nice manners. Always call you 'sir,' even when they're bustin' your balls."

Ignoring him, Zarnicki moved two stools over to make room for his boss. Alcott frowned, sniffed once, and sat.

The bartender returned with a fresh drink. Parnelli gave me a bemused look, again indicating the stool to his right. I chose instead to lean with my back to the bar.

"Suit yourself." Parnelli loudly sipped his drink.

"Feel better?" I asked. "Good enough to tell me how the hell you ended up defending John Jessup?"

Alcott chimed in. "I'm curious myself, Parnelli. You're with the DA's office here in town, right?"

"That's right. Couple years now. But I started as a public defender in New York. I'm Brooklyn born and raised."

"Yeah, I noticed the accent."

"Hard to miss. Though every year in Pittsburgh grinds it down a bit." He shook his head sadly. "Anyway, after I left New York, but before moving down here, I worked in the private sector. A huge corporate law firm called McCloskey, Singer, and Ganz. You guys remember them, don'tcha?"

"Oh yeah," I said flatly. Alcott nodded, too. The firm's name and reputation had figured prominently in the bank robbery case during which he and I met last summer.

"Then you might also remember how shitty I felt bein' associated with that motley band of big shots. Besides, after a year of corporate work, I couldn't wait to get back in a courtroom. So I started lookin' around for another place to hang my hat. Right around then, a buddy of mine in Legal Aid in Cleveland—we went to law school together—tells me about John Jessup. How he's accused of multiple rapes and murders, and the woman public defender who's caught his case just went on maternity leave. So did I want to come to Cleveland and defend Jessup, *pro bono*? At least it would get me back in front of a judge and jury. Nobody else in Legal Aid wanted to defend the bastard, anyway. So I said yes."

Parnelli paused to knock back the rest of his drink. Tapped the glass on the counter. The bartender appeared.

"Sure I can't get you guys anything? I'm runnin' a tab here and it's gettin' lonely."

Alcott and Zarnicki declined, but I ordered a draft Iron City. Somehow listening to Parnelli made *me* thirsty.

After our drinks came, and the ADA took a healthy swallow of Mr. Daniels' finest, he went on with his tale.

"Now, believe it or not, I did my best for Jessup at the trial, but the evidence against him was overwhelming. Didn't help that the prosecution had this female firecracker arguing their case."

"Claire Cobb," I said. "She's just upstairs."

"No shit? Ya shoulda brought her down to say hi. Ya wouldn't know it to look at her, but she's a cruise missile in the courtroom. By the time she finished her summation to the jury, *I* wanted to string Jessup up by his balls."

He paused then, a shadow passing over his eyes as he stared down at his drink.

"Not that I needed much persuading. Jessup was a cold, unfeeling bastard. Every minute of pretrial prep with him was goddam awful. That flat, empty stare…"

Parnelli finished his drink in one swallow.

"Point is, it was pricks like Jessup that helped make up my mind to switch sides, go over to prosecution." He gave me a collegial smile. "I think I told ya my sister lives here, right? I figured, why the fuck not? So I moved to town and went to work for the DA's office."

Alcott stirred, which is when I realized he'd been silent during Parnelli's entire story.

"Doesn't matter what you're doing now, Parnelli. As far as our killer's concerned, you failed to successfully defend Jessup at trial. We assume he blames you as much as anyone for what happened to him."

Parnelli shrugged. "Maybe you're right. But there's no way I'm gonna stay cooped-up in some FBI hotel room for the duration. Even if you gave me the key to the mini-bar. Hell, it could take weeks to catch this guy. *Months…*"

"No it won't." Alcott's voice grew hard as a blade's edge. "But even if it did, cooped-up is better than dead."

I put my hand on Parnelli's forearm.

"C'mon, you gotta agree you're a likely target for the killer."

"What if I am? Fuck him." His words slurred now, laced with alcohol-fueled bravado. "Besides, did I *ask* for FBI protection?

Nope, I was just sittin' in my office, mindin' my own business, when Junior here showed up…"

Alcott looked past him at me. "Son-of-a-bitch is drunk."

"Ya think?" I kept my grip on Parnelli's arm. "So what's your plan, Dave? Figure you'll just stroll around town, waiting to get shot in the head?"

"Not a bad plan, Danny boy, but I see some flaws in it. How 'bout this? J. Edgar here assigns an eager G-man or plainclothes cop to be my bodyguard. Some Clint Eastwood wannabe who'll shoot first and ask questions later. Now *that's* a plan. Ain't it?"

I took a pull of my beer and tried again.

"What about Sinclair? What did he say?"

Leland Sinclair, Pittsburgh's ambitious district attorney, was Parnelli's boss. And not a man who suffered fools lightly.

"Haven't asked him." Eyes blinking as he struggled to maintain focus. "Thing is, Lee's up in Boston for some political fundraiser. Brown-nosing the party bigwigs." He leaned in, conspiratorial. "Ya know what I think? I think Lee's gonna run for governor again."

Parnelli was probably right, but it was hardly the point at the moment. With a grunt, I helped him sit upright again. It was like hefting a big, shifting bag of sand.

Meanwhile, Alcott had had enough.

"Zarnicki, take Mr. Parnelli upstairs to the suite till he sobers up. Maybe get some hot coffee into him. Then I'll have another talk with him."

As the young agent took hold of Parnelli's other arm, the ADA glared hotly at him.

"Where are we going? Are we done here?"

I leaned in close. Buddies. *Paisans.* "Go with Agent Zarnicki, will ya, Dave? The Feds need your input on this case. You spent time with Jessup. You might even have some idea who'd been sending him fan letters in prison."

He nodded importantly. "Ya know, I might at that…"

I smiled encouragingly. "So go on upstairs and give it some thought, okay?"

Without waiting for his reply, Zarnicki pulled roughly on the older man's elbow and yanked him off the stool.

"Hey!" Parnelli yelped. "Watch it, Junior!"

Alcott growled. "*Now*, Agent Zarnicki."

Parnelli wobbled a bit, but Zarnicki steadied him and began leading him out of the bar. Once they'd cleared the door, Alcott turned back to me. Made a point of showing how beleaguered he was.

"Figures he'd be a friend of yours, Rinaldi. Another pain in the ass."

"Maybe. But Parnelli has a point. I mean, how long can you keep these people under wraps? They have work, lives. And the Bureau's resources aren't unlimited."

"Tell me about it."

"Besides, now that the story's leaked, the killer might go underground. Or at least slow his pace. He might wait months to go after the next victim on his list."

"That thought *had* occurred to me."

But his words had no bite. Alcott leaned back on his stool, hands on the bar, head sinking down between those linebacker shoulders. The fatigue he'd fought for so long finally asserting itself.

"Time's on *his* side, Rinaldi," he said at last. "And the killer knows it."

Before I could respond, a heavy tread on the bar's hardwood floor behind me drew my gaze. It was Harry Polk, buttoned up tight in his Army surplus coat. As he neared, I noticed he was also carrying another winter coat.

Mine. The one I'd left up in the hotel suite.

He and Alcott exchanged perfunctory nods, then Harry turned to me. Held out my coat, bunched in his hands.

"Here, Doc, you're gonna need this."

"Where am I going?"

"On a little road trip. To Steubenville, Ohio. Ain't that exciting?"

"Why?"

"I gotta go talk to our eyewitness to the Cranshaw shooting, and you're comin' with."

Chapter Twenty

Ash-gray snow was piled high and wide on either side of US-22 West, the waning sun offering just enough light to make the frost on the hood of Polk's unmarked sedan glisten. Beyond and behind us, the empty fields shone like white satin sheets.

"Looks like a Christmas card, don't it?" Harry drove with one hand, the other holding the dash lighter to the end of a Camel unfiltered. With the windows shut tight and the heater on high, after two puffs from his cigarette you could've smoked a ham in the car's interior.

"Out *there*, yeah," I said, waving away smoke. "Just like Christmas. In here, not so much…"

Polk gave a grunt, his version of a disinterested rebuke. I turned my attention back to the view.

We'd crossed the state line into Ohio ten minutes before, though the scenery wasn't dissimilar. The highway passed towns of various sizes and levels of prosperity, and more than a few well-tended farms, but most of the region's industrial vigor had fled. Like many other parts of the country, the tri-state area's manufacturing base had been transplanted overseas, and its agricultural bounty had been co-opted by conglomerates. Between outsourcing and the rise of agribusiness, the economic landscape of states like Ohio and Pennsylvania had changed radically, even while the actual landscape had not.

Which was what made the view so mournfully evocative. It looked exactly as it had when I was kid, when my dad had driven the two of us—lonely father and motherless son—to visit family in Cincinnati for the holidays. The weather reliably cold and snowing, the roads thrillingly icy, the cloudless night sky as blank as a blackboard. A blankness waiting, in that same child's imaginings, for the words of a hopefully-exciting story—the narrative of his future—to be written on it.

"You with me here, Doc?"

Polk's sharp voice shredded the skein of my memories.

I turned my head away from the gathering dusk.

"Just thinking, Harry. You ought to try it sometime."

"Uh-huh. Speakin' o' which, you give any thought to why I might've asked you along? It sure as hell ain't for your delightful company."

"I figured that. So why *am* I riding shotgun? You need back-up in case Vincent Beck gets violent?"

Another noisy smoker's laugh, somewhere between a gasp and a hack.

"If I needed backup, I'd get me a couple actual cops. Not some shrink with a hero complex."

"I'm a psychologist, not a shrink. Jeez, Harry, we've been over this."

"Like I give a fuck."

"And I'm nobody's idea of a hero, believe me."

"You get no argument from me, Rinaldi. I'm just makin' a point here."

"Wish I knew what the hell it was."

He took another drag on his cigarette, burning it half-way down. When he exhaled, the dash heater swirled the smoke in eddies before our eyes.

"I just wanted to get you alone," Harry said at last. "So we could talk."

"*You* wanna talk? Since when?"

"Since I noticed how you and Detective Lowrey been actin' around each other."

"Eleanor and me?"

"Gimme a break, will ya, Doc? You've been checking out her inventory, on and off, since last summer. Which makes sense, since she's a great-lookin' woman, even if she is my partner. My problem is, I think she kinda likes you, too."

"Look, even granting that it might be a problem, how is it *your* problem?"

"It's my problem 'cause I don't need the aggravation. You go breakin' her heart or some shit, and it'll be my job to pick up the pieces."

I considered this.

"Harry, are you asking me what my intentions are regarding Detective Lowrey?"

"Christ, you make it sound like we're on *Masterpiece Theater*...but, yeah. I guess I am."

"Okay. Then let me ask *you* a question: Does the phrase 'It's none of your business' mean anything to you?"

"Don't mean shit. Lowrey and me are partners. Which means we watch each other's backs."

"I appreciate that, Harry, but—"

"There's somethin' else." Polk gave me a sidelong look. "I don't wanna tell tales outta school here, but Lowrey...I mean, it ain't exactly a secret that she swings both ways."

Actually, I'd thought it was. Given how zealously Eleanor guarded her private life, I was surprised Harry knew. Though Eleanor once told me that some of her fellow cops suspected. Maybe Harry had just picked up on the rumors. Or maybe she'd told him herself. As Harry'd said, they *were* partners. And had been for a long time.

Regardless, I wanted to see where Polk was going with this. "What are you talking about, Harry?"

"You know damn well what I'm talkin' about. Sometimes she drives stick, sometimes she don't. I'm just sayin'… Hell, no need to get *your* heart broken, either."

"Why, Sergeant, I'm touched."

"You're touched, all right. In the head. But this thing between you and Lowrey...I just want you love-birds to know what the hell you're gettin' into. Far as I'm concerned, everybody would be a lot happier if you two just gave it a pass."

I suppressed a smile. "I'll take it under advisement."

"See that you do."

With that, he opened his window to toss out the spent cigarette. Exposing us to a blast of bone-chilling cold.

"Now, about this Vincent Beck mook." Polk quickly rolled up the window. "He's the only eyewitness we got, so I don't wanna spook him. This interview calls for a kid-gloves approach. A little finesse."

"Probably why they sent you."

He wisely ignored me.

"Anyway, my gut says Beck didn't cough up everything he knows. That's why we got Alcott to pull rank on the Steubenville PD and let me re-interview him."

"I'm guessing they're not too happy about some Pittsburgh cop playing in their jurisdictional sandbox."

"Good guess. Which is why we gotta make a pitstop first at *their* house, so I can kiss the captain's ring."

◇◇◇

Initially, it was hard to pick out Vincent Beck from the dozen or so other delivery drivers at the warehouse.

They were all on the young side, bundled into thick coats and scarves against the numbing cold. Some even wore ski masks under their assorted caps and hoods, wind-dried eyes peering out in the gathering dark, making them look like a team of cat burglars.

After Polk's obligatory call at Steubenville PD's downtown precinct, we'd driven to an industrial area just outside the city. Rows of warehouses and factory outlets, lights blazing, stood against the winter's night sky.

The warehouse where Beck worked belonged to a well-known grocery chain, whose business had apparently transitioned over the years into primarily a delivery service. The long, low-slung building huddled at the far end of a broad graveled lot, which was dotted with steepled, melting islands of snow. A huge semi, wheels pock-marked with icy sludge, was parked with its rear doors opened to the warehouse's cavernous mouth.

Polk shut off the engine and pointed to a tall, gangly guy engulfed by a heavy coat and muffler, and wearing a Bengals cap. He was loading boxes from a handcart into the back of the truck.

"That's Beck," Polk said. "Big Bengals fan. Local PD said he even kept the cap on in the interview room."

His hand on the driver's side door, Polk turned to me. "I guess there ain't no chance you'd stay in the car?"

"None whatsoever."

"Lucky for you, I'm too fuckin' tired to argue about it. But keep your mouth shut, okay?"

"Don't I always?"

Harry growled something unintelligible and wrestled himself out of the car. I got out on my side and joined him, quickly buttoning my coat against the frigid air. Since the sun had gone down, the temperature must've dropped fifteen degrees.

With Polk in the lead, we crossed the ice-glazed gravel, stepping over heavily-indented tire tracks, until we reached the lip of the loading area. Vincent Beck was bent over the handcart, lifting the last of the boxes.

Glancing past him, into the shadowed maw of the great building, I saw towering rows of shelves, holding hundreds of brand-name products. The other delivery men—they were all male, I noticed, and all similarly bundled against the cold—hurried along the various stacks. Putting items into boxes emblazoned with the store's logo, climbing ladders for the upper shelves. Long, buzzing fluorescents hanging from the ceiling creating as much dense shadow as pools of unnatural light.

For some reason, Polk waited until Beck had secured the final box into the belly of the truck. Then Harry called him by name and flashed his badge.

It wasn't until Beck had jumped down from the loading dock and unspooled his muffler that I got a good look at him. He was as young as I'd first thought, barely twenty, with cheeks burned by the cold. Deep-set, troubled eyes. A thatch of unruly hair shoved down by the Bengals cap.

He was instantly on his guard, nervously shifting his weight from one foot to the other. Gloved hands patting before him, the muffled applause of anxiety.

"I told everything to the other cops already." His voice thin, a bit nasal.

"I know, but now you gotta tell *me*." Polk glanced around, taking in the other workers on the dock. A second truck now slowly backing up against a warehouse further down the line. "Is there somewhere we can talk, Vince?"

"Vincent." The younger man corrected him, rubbing his red nose. "And here's fine. Nobody pays no attention. We all got enough to worry about, gettin' the delivery right. Ya don't know what these customers are like. If anything's missin' from the order…Like I said, ya don't wanna know."

Polk nodded, uninterested, and motioned Beck a few feet back, so that we were all three standing between the rear doors of the truck and the dock. Our breaths formed frosted puffs that co-mingled in the tight confines.

Beck gestured at me. "Who's this? Your partner?"

"Christ, no. This is…uh…his name's Rinaldi, and he consults with the department."

"Dan Rinaldi." I shook Beck's hand. "Nice to meet you, Vincent. Sorry you're mixed up in all this."

"Yeah. Whatever." Never taking his eyes off Polk.

The detective returned the favor. "Look, Vincent, I gotta be honest about somethin'. Ya sure waited a long time before comin' forward about the Cranshaw murder."

"I know. It's just…I mean, I was so scared. But then I told Father Healey about it in confession, and he said I hadda go to the police. Tell 'em what I knew. Then he gave me ten 'Our Father's' and ten 'Hail, Mary's.' *Ten* each." An aggrieved sigh. "He don't play, that Father Healey."

"Sounds like a real hardass, all right." Polk cleared his throat. "Anyway, Vincent, I read your statement about the day of the shooting. It was about eight in the morning, and you were making a delivery at a house three doors down from Earl Cranshaw's place. Right?"

"That's right. My first delivery of the day. Huge order, the lady was plannin' a party or somethin'. I been up since six loading the truck."

"Fascinatin', but I'm mostly interested in what happened to Cranshaw. You told the Steubenville cops you noticed him comin' outta his house, in his bathrobe with a coat over it."

"Yeah. And big boots, with the laces loose. He musta just thrown stuff on to go out on the front porch and get the morning paper."

"Did he see you?" I found myself asking.

Polk shot me a warning look, but Beck answered anyway.

"If Cranshaw saw me, he didn't let on. Didn't wave or nothin'. Just bent down, got the paper—they had it wrapped in plastic, 'cause o' the snow—and headed back inside."

Beck shivered, but not from the cold. "He never made it."

Harry edged closer.

"Now what happened then? Exactly. I know it's hard, Vincent, but try to remember everything."

Polk's voice was unusually solitictous. Sympathetic. Must've been that "finesse" he'd talked about.

But all it did was make Beck more anxious. He ducked his head, jaw disappearing beneath the collar of his heavy coat. Gloved hands rubbing the sides of his jeans.

"Easy now, Vincent." Polk kept the impatience out of his tone. "Just give it to us, step by step."

"Well…" The young man glanced quickly to his left and right. "All of a sudden, I hear a car engine rev up. And before I knew it, I seen this Chevy sedan come roarin' down the street. Musta been parked down the block, 'cause it only took a few seconds and it was barrelin' up to the Cranshaw place. I know Cranshaw heard it, too, 'cause he stopped at his front door and turned around. He was lookin' right at the car as it pulled to the curb. And then the driver stuck out his hand…and I saw the gun—"

Polk stopped him by raising a forefinger.

"Tell me about the driver. The guy with the gun."

Beck shook his head slowly. "It all happened so fast. The guy sticks his gun out the driver's side window and fires. Twice, I think. I couldn't even believe what I was seein'. Like it couldn't be real, ya know? I hear the shots, see the little puffs of smoke or whatever. And then I see Cranshaw, stumblin' back against his own front door. Grabbin' his chest…there was blood…"

He almost choked, as though the words were piling up in his throat. Constricting his breath. Strangling him.

I reached out and touched Beck's shoulder.

"It's okay, Vincent. You're doing fine."

"Yeah." Polk forced a smile. "Real good, Vincent. Now what happened after you saw Cranshaw get hit?"

Beck recovered himself somewhat, taking a gulp of freezing air deep into his lungs.

"He…Cranshaw…he kinda crumpled to the porch. I remember seein' his leg twitch. Plus I could see his whole chest was covered in blood. I…I know I shoulda run over there, see if I could help…"

I found his eyes with my own.

"He was probably beyond help, Vincent. I doubt if there was anything you could've done."

"Maybe, but…" Letting his words die out.

Polk spoke up. "What about the shooter? In the Chevy?"

"I guess I was still lookin' at Cranshaw when I heard the car rev again, 'cause when I turned back he'd already taken off down the street. Like a bat outta hell."

"But can you tell us anything more about him? Did you get a good look at him? The gun? Did you notice the car's license plate?"

Another slow head shake. "No, I didn't notice the license. Like I said, it all happened so fast, and I was so wigged out by the whole thing…"

"What about the guy himself? Was he wearing a mask, or a scarf or anything? Could you see his face?"

Beck abruptly fell silent, eyes averted. Jaw working anxiously behind his coat collar.

"Vincent...?" I leaned in again, seeking his face.

His response was barely audible.

"What was that, Vincent?" Polk asked sharply.

"I said, I don't wanna talk no more. I don't got nothin' else to say."

Harry's face reddened, grew hard. He took a step closer to the younger man.

"Listen, Beck, if there's anything more you know about this guy. Anything you can tell us—"

"*I said I can't!*" Voice thick, threaded with fear. Despite the cold, he pulled off his cap. Ran his other gloved hand through sweat-matted hair. "I told ya all I saw. I told ya I just—"

Those were Vincent Beck's last words on this earth.

Suddenly, a sound like a branch snapping in two sliced through the icy air. It took me a second, maybe less, to register it. Give it meaning.

Gunshot.

Beck heard it, too. I saw it in his stricken eyes.

Before the top of his head exploded, spewing blood and brain matter on Harry Polk and me.

Chapter Twenty-one

Beck wheeled into my arms, dying even as I clutched him to me. We fell as one to the hard, frozen ground.

Out of the corner of my eye, I saw Polk reach for his service weapon. At the same time scanning the warehouse roof, just above us and to the right.

Before his gun cleared his holster, another shot boomed. Polk cried out, and grabbed for his shoulder.

"Harry!" I called.

The gun spiraled to the ground, and I saw his knees buckle beneath him. He fell with a thud and rolled, gasping, under the truck carriage. My arms still clinging to Beck's lifeless body, I used my legs to scrabble underneath as well, between the huge rear wheels.

Only then did I hear the shouts of the other workers, coming from within the warehouse. Panicked cries. Footsteps pounding, men leaping from the loading dock, stumbling, scrambling for cover.

As another shot took a divot out of a curve of fender not inches from my head. The loud, metallic ping echoed.

I ducked down low. "You okay, Harry?" Polk lifted his hand from his wound, fingers painted with blood.

"I'll live. You?"

"Fine. But Beck's gone."

He nodded. No surprise, since a bloodied, crescent-shaped shard of Beck's skull lay not a dozen feet away. Vivid as a scar on the snow-frosted ground. Just beyond, as though marking his grave, the forlorn Bengals cap.

Unwilling to look at Beck's face, I opened my arms and gently rolled him off me. Looked down at my hands, spackled with his blood. Bits of bone, brains. I rubbed them roughly against the sides of my coat, all the while fighting the urge to retch.

"Fucker must be on the roof." Polk shifted where he lay, favoring his shoulder. "Couldn't spot him, though."

Wincing from the pain, he reached across his body with his good hand and retrieved his cell. It was crushed.

"Musta fell on it. Piece o' shit. Gimme yours."

I handed him my phone, then hunkered down lower as he called the Steubenville PD for backup. There hadn't been another shot for over a minute.

"Guy might be gone," I said, after he'd hung up.

"And might not." Polk's breathing was labored. His wound was worse than he'd let on. His fading grip on it couldn't slow the blood seeping through his fingers.

"Here." I reached over and undid his bulky scarf, then wrapped it around the wound. Knotted it tightly.

"Press down on this. Oughtta help."

Polk didn't answer, but did what I asked.

After another minute, I said, "I think he's gone."

I had to know.

Steeling myself, I slid a few inches out from under the truck fender and leaned up. Just enough for me to see out. Scan the roof edge.

Nothing.

But that had to be where he'd fired from. Given the angle of the shots. They'd come from somewhere above us.

So maybe he *was* gone—

Then I saw him. Not on the roof. Inside the warehouse. Far back from the loading dock, perched atop a ladder braced against one of the high shelves.

Face concealed under a hat. Wearing a coat, muffler, and gloves. Like any of the other workmen.

And aiming down the barrel of a hunting rifle.

At me.

I froze. Dead meat.

He pulled the trigger. Nothing happened.

The gun had jammed.

Before I could react, he'd thrown the rifle aside and quickly started down the ladder. Half-sliding, feet slipping on the rungs.

I'd instinctively followed the rifle's arc as it fell to the warehouse floor and skittered noisily to a stop. Rousing myself, I looked up again and saw the shooter running into the shadows of the building.

Then I did something stupid. I went after him.

Bolting from my hiding place under the truck, I hoisted myself up onto the loading dock.

Polk's pain-shredded voice followed me.

"Rinaldi! What the fuck ya doin'?"

I ignored him and headed into the sprawling warehouse, the darkness within serrated by pockets of harsh light from the fluorescents overhead.

The building's massive interior was a maze of high shelves, intersecting at severe, irregular angles. Stacks of boxes, placed unevenly on the floor, reached to my shoulders. Emptied of workers, of the sound of human labor, the heart of the warehouse was a cold, bewildering array of shadowed corners, dead ends, and looming towers.

He was in here, somewhere.

Adrenaline pumping, fists clenching and unclenching, I went slowly forward. Eyes straining to see. Ears pricked for any telltale sound.

With every other step, I was either bathed in that stark light, or plunged into an opaque darkness. Through the spaces between rows of high shelves—stacked to the roof with canned goods, paper products and plastic bottles—I caught sight of the building's undraped windows. Huge, black-paned squares set high in the walls, reflecting the unyielding darkness beyond. And, like the walls themselves, offering no shelter from the bone-chilling cold of deepening night. A cold that permeated everything in the vast immensity of the place.

Shivering now—either from the chill or my own growing dread—I neared the end of an aisle formed by two high shelves and turned the corner.

Nothing. Boxes piled against the walls. The flickering of a fluorescent directly above me, its light dying.

I went on. Peering down the next aisle.

Again, nothing. I tried to remember to breathe.

Another dozen paces in, and then—

A sound. Loud, rumbling. An old engine sputtering to life, revving.

I whirled, straining to see down a corridor formed by two facing ceiling-high shelves. A narrow aisle whose utter darkness was bisected by an angled column of light.

The engine's roar grew louder, and then I saw it. Emerging out of the shadows, its great twin tines—like two silver spears, pointed and waist-high—flashing in the bright light.

A huge forklift, smoke belching from its engine, was hurtling down the corridor. Toward me.

Nearly as wide as the space between the two towering shelves, the forklift offered no escape on either side. No way for me to avoid its remorseless advance.

I sensed rather than saw the wall behind me. Knew there was nowhere to run. That within seconds I'd be crushed against its exposed bricks, caught between the metallic pincers of a rattling, two-ton behemoth.

Without thinking, I turned and leapt to the broad base of one of the shelves. Started climbing, fast as I could, using the shelves and struts as a ladder. Pushing aside boxes, grabbing for hand-holds. Scrambling upward.

Hanging tightly to the quivering aluminum tower, hoping my weight didn't pull it over, I glanced down in time to see the forklift rumble by barely beneath my feet.

With an ear-splitting whine, it crashed into the wall, burying its tines into the rough bricks. Engine chugging impotently, wheels spinning on concrete, the machine rocked on its chassis as though a live thing. Thwarted. Enraged.

And empty. No one in the driver's seat.

I released my grip on the shelf and dropped down into the forklift's open cab, behind the steering wheel. A man's belt had been used to secure the wheel in place, making sure the machine stayed on course.

I found the key in the ignition, turned it off. The engine choked a few times, sputtered, and went silent.

A deafening, echoing silence.

Taking what felt like my first breath in the past two minutes, I climbed from the cab. Peered down the aisle in the direction from which the forklift had come.

Nothing. No one.

I moved cautiously down the aisle, hands lightly grazing the shelves as I walked, as though for some kind of mental support. When I finally reached the open area at the other end, I paused, my gaze sweeping from left to right.

Nothing. No one.

Was the killer gone? Had he bought enough time by sending the forklift down at me to make his escape?

I kept moving. Going slowly down a line of shelves, past more stacks of boxes, another forklift half-hidden in shadow. A few handcarts. A row of vending machines along the near wall.

I'd just decided for certain that the killer was gone when I heard—

Soft, muffled. The rustle of clothing. The scrape of a shoe on concrete.

I stood, unmoving. Listening so hard my face hurt.

Finally, I risked turning my head. Squinted in the half-light down the mouth of another aisle formed by two shelving units.

There, at the far end. Where a shaft of light fell from overhead. The tip of a workman's boot.

Him. Hiding behind a six-foot-high pile of broad wooden crates.

Afraid even to swallow, I crept down between the shelves. Carefully placing my feet on the concrete, one slow, measured step at a time.

Making my way toward where he stood, shielded by the tower of heavy crates. Never taking my eyes off that workman's boot. The tip gleaming in the light.

Until I was standing not two feet away. My back to the stacked crates behind which he hid.

Hearing his frantic, labored breathing.

Which caught me off guard. Suddenly he came rushing out from behind his hiding place, yelling. Voice a garbled, viscous cry of panic.

He was holding something. A thick crowbar. In both hands, like a baseball bat.

As he stumbled forward, raising it high—

Without a thought, I ducked as he swung the crowbar at my head, missing me by a wide margin.

Then my old instincts took over. The feints and parries, learned at great cost in the ring. When I was just a kid in a man's sport, an amateur whose father bellowed caustic, belittling instructions from the corner.

Words that must've stuck. I used my forearm to block the next pass of the crowbar. Then, pulling my head down into my shoulders, I charged forward, grappling my assailant around the waist. Bringing us both down hard.

The crowbar flew from his grasp, clattering somewhere behind us on the concrete. Using my full weight, I pinned him beneath me. Fists clutching his coat collar, I stared down at his wide, frightened eyes.

He was wearing a heavy coat, gloves, and muffler.

Like the other delivery men. Like the shooter.

Like every other goddam person on earth, seemed like.

Rage boiling up in my throat, I pulled the muffler from around the lower half of his face.

He was a kid, younger even than Vincent Beck. With a kid's face. Unformed. Acne-scarred.

And utterly terrified.

"Please, mister! Please don't kill me!"

I was still gasping for breath, my fists at his collar, pressing hard against his sternum. My own face inches from his.

"*Please*, mister!" A thin line of spittle trailed from his lips.

I squeezed my eyes shut, mind reeling. I didn't know who this kid was, or what the hell he was doing here, but my gut told me one thing for sure.

He wasn't the killer.

At almost the same moment I had that thought, I heard the rising wail of sirens. Outside the building. The backup Polk had called for. The local cops, moving in.

I looked down at the shivering kid beneath me.

"Listen, that's the cops, and—"

My voice caught, as I heard another sound.

Sharp. Distinct. And nearby.

The staccato rap of footsteps, behind me. Receding.

I reared up, struggling to separate the sound from that of the approaching sirens.

Craning my head around, I could just make out—across the wide expanse of the building—a running figure.

I rolled off the frightened kid, who'd begun weeping copiously, and swiveled in a crouch. Staring hard down the length of the warehouse floor.

I saw him more clearly now. At a far corner of the building. The shooter. In coat, muffler, and gloves.

The disguise he'd used to hide in plain sight. To blend in at the warehouse.

To kill Vincent Beck.

I fell to my knees. Winded. Frustrated. Done in.

As though sensing this, the shooter stopped and looked back across the cold, empty distance at me.

It was then that I noticed he was standing by a metal exit door. Hand resting on the handle.

Then, slowly, deliberately, as though wanting me to see, he stepped through the door. And disappeared.

Chapter Twenty-two

"What the hell were you thinking, Rinaldi? Going after the shooter like that?"

Lieutenant Stu Biegler, Pittsburgh Robbery/Homicide, glowered down at me. He was past forty, but with an oddly unlined, youthful face, which made his attempt to project authority difficult to take seriously.

At least it's always been difficult for me.

"I told you, his rifle jammed. So I figured it was safe. Besides, at the moment, I wasn't exactly thinking—"

"That's for goddam sure! What if he had another gun on him? Some pocket piece. That ever occur to you?"

"Well, sure, now that you point it out…"

He waved a hand in disgust and glanced over at Eleanor Lowrey, who slumped in a corner chair. Barely listening.

According to the waiting room wall clock at Steubenville's All Saints Hospital, it was just after nine p.m.

Harry Polk had been in surgery for over an hour.

I sat on an over-stuffed green sofa, sipping bitter vending machine coffee. My winter coat, spackled with blood and gore, had been tagged and bagged by the CSU team still working at the warehouse. Same with my gloves. The leather jacket I'd borrowed from one of the EMT guys on-scene lay folded on the chair next to me.

Biegler hadn't bothered to unbutton his own London Fog coat since he'd arrived, and the building's central heating had

layered a sheen of sweat on his smooth brow. Though he didn't seem aware of it.

The night outside the stuffy room's single window hung like a painted backdrop, flat black, starless. I hadn't paid much attention to my surroundings in the ambulance racing here with Polk, but I got the vague impression of an industrial-park-like monotony. Squat, somber buildings. Mini-malls. Tract houses.

Since Biegler and Lowrey had driven straight here from Pittsburgh, after getting the report about the warehouse shooting, there hadn't been much for the three of us to do but wait for the results from Polk's surgeon. And to go over my description of events. Over and over.

"Look," I said now, "I've given Steubenville PD my statement. I've gone through it a half-dozen times with you two. But like it or not, the details aren't gonna change."

"And neither are *you*, apparently."

It was Eleanor's first words in quite a while. Though despite the stern look she was aiming in my direction, I detected the concern in her voice. More worry than anger.

"I mean, Jesus, Danny, this kinda thing is becoming a habit with you. Taking stupid risks, and—"

"And interfering with proper law enforcement," Biegler finished for her. "Though I'm just as pissed at Sergeant Polk. No way he shoulda let you take part in his interview with Beck. He shoulda locked your ass in the car."

"Hey, don't blame Polk. He tried."

Scowling. "You think this is funny, Rinaldi?"

"Hell, no. Not with Harry in surgery, at risk of losing use of his arm." I half rose from my chair. "What I *think* is that you're dumping on me because you're nowhere with finding the killer."

Eleanor raised a hand.

"Whoa, Danny. Chill." A sidelong glance at Biegler. "We're all worried about Harry, okay?"

Biegler looked as though he wanted to say something, but thought better of it. Instead, he turned away from me and folded himself into a chair a few feet from Lowrey's. Which left the three of us more or less in separate corners of the room, staring at each other.

Finally, Eleanor broke the silence.

"Look, I spoke to the local detectives on-scene on our way here. They're still piecing things together, but I think we got a pretty good fix on what went down."

Without waiting for a response, she withdrew her notebook. "They have statements from all the men working at the warehouse when Beck got shot. Plus the shift foreman, who was in his office at the far end of the building. He claims not to have even known anything had happened till he heard the police sirens."

She flipped some pages, then looked at me.

"Apparently, they're still questioning the warehouse worker you tackled, but he appears clean. Name's Jimmy Talbot. He's been employed there since high school. No sheet. Not even a traffic ticket. According to Talbot, he was terrified when the shooting started. He was in the rear area of the building, so instead of running, he just hid behind some crates. Actually pissed his pants, which he was quick to show the officer taking his statement."

"I don't care how wet his pants were," Biegler said, "he was also holding a weapon. Came out swinging a crowbar at the doc here." He turned to me. "By the way, you wanna press charges for assault?"

I shook my head.

"He was scared shitless, Lieutenant. Probably thought I was the shooter, sneaking up on him. So he panicked, grabbed the crowbar. Hell, maybe the kid's got a case against *me*."

Biegler smiled. "Well, if he ever needs a character witness against you, I'm so there…"

Eleanor put down her notebook and looked at him.

"Sir, with all due respect…"

I'll never know what she was going to say, for at that moment her cell rang. She took the call, listened intently, made a few notes, then clicked off.

Her boss sat up straighter in his chair. "What is it?"

"We just got an ID on the rifle the shooter used, *and* where he got it. It's a hunting rifle, as Danny guessed. A Remington.

Mid-range scope. It was stolen about an hour before Beck was shot. From a gun store two miles away, in a mini-mall."

"The shop owner get a look at him?"

"The shooter got lucky. The place was closed. He just smashed a window, went in and took what he needed. The weapon and some shells."

"Closed? At four in the afternoon?"

"The owner says he'd closed up early to celebrate his birthday. Besides, the weather's been bad for business."

"Did the place have an alarm?"

"Yes. But the shooter was in and out in a minute."

"Tell me there's video from inside the store."

"There is. All you can see is a guy in a winter coat, muffler and gloves. Just like the guy Danny saw go out the exit door in the warehouse."

"Gloves," Biegler repeated, as much to himself. "So no prints on the rifle."

"Afraid not, sir."

I stirred, which brought their gaze in my direction.

"So now the killer's improvising. Off his game. Which could be good for us. No stolen car. Not using his regular weapon of choice, the Taurus 44M."

"Which means he had to think on the fly," Eleanor said. "Make it up as he went along."

"Right. Somehow he finds out Pittsburgh PD is sending someone to talk to Vincent Beck, and—"

"But how would he know that?" Biegler asked.

"Beats me. But the shooter was worried enough about it to dress like one of the other delivery workers, break into a gun shop for a rifle, and get to the warehouse. To stop Beck before he spilled something important."

I paused. "Which also tells us a couple other things. How could the killer know what the other workers looked like, unless he'd been to the warehouse before? Seen how the guys bundled up against the cold in there. Which means he already knew where

Vincent Beck worked. Even *before* he'd learned that Pittsburgh PD was coming to talk to him."

"Good point." Eleanor made a note.

Biegler stared at me. "What's the other thing?"

"I'm less clear on this, but why didn't the killer use the revolver he's been using all this time? The Taurus 44M. If this guy is as methodical as I think he is, he's not just following an M.O. He's formed habits."

"So?"

"I think the only reason he didn't use his usual gun is that he didn't have it with him at the time. That when he learned about Polk's trip here, he was away from where he keeps the gun. Maybe he was away from home, on the road or something."

Eleanor nodded. "Wherever he is when he finds out about the interview with Beck, there's no time to go get the Taurus. All he can do is head for the warehouse as fast as possible, stopping only to break into a gun shop and get a weapon. Maybe seeing the rack of hunting rifles gives him the idea of taking a shot at Beck from a safer distance. Which means a better chance of getting away afterwards."

"You could be right," Biegler said officiously. "But then how did he get to the warehouse, and get away again?"

"If he was in as big a rush as we think, he wouldn't have time to steal a car. Not without risking being seen."

"So what are you saying, Detective?" Biegler's face darkened. "He took a cab?"

Eleanor shrugged. "Or just drove his own car."

I finished my coffee and got up. Gingerly. Feeling the early aches from my struggle with Jimmy Talbot. The sore muscles, the tender ribs from when we both hit the concrete floor. I knew they'd only intensify as the night wore on.

I'd be damned if I'd let Biegler see it, though. I stood to my full height, and put some grit in my voice.

"Now I have a question for *you*, Lieutenant. Did anyone outside the investigation even know a witness to Cranshaw's murder had come forward?"

"Hard to say, given the leaks we've been dealing with. Beck's name never appeared in the media, that's for sure. Or we'd have known. Other than that…"

Biegler fell silent.

"Regardless of how he found out about him," I went on, "the killer obviously feared Beck knew something. So was he right? Maybe Beck saw the killer's face the morning of the shooting, but had been too scared to say anything."

"So far," Eleanor said. "But the killer couldn't take the chance that Beck wouldn't at some point tell what he knew. He had to get to the warehouse and silence him."

"And for a spur-of-the-moment plan," I added, "it wasn't bad. Bundled up like the other workers. Everyone scurrying around, loading trucks. Most even with their faces covered by scarves or ski masks. Who'd notice him? From what I saw, the workers just wanted to load their trucks as fast as possible, climb behind the wheel, and get the hell out of the cold."

Biegler absorbed this. "But *had* Vincent Beck seen the killer's face? Had he seen anything at all?"

"We'll never know." Eleanor's voice grew soft. "He was just nineteen, poor kid."

I thought then of Beck's story about confessing to his parish priest that he'd witnessed Cranshaw's murder. And that now the same priest who'd urged him to go to the police would have the sad duty to preside over Beck's funeral Mass and burial.

Priest and penitent. Both victims of a higher law.

The arbitrary, remorseless law of unintended consequences.

◇◇◇

It was nearing ten when Polk's surgeon, Dr. Alice Yu, came into the waiting room to update us on his condition.

She hadn't taken two steps through the door before Biegler, Eleanor, and I rose to our feet and formed a semicircle around her.

Dr. Yu was tall, slender, and probably a bit younger than you'd want your surgeon to be. But her solemn eyes and brisk manner conveyed both confidence and maturity, as well as the expected level of impatience with us lesser mortals.

"Sergeant Polk will make a full recovery," she announced. "Luckily, there was no nerve damage. The muscle tearing was severe, but he should heal adequately. However, his recuperation will take time."

Biegler clucked his tongue. "So he'll be out of commission for a while?"

Dr. Yu smiled. "I believe that's what I said."

"But he'll be fine, right?" Eleanor's relief was palpable. "Can we go in and see him?"

"Not until tomorrow morning, at the earliest. Even then, he'll be heavily sedated. And in considerable pain."

Eleanor nodded soberly. Then, to my surprise, she reached and squeezed my hand. I squeezed back.

"I'm glad he's okay, too," I said simply.

A brief smile. Then, as though suddenly mindful of Biegler's presence, she slipped her hand from mine.

Chapter Twenty-three

A fresh, unexpected snowfall sifted down into the night as the police cruiser crossed the Allegheny into mid-town. Pittsburgh in winter, at midnight, and cloaked in seasonal cold, was a study in contrasts. Poised between two very different centuries, it was an amalgam of sleek, light-bejeweled towers and muscular, shadowed structures built low to the ground. Dusted now with soft new snow that fell like a benediction on the sleeping city.

At least that's how it felt to me, sitting in the passenger seat of the Steubenville PD black-and-white. Since the rookie uniform assigned to drive me back to town wasn't much for conversation, I passed the time watching the weather subtly change as we crossed the state line into Pennsylvania.

Lieutenant Biegler and Eleanor Lowrey had stayed behind in Steubenville, conferring with the local cops about the warehouse shooting. I could tell Biegler had wanted to re-interview Jimmy Talbot, the kid I'd tangled with, and Eleanor wanted to get a personal look at the crime scene. Which meant they'd probably end up staying the night in town. I figured this would be fine with Eleanor. No doubt she was anxious to be at Harry Polk's bedside the next day when he woke up.

My taciturn chauffeur dropped me off at the entrance to the Hilton parking lot, then pulled his vehicle around the corner and parked in the fire zone. As I stood under the gently-falling snow, trying to remember where I'd parked my car, I saw him

hurry out of the black-and-white and into the hotel's coffee shop.
A caffeine refueling for the hour's drive back home.

Shivering in the too-thin borrowed EMT jacket, I jammed
my hands in my pockets and trudged across the lot. It took me
a full minute to find my Mustang, and another five to get the
engine—and me—warmed up enough to drive.

I slid a Grover Washington CD into the dashboard deck and
carefully pulled out into the road.

As I circled the Point's mammoth construction site, heading
for the Fort Pitt Bridge and home, my cell rang.

It was Angie Villanova.

"Well, I hadda call in a few favors, but I did it."

Her voice wired, breathless, but tinged with fatigue.

"Did what?"

"Got you the interview with Wes Currim. That nutcase who
put his victim's head on the snowman."

"Jesus, Angie, I didn't—"

"Luckily, the interim DA in Wheeling is kind of a fan of
yours. Especially since you cooperated with the cops and accompanied Currim to where the vic's remains were. She thinks you're
a real standup guy. Or at least she did, before I set her straight."

I listened to her hoarse chuckle as I wheeled my car to the
curb. I don't like driving while pissed.

"Goddam it, Angie, I never agreed to see Wes Currim. I only
told his mother that I'd consider it."

"I know. Maggie Currim called me right after she saw you.
Truth is, you were kind of a disappointment to her."

"I got that feeling."

"You shoulda heard her cryin' to me on the phone. She said
that you'd been her last hope."

"I *am* sorry for what she's going through."

"Yeah, whatever. Anyway, I sorta felt responsible, since I'd
set up the appointment with you. So I told her I'd do my best
to get you in a room with her son."

"Without checking with me first?"

"Sometimes you gotta make a command decision. So I ran it past the assistant chief, who put in a call to Chief Block in Wheeling, who kicked it up to the DA's office. Then I got on the phone and closed the deal. Me and the DA. Woman to woman, ya know what I mean? Mother to mother."

I paused, letting my anger subside.

"So it's a done deal?"

"Done and done, like they say."

"What if I don't go along with it?"

"Then one of us looks like an asshole, Danny. Guess which one?"

I sighed loud enough for her to hear it.

"Shit, don't even try. I've heard tortured sighs from Italian men all my life. I'm immune."

Despite myself, I smiled. Imagined her patting her laquered cloud of hair in self-congratulation.

"Okay, Angie, I give up. When and where do I meet Wes Currim?"

"Eleven a.m. tomorrow. Wheeling PD's main lockup. Until they set a trial date, they're keepin' Wes outta prison. Probably save him takin' it up the ass, too. He's young, skinny, and a freakazoid. Hard-timers love meat like that."

"Tell me about it."

We exchanged a few more playful insults, argued about the next time she could expect me for dinner, and hung up.

I stayed parked at the curb, engine running, and thought about what it might be like meeting with Wes Currim tomorrow. What, if anything, I could say to persuade him to recant his confession. If, in fact, it wasn't true.

More to the point, I thought, *if he really didn't murder Ed Meachem, why the hell does he say he did?*

◇◇◇

Despite the Arctic chill and new snow, Noah's Ark boasted a decent-sized crowd. A half-dozen tables and most of the barstools were occupied, though few patrons were paying attention to the trio playing in the far corner. Working their way through an uninspired yet deafening cover of Brubeck's "Take Five."

I was still brushing wet snowflakes from my jacket shoulders when Noah signaled for me from behind the bar. Stopping only to get a peck on the cheek from a harried Charlene, hefting a tray of drinks, I joined him there.

"Glad you showed up, Danny." Noah planted his forearms on the bar. "I'm close to havin' an episode here."

A customer on a stool next to me glanced up, curious. Noah scowled at him and he went back to his beer.

"What are you talking about?" I peered hard into his eyes. On the lookout for crazy. "You taking your meds?"

"'Course I am. If I didn't, Charlene'd kill me."

"Only after *I* got done kicking your ass."

The trio behind us was so loud that it was hard to be both audible and private. Especially since the drummer had begun an ear-pummelling solo.

I leaned further across the bar, mouth next to Noah's ear. "So what's the problem?"

"Hate to say it, man, but it's you."

"Me? What'd I do?"

He turned away, then back again. As though reluctant to speak the words.

"Look, Danny, I don't wanna hurt your feelin's, but you gotta stop recommendin' this place to law enforcement types. It's lowerin' the caliber of clientele."

"You mean Dave Parnelli?"

"He's bad enough, but now I got G-men stinkin' up the joint."

"What?"

He jerked a thumb in the direction of the back wall. Special Agent Neal Alcott sat alone in a booth for four, nursing a Scotch. A stack of manilla folders at his elbow.

"Says you're workin' with him and the FBI. You wanna be cozy with the cops, okay, but the fuckin' *Feds?*…"

"Sorry, Noah. I didn't expect to see him here."

"I mean, shit, what's next? Secret Service? CIA?"

I waved him off and made my way through a clutch of crowded tables to Alcott's booth. Slid in across from him.

"Slumming, Agent Alcott?"

He rubbed his reddened nose. Sniffed.

"Just curious about the place, since it's your regular watering hole. Thought it might help me figure you out."

"Any progress?"

"Minimal. Got something for you, though."

He shoved the stack of files across the table.

"I realized I forgot to give you John Jessup's files. The ones I showed you in the car the other night. Might help if and when you get the chance to work with Barnes, since it was his last case. It could be connected to why he freaks out when he falls asleep."

"Could be."

"There's also one on Barnes himself. His FBI dossier. All the sensitive stuff's been redacted, of course. But you'll find the pertinent biographical details on the guy. That oughtta help, too."

I eyed him suspiciously.

"You've had a conversation with the director, haven't you, Neal? Along the lines of your being more supportive of my involvement…?"

He threw back the rest of his drink, tapped the glass irritably on the tabletop. I'd gotten my answer.

"Hell, the whole thing's moot, anyway." Alcott craned his head around, looking for Charlene. "We're no closer to finding Lyle Barnes than we were two days ago. We've sent people up to Franklin Park, even had our Illinois office reach out to his son in Chicago."

"Any luck?"

"Barnes' kid has no idea where his old man is. And doesn't care. Turns out, they haven't spoken in years. The prick hasn't even met his grandchildren."

I didn't comment. I figured Lyle Barnes was still my patient, at least theoretically, which meant I wasn't about to discuss his personal life. Least of all with Alcott.

The agent finally caught Charlene's eye, and ordered himself another round. I ordered a draft Iron City. After which, Alcott and I sat in an uncomfortable silence until she returned with our drinks. And departed again.

"By the way," Alcott said at last, "I heard about the debacle in Steubenville. How you and Polk let the witness get killed, and the shooter get away. Nice work."

"You had to be there."

"Believe me, I wish I had." He sipped his drink. "We lost a real opportunity to collar this bastard. You don't get many breaks like that. I don't blame *you*, of course. You're a civilian. Shouldn't have even been there. But Polk screwed the pooch on this, no question."

I raised my beer, took a long pull. "He's fine, by the way. Thanks for asking."

Alcott laughed shortly. "Like I give a shit. This whole investigation has been a nightmare. The joint task force is a joke. Undisciplined. Too many chiefs. We've got no leads, and more leaks than a sieve. Plus it took forever to get forensics on the letters Jessup got in prison—"

I indicated the files in front of me.

"Is that new data included in this?"

"Don't worry, it's all in there. Just got updated."

He barely got those last words out before sneezing violently. "Goddam cold's getting worse."

Muttering curses, he took out a handkerchief and wiped his sore nose. Then downed the rest of his drink.

"Now on top of everything," he continued, "our only eyewitness gets himself killed. This perp's making us all look like clowns."

"Speaking of the perp, what's the status of his next potential victims? Especially Claire Cobb. Parnelli."

He shook his head in disgust. "Don't get me started on those two. Claire asked to be moved again, so we have her in a motel in Wilkinsburg. No room service, so she's gonna have to live on take-out. Serves her right."

"And Dave Parnelli?"

"The other pain in my ass. He insisted his workload demanded constant attention. So *I* insisted he has one of our field agents with him at all times. Plus his movements are restricted either to his office or his home."

No bars? I thought, but didn't say.

"What about the rest? Others who might be on the killer's hit list?"

"The jury foreman and the two cops who arrested Jessup are under wraps in Cleveland. No hotel this time. One of our permanent safe houses. All three of 'em happy to be let off from work and under constant guard."

I considered this. "Makes it harder, doesn't it, not knowing for sure who's even on the list…"

"You got that right, Rinaldi. Not to mention all the manpower we've wasted in the last forty-eight hours looking for Lyle Barnes. At this point, I say to hell with finding him. Let him take his chances with the killer."

"But what does the director say?"

Alcott frowned bitterly. "He and Barnes went through the Academy together. They're old friends. That's why he wanted you to help him out. Cure him, or whatever."

"Cures are pretty tough to come by. I just hoped to help Barnes manage his symptoms. Or maybe, with luck, get to the root of them."

Alcott blew his nose, then abruptly got to his feet.

"Yeah, well, to do that, we'd have to find him. And we're havin' as much luck with that as we are with finding the killer."

He threw some bills on the table. But I wanted to stay longer, have another beer. I tapped the files before me.

"Thanks for these, by the way. They'll help me get up to speed on John Jessup. And Lyle Barnes."

A shrug. "One thing the Bureau's good at is compiling files. We got files on everybody."

He buttoned his coat and turned to go. Turned back. "Hell, Rinaldi, you oughtta see the one we have on *you*."

◇◇◇

By the time I got home, two hours later, I was dangerously exhausted. The three beers I'd had before Noah closed up hadn't helped. I made my way into my darkened living room, put the files Alcott had given me on the rolltop desk, and went straight to bed, stopping just long enough to get out of my shoes and coat. Then I fell, fully clothed, on top of the covers. And didn't stir.

I was thoroughly spent. Though my mind raced. Jumbled, incoherent thoughts crowding each other out. I knew I was experiencing a delayed reacton, emotionally and physically, to the past twenty-four hours' stunning events. The shooting at the warehouse, Vincent Beck dying in my arms, my frantic pursuit of the killer, the violent struggle with Jimmy Talbot. Not to mention what had happened to Harry Polk.

It was hitting me now. All of it. Images of blood and death. The fear, the dread. Sending long-suppressed shudders of anxiety coursing through me. The thickness in my chest hardening, like drying cement, as I drifted down into the black void of a deep, fathomless sleep.

Chapter Twenty-four

I knew, as I pulled onto the highway, that the drive down to Wheeling, West Virginia—which usually took about an hour and change—was going to last a lot longer.

During the night, the weather had turned angry. Fierce winds, hurtling snow, low visibility. Another winter storm thrashing the city, gathering strength as it rolled east.

It was just past nine in the morning, and I was on my way to see Wes Currim.

Fueled by three cups of black coffee, wearing my other Thinsulate coat and gloves, and with the dash heater on high, I drove slowly and deliberately through the blur of the storm. Heavy traffic made the slog from downtown to I-70 East even more ponderous than the radio had warned, so I was glad now, at last, to be out of the city.

The highway itself was barely discernable, merely thin lanes of powdered white, cinder-block snowdrifts forming tunnel walls on either side. I drove in a kind of concentrated silence, hands at ten and two on the wheel, the only sound the metronome-steady squeak of the wipers. Though they fought a losing battle with the frost caking the windshield, testament to the numbing cold outside.

As I crossed the state line, traffic thinned in both directions, though the storm's intensity had increased. By the time I'd register the high beams of an approaching car or truck, emerging out of the swirling cloud of snow, our two vehicles would just about pass each other.

I tightened my grip on the steering wheel, peering with renewed focus on the road ahead.

So naturally my cell rang. It was in its dash holder, and I could see the caller's number. Eleanor Lowrey. I pushed the button for the hands-free app.

"Where are you, Danny?"

"On my way to see Wes Currim. In Wheeling."

"I heard about that case. Should I even ask why you're visiting a confessed murderer?"

"I wouldn't bother. Long story."

"Can't wait to hear it. Meanwhile, the *real* news is that Harry's fine."

"That's great, Eleanor."

"I just left his room. He's still groggy, high as a kite on pain meds. But Doctor Yu says he'll definitely make a complete recovery."

"Do they know how long he'll be out of commission?"

"You know docs, they never want to make promises they can't keep. But looks like Harry's gonna need at least a month to recuperate."

"Which means he'll give himself a week, right?"

"Not if *I* have anything to say about it. He's gonna get the rest he needs, even if I gotta tie him to his bed. Though Biegler's bummed as hell about it, since the department's stretched pretty thin at the moment. With the shooter still out there and the FBI detailing every spare cop to help look for that Barnes guy, losing a veteran like Harry is a real blow."

"Speaking of which, how's the investigation going?"

"It isn't. We're fielding every tip we get, chasing every lead, but coming up empty. It's gotten so bad, we're recanvassing all the crime scenes again. Cranshaw, the judge, and Claire Cobb. And the warehouse where Vincent Beck was killed."

"Maybe you'll get lucky."

Her reply was a wry chuckle. If there was one thing this investigation was lacking so far, it was luck.

"Listen, Danny—"

Just then, a quartet of blazing lights appeared up ahead, glazing my windshield. A huge semi, heading west, rumbled past me. The wind shear made my Mustang's chassis shudder, doors rattling in their hinges.

I heard Eleanor gasp over the cell's tiny speaker.

"What the hell was that?"

"Semi. Big sucker."

"I assume you have tire chains."

"Put 'em on myself this morning."

"Good, 'cause I want you back in town in one piece. See, I remembered what I wanted to ask you the last time I called. Once I knew Harry was okay, it came back to me."

"What's on your mind?"

"Remember when we talked about working out together? Us two quasi-jocks? Last summer?"

"If I recall, it was more like a challenge. So?"

"Well, we never got around to it. We've both been busy, plus I had all that grief with my family…"

A long pause from her end. My turn, I guessed.

"Are you asking me out on a date, Detective?"

"Don't flatter yourself. I just figured…I mean, I was planning to hit the gym later this afternoon, anyway. Helps me think. Clears the cobwebs. I thought you might want to meet up there. If you're free."

"I don't know…sounds suspiciously like a date to me."

"Jesus, Rinaldi. How tough you gonna make this?"

I laughed. "I'm just screwing with you, Eleanor. Time and place?"

"The precinct gym, near the Old County Building. They just renovated the place. It's pretty nice. How's four?"

"Four o'clock it is. I should be down and back long before then."

"Good. Machines and free weights. And, Danny..?"

"Yeah?"

"Don't worry, I won't show you up too badly."

Her laugh was as warm and inviting as any man could want. A sound that stayed in my mind for more than a few moments after we hung up.

I took a long breath, brought my attention back to the road. Eleanor Lowrey and I had been dancing around each other's lives since last year, though duty, family, and circumstance seemed to conspire against us. Not to mention the fact that she was a cop, and I consulted with the department, which made us colleagues. Sort of.

Great, I thought. If there's a way to complicate things, I'd find it. Maybe it was the therapist in me. Though I sure as hell hoped not.

A road sign appeared out of the storm on my right.

Wheeling, fifteen miles.

I smiled to myself. Between my intense focus on driving and the conversation with Eleanor, I hadn't even noticed I'd crossed the state line into West Virginia.

Feeling more settled, I reached into my CD stack and took out a—Suddenly, a dark shape filled my rear view mirror. Large, metallic. High beams blazing.

The grille of a truck. Coming up fast behind me.

Even with my windows sealed tight and the heater blasting, I heard its ominous roar.

Gutteral. Insistent.

I tore my gaze from the rear view, risked craning around to see.

It was a junkyard pickup, battered, salt-pitted. License plate held by one screw, twisting in the wind, unreadable. Headlights flashing on and off.

I couldn't see the driver behind the cracked, ice-caked windshield. Just the massive front of the truck getting closer and closer, bearing down on me.

My temples pounding in my ears, I turned back to the road ahead. Nothing but a grey, nightmarish billow, from which came an unending rush of snow. Swirling, cascading.

Without a thought, I sped up. Racing blindly into the maw of the storm.

A glance at the rear view. He was accelerating, too.

Gaining on me. Faster and faster.

Fucking lunatic! Was he going to—?

The sickening sound of metal against metal as he rear-ended me. The Mustang lurching forward.

I felt the powerful jolt, pain spider-webbing up my back. Panic rising, I gripped the wheel tighter, struggling to maintain control as he rammed me again from behind.

This time, my car's chains spun uselessly and I careened into the oncoming lane. Taking every ounce of strength to right myself again. Pumping the brakes.

Just as another quartet of high, nova-bright lights emerged from the storm. Another semi, barreling toward me. I was in his lane, struggling to slow down. Regain control.

He wouldn't even see me until it was too late.

A cry I didn't recognize tore from my throat as I swung the wheel with all my might, angling back toward my own lane. Swerving to avoid those twenty relentless tons of steel and rubber.

The semi roared past on my left, missing me by the width of a hand. Wind shear was twice as potent as I'd felt before. My car shaking, as though it might come apart.

Not even daring to breathe, I focused on steadying myself in my lane. Then slowly accelerating. Pulling away.

I didn't make it.

The pickup filled my rear view again. Engine whining louder than the storm's wail, it rammed me again.

The impact lifted me half out of my seat, steering wheel spinning under my fingers. I managed to grab it, hold it steady. A death grip.

Too late. I was fishtailing on the icy asphalt. Skidding. Chained tires screaming in protest, I tried to turn in the direction of the skid.

No luck. As though caught in a vortex, I went into a 360-degree spin. The world outside my windows rushing in a formless, circular whirl.

The air pushed out from my lungs. Time became fluid, unreal. There was only the feeling of directionless motion. Unstoppable. Going faster and faster.

By the time the car righted itself, coming out of the spin, it was hurtling in a diagonal across the oncoming lane. And then I was bumping off the side of the road, plowing through the banked snow at full speed. Tilting and rattling as I hit the white-blanketed woods beyond. Ice-glazed branches scraping the windows, clawing the sides of the car. Loud, hawk-like screeches.

Until, finally, the Mustang's nose buried itself in a shallow ditch full of snow and frozen mud. And shuddered to a stop.

Gasping, head thudding painfully, I scrambled from behind the wheel. Stumbled out into the ceaseless cold, the buffeting wind. Ice cracking beneath my boots.

Clutching the door frame, I peered out onto the snow-shrouded road, just in time to see the rear lights of the pickup as it roared by.

Vanishing into the belly of the storm.

Chapter Twenty-five

"Meth freaks. Hadda be."

Chief Avery Block, Wheeling PD, came around his desk holding two steaming mugs of black coffee. Behind him, the carafe burbled noisily, sharing shelf space with a photo of some lakeside cabin, a small plastic replica of City Hall, and a bronzed bowling trophy.

I gratefully took a mug between my two chafed hands.

"I heard there're a lot of meth labs in the area." I swear my teeth were still chattering. Post-impact stress.

Chief Block snorted, then sat on the corner of his desk. Weary gaze angling down at me, sitting in the room's only other chair.

"Shit, it's a growth industry around here. Only part of the economy still goin' strong, I guess."

The chief's office at the main precinct was larger than I'd expected, but otherwise bore all the familiar markers. Wood-paneled. Shoulder-high metal files. The governor's official photo on the wall, framed importantly between the American flag and the state one.

Standard issue or not, the office had a good working heater, and at the moment that was all I cared about. That, and the unlikely fact I was still alive.

After the crash, I'd no sooner tried climbing out of the road-side ditch than I felt a rushing wave of nausea. I stumbled, fell forward, gasping. My vision was blurred, and a sudden, searing pain buckled my neck. Whiplash, maybe.

Aching and shivering, gulping frigid air, I staggered up the embankment to the edge of the road. Instinctively rubbing my sore neck, I just sat there, winded, knees drawn up. Listening to the hollow pounding of my heart.

Finally, I managed to call AAA on my cell and ask for a tow truck. Then I phoned Chief Block and explained that I'd be a bit late in arriving, though I didn't tell him why. Not then.

When the tow truck showed up, the driver got out, took one look at my car, and shook his head.

"Well, it ain't totalled, mister. But damned near."

I'd gotten shakily to my feet to help him secure a tow line to the rear of the Mustang, but he waved me off. Luckily, the ditch was shallow enough that pulling the car out wasn't too difficult. But it was plainly undriveable.

I gingerly joined him in the front seat of the truck and we towed my car to an auto repair shop the driver knew. Once there, I spent another twenty minutes with the shop's service manager, who explained he'd need until Monday afternoon— at the earliest—to call me with an estimate. Given his look of barely-contained glee, I knew the repairs would be costly.

Not that I had much choice. So I signed some papers, shook hands with the guy, and asked if there was a car rental place nearby. He pointed to the peak-roofed building across the street.

By the time I'd rented a late-model Ford sedan and gotten back on the road, it was nearing noon. The storm had abated. Winds decreasing, snow thinning to flurries. Pale fingers of sunlight reaching through the trees.

Thankfully, my vision had cleared by then, though my neck had grown stiff, throbbing painfully. Every time I turned the wheel, I felt my shoulders pinch, as though snagged on something.

I stopped at a local store for Motrin, downed three pills with some bottled water, then drove on to the Wheeling precinct, where a bored, chinless desk officer directed me to Chief Block's office.

"Goddam meth dealers think they rule the roads," the Chief was saying now, between tentative sips from his mug. "We hear of somebody gettin' hassled about once a week. Not just tourists, either. Business people, families. Hell, last year a couple o' them joy-ridin' sons-o'-bitches ran a squad car off the road."

"So you don't think this was maybe somebody trying to stop me from talking to Wes Currim?"

He laughed bitterly.

"Listen, Doc, if it was in my power, *I'd* stop you from talkin' to Currim. But the order came from upstairs, so my hands are tied. Though I still think it's bullshit."

"Why?"

"'Cause the crazy bastard confessed! He's guilty, and he knows he's guilty. So do I. So does everybody."

"His mother tells a different story, Chief."

"Yeah, well, she would, wouldn't she?"

Rousing himself, he hauled his heavy frame off his desk and re-took his seat behind it. As he leaned back, the wheeled leather chair squeaked in protest.

"Now don't cause no trouble, okay, Doc? This visit with Currim is just a formality. A favor our bleedin' heart lady DA is doin' for the bleedin' hearts up your way. I mean, we appreciate your helpin' out with Currim before, but here's where it ends. You good with that?"

I nodded. "Believe me, I see it pretty much the same way. One short meeting with Currim and then I'm gone."

This seemed to mollify him, for he gave me his version of a smile and pushed a button on his desk phone console.

"Hey, Harve…? Ya wanna step in my office?"

In moments, Sergeant Harve Randall entered, a bulky fur-collared parka over his police uniform. I rose and we shook hands. He was as spare and wiry as I remembered.

"How's it hangin', Doc?" Randall grinned. "Sure didn't expect to see *you* again. After what we found up at the old house, poor Ed Meachem hacked all to pieces, I figured you'd seen 'bout enough of this place."

"I'm kind of surprised myself, Sergeant."

Block looked up as he casually unwrapped a stick of nicotine gum. "Do me a favor, will ya, Harve? Escort the doc over to lock-up. He's here to see Wes Currim."

Randall frowned. "No shit? What for?"

"That ain't our concern, Sergeant. Now just do what I asked ya, okay? The sooner he sees Wes, the sooner he can be on his way."

Block popped the gum in his mouth. "No offense, Doc."

"None taken."

◇◇◇

Slapping his arms against the cold, Randall led me across the plowed precinct lot to the adjacent building. The lockup was a predictably bleak, block-long structure, all gray brick and barred windows. Pockets of snow rounded its corners, icicles hung from its low eaves. Though I doubted it looked any less forbidding in the summer.

"Don't mind Chief Block." Randall's breath was coming in puffs. "He's nearin' retirement, and lately he just hates aggravation. This Currim thing—"

"A bit too public for the chief, I'll bet."

Randall chuckled. "Damn straight. They practically had to drag him in front o' the camera when the DA gave her press conference."

"I saw. *You* didn't look too happy, either."

"No, sir. Not one bit."

He stopped then and spread his hands, taking in the near-deserted lot.

"Anyway, that was the last straw for the chief. Past couple days, this place was swarmin' with reporters, TV news vans. He finally put his foot down, had the mayor tell 'em to clear out. We weren't grantin' any more interviews, and havin' all that ruckus here was interferin' with the investigation."

"Looks like it worked."

We'd arrived at the heavy double doors fronting the building. Plexiglass windows interlaced with wire netting.

Randall paused again, gloved hand on the door knob.

"Look, Doc, I ain't no shrink, but if you want my advice, don't say nothin' bad to Wes about his mother. She was in here yesterday, and one o' the guards musta said somethin' about her, 'cause Wes kinda lost it. Yellin' and screamin' like all get-out. Hadda be subdued."

"Is he okay? Was he hurt?"

"No, nothin' like that. He calmed right down, sounds like. But, man, he's got some kinda weird thing with her. Ya know? Like he's her little husband or some shit. Totally fucked up."

I didn't reply. After a moment, Randall shrugged, feigning disinterest, and pushed open the door.

I followed him into the small front lobby, where he introduced me to the desk officer and had me sign in. Then he directed me to a narrow corridor.

"Go on down and make a left, and you'll see the cell block door. Guard there will take you to the visitors' area and bring Wes in to you there."

I thanked him and started down the corridor. He called after me. I stopped, turned.

"Listen, Doc," he said, voice oddly tentative. "Ya want me to look into that thing with the pickup? Maybe try to find out who ran you off the road?"

"I appreciate the offer, Sergeant. But you're probably not going to find anything, are you?"

He sheepishly scratched his ear. "Probably not."

I nodded and headed back down the corridor.

Chapter Twenty-six

"Ya know, I don't gotta say nothin' to nobody."

"That's true, Wes. You don't."

Wes Currim and I sat across from each other at a smooth pinewood table. Aside from our two chairs, it was the only stick of furniture in the small, featureless room.

In contrast to the wintry temperature outside, the air was warm to the point of stifling, thanks to a huge heating vent in a near corner.

There was also a single window, high and rectangular, through which I could see a guard standing in the adjoining room. His gaze narrow-eyed and suspicious.

Wes had been seated when I was ushered into the room, and hadn't risen to shake hands. Had barely raised his head in acknowledgement when I sat down.

He was less anxious and jangly than he'd been in the patrol car on our way to Meachem's body. But not by much. He hadn't shaved since then, so that his face seemed narrower, more wan, under the bristles. And his eyes were blinking rapidly, as though stung with something acidic. Trying to manufacture tears.

"If you don't want to talk," I tried again, "then why am I sitting here?"

A cool smirk. "My lawyer, Mr. Hansen, forced me to let you come. Says it'll look good to a jury that I wanted to confide in someone like you."

"Are you going to confide in someone like me?"

"Fuck, no. Hansen's an asshole. He don't give a shit what happens to me. But I'm supposed to be all grateful to my brothers for hirin' him. Well, I'm not, and I hope he ends up costin' 'em a fortune in lawyer's fees."

"You don't like your brothers?"

"Goes both ways. They don't like *me* much, either. Think they're better n' me. Always have."

I leaned across the table, staring hard at him until he had no choice but to look back.

"Listen, Wes. Truth is, I'm not sure *I* give a shit what happens to you. But your mother does. And she swears you're not guilty. That you were at her house, helping her clean out the attic, the night of Meachem's murder."

"Well, she's lyin'. That's what I told Hansen, that's what I told the DA, and that's what I'm tellin' you."

"Why would she lie?"

"What are you, a fuckin' moron? To protect me. I'm her son and she loves me."

"So she'd lie to keep you out of prison?"

"My mother'd do *anything* for me. Just like I'd do anything for *her*. Anything!"

I watched the pulse jumping in his neck, his level of agitation rising.

It didn't help that the over-heated air was bringing beads of sweat to his brow. And to mine. I suddenly wished I'd asked the guard for some water before entering.

"It's been that way for a long time, hasn't it, Wes? You and your mother, taking care of each other."

"That's right. Long time."

"Since your father ran away with his girlfriend?"

"Even before that. All he ever cared about—" His jaw tightened. "He *never* treated her right. Never! Then he starts fuckin' his secretary, for Christ's sake, right behind my mother's back…"

He paused, rubbed the hairs on his cheeks. "I mean, after all she did for him…he goes and runs off with this little cunt. Broke my mother's heart."

"And you never heard from him again?"

"Nope. Not a word. Not a goddam word."

He fell silent for a long moment. Calming himself. Hands splayed flat on the table.

"Wes," I said quietly. "Did you kill Ed Meachem?"

"Yes."

"Did you assault him in that supermarket parking lot, knock him out, and take him to your uncle's house in the woods?"

"Yes."

"Why?"

"Like I told the cops. Like I told everybody. I was gonna hold him for ransom."

"Why?"

"Another stupid question. For the goddam money."

"What happened?"

"He came to and tried to escape, so I killed him and cut him into pieces."

He swallowed hard, as though his throat hurt.

"And you got the idea to do this because of the Handyman's crimes? How he'd dismembered his victims?"

"Yeah. Everybody knows about that. He's famous. But only *I* thought o' puttin' Meachem's head on the snowman. That was *my* idea. All mine."

"And you did all this—the kidnapping, the murder—just for the money? For drug money?"

"I didn't do it for *fun*, if that's what you think."

A thin, wayward smile. "Except for the last part. The thing with the dude's head. *That* was fun."

The pulse in his neck was nearly vibrating, it was pumping so fast. Excitement at the memory? Pleasure at the thought he was shocking me?

"So you're this stone killer," I went on. "You need money and decide to get some. You methodically pick your victim out because he looks rich, drives an expensive car. You bring him to an isolated spot, planning to hold him for ransom, but things go wrong and he ends up dead. So you hack the body to pieces.

Then, just for fun, you build a snowman and put the victim's severed head on top."

"That's pretty much it, Doc. Ya got me."

Palms rubbing the table now, as though cleaning it. Placid smile intact, belying his anxiety.

"Then I just have one question," I said. "One thing that's bothered me from the start. Why the hell did you turn yourself in?"

His smile deserted him. Palms stopped moving.

"What?"

"Why did you confess? Meachem had been missing for a week, the police had no leads. Suddenly you show up and say you did it. You're even willing to show the cops where you left the remains. Why?"

He swallowed again.

"I—I felt guilty. I mean, I fuckin' *killed* a guy. I never planned on killin' nobody. I just wanted the money."

"So why wait a week before going to the cops?"

"'Cause I was scared. I knew that if I turned myself in, I was lookin' at life in the state pen. Hard time. Shit, man, I was just…I didn't wanna do it. But then…"

"Then what?"

He took a deep, slow breath. As though it was the first he'd taken in a long time.

"I kept seein' the story on the news. The guy's family cryin' on TV, askin' for help findin' him. Sayin' if anyone out there knew anything…ya know what I mean…"

I nodded.

"I couldn't sleep, couldn't eat…felt sick all the time, like I was gonna throw up. Plus I figgered, hell, they're gonna find the body sooner or later…"

"Maybe. But here's what I don't understand. Let's say the police *did* find the body at your uncle's house. In that case, you had to know they'd start questioning you, your whole family. Anyone who might have known about the house, or had access to it."

"That's right."

"So why did you leave the remains there? Why not put all the body parts in some trash bags and get rid of them?"

He hesitated for a moment. A long moment.

"Jesus, I don't know," he said at last. "I wasn't thinkin' right. I guess I shoulda done that. I probably shoulda got rid o' everything, and…Like I said, I just wasn't thinkin' right…"

Then, as if flipping a switch, he grew animated. Flashed me that same dark, unnerving smile.

"Fuck it, maybe they're right about me, after all."

"What do you mean?"

"I mean, maybe I'm just crazy, like everybody says." He sat back then, hands behind his head. "They don't put you in the big house if you're crazy, right?"

I didn't say anything. Just watched him watching me, a strained, empty silence settling between us. Filled only by the cotton-soft hiss of hot air rising from the wall vent.

When he finally spoke, his voice was clear. Defiant.

"Or maybe I'm just playin' ya, Doc. Playin' *all* o' you. Ever think o' that?"

"I've considered that possibility. Which means you're guilty. That you've been guilty all along."

He gave a hoarse laugh. "Christ, Doc, that's what I've been tryin' to tell ya. Shit, how many times does a guy gotta confess around here?"

"Then I guess I'm wasting my time."

"Guess so."

Currim sat forward again, hands once more palms-down on the table between us. Then he quite deliberately began drumming his fingers.

"Any more questions, Doc?"

"Just one." I slowly got to my feet. Looked down at him. "What do I tell your mother?"

The drumming stopped. Sudden sorrow veiled his eyes.

"Tell her…" A slow, measured breath. "Just tell her I'm sorry."

Chapter Twenty-seven

I didn't make it to the new precinct gym until four thirty. On the way back to Pittsburgh, I realized that having to drive a rented sedan had one advantage over my Mustang. Given how banged up I was, it was nice not to be wedged into a bucket seat.

The lot behind the Old County Building was nearly deserted, so I had my pick of parking spots. I figured that every available vehicle, marked and otherwise, was in use. Part of the massive joint FBI-Pittsburgh PD investigation into the identity and whereabouts of the elusive shooter, who even now could be planning an attempt on the next victim on his list.

After locking the car, I stood in the freezing air of the open lot, picturing the killer in my mind. When I'd actually *seen* him, hidden under his bulky coat and hat, standing casually at the warehouse exit door. Staring frankly at me across the lengthy, shadowed floor.

There was something implacable, unswerving in his stance. His faceless, determined gaze. The way his gloved hand rested easily on the door handle.

He won't stop, I realized suddenly. No matter how intense the manhunt for him, how many law enforcement personnel and resources were brought to bear. The killer would not stop until he'd crossed off every name on his list. Until, for whatever inexplicable reason, his need to avenge John Jessup's imprisonment and death had been satisfied.

I blinked up at the glare of sunlight threading gray, weary clouds. The temperature was dropping by the minute, though the latest forecast had promised no new snow.

Fine with me. Pulling my coat collar up against the icy chill, I hurried across the lot.

◇◇◇

The departmental gym was housed in a two-storied structure adjacent to the Old County Building. Though I'd never been inside before, it was obvious that it had been recently renovated. The walls were freshly painted, and all the equipment boasted a still-new chrome gloss. Even the free weights looked like they'd just come out of their packing crates.

As I expected, the gym was as deserted as the parking lot. Maybe a half-dozen officers. Men and women in sweats, departmental t-shirts, and tank tops using the treadmills, Nautilus apparatus, and barbells. One guy—and there's always at least one in every gym in the world—looked totally 'roided-out, veins popping on his forearms and neck as he pumped iron in front of a wall mirror.

I looked around. Maybe I'd beaten Eleanor here after all. Not that it mattered. No way I'd be working out today.

Then I saw her, sitting at a workout bench in a far corner, away from the others. She was in a sport bra and sweats, bent at the waist, elbow on knee, doing biceps curls with her right hand. Her concentration on her form was so intense, she didn't even register me until I was only a few feet away.

"Enjoying the view?" She didn't look up as she smoothly lifted the multistacked hand weight. Her breathing slow and steady.

"Looks heavy."

"Nah. Just warming up."

She smiled at me, then, with a quick motion, shifted the weight to her other hand. Then her left arm began the clean, rhythmic curls.

"Now you're just showing off."

"Hmm. Somebody sounds intimidated."

"Maybe. Though if this fancy-ass place has a speed bag, I'd be happy to return the favor sometime."

She finished her set and placed the weight back in its rack against the wall. Then she sat up straight on the bench, rolling the kinks out of her shoulders.

"Good burn?" I said.

"The best. I'd ask you to go change and join me, but you don't look so hot. What happened?"

I told her, and she made the appropriate commiserating noises. "You oughtta see a doctor."

"If I start feeling worse, I will. Promise."

She leaned back on her elbows, a stray wisp of hair dangling. Face, arms, and belly sheened with sweat. All sweet curves and lean, defined muscle.

I was staring. I owned it.

"Still, the day isn't a total loss. The view and all."

She shrugged. "Good genes. Plus varsity track and field in college. Guess I've always liked being strong. In shape. Even before I joined the force."

"Too bad you've let yourself go."

She smiled again. But it was her gaze that held me. Managing to be both frank and warm at the same time, with just the hint of wry amusement.

"How long are we going to keep doing this?" she said at last.

"Doing what?" I finally moved, as though freed from a spell, and found a seat next to her on the bench.

"This," she said. "Flirting. Mating dance. Whatever. 'Cause, man, the suspense is killing me."

"Not doing me much good, either. But aren't you the one who's been busy? Unavailable. With work—"

Her smile faded. "And family stuff. I know."

Eleanor sat up again, reached for a towel hanging next to the free weights rack. Dabbed the sweat from her face.

"The thing is, Danny, my life is complicated. As you know better than anyone. Besides, I don't know if I'm over what happened last summer yet…"

"I wondered about that myself."

That damned bank robbery case had unearthed some old hurts for a number of people, myself included. But perhaps Eleanor most of all. Something neither one of us had mentioned much since.

Now, making an effort to brighten her voice, she looked at me through the folds of the towel.

"On the other hand, I can't seem to stop thinking about you. Crazy as it seems."

"Or not. And I'm an expert on crazy."

She chuckled ruefully, tilting her head until it gently touched mine. "Let's face it, Danny, our timing sucks. With the shooter out there, the joint task force scrambling, all the political pressure to make an arrest—hell, the only reason Biegler gave me the afternoon off is 'cause I haven't had a break in about thirty-six hours."

"Which means you're back on duty by dinner, and probably looking at another double shift."

"At least. See what I mean? Not exactly a good time to hook up."

"Or else it's the *best* time."

She grinned. "Christ, that's both lame *and* desperate. You need to get laid that bad, I'm sure Harry knows the names of some primo hookers. If you can afford them."

"Speaking of which, how *is* my favorite sergeant?"

"Pretty well, thank God. I saw him this morning. They're keeping him in All Saints for another two days, then he can be transferred back home."

"How's he taking it?"

"He probably hates being stuck in Steubenville, away from all the action. But he's too sore and doped up to make much of a fuss about it. The last time I saw Harry this docile, he was passed out drunk on my living room sofa. I remember, Luther took one good sniff and just—"

Suddenly my cell rang. It was Neal Alcott.

"Rinaldi?" Breathless, agitated. Like I'd never heard him before.

"What is it?"

"Claire Cobb. You gotta get over here."

"What's happened?"

He told me.

"Keep her warm, comfortable. Get her to breathe in a paper bag," I said. "Where are you?"

"Majestic Motel. On Third, in Wilkinsburg."

I gave Eleanor a quick glance. In lieu of explanation.

"Be right there."

Chapter Twenty-eight

Based on the symptoms Alcott described on the phone, it was clear that Claire Cobb was having a panic attack.

And based on what I was hearing on the all-news radio station as I drove across town, I wasn't surprised.

Since the story had leaked about the shooter targeting those he held responsible for John Jessup's death, there'd been ongoing media speculation about who might be on the hitlist. From sober analysis on mainstream interview shows to reckless guesswork on various Internet sites and blogs, the crimes had become fodder for the nation's pundits.

Once the link had been made between the murders of Earl Cranshaw, the guard who'd killed Jessup in prison, and Ralph Loftus, the judge who'd put him there, it had been easy to see the failed attempt on Claire Cobb in the same context. She'd been his prosecutor.

Which then made it likely that Dave Parnelli, who'd unsuccessfully defended Jessup, was also on the list of potential victims. As well as the cops who'd arrested him, and the jury that had convicted him. Moreover, while the FBI only had the jury foreman under its protection, some commentators feared the entire jury might be at risk.

In the past two days, whenever I happened to check in on the news coverage, it seemed the theories about the killer's list were growing more provocative. And personal. One Cleveland print reporter who'd covered Jessup's trial—and was among the very few who'd done so—wrote in her blog about buying a gun, in case the killer might bear some grudge against her as well. Even the courthouse's veteran bailiff had expressed concerns about his safety in a paid interview he granted to the *National Enquirer*.

I found myself recalling these stories as I drove in a gathering dusk toward Wilkinsburg. While these and dozens of others were either trivial, exploitative, or merely ludicrous, they were just part of the fog of reportage in the age of the endless news cycle. The usual chatter that nowadays bedeviled the serious investigation of a case, or the issues it raised. *Vox populi* turned to white noise.

Until two hours ago, when a popular—though anonymous—"true crime" blogger opined that, if *he* were the unknown shooter, he'd want another crack at ADA Claire Cobb. That anyone who's ever worked from a list knew you couldn't move down to the next item until you'd crossed out the one above. "Anything else," he cheerfully wrote, "is just plain sloppy."

Predictably, the incendiary post went viral. And was soon picked up by the mainstream media, who decried its jocular tone even as they quoted from it. Endlessly.

After making the turn onto Penn Avenue, cobblestones slick with a crust of ice, I tried to imagine Claire's reaction. Maybe she'd seen it online herself, or watched a local news report on the motel's TV. Maybe she'd overheard one of her FBI handlers talking about it.

It didn't matter. Given her mounting fears and her legitimate concerns about the bureau's ability to protect her, the cruel story was bound to trigger a convulsive, overwhelming panic.

New snow flurried and wheeled in the dying sunlight as I merged into slowing traffic. This was the gray, defeated, disavowed part of Wilkinsburg, an area passed over in Pittsburgh's rush to gentrify its older neighborhoods. On either side of me, angry, desperate men lounged before empty storefronts, or in the doorways of run-down rooming houses. Smoking, arguing, killing time.

Ahead of me, the once proud Penn Lincoln Hotel, long gone to seed and now marked for demoliton. Beyond its faded façade, garish billboards blocked the waning sun. Narrow alleys snaked between somber, chipped-brick buildings. Boarded windows lined the upper floors. Neon signs flickered above corner bars, mini marts, pool halls, and single-storied motels.

Claire Cobb was in one of the latter, though it took a full ten minutes for traffic to move enough for me to locate it. The Majestic was on a side street, just past a mom-and-pop store on the southwest corner.

There were maybe a half-dozen cars in the lot fronting the low-roofed motel, its rough stone and aluminum siding showing the result of many years' exposure to Pittsburgh's muscular weather. The word "Majestic," written in a carved-wood cursive, was backed by a metal trellis that rose above the entrance. Pillows of snow ringed the building's walls and splayed in strands across the cracked asphalt.

I'd just parked and locked the rental when Agent Green came out of the frosted double doors to meet me. For some reason, he felt the need to elaborately shake my hand. Perhaps the director's admonishment about me to Neal Alcott had made its way down the chain of command.

"Glad you're here, Doc," the younger man said, before hustling us both back inside, out of the cold.

◇◇◇

I was taking Claire Cobb's pulse.

"Okay, Claire. Just keep breathing. Deep breaths."

We sat next to each other on the motel room's sagging bed, my fingers on her wrist. I raised the forefinger of my other hand before her moist, blinking eyes.

"Now just follow my finger, without moving your head."

She did, as I traced a horizontal path in the air, to the left and then the right.

As both her breathing and pulse rate slowed, the color rose in her cheeks. Along with an embarrassed grimace.

"I've had panic attacks before, Doctor Rinaldi. You'd think I'd be used to them."

"Nobody ever gets used to them. Were you prescribed medication to help?"

She nodded. "Xanax. Ran out yesterday. I've been taking them on spec."

Claire took another deep, cleansing breath, at the same time shifting her bulky shoulder sling. The bandages had already started to fray, lose their adhesion.

I sat back, then glanced over at Agents Alcott and Green, who stood in almost identical poses at the shuttered window. Hands behind their backs, feet planted apart on the threadbare carpet. Their discomfort palpable.

In contrast, sitting forward anxiously on a nearby chair, was Gloria Reese, the agent personally assigned to Claire. Hands clasped on her lap, she looked over at her charge with what seemed like genuine concern.

Finally, Alcott spoke up. Nodding at Claire.

"Is she okay now, Doc?"

Claire answered him. "*She's* fine, thanks. Good to go."

Unamused, he kept his gaze on me. "Can you stay with her for a few minutes? We have to go arrange transport."

I peered at Claire. "You're moving again?"

"After that online post about me? Damn right I want to move. Out of the city."

Alcott took a few steps toward the bed, oversized fists clenching at his sides.

"Jesus, I'd like to get my hands on the prick who wrote that thing. Practically daring the shooter to try and finish what he started with Ms. Cobb."

"Fuckin' Internet." Agent Green's informed assessment of the situation. After which he turned and carefully peeked out between the shutters to the street beyond.

I suppressed a small gasp as I got to my feet and faced Alcott. Still favoring my sore neck.

"You okay, Rinaldi?"

"I'll live. Listen, even *you* can't blame Claire for wanting to change locations again. Where to?"

"Sewickley. Outside the city limits, but close enough to maintain control of the situation. A night in a B&B we booked there, then transport to the Ohio safe house where we have the jury foreman and the two Cleveland cops."

Claire shivered noticeably. "Good plan. This way, all four of us will be conveniently located in one place. Makes things easier for the killer when he finds us."

"He *won't*, Ms. Cobb."

With a weary sigh, he took out his pocket handkerchief and blew his nose. The persistent cold had made his eyes look strangely old. Red-veined, fatigued.

"Hell, the location of the safe house is a secret even to most field agents. Strictly need-to-know basis."

She looked unconvinced, but said nothing. Merely let her head fall, eyes on the scuffed carpet.

I bent and took her pulse again. Elevated, but not bad. Appropriate to the situation, I figured.

Meanwhile, Alcott had stepped purposely to the door, motioning for the other two agents to follow.

"Back in five, okay?"

Without waiting for an answer, he strode out into the deepening darkness, Green and Reese at his heels.

"Really inspires confidence, that guy," Claire said, with feigned humor. Her skin had begun to pale again.

Though her outward symptoms had subsided, I knew she was barely keeping it together.

"Looks like they've got a good plan." Wishing I sounded more convinced. "Besides, you're probably tougher than you think. Your opposing counsel in the Jessup trial, Dave Parnelli, called you a cruise missile. And he doesn't exactly pour on the compliments, if you know what I mean."

Her expression changed. Grew pensive.

"Tough? I don't feel so tough now. I've never been through something like this. All of a sudden, it's like the real world has broken through. Invaded my controlled little life."

"But you've dealt with crime—and criminals—your whole career."

She shook her head. "It's not like a court room. It's not the brutal civility of people in power suits, arguing before a jury. It's mad men with guns leaning out of a car, aiming for your head."

Her gaze went to the shuttered window. What I suspect she imagined might be right outside, beyond its thin glass.

"I'm ashamed to say it." Her voice dropping. "But I'm afraid. Really afraid."

I resumed my seat next to her on the bed. Kept my own voice measured, matter-of-fact.

"No need to be ashamed, Claire. I'm afraid myself a lot of the time. It's a scary world."

"You don't seem that scared to me. Jesus, what kinda guy bullshits a damsel in distress?"

"No bullshit. Truth is, I think fear's gotten a bad rap. Years ago, right after grad school, I did a little mountain climbing out west. The Tetons. I was with a friend of mine, an experienced mountain guide. First time out, I almost couldn't do it. I had to admit to him that I was afraid. Know what he said? He said he wouldn't climb with anyone who wasn't."

"And that helped?"

"Yes, because he was right. Fear gives us the edge we need to stay alert, to recognize what's coming. It helps focus our attention. It's only a problem when it paralyzes us. Makes us feel impotent to act."

"Well, I'm there, Doc. Paralyzed and impotent. Sounds like a bad law firm."

She sighed. "But I guess you're right about fear. I remember when I did my first three-way. With some guy and his skinny girlfriend. In case you haven't noticed, I'm a big woman. I was afraid I'd roll over in the heat of the moment and squash the poor thing."

"Uh-huh."

"True story."

"No doubt."

She summoned a wan smile. "C'mon, I figured we could use a little levity right about now."

"Good coping skill."

"Maybe. Unless it's just empty bravado. Like whistling in the graveyard. 'Cause I'm still scared shitless."

I took her hand, squeezed it hard.

"You're gonna come through this, Claire. At least if *I* have anything to do with it."

"Talk about empty bravado. Christ, now you sound like Agent Alcott."

"Well, if you're gonna start insulting me…"

But her smile had long since faded. She turned and stared once more at the somber, shuttered window.

◇◇◇

Ten minutes later, Claire Cobb and I were sitting together in the back seat of an SUV with tinted windows.

Our driver, alone in the front seat, was Agent Green.

We'd just pulled out of the motel parking lot, right behind Alcott and Reese in a nondescript sedan. Given the knot of traffic and the increasingly dense snowfall, soon their blurred rear lights were all that was visible through the driver's windshield. Then they too seemed to vanish into the milk-white sheeting of the storm.

"Weather's gettin' worse." Agent Green hunched forward, steering with one hand, using the other to palm away a coating of fog from the windshield. "Bad break."

"Why am I not surprised?" Claire murmured.

I spoke up quickly. "How far to the B&B?"

"Figurin' traffic and this new storm, I don't see us reachin' Sewickley in less than an hour."

As if to emphasize his point, Green slammed on the brakes, nearly rearending the hatchback that had slid into line in front of us.

"Asshole never hear o' runnin' a yellow light? Damn!"

Green pounded the wheel with his fist, then let out a long exhalation.

Claire gave me a wry smile. "Gonna be a *long* goddam hour…"

But she was wrong.

I felt the other car pull up alongside us almost before I saw it. A dark-hued panel truck, the driver peering right in at us through his opened window.

Opened window. In this weather—

It was *him*. The coat, ski mask, and gloves.

The gun.

"Go!" I shouted at Green. "Get moving—!"

"What? We're jammed in. I can't—"

I turned and threw my arms around Claire, pushing us both down hard. Just below the shooter's line of sight.

The first shot blew out the front passenger side window. Loud as a thunderclap. Glass shattering, spraying.

Claire's screams echoed the lingering sound of the gunshot. Then rose louder, choked, gasping.

Agent Green shoved the car into park, his other hand reaching into his jacket. He didn't make it.

Another shot boomed, more glass flew. And a scarlet streak edged the side of his skull. He cried out.

Keeping Claire's head down beneath the seat, I tried to raise myself up enough to see how badly Green had been hit. He slumped forward on the wheel, unmoving.

Beneath me, I felt Claire's whole body quivering. Heard her anguished, wracking sobs. Panic rising.

Then another shot pierced the rear passenger window, whistling over our heads. Glass exploding. Shards slicing my hands and face.

Claire was wheezing, hyperventilating. I bent and cradled her, ignoring the rivulets of blood spreading across my knuckles. Bracing for another gun shot.

It didn't come.

Suddenly, Claire wriggled up from under me and squinted out the shattered window. Face smeared with tears, tattooed with an ugly bruise.

"He's not there!" Words coming in short gasps.

I followed her gaze. The panel truck was still beside us, wedged in by the stalled, motionless traffic. As were we. But the driver's seat was empty.

Claire turned to me, her anguished look as fierce as it was stricken.

"He's coming! For me! I've gotta get away!"

She began beating my head and arms with her fists, fully in the grip of a maddened, intolerable panic. I grabbed her wrists, held her.

"Maybe he's gone! Maybe—"

Another shot boomed, piercing the rear window on our other side. Glass pelted us. Claire screamed, pulling free of my grasp.

Disoriented, I swiveled around, trying to make out where he was. Behind the car? Closing in—?

But all I could see was a whirling, roaring cascade of snow. All I could hear was the shrill honking of car horns.

Then, abruptly, I felt Claire moving beside me. I turned back to her just as she bolted out of the seat and pushed open the door on her side. And ran.

"Claire! No!!"

Too late, I scrambled out after her. Frantically looking about me for some sign of the shooter.

But I saw nothing. Heard nothing.

Just kept running.

In my haste, I slipped on the ice, losing my footing. By the time I righted myself, Claire had managed to put some distance between us.

But not enough. I spotted her.

She'd threaded her way through the stopped traffic, the choked snarl of cars in the intersection. Through the growing crowd of stunned, curious on-lookers and drivers climbing out of their own cars. Into a howling wind and blowing snowstorm, beyond which rose the high whine of approaching sirens.

Then she was gone, slipping into a canyon of looming, dilapidated buildings. Disappearing into a maze of forlorn alleys, shuttered shops and single-lane side streets. Into the veins and arteries of the district's broken, forgotten heart.

I followed her.

Chapter Twenty-nine

I'd just caught sight of her, moving haltingly down a narrow alley through the flying snow, when I heard the gunshot. Instinctively, I ducked my head, but kept running after her.

Claire must have heard it, too. She hesitated for a brief moment, head swiveling back and forth, then turned and vanished around the corner of a deserted tobacco shop.

I sped up, feet slipping on the soft accumulaton of new snow. Not daring to look up or around me, I arrived at the same corner. Expecting at any second to hear another shot. Feel the sudden, searing burn of a bullet.

But there was only the wild sigh of the wind, the billowing whiteness of the storm. Where had the shot come from? Behind me, from the street? From one of the smudged windows overlooking the alley? A rooftop?

I tried to think. The shooter must have seen Claire get out of the car. Then followed her into the clutch of old, semi-abandoned buildings. A perfect killing floor, emptied of everything but hurrying snow and an ominous, flooding darkness. Determined to finish what he'd started.

I peered around the corner of the shop, down into another alley. Narrower, barely discernable in the dim glow of the streetlight at its other end. Claire had stumbled halfway down its length. I saw her curled on her side in the snow, free hand rubbing her knee.

I almost called out to her, then realized that my shout might give the shooter a new fix on her location.

Instead, I moved in a crouch down the alley toward her, at the same time glancing from one side to the other.

Looking for the movement of a shadow. The glint of a gun barrel. Anything.

I tried to hurry, gasping in pain with every step.

My sides ached from the exertion, my blood-smeared hands stung. I never felt so vulnerable, exposed.

By the time I reached her, Claire had just managed to get up. Her eyes wide with terror. Her breathing quick, shallow. She practically swayed on her feet.

Gripping her shoulders, I tried to steady her. Peering into her oblivious, panic-stricken face.

I noticed that her glasses were gone. Probably lost in the snow when she fell. No time to look.

But my gaze had spotted something. A dozen yards ahead, on the right. Cover.

"C'mon!"

Her legs started to buckle, so, dropping my hands to her waist, I half dragged, half carried her to the large, weather-battered trash dumpster. Wheels long rusted, lid piled high with a month's undisturbed snow. It stood against the side of a squat, brick-and-mortar apartment building whose windows were barred and caked with ice.

I pulled us down to the ground, crouching low and tight against the cold metal skin of the dumpster. Behind us, at the end of the alley, that lone streetlight. Our only way out, agonizingly far away.

Claire's sudden death grip on my arm drew my gaze back at her. She huddled, trembling, breathless. Paralyzed by engulfing, immeasurable fear.

Suddenly, the sharp crack of a gunshot pierced the wail of the storm. A bullet pinged off the lip of the dumpster, just above our heads.

He knew where we were.

Claire began to weep uncontrollably, between sharp intakes of breath. I pulled us lower to the ground.

Steeling myself, I risked leaning out and squinting down the alley's length. Back the way we'd come.

At first, I saw nothing.

Then, a subtle movement. A blurred figure emerging from the hellish storm. Coming toward us.

I drew myself back. My mind raced, trying to conceive of a plan. See any kind of move.

We were unarmed. He wasn't.

We were huddled behind the alley's only obvious cover, with at least twenty yards between us and the near corner, and the broader street beyond. And the streetlight on that corner, providing the only illumination, would reveal us to the shooter if we tried to move.

We were trapped.

Then, even as that thought registered, I knew that our pursuer must have realized the same thing. Which forced me, as though against my will, to risk another look.

He was getting closer. Walking slowly, taking one measured step at a time in the soft snow. Ugly gun glinting in the dimness.

He seemed unreal, other-worldly. In that same thick coat, ski mask, and gloves. Eyes invisible, shielded beneath his hat's brim.

Suddenly, inexplicably, I thought about Lyle Barnes. The missing FBI profiler. Had his night terrors been like this? Had he been visited in his tortured sleep by such implacable, seemingly unstoppable creatures? Silent. Masked. Nightmarish juggernaults stalking the sleeper's pitiless, unending dreamscape...

Christ! I involuntarily shook my head, as though to push such thoughts from my mind.

Because this was real. The shooter, coming toward us out of the night and the storm, was real.

And closer now. Perhaps twenty feet away. Holding the revolver with both hands. The hunt ended. His prey caught.

I didn't see a choice. I'd have to time it perfectly.

Wait till he was almost upon us. Look for telltale signs. Like planting his feet. Bringing the gun to eye level.

Then making my move, such as it was. Jumping him. Fighting for his weapon. Somehow...*stopping* him.

He took another step closer.

Pressure crowding my chest, I sank back, readied myself. Claire's bandaged shoulder pressed next to mine.

"Don't move," I whispered.

But she just stared at me. Glassy eyed. Shivering with panic. With sheer, unyielding terror.

That's when it happened.

Suddenly Claire was staring out at something. Just to her left. Her breath quick, serrated.

I followed her gaze. A tall building across the alley, a hulking structure shadowed black against the night.

Then I saw what she did. A fire escape. Old, rusted, hanging from iron struts embedded into the building's bricks. The ladder had been left unhinged, its lower section extended, rungs reaching almost to the ground.

"Claire, no!"

She turned her eyes toward mine for just a moment.

Enough for me to see their crazed determination. Their desperate, inconsolable fear.

Another bullet sliced the air, burying itself in the bricks above us. As I instinctively ducked my head, Claire bolted from behind the dumpster and ran out into the alley. Stumbling blindly, hand outstretched, toward the bottom of the ladder.

I hauled myself up, unthinkingly. Never taking my eyes off her as she grabbed the ladder's sides and put a foot on the first rung.

The sound of boots scraping the snow-scrabbled ground snapped my head around. Back toward the alley.

The shooter stood calmly, having come even with the edge of the dumpster. Not five feet from me. Gun upraised. Aimed right at me. Pinned there.

I looked across the alley at Claire, who was clumsily climbing up the ladder. She'd only reached the third rung, the effort nearly exhausting her.

The shooter saw her, too. Head held perfectly still, profiled against the falling snow, watching. Just watching.

While keeping his weapon pointed at me.

Suddenly, Claire gave an anguished, terrified gasp. Her bandaged arm hindering her, she'd collapsed, a leg entwined between two rungs. Clinging desperately to the ladder. As its corroded metal groaned and swayed.

It was then that the shooter finally swung his gun away from me. Toward her.

Now or never.

With a hoarse shout, I took two broad steps into the alley and hurtled myself at the shooter. Wrapping my arms around him, I let the momentum carry us both to the brick wall on the other side. We collided against it with a thudding, jarring impact.

Intense pain exploded in my shoulders and neck, and for a moment I thought I might black out. Then, twisting violently, the shooter broke from my grasp. Staggered away, gun still held tight in his fist.

Struggling to stay upright, I lurched toward him again. But he was ready this time. He swung his gun-hand in a clean, swift arc and clipped my jaw with the butt.

I went down hard. Tasting blood, even as I fought to stay conscious…

Then I saw him turn his gaze once more to Claire.

I cried out, my voice a strangled, impotent cry against the storm. The darkness. The inevitable.

The shooter raised his gun, supporting the butt with the palm of his steadying hand, and fired. Twice.

I could only watch in horror as Claire Cobb, hanging helplessly on the lower section of the ladder, screamed in agony. Twin splotches of dark scarlett sprouted on her chest. Blood bubbling across the curve of her bandaged arm.

For a long, awful moment she hung, suspended, in the same position on the ladder. Leg coiled awkwardly between the rungs. Free arm clutching the ladder's side.

And then, as if only now realizing what had happened, she released her grip on the ladder.

And fell.

My heart stopped.

Unthinking, choked with rage, I climbed to my feet. Stumbled toward her. Out into the open—

The shooter turned back to me. Raised his gun a second time. For his second kill.

I froze in mid-step. Looked at him. At the black ski mask that hid his face. At his shadowed, unseen eyes.

When, from the far corner of the alley, I heard a familiar voice call out. Young, strong. Angry.

"Drop it! FBI!"

It was Agent Green, standing unsteadily beneath the street-light at the end of the alley, two-handing his service weapon. Pointed determinedly past where I stood, at the shooter.

"I said, freeze, motherfucker!"

Hesitating only a second, the killer suddenly crouched and fired at the agent.

Wildly. Missing him.

But the shots forced Green to hit the ground. Giving the shooter enough time to turn and start running at full speed back down the alley.

Within moments, he'd vanished into the storm-threaded darkness. As if he'd never been.

Rousing myself, I made my way to where Claire lay on the ground. Bending over her prone body, I cradled her head in my hands. Blood pooled thickly, spreading across her chest.

Meanwhile, Agent Green had gotten to his feet and was coming up the alley toward Claire and me. His breathing labored, his head wound still bleeding freely, he stared in horror down at her.

I cast him a warning look, then bent over her again.

As I heard Green step a few feet away, and start talking into his cell. Calling for backup. An ambulance.

Though I was sure he knew, as I did, that it was too late.

I took her hand.

"Claire…I'm so sorry…"

Strangely, the panic had left her eyes. Replaced with a sad, disquieting calm.

With supreme effort, her mouth moved. A half-smile.

"Told ya, Doc…I knew. I knew it all along…"

Then, lips still parted, she grew still. Eyes going dull, empty. In the bitter cold, the ceaselessly falling snow. And the close, impenetrable darkness.

I lay her gently back down. On my hands and knees, I crawled a short distance away in the soft carpet of new snow. Head down, staring at the ground. At the crumbled cobblestones and cracked asphalt beneath the cold skin of smooth, translucent white.

A whiteness marred by the blood dripping from my swollen mouth, oozing from my cut, throbbing hands. Each drop a reminder of what just happened. Of what I'd allowed to happen.

Of my guilt.

I felt like a fraud. A failure. What had I told her, just hours before, in answer to her fears? I'd assured her that nothing would happen to her. That she'd be okay.

"At least," I'd said, "if *I* have anything to do with it…"

Well, I'd *had* something to do with it, all right. And this was the result.

The shooter was still at large.

And Claire Cobb was dead.

Chapter Thirty

Agent Green winced as he patted the new bandage covering the side of his head.

"Sorry about Ms. Cobb, Doc. She was a nice lady."

I nodded dumbly. We were still on-scene and sitting across from each other in a city ambulance. The EMT—young, male, and cooly efficient—had just finished with Green and was attending to me.

"I'm fine," I said stiffly.

The EMT clucked his tongue distractedly and went back to checking my vitals. Grunting occasionally with satisfaction. Then he began picking tiny bits of glass from my knuckles with a medical tweezer.

Through the slitted windows of the ambulance, I could see the flashing lights of patrol cars, CSU techs lugging their equipment, uniforms unspooling crime scene tape across the mouth of the alley. I also made out the M.E's wagon, in which Claire Cobb's body lay in a zippered bag.

Until the EMT none-too-gently took my jaw and turned my head back to face him. Ignoring my grimace of pain, he shone a penlight in my eyes. Another satisfied grunt, and then he was wrapping thin gauze around my hands, securing it with bandages.

Finally, he swiveled on his haunches and directed his opinion to Agent Neal Alcott, who sat with his back to the driver's seat. Looking utterly spent.

"They're both okay, under the circumstances. Luckily, the shooter just grazed Agent Green. Though he'll need looking at when we get to the hospital."

Alcott barely acknowledged him. The EMT coiled his stethascope around its hook just behind my head and moved smoothly up to the driver's seat. Started the engine.

"We're stretched pretty thin 'cause of the storm," he announced. "So we're down to one tech per vehicle."

Nobody answered him. Instead, Alcott stared at his junior agent as the EMT pulled the ambulance away from the curb. The traffic had thinned somewhat as the night had lengthened, and we moved slowly but steadily toward town.

I slumped back against my seat, arms and legs emptied of feeling. Closed my eyes. Welcoming the low growl of the engine, the hum of the tires on snow-carpeted asphalt.

Abruptly, Agent Green stirred. Spoke to his boss.

"It was my fault, sir. After the attack, it took me a few minutes to come to. By the time I realized that Claire and the doc were gone, and I was able to find them, she'd already been...she was already dead." A bitter sigh. "It didn't help that I went down the wrong goddam alley and had to come around the other way."

"It's not about fault," Alcott replied. "At least not yours alone. Reese and I got stuck up ahead of your SUV in traffic. So nobody caught sight of the panel truck until it was too late. Between that and the storm..."

Despite myself, my eyes opened. "But the panel truck came up alongside us as soon as we left the motel parking lot. No question, the shooter knew which car we were in. And when we were leaving."

Alcott was grim. "No question, all right."

Another thick, uncomfortable silence.

"I assume the pattern still holds," I said, "and the panel truck had been stolen."

"That's right. Just got word."

Alcott looked off and spoke to the air.

"She didn't like me, did she?" Voice subdued. Holding more puzzlement than sorrow. "Claire. She didn't like me."

Lost in my own thoughts, I didn't offer a reply.

◇◇◇

I was alone at a table in the ground-floor lounge at the Old County Building, flanked on either side by scuffed, mottled vending machines. Spindly cracks spreading out from beneath them on the linoleum.

I'd just spent the past hour in the ER at Pittsburgh Memorial. While Agent Green was taken for a more thorough exam of his head wound, I was given a checkup by a newly-minted resident. He redressed my bandages, then assessed me for concussion. When I told him about my recent car accident, he gingerly tested my neck and shoulders for whiplash. He didn't seem sure one way or the other, but prescribed some Vicadin anyway. In case the pain worsened.

Now, an untouched paper cup of coffee in front of me, I used my cell to check my voice mail. No messages from any of my regular patients, thankfully, but there *was* one from someone else.

Maggie Currim.

"I just wanted to tell you how disappointed I am, Dr. Rinaldi. I counted on you to help me, to convince my poor Wesley to change his story. To take back his confession. *Because he didn't do it.* And you…well, as I told Angela Villanova, you were my last hope. Now all I can do is pray to the Lord for His mercy and His justice. And I suggest you do the same."

I clicked off, and sat looking at the phone. Though I was genuinely sorry that I'd let Maggie down, it was hard to hear it right now. Not when I was still reeling from the tragedy of Claire Cobb's death, and what I felt was my own culpability.

It wasn't merely guilt. It also flew in the face of my own self-concept. Over time, belief in yourself and your actions becomes a habit. A hard one to break, especially once you've allowed yourself to be seen as someone who usually comes through. Once you believe too much in your own skills, your own convictions. Your own publicity.

Is that what I'd been doing the past few years, involving myself in these police cases? Making promises I couldn't keep? Turning my desire to help those suffering from trauma into some absurd pseudo-heroics? Mere ego disguised as courage, narcissism disguised as compassion?

Probably not questions I could ever answer. Not for sure, anyway. No matter how hard I explored my own motives. As the Buddhists say, "The eye cannot see itself."

But they *were* questions worth thinking about, if nothing else. Worth keeping in the forefront of my mind.

Or else Claire Cobb's death would be even more obscene, more senseless, than it already seemed.

I pushed myself back in the chair, plastic legs scraping the linoleum, and got up. I was late for the debriefing upstairs in the main conference room, called by Lieutenant Biegler and Special Agent Alcott.

And my attendance, I'd been informed, was mandatory.

Chapter Thirty-one

When I stepped off the elevator on the top floor, I saw Eleanor Lowrey standing in front of the closed double doors of the conference room. I joined her there.

"I wanted a moment with you alone, Dan." She gave me a sad smile. "I'm so sorry about Claire Cobb."

"Me, too. I can't help but feel responsible. I really hoped… well, I hoped she'd come through this okay."

"We all did." Her glance fell to my bandaged hands. "But what about you? Are *you* okay?"

"Define your terms. At least I'm still in one piece."

"Which just means you got lucky. No way you should've gone after Claire when she jumped out of the car."

"No way I *couldn't* have. Not if I wanted to live with myself afterwards."

Eleanor sighed. "I figured you'd say something like that. But I had to go on record that it was crazy stupid."

"Duly noted. Meanwhile, how's Harry Polk doing?"

"The docs are releasing him from the hospital in the morning. Biegler's having a uniform go pick him up in Steubenville and bring him back."

"But he'll be on leave, right?"

"At home. Recuperating."

"Bet he's not taking that well."

"That's putting it mildly. I just spoke to him on the phone and he's furious. He hates being sidelined in the middle of all this. I promised to keep him in the loop, but it didn't do much good. Finally, I told him to chill out before he gave himself a stroke."

"Harry? Chill? Not enough pain meds in the world."

We shared a brief smile, then, reluctantly, she smoothed her hair back with both hands. Prepping her game face for the meeting.

"Do me a favor?" Her violet eyes finding mine. "Don't get yourself killed any time soon. Okay?"

Then she turned and pulled open the doors.

◇◇◇

We stepped into the spacious, paneled room just as Lieutenant Stu Biegler was hanging up the phone.

Along with Neal Alcott, Agents Green, Zarnicki, and Reese looked up expectantly at the lieutenant from their seats at the oval conference table. Taking little notice of Eleanor and me as we each pulled out a chair, though I did catch Gloria Reese peering at my hands.

"That was the assistant chief," Biegler announced. "Who's just conferred with Chief Logan and the mayor." He looked over at Alcott. "*And* the director."

"I know." Alcott's elbows bookended a tidy stack of files. "I debriefed the director an hour ago, and he decided to speak personally with Pittsburgh PD. To clarify the situation for all concerned."

Biegler kept his gaze narrowed, skeptical. I could tell this was supposed to unnerve the FBI agent. It didn't.

Alcott scanned the room, stopping once to give me a brief, acknowledging smile.

"I asked that you be included in this meeting because, like it or not, you've been significantly involved in this investigation. And so your input may have some value."

Biegler scratched his chin. "By 'significantly involved,' he means you've been shot at. On two separate occasions. Not to mention all the goddam cuts and bruises. Whatever. How valuable that makes your so-called input is open to dispute."

Eleanor gave me a sympathetic look, but I pretended I hadn't seen it. Kept my own eyes on Biegler.

"You know, Lieutenant, as much as I normally enjoy trading insults with you, I'm not really in the mood right now. A good person was killed just hours ago, right in front of me. A person who was constantly assured by the people in this room—including me—that she'd be safe. Protected."

"Yeah, I know. So?"

"So let me just say, from the bottom of my heart, go fuck yourself."

Bristling, Biegler got to his feet. Fists pressing down on the table, knuckles going white.

"Listen, you arrogant piece of—"

"Lieutenant!" Alcott had risen, too, squaring his big shoulders. "Shut the hell up! I don't care what your beef is with him, this isn't the time or the place."

Still fuming, Biegler whirled to face Alcott.

"Since when did you start kissing Rinaldi's ass?"

"Since the director ordered me to cooperate with him. To include him in the investigation."

"But he's a goddam *civilian*—!"

"Paid consultant," I corrected him, turning to Alcott. "Though I don't think the lieutenant has ever gotten over it. I swear, he brings it up every time we're in the same room. In my clinical opinion, it's becoming an obsession."

I could sense Eleanor, frozen in her seat, gazing up at me. Whether in alarm or amusement, I had no idea.

"Like I give a shit," Alcott snapped. "About either one of you. Especially not now. Understood?"

I paused only a moment before giving him a slow, solemn nod. Then I glanced at Biegler.

"How about it, Stu? All good?"

Even Biegler was smart enough at this point not to take the bait. Instead, he merely shrugged, though he couldn't resist shaking his head in disgust as he re-took his seat. With a heavy sigh, Alcott did the same.

Which signaled his three subordinate agents that they, too, could risk taking a breath. I'd noticed how they'd each sat perfectly still, like trained guard dogs on alert, while Alcott and Biegler argued. As though just waiting for the signal to act.

And do what? I wondered. Join the debate? Toss Biegler out the window? Interagency cooperation, my ass. It was just as I'd first thought. As far as the FBI was concerned, local cops were the enemy. And always would be.

Alcott sniffed loudly, getting our attention, then opened one of the files in front of him. Sitting opposite him, I could make out the photos paperclipped to the report. Crime scene images of Claire's bloody corpse.

"Just so you know," Alcott began in a quiet tone, "Chief Logan and the mayor are going to hold a joint press conference in the morning. As you can imagine, Ms. Cobb's death has intensified the scrutiny this investigation will be getting from the media. Not to mention the director."

He rubbed his chafed nose. "And, on a personal note, I want to express my outrage and dismay at what happened to Ms. Cobb. And I know I'm not alone in these feelings."

Agent Green grunted his assent, fingers distractedly touching his bandaged head. Beside him, Gloria Reese kept her face composed, concealing…what? Guilt? Sorrow?

Alcott went on. "Moreover, I want to let everyone in this room know what I said to the director. That this joint FBI-police task force will redouble its efforts to nail the sick bastard behind these killings. I want this man caught, people. Hell, I want my hands around his goddam throat."

He'd actually lifted his huge, athlete's hands over the files. They hovered as though having risen of their own volition. Agent Zarnicki, at Alcott's left, gave his boss a wary look. But Alcott didn't seem to care.

"The politics of this case are clear. For the bureau. For Pittsburgh PD. But frankly, I don't give two shits about any of that. I just want to nail this fucker."

Even Agents Green and Reese seemed surprised at his words. I realized they were unaccustomed to both this kind of language and this level of feeling coming from their normally polished, tightly-wound boss.

I had to admit, it was fascinating to watch the change that had come over Neal Alcott since this case began. As he went from being one of the bureau's most self-assured, articulate spokesmen—a slick, media-genic rising star—to this frustrated, emotionally exhausted, and bitterly determined law man. In other words, a human being.

I smiled grimly to myself. Who was I kidding? I'd practically described myself. I was obviously projecting my *own* feelings. My own grief, regret, exhaustion. My own determination to make sure, if I could, that Claire Cobb's murder didn't go unpunished.

"That said," Alcott continued, his voice once more assuming its professional tone, "the director and Chief Logan have agreed to a new set of protocols for this investigation. *And* a new set of priorities."

Reese said, "What does that mean, sir?"

"First, we've decided to call off the search for Agent Lyle Barnes. Given the director's personal relationship with him, this is, of course, a difficult decision for him to make. But we can't spare the manpower, and have to trust that Agent Barnes, no matter where he's hiding, has the field experience to keep himself safe. While we believe he's high up on the shooter's hit list, it's no longer feasible to expend Bureau resources looking for him."

"About time we let that old fool fend for himself," Biegler said, to no one in particular.

I noted Agent Green's subtle nod of agreement, though my own reaction was decidedly mixed. While Lyle Barnes was ostensibly my patient, I'd never had the time to form a proper clinical bond with the retired FBI profiler. If anything, he'd seemed clearly resistant to the idea of working with me.

On the other hand, it was obvious he suffered from severe and pervasive night terrors, which affected both his health and his emotional stability. With his whereabouts unknown and a target on his back, his sudden flight had only intensified the risk. As long as the shooter was at large, Barnes was in danger.

Then there were my personal feelings about the man.

Which were complicated. While I didn't exactly like him, I liked him. If that makes any sense.

Eleanor spoke up then, drawing my thoughts back into the room. And the present. "What about the rest of the potential victims on the killer's list?"

Alcott flipped open another file. "I'm getting to them, Detective. As of now, we're doubling protection on the remaining possibles. Which includes moving the people we have in the Ohio safe house to another undisclosed location. I'm also changing the directive regarding ADA Dave Parnelli. I don't care what the son-of-a-bitch says, he's being sequestered there along with the others."

He hesitated a moment, and then closed the file. Folded his hands over it.

"Which brings me to our main concern."

"The fact that the killer knows every move we make," Zarnicki said flatly. "Usually before we make it."

"That's right," Eleanor agreed. "He knew that Sergeant Polk was going to Steubenville to interview Vincent Beck. And was there waiting."

"Just like he knew the motel where we'd placed Claire Cobb," Green added, "*and* when we were making the transfer. Even which vehicle we were using."

"Which means the killer could be someone fairly high up in the task force," I said. "Or else has a connection to someone on the inside, who's funneling information to him."

"Great," said Reese wearily, rubbing her eyes.

Alcott grew pensive. "Yes. By this point, it's obvious the investigation has been compromised, perhaps from the outset. And though the director has assigned a special unit to scour all the task force intel—the relevant emails, faxes and phone records—we can't risk another breach like tonight's. The chance of another murder."

"So what are you saying?" Biegler folded his arms.

"I'm saying, the tri-state online interface is too vulnerable. Everybody involved in the investigation knows everything. So the only reasonable decision is to shut it down."

Agent Green blinked at his boss in confusion.

"You mean, all three states on the grid? Pennsylvania, West Virginia, and Ohio?"

"The servers are being shut down as we speak."

Then Zarnicki waded in. "Sir, with all due respect, is the director serious? Without the interagency network, there's no way to coordinate the operation."

Eleanor leaned forward in her seat. "He's right, Agent Alcott. If we shut down the interface, we reduce the amount of input from the various jurisdictions involved. Which means reducing the number of possible leads."

"I agree with all of you," Alcott said calmly. "This seriously hamstrings our ability to gather intel, as well as collate evidence. But the director believes it's worth it in terms of security."

Biegler frowned. "Then how the hell do we do our jobs? We have half the force working the case. Interviewing the vics' families, friends, coworkers. Responding to hundreds of anonymous tips. Going over every inch of the various crime scenes. Not just us, but Cleveland and Steubenville PD, too. And we all gotta communicate, so we don't end up tripping over each other's feet."

"Same goes for *our* people, sir," said Zarnicki. "Right hand's gotta know what the left hand's doin'."

Alcott drew himself up. "Look, I'm well aware of the downside. So is the director. But we're gonna have to switch to a need-to-know basis. Close the circle. At least till we get some kinda handle on how the killer's been staying one step ahead of us."

He paused then, as though awaiting further questions. Or objections. None were forthcoming.

Because we all knew Alcott was right. As were the people above him, from whom he took his orders.

Given the past three day's events, either the killer had someone inside the investigation providing him with information. Or else the person on the inside was the killer himself.

Perhaps, I realized, even someone in this room.

Chapter Thirty-two

I'd just pulled up to the curb opposite Noah's Ark when my cell rang. I looked at the display. Then, with a twinge of guilt, I let the call go over to voice mail.

After waiting a minute, I checked the message. It was meaningfully brief.

"Hi, Danny. It's Nancy. See if you can guess why I'm calling."

Then she'd hung up. I replayed it, smiling now at Dr. Nancy Mendors' mock-severe tone.

Truth is, I was surprised she'd waited this long to call and chastize me for getting mixed up—once again—in a police investigation. Ever since my involvement in the Wingfield case, she'd shared Noah Frye's disapproval of what she saw as the foolhardy risks I sometimes took.

As a psychiatrist and longtime colleague of mine, she was right, of course. Though her concern wasn't completely professional.

Years before, when we met at Ten Oaks—the private psychiatric hospital at which she's now clinical director—we'd fallen into a brief but passionate affair. I was still dealing with the death of my wife and Nancy had recently divorced her abusive husband. And though our physical relationship ended almost as quickly as it had begun, we've remained friends.

Then, last summer, she became engaged to Dr. Warren Sackheim, a pediatric surgeon at Children's Hospital. After some surprising reluctance on both our parts, we arranged to have dinner so that Warren and I could meet.

It went fine, especially since it was immediately apparent that Nancy hadn't shared all the details of our prior relationship with her fiance. Warren himself turned out to be okay, too, if you like smart, articulate guys who've dedicated their careers to saving children's lives. He also knew a lot about wine. And loved the Steelers almost as much as I did.

Now, still sitting behind the wheel, I debated whether to return her call and subject myself to another of her stern lectures about my self-destructive impulses. Then I remembered she'd told me right before Christmas about a ski trip up at Seven Springs that she and Warren were planning for the holiday break. As a kind of prewedding honeymoon.

Given the past weeks' heavy storms, the resort's slopes were sure to be amply layered with new snow. And she'd sworn to keep her iPad and laptop at home, and only use her cell phone to check for clinic emergencies.

Knowing Nancy wanted the trip to be a real romantic getaway, I guessed she also hadn't paid much attention to the news. Until now.

Regardless, I didn't have the stomach to call her back. Not when the image of Claire Cobb zipped up in a body bag still burned before my eyes.

Besides, Nancy was getting on with her life, and it was best I let her keep doing so.

◇◇◇

"This one's on the house, Danny." With an exaggerated flourish, Noah put a draft Iron City on the bar in front of me. Gave me a bearded grin. "I hear havin' a death wish really works up a guy's thirst."

I grimaced, but gratefully lifted the foaming mug to my lips. It was my third beer in twenty minutes.

"I take it you saw the news?"

"Who didn't? It's all over the tube. Ya know, for such a smart guy, you're a real idiot sometimes."

"So people keep telling me."

"Maybe you oughtta listen." He leaned across the bar, massive forearms crossed. "*I'm* supposed to be the crazy one, remember? You keep chasin' bad guys down dark alleys and they'll put *you* on meds. And not the fun kind."

"Might not be a bad idea." I looked at the brew in my hand. "Though for now, I'm happy to get hammered."

Noah sighed, clearly disgusted. He glanced up and down the bar, making sure the few other customers were too wrapped up in their own dramas to pay us much attention.

With the temperature outside at zero, and midnight having come and gone, the saloon was pretty quiet. Especially now that the jazz trio had played their last set and departed.

"Look, man," Noah said carefully, "I know you feel bad about that lady attorney gettin' killed. Who wouldn't? She sounds like good people. They've been runnin' her picture and life story all night long on the news. Why the hell you think I turned the damn set off? I didn't wanna hear about it any more."

"Feeling bad about it isn't a crime. In fact…" I took a long pull of my beer, draining it. "In my clinical opinion, it's appropriate."

Noah frowned. "Christ, you guys love that goddam word. Well, maybe feelin' bad is 'appropriate,' but self-pity isn't. It's bullshit. And that's *my* clinical opinion."

"Yeah?" I tapped my empty mug on the counter. He ignored me, and leaned in further.

"Yeah. It's bullshit. And I oughtta know. I used to be the poster child for self-pity. They coulda thrown a telethon for my sorry ass. But now, thanks to therapists like you, and my sweetie Charlene, and a fuck-load o' meds, I ain't like that no more. I'm just your garden variety paranoid schizophrenic. And the good news is, I don't feel too bad for myself about it anymore."

"Glad to hear it. Now, about that refill…"

His eyes narrowed.

"I mean it, Danny. Why don'tcha stop pissin' and moanin' and go do that thing you always do? Help the cops get the bastard who killed the lady. Nail him before he can hurt anyone else."

I paused. Looked down at the empty mug.

"I think my crime-busting days are over, Noah."

"Like hell. Before you know it, you'll be on the news again. Talkin' to some hot anchor babe."

"Right."

"Trust me, man. Gonna happen. But, listen, next time you're on the tube..." Voice lowered again. "Two words: Grecian Formula. And I say this with love."

He tilted his head, eying me, waiting to see if I'd smile. So I did. I figured, why not make the guy happy? He was trying his best.

"You're a good friend, Noah."

"Damn right I am."

"Now be a *great* friend and bring me a Jack Daniels. Straight. The beer isn't cutting it."

And it wasn't. Because I could still see Claire Cobb's face in my mind, still hear her last words as she died in my arms. Just as I still felt the dull ache of remorse, the numbing pain of loss. I needed something strong enough to change that. To obliterate the hurt and anger.

Though I knew better, I wanted whatever it would take not to feel anything at all.

Noah waved his hand in irritation, or else maybe just surrender, and shuffled down the bar to get my drink. At the same time, I heard the front door open. Felt the frigid breath of the night raise prickles on the back of my neck, making me turn. It was Eleanor Lowrey.

I held out a stool for her as she joined me at the bar, pulling off her overcoat. Even in the saloon's dim amber light I could see the fatigue etched on her face.

"Geez, Danny, looks like you started without me."

"If you hurry, you can catch up."

"My plan exactly."

When Noah returned with my drink, I ordered one for Eleanor as well.

"Make it a double, Noah." She rubbed her temples.

"Bad news?" I asked.

"Is there any other kind? The mayor's still awake, which is never a good sign. That means he's chewing out the chief as we speak. I also hear he phoned District Attorney Sinclair up in Boston. Wants him back here ASAP."

"What about Neal Alcott?"

"Apparently, *he's* getting torn a new one by the director. Who just got reamed himself by Ohio's governor."

"Makes sense. Though Claire Cobb and Judge Loftus were killed here, all four victims—including the eyewitness, Vincent Beck—were Ohio residents."

"Right. And the governor is an old crony of the president. So you can imagine the heat coming down on the bureau. Agent Reese confided in me that there's a rumor Alcott might be replaced."

"I'm not surprised." And I wasn't.

Our drinks came, and we drank in a subdued, somber silence. Not necessarily a bad thing. Given our shared levels of stress, grief, and fatigue, it was almost a relief. Like two fellow soldiers in a foxhole, after the most recent battle. Gathering strength for the next one.

We stayed there till last call, going over elements of the case in murmured half-sentences. Eleanor also shared, between succeeding rounds of Scotch, more details of her brother's struggle with addiction. Her family's mixed, often unsupportive reaction. The toll this divided response had taken on everyone, especially her mother.

"I think you're caught up," I said finally, watching her roll her empty shot glass between elegant fingers.

"Only 'cause you let me, you big softie. You dogged it the last couple rounds."

She'd seriously slurred her words. Maybe I had, too. At this point, I wasn't exactly sure.

No question, we'd both had too much to drink. I swear I could feel the room tilting.

"I'll have Noah call us each a cab, okay?"

"No." She didn't look at me. "Just one. To my place."

Chapter Thirty-three

It wasn't as I'd imagined it.

I'd thought it would happen unexpectedly. In some heated, careless moment. That the sex would be sudden, unthinking, explosive.

With plenty of mutual regret after the fact. Not for the act itself, but for the problems it inevitably presented. The lines now forever crossed. The effect it would have on our professional relationship.

Two competent adults who should've known better. Now regrettably facing the consequences.

But that's not the way it happened.

◇◇◇

Leaning against the doorway to her apartment, Eleanor apologized as she fumbled for her keys. I stood just behind her, hands on her shoulders. Reassuring her that she had nothing to apologize for.

We hadn't sobered up much on the cab ride from Noah's to her apartment building on the South Side. I still felt a potent, serious buzz from the drinks. More than that, I welcomed it. Wanted my thoughts to be blurred, unfocused.

No sooner had Eleanor turned the key in the lock than a low growl came through the door.

"Luther?" I asked.

She smiled and nodded.

"Let me go in first and lock him in the second bedroom. Unless you want to be a late-night snack."

"I like your idea better."

Eleanor slipped inside the darkened apartment and quickly shut the door again. My ear against the polished wood, I could just make out her warm, affectionate murmurs to her Doberman. Followed by footsteps and the muffled sound of a door within the apartment softly closing.

I stepped back as she re-opened the front door.

"All secured." She extended her palm behind her, welcoming me in.

Her gesture had been slow, deliberate. As was my slow nod in response. There was a curious formality to the way we interacted now. Diffident, mannered. As if to bely the mind-numbing, incautious effects of the alcohol.

She led me carefully through the dimly-lit front room, a single table lamp its only illumination. I stumbled once, slightly, before managing to right myself against the edge of a wall-length cherrywood bookcase. She went on into the room, while I let my eyes grow accustomed to the dimness.

Her apartment was simply but tastefully furnished, and not as cooly functional as I might have guessed. Perhaps because the no-nonsense demeanor she displayed on the job conflicted with the number of homemade crafts items placed carefully about. Even in that shadowed room, I could make out the needlepoint throw pillow resting on a corner chair. For some reason, I knew instinctively that her mother had made it for her.

At the far end of the room, a wide sofa stood before a rough-stoned fireplace. Atop the marble mantlepiece were photos of family and friends, including one unlikely shot of Sergeant Harry Polk, in a Pirates t-shirt and baggy shorts, tossing a Frisbee at some departmental picnic. There was also a pride-of-place mounted photo of Eleanor as a rookie cop, after having just been sworn in.

I found a seat on the sofa and watched as she crouched in front of the fireplace. Neither one of us had removed our coats.

Nor spoken, since we'd entered the room.

It took a few minutes for her to get a fire going, but soon the modest flames were sending angled shadows scurrying around the pale walls.

Eleanor rose, her back still toward me. Then she turned, at the same time unbuttoning her coat.

"Can I make you a drink?" she asked.

I shook my head.

"Good," she said. And smiled again.

She stood, unmoving, and let her coat fall to the floor. Instinctively, I reached to catch it. Missed.

"Leave it, okay? Leave all of it."

I eased myself back against the sofa cushions as she slowly peeled her long-sleeved sweater up and over her head. It too dropped to the floor. I let it.

Backlit by the flickering fire, she reached behind her and undid her bra. Freeing her full breasts.

I must have opened my mouth to speak, for her finger went to her lips. I stayed silent.

Slowly, unself-consciously, she stepped out of her boots and jeans. Wholly naked. Smooth black skin shimmering as she moved toward me. Reached out her hand for mine. I took it. Stood. Suddenly indifferent to any hurts, pains.

I watched, stunned by alcohol and arousal, as she closed her eyes. Just let herself breathe deeply, in and out. The mounds of her breasts rising and falling. The heat from the fire behind her enveloping us. Embracing us in its warm, insistent glow.

Then, finally, her eyes opened.

"Now," she said.

◇◇◇

I loved how sinuously, how achingly slowly her body moved under my touch. We were both naked now, on the floor in front of the fire, Eleanor having undressed me as deliberately as she had herself.

In the dimness of firelight, we explored each other's bodies with our fingers, our tongues. A sweet, unhurried hunger. Until

I drew my hand up between her thighs, cupped her. Felt the moist heat of her.

Then I was inside her, feeling the swell of her breasts against my chest. The press of her nipples. Her strong arms encircling me.

Without a word, we found a slow, undulating rhythm that was all movement and breath and yearning. As though whatever our private griefs, our sorrows, our nameless needs, they fused into one. A hallowed, shared passion.

For escape? Release? For each other?

I didn't know, or care.

And then I felt her long, deep shudder beneath me, and I let myself come with her. Let myself dissolve, unravel. Disappear into her as she had into me.

"Stay inside me," she whispered.

I did.

◇◇◇

It was an hour before dawn. We'd made love again, and lay on our sides, facing each other. I reveled in the feel of her taut belly, of her long thighs entwined with mine. The pure physicality of her.

She seemed to sense my thoughts. Gave me a knowing, though slightly unfocused, look. A hazy attempt at a leer.

"Jock sex, Danny. Once you get a taste, you never go back. Or so they tell me."

She carelessly brushed her lips against mine.

I smiled. "You're not used to drinking, are you?"

"Is it that obvious? I still feel like I'm…floating. What about you? Are you sober yet?"

"Not yet. But I'm in no rush."

The room was blanketed in darkness. The fire had long since died, leaving only the acrid smell of the embers.

In these past hours together, she hadn't just shown me her body, her subtle and compelling sensuality. She'd also given me a rare glimpse into another part of herself. Her wry humor, openness, vulnerability. The part of her that her job, her professionalism, didn't allow her to expose. That, as a female in a still predominantly male world, she often had to suppress.

"I want to stay like this forever." Her voice now plaintive, whisper-soft. "Just as we are. But we can't."

"I know."

"And, please, Danny. I know we have to talk about this… but not now. Okay? I don't want words. I don't want to think beyond this moment."

"Neither do I."

She shifted position. I grew an inch inside her.

Her eyes smiled. "Love to, mister, but somebody's gotta feed the poor dog."

"You do take your responsibilities seriously, don't you, Detective?"

"You're one to talk. Sometimes I think you get off on taking the world on your shoulders."

"Actually, according to Noah Frye, I get off on being a TV celebrity."

"Well, that goes without saying…"

She gave a quiet laugh. We kissed again, deeply.

Then, from the bundle of clothes beside us, a cell phone—maybe hers, maybe mine—began to ring.

Chapter Thirty-four

Turned out, it was Eleanor's. She recognized the ring.

Reluctantly, she pulled away from me and rummaged in her clothes for her cell. Found it.

"Yes, this is Detective Lowrey...Okay. Right. Give me thirty minutes. Right, see you then."

After clicking off, she sat up on her elbows. Eyes grown solemn, she'd undergone within moments the familiar alchemy of modern life. The personal giving way to the professional. The inevitable, purposeful return to duty. Unmindful of the way her naked breasts gleamed in the suffused, predawn light.

"Biegler or Alcott?" I reached for my own clothes, mingled with hers in the pile.

"Agent Zarnicki, speaking for both of them. All top level task force personnel are meeting at seven a.m. Federal Building, downtown. To implement the new security protocols and refocus the hunt for the shooter."

"What does that mean?"

"It means we better have something concrete to present to the director and City Hall. A new approach to the case that will get results."

"*And* one they can sell to the media. And the public."

Sitting cross-legged on the floor, Eleanor began separating her clothes from the pile. And suddenly froze. Stared at the bundle in her hands. Then up at me, bleary-eyed. Trying to focus.

"Wait, I was so drunk…I think I remember…Jesus, Danny, did I…did I *strip* for you last night…?"

"Well, I was fairly blitzed myself…"

She buried her face in the wad of clothes. "I don't believe it! That's so cheesy, so—so *not* me…"

"If you say so…but it was pretty great."

Growling, she playfully hurled her balled-up sweater at me. "This is all *your* fault, Rinaldi! I swear to God, I'm never having another drink. Never!"

"I believe you." I leaned forward and kissed her softly. "Honest."

She kissed me back, just as softly. Then lowered her chin, so that our foreheads touched.

"Danny, I gotta see to Luther, take a shower, and hit the bricks. It's gonna be a brutal day."

"I should get going, too. See if I remember where I live. Don't seem to be spending much time there lately."

I rose stiffly, then helped her to her feet.

"Besides, now that the fog's lifting, I seem to remember we each left our cars parked outside Noah's Ark."

Eleanor groaned. "Shit, I forgot…"

"No problem. I'll get dressed and call a cab. Have it waiting for us by the time you're ready."

Which I did.

◇◇◇

We parted outside Noah's bar in the icy cold blue of early dawn. I'd had the cab drop her at her unmarked first, then watched as she pulled out onto an empty Second Avenue.

Hands jammed in my overcoat pockets, I made the short trudge along the riverbank, leaving the day's first footprints on the snow-powdered asphalt, to where my rental was parked. I actually had to scrape a thin glaze of ice off the door handle with a fingernail to insert my key.

Driving cautiously across the bridge to the foot of Mt. Washington, I used my cell to check my messages. Again, nothing from patients, other than a potential new one calling to make an appointment. But there *was* a message from Angie Villanova, left late last night.

I called her back.

"You know it's not even six, right, Danny? It's barely light out."

"You sounded pretty concerned in your message."

"Well, I am concerned. For *her*…"

I took a guess. "Are we talking about Maggie Currim?"

"As a matter of fact, yes. She and I are sorta bonding, ya know what I mean? She's really opening up to me. Sharing her troubles. It's not like she has anyone else, since you bailed on her."

"I didn't exactly bail, Angie."

"And you didn't exactly step up, either. Besides, believe it or not, this isn't about you, Mr. Wonderful. But maybe you can try to pay attention anyway."

"Sure. I'll try anything once."

Great, I thought. Banter with my third cousin, twice removed, after an exhausting night without sleep and before my morning coffee. Squinting through the bleak, wintry light of a recalitrant sunrise, I hoped against hope for the familiar Starbucks sign.

"But pull over first. I want your complete attention."

I did as requested, finding a side street just past the mouth of the Incline. I pulled to the curb.

"As you know," she began pointedly, "her son Wesley's arrest is the biggest thing to hit West Virginia in years. The TV, local talk radio, the Internet. There's even a Facebook page devoted to the murder victim. The Ed Meachem Memorial Page. So friends and family can post condolences, share fond memories of him. That kinda stuff."

"I imagine people are also posting horrible things about Wes Currim."

"Oh, yeah. He's condemned to the fires of hell on a daily basis. Usually by people who believe he should be boiled in oil first, or buried upside down in an ant hill, or fed to a wood chipper. Man, those good, decent, down-home folks sure are a colorful lot."

"Must be pretty hard on Maggie. I wish she could be convinced not to read that garbage."

"She doesn't. Not anymore. But what really hurt her is a YouTube video put up by the Greer family."

"Who?"

"Mr. and Mrs. Leonard Greer. A Wheeling couple whose daughter disappeared a few years back. Her name was Lily. She was only twenty-three years old at the time."

"I'm sorry for their loss, of course, but what does this missing girl have to do with Maggie Currim?"

"Lily used to work for Maggie's husband Jack. At their auto parts store. She was his secretary."

Now I began to see where this was going.

"So Lily was the girl Maggie's husband was having the affair with."

"That's right. Maggie told me she explained all this to you. How Jack had been sleeping with his secretary. And that when she found out about it, and confronted him, Jack and Lily ran away together."

"And nobody knows where they went?"

"Neither one of them was ever heard from again. Though Lily had applied for a passport in Wheeling before they disappeared. So most people, including her family, figure she and Jack are overseas somewhere. Asia, South America, Europe. Who the hell knows?"

"But what about this YouTube video? What's on it?"

"I've seen it, Danny, and I gotta admit, it's a throat-grabber. It shows Mr. and Mrs. Greer sitting together, talking to the camera about what a sweet, wonderful girl their daughter was. All the while showing photos and videos of Lily as a cheerleader, helping out at a homeless shelter on Thanksgiving, behind the wheel in her first car. A beautiful, adorable kid. Believe me, it's a goddam ten on the heartbreak scale."

"Sounds like it."

"Yeah, until the last part. Where they show a photo of Jack and Lily that was taken at some holiday party at the store. The horny bastard has his arm draped all over the poor girl. Both of 'em with big, dopey smiles. Then they show a mug shot of Jack, from when he got a DUI a few years before. He looks like shit, Danny. Old and mean. Every parent's nightmare."

"Poor Maggie…"

"It gets worse. Somehow they morph this photo into a mug shot of *Wes* Currim, taken at his arrest last week. Like father, like son, see? Then we cut back to the grieving parents, holding hands, as the father looks straight at the camera and says—and I wrote it down, so this is the actual quote—"It's no wonder Wes Currim is charged with a brutal, unthinkable murder. Evil runs in their blood. Jack Currim stole our daughter from *her* family, and now his son Wes has stolen Ed Meachem from *his*.' End quote. Then the screen goes black."

"Jesus…" I gave it some thought. "Wait a minute. How can they post something like that? What if potential jurors happened to see it..?"

"I know. That's why, at the very end, a written disclaimer appears reminding viewers that Wes Currim is only *allegedly* guilty of murder. That all suspects are presumed innocent. Just to cover their asses legally."

"I assume the video's a hit?"

"Fifty, sixty thousand views. Now the Greers are getting invited to go on talk shows. To tell their story."

"I'm not surprised. And while I understand their rage at Jack Currim, the connection to Wes' arrest for murder is just guilt by association."

"That's how Maggie sees it, too. Especially since she still maintains that Wes is innocent."

I looked out at the curve of river visible between the silent houses. Even in the heart of the city, there was something timeless in this primeval image of the world that nature presented in earliest morning. A quality of the light, the air. The pristine, untracked hills. As it must have seemed, in Conrad's words, in "the first ages."

Not the world Angie and I, nor anyone else, inhabited.

Nor had for a long, long time…

"You still there, Danny?" Angie's throaty impatience crackled over my cell's speaker.

"I'm here." I reached and turned the rental's dash heater up. "I was just thinking about Wes Currim."

"What about him? C'mon, don't keep a lady in suspense. Is he guilty or not?"

"Hell, I don't know. I think so. There's nothing to indicate he isn't."

"Except a mother's faith. I know that sounds like some horse-shit Hallmark movie, but it's pretty much the deal. Maggie's sure her son's innocent, and nothing will convince her otherwise. Not even Wes himself. Damndest thing."

Yeah, I thought. It sure was.

◇◇◇

Maybe it was because I was slightly hungover, but I didn't think about what happened between Eleanor and me until I pulled into my driveway. Even then, I had no idea what, if anything, I *did* think about it.

I shut off the engine, but stayed behind the wheel. Replaying the long night's events. I knew she and I could probably put off discussing things while the investigation was ongoing. Hell, if we were lucky, maybe even beyond that. However, given the kind of people we both were, it was going to happen at some point.

But, thankfully, not now. All I wanted to do now was take a hot shower and grab as much sleep as I could.

I got out of the car into a razor-sharp cold, and walked briskly to my front door. Bending to pick up the morning's *Post-Gazette*, I saw a front page sidebar about the continuing frigid temperatures. Apparently, no relief from the region's winter weather was in sight.

Of course, the headlines were all devoted to the hunt for the elusive shooter—the lead story being the death of his latest victim, Cleveland ADA Claire Cobb. I got all this from a quick glance, after which I tucked the folded paper under my arm. I didn't have it in me to read more.

Once inside the house, I switched on a table lamp, tossed the newspaper on a chair, and headed across the front room. Until, for some reason, I happened to glance at the rolltop desk.

And then, suddenly, stood very still.

The stack of manilla folders—the files on John Jessup that Agent Alcott had given me—was gone.

Taking a long, deep breath, I tried to remember if I'd moved the files myself. Maybe taken them into the bedroom.

But no. I'd left them here, on the rolltop.

Instantly, my heart quickened. I shook off my fatigue, ignoring the ache in my shoulders, and stepped further into the room. Scanning the hallway opening to my left. Glancing down the corridor to my right, which led to the garage.

Nothing.

Maybe, I thought, whoever took the files had come and gone. But some primal instinct told me otherwise.

Someone—whoever it was—was in this house. *Now.*

My fists clenching involuntarily, I crossed to the other side of the room. Stepped into the main hallway. Unlit, carpeted, silent. Leading on the left to my bedroom, on the right to the kitchen.

I turned right, and saw it.

A light, coming from the kitchen. Too bright for the morning sun. Not this early.

I crept carefully down the hallway to the kitchen entrance. Paused just outside the threshold.

Then, steeling myself, I went in.

There was a man sitting at the kitchen table, under the overhead light. The opened files spread out before him. A steaming mug of coffee in his hand.

Lyle Barnes.

I gaped at him, surprise replaced by anger.

"Barnes! What the—Christ, half the bureau's searching for you! Where the hell have you been hiding?"

He looked up at me with sleepy, half-lidded eyes.

"Here, Doc. I've been right here."

Chapter Thirty-five

Lyle Barnes kicked the chair opposite his toward me under the table.

"Maybe you oughtta park it, son. You look like crap. What happened, you get hit by a truck?"

Momentarily stunned, I couldn't think of anything else to do. So I sat.

"Just don't touch these files on Jessup, okay? I'm working on 'em." He raised his coffee mug. "By the way, we're low on coffee."

"*We?*"

"Well, I mean you, of course. Though I've replaced any other stuff I've eaten."

I put my bandaged hands to my temples, trying to quell the sudden throbbing in my head.

"What are you talking about? Are you telling me you've been hiding out this whole time *here*? In my house?"

He shrugged. "Turns out, it was a smart move on my part. You're practically never here. Or else you just come home to crash for a couple hours."

I could still feel the anger burning in my chest.

"Give me one good reason I shouldn't kick your ass outta here," I said. "And then sic the bureau on you."

"I can give you two. First, I'm sorta your patient, and you don't strike me as the kinda therapist who throws his patients under a bus." He sipped his coffee. "And second, you're curious as hell to find out how I did it."

I considered this, my gaze meeting his over the rim of his mug. I had to admit, the smug son-of-a-bitch was right. On both counts.

"Okay," I said at last. "Truth is, I *do* want to know what happened. Besides, the bureau's stopped looking for you anyway."

"Good. They shoulda called off the search days ago. It was a stupid waste of resources."

He drained his mug, then went about arranging the files in front of him. Which gave me the opportunity to examine him more closely.

Not surprisingly, he looked like hell. His lined face had thinned in the past four days, and wore a yellowish pallor. His red-rimmed eyes and slight hand tremor bespoke the countless sleepless hours he'd endured since leaving the hotel that night. Even his voice, while still threaded with sarcasm, carried the telltale rasp of exhaustion.

He was also wearing the same suit I'd last seen him in, minus the tie. Both the jacket and white shirt beneath were wrinkled, darkly outlined at the creases.

"Have you slept at all since you slipped away from Alcott?" I asked him.

"Not if I could help it. Couple hours here and there."

"And...?"

"What always happens. The seven circles of hell." A bitter smile. "Luckily, you were never here when I woke up screaming. Even *you* wouldn't have missed that clue."

I sighed. "There you go, pissing me off again. What *is* it with you, anyway?"

"Lousy people skills. Sue me."

He rose abruptly and went over to where the coffee carafe— *my* coffee carafe—burbled on the tiled counter.

Barnes poured himself another cup, then turned to me.

"You want a cup? You look like you could use one."

"Sure, thanks. Black. The cups are—"

"Hell, I know where the cups are." Reaching into the cupboard to his right and getting one.

He returned and placed two fresh steaming mugs of coffee on the table, positioned carefully within the array of opened files. I could see where he'd made notes with a pen on some of the typed pages.

"Mind if we start at the beginning?" I gratefully inhaled the coffee's rich aroma. "From when you ran out on us at the Marriott? What happened, you didn't like the room service?"

He frowned. "You gonna make smartass remarks, or you gonna listen to the story?"

"Knowing me, I'll probably do both. But go ahead."

I could tell that the authoritative, G-man part of him bristled at my tone, but I didn't give a damn. Apparently he'd been squatting in my house, without my permission, for days. I figured I was entitled to some attitude.

"Start with why you took off in the first place," I went on. "It can't just have been your lack of respect for Neal Alcott."

"It wasn't. I mean, don't get me wrong, he's a self-satisfied little shit, but that wasn't why I did it. John Jessup was my last case, my last collar, before I retired from the Bureau. Now some whack job was going around killing people because of what happened to him? No way I was gonna cower in some safe house while my idiot colleagues mishandled the investigation."

"I thought it was something like that."

"Good for you. Though it wouldn't exactly take a genius to figure it out. Personality Assessment 101."

I gave him a smile. "You know, I've really missed our little talks, Lyle."

"I'll bet. Anyway, once I ditched you losers at the hotel, I walked about ten blocks away and flagged down a cab. So the doorman wouldn't happen to see which cab company I used—or, even worse, recognize the driver. Cabbies are creatures of habit, and the smart ones know to cruise the better hotels. Improves the chances they'll get a pricey fare to the airport. After a while, the doormen and parking valets get pretty familiar with the cabbies' faces."

"Makes sense."

"Anyway, I had the driver take me to the nearest electronics store. Luckily, I had some cash. No more using credit cards to buy anything from that point on."

"So no way to trace your movements."

"Right. I bought a throw-away cell phone at the store and called a buddy of mine at Quantico. Bob Henderson. I knew I had to get whatever I needed from my bureau contacts fast, before the word went out that I'd skipped. Like I thought, it took Bob about thirty seconds to give me your home address."

"The bureau has my home address?"

He laughed. "What are you, an infant? Of course."

Then I remembered Alcott's comment back at Noah's Ark, about the file the FBI had on me. It was no lie.

"Wait a minute," I said. "You had to know that soon Alcott would have everybody looking for you. Checking on your friends and family. *And* your colleagues at the bureau. What if they talked to this so-called buddy and he told them he'd given you my address?"

"I knew he wouldn't do that."

"Why? Because he's such a loyal guy?"

"No, because I happen to know that Bob goes up to George-town once a week to pay a dominatrix to smack him around. And he *knows* I know. Not exactly the kinda thing that would look good in his personnel file. I figure, I keep his secret, he'll keep mine."

"But why come here, to my place?"

"Because I knew they'd never think to look for me here. And I was right. Alcott and his kind are a perfect fit for the bureau's herd mentality. Nowadays, it's all about hard-target search protocols. I knew they'd check my credit cards, the calls and GPS on my cell. They'd search the airports, homeless shelters, motels. I also knew they'd talk to all the cab companies, so I tipped my cabbie an extra hundred to keep his mouth shut in case they started showing my picture around."

"Was this before or after he drove you up here to my house?"

A puzzled stare. "Why would I be stupid enough to take the same cab? Why give the cabbie information that he could reveal, despite the size of his tip?" He shook his head. "Really, Doc. Are you always this trusting? How the fuck do civilians like you survive?"

"Then how did you get here?"

"Like the rest of the average joes in this fair city. I took the bus. Two, in fact, which got me up here to Mt. Washington, and then I walked the eleven blocks along Grandview till I found your address."

"In this weather?"

"My ancestors come from Norway. I'm part polar bear."

Which reminded me that he'd also had an overcoat and gloves. At least when he was at the Marriott. Even so, the trek along Grandview must have been arduous. Yet I could see him doing it.

"Okay," I said, "so now you've arrived here. How did you get in?"

"Easily enough. I figured your front door would have both a good lock and a deadbolt. So I went around to the rear of the house and climbed the trellis up to your deck. Great view of the Three Rivers, by the way. But the door leading out to the deck from here…" Indicating the kitchen where we sat… "Well, let's just say there're some security issues. I used the edge of a credit card and the corkscrew from my Swiss Army knife to pick the lock."

He withdrew a familiar red Swiss Army knife from his trouser pocket and put it on the table.

"Word to the wise, Doc: Never get dressed in the morning without one of *these*."

"But where have you been staying? And how come I didn't know?"

"Like I pointed out before, you haven't been here much these past few days. Even when you are, it's mostly to eat, sleep, and take a shower. That means kitchen, bedroom, and bath. So I've been camping out down in the basement. Then, when I hear you leave the house, I come up and do what I need to do. Eat, use the bathroom. Just like you."

"Except for the shower."

He laughed. "Yeah, I must smell like shit by now. But I couldn't risk taking a shower. You might've come home when I was using it. Besides, you could've spotted any dampness or water drops afterwards."

"So you've been my secret roomie all week?"

"Pretty much. I ordered delivery. Using your land-line phone. Always paying cash, of course. And always getting uncooked food, sandwiches, cereals and the like, so there'd be less chance of any latent smells."

"Very clever."

"Naturally, I washed any cup or utensil I used. I also made sure everything looked exactly the same as the last time you'd used it. I happen to be pretty damn compulsive when it comes to cleanliness, so it wasn't hard to do. Especially given my eye for detail. After all those years at the Bureau, I'm good at noting exactly how a room is set up, where items are placed, and replicating it."

I let out a low whistle. "It's unbelievable."

"Believe it."

He got up to get another refill. I couldn't even imagine how much caffeine he'd been consuming. All in an effort to stay awake.

"I can see how you've gone through the coffee. I guess you had it delivered, too."

"Yes. And poured it into your large cannister here, so that the level stayed the same. I also bagged all my trash separately and walked the bags down the block. Tossed them in one of your neighbor's bins."

"You're lucky they didn't see you."

"I was careful to make sure they didn't. But it wasn't hard. Who goes out in this weather?"

He rejoined me at the table. "Regardless, you did almost catch me once. Couple nights back."

"I did?"

"I was in the basement, same as always. I use my overcoat down there as a makeshift mattress. When I can't keep myself awake anymore, and have to rest. I mean, I tried using the workout bench to sleep, but the leather's so cracked and worn it hurt my back."

"My apologies."

"Really, Doc. You gotta spring for some new equipment someday. It's embarrassing. Anyway, I heard you up here. You'd showered, gone to bed. But I guess you couldn't sleep, because all of a sudden I hear you open the door to the basement. Start coming down."

"You're right. I was too wired to sleep, so I went downstairs to work out."

"Luckily, I wasn't asleep either. I grabbed up my coat and ran into the furnace room. I'd just closed the door when you flipped on the track lights."

I absorbed that. "You mean you were crammed into the furnace room the whole time I was working out?"

"Oh yeah. Hotter than hell in there, too. Stifling. Kinda ironic, given how goddam cold it's been all week. I thought I was gonna asphyxiate. Finally, you wore yourself out on the heavy bag and went back upstairs. Man, I was never so glad to get outta someplace in my life."

Barnes sat back in his chair, gesturing at the files he'd spread on the table.

"When you didn't come home last night, I figured you'd crashed somewhere else. Girlfriend's house or whatever. So I started looking through the files."

"Is this the first time you've gone through them?"

"Yeah. The thing is, I only just caught sight of them on the rolltop yesterday. I'd always made a point of staying out of the front room, or any room I didn't need to be in. But then, coming out of the bathroom, I spotted the stack of folders out of the corner of my eye. Different angle of the light or something. I couldn't be sure what they were, but I had to check them out. Just in case they related to Jessup."

"Alcott gave them to me. He said they were updated to include the latest forensics on the letters Jessup received in prison."

"I can see that. I've just given them a cursory look, but I may already have a few ideas…"

"God knows we could use them," I conceded.

His voice slipped into a lower register. "Yes, I heard about Claire Cobb on your radio. Damn shame."

"I know. I screwed up. Badly."

"You also look like you paid the price for it. What exactly happened, anyway?"

I told him. He listened without comment.

Then I looked down at the mug in my hands. "I only knew Claire a short while, but I liked her. A lot. She was…" I hesitated. "I know this is stupid, and banal, but she was too goddam young to die. Especially like that. Just a senseless waste of a life."

To my surprise, when I glanced up again, Barnes' returning gaze was somber, reflective. Sleep-deprived eyes pale and moist.

"A senseless waste," he said quietly. "Yeah. I know what you mean. I felt the same way when my wife…when she died. Cancer. Afterwards, I just…I mean, I didn't know such pain was possible. Or bearable. What really made no sense to me was how I was supposed to go on. Or why." He paused. "I guess that's something *you* can relate to, eh?"

"Yes. Unfortunately."

No doubt my late wife's murder, and how I fell apart afterward, figured prominently in the bureau's file on me.

I was also struck by this sudden illumination of his inner world, this unexpected disclosure of feeling. Whether due to simple exhaustion, stress, or the lingering effects of his punishing night terrors, Barnes was letting me see a rare, unalloyed vulnerability. Giving me a window into his carefully crafted solitude.

"Not that I ever let her know how I felt when she was alive," he went on. "Hell, she used to say she wondered if I ever felt *anything*…"

I shrugged. "In my experience, sometimes it's men like that who feel more deeply than anyone else."

"Or else that's just therapeutic bullshit." He straightened in his chair, as though physically pulling himself back from his past and its sorrows. "I warned you, Doc, don't try building some lame-ass clinical rapport with me. Last thing I need is therapy."

"Maybe." Bringing some edge to my own voice as well. "But what you *do* need is a shower. And a change of clothes. I have some in my bedroom closet that might fit. Now that you're officially my house guest, please feel free…"

A brisk smile. "At last. Providing something I can actually use. Won't they kick you out of the Fraternal Order of Therapists for that?"

"Damn, and I just renewed my membership…"

He wearily got to his feet. As he headed for the door, I called after him.

"Just one thing, Lyle. Something to think about in the shower."

He leaned against the doorframe, arms folded.

"Shoot."

"You said you chose this place because you knew Alcott's people would never think to look for you here. But a smart, experienced agent like yourself could've found a hundred different places to hide out. Yet you picked *my* house. Makes a guy like me start to wonder."

He grimaced. "Let me guess: Unconsciously, I *wanted* your help. Or maybe it's because your house represented some kind of psychological safe haven. A refuge for my poor, shattered psyche."

"Couldn't have said it better myself. So you concur?"

His eyes narrowed.

"You're not gonna give up, are ya, Rinaldi?"

"Probably not. And, believe me, you don't want me to. Not if you ever want to sleep again."

Chapter Thirty-six

While Barnes was in the shower, I poured myself a second black coffee and considered the situation.

Of course, the logical—and appropriate—thing to do was to call Neal Alcott immediately and tell him I'd found his missing retired profiler. After which Barnes would be hauled off to an undisclosed location and kept under constant guard. For his own safety, naturally. Also to spare Alcott and the bureau any further embarrassment.

As it happens, I don't always do the logical or appropriate thing. As a therapist dealing with patients, I tend to work on a case-by-case basis. Clinically speaking, there is no one-size-fits-all approach to doing therapy. Every patient is different, as is my subjective experience of them. And theirs of me. In my view, good therapy is only possible in this kind of relational context.

Now, thinking about what to do with Lyle Barnes, I felt a similar desire to serve our relationship first. Which meant I truly believed I had the best chance to help him with his night terrors by maintaining his trust. To someone with his views concerning loyalty, turning him over to Alcott would be perceived as a betrayal. It would also be the end of any possibility of my treating him.

Besides, I told myself, Lyle Barnes was probably as safe here as he'd be anywhere. If the FBI hadn't considered looking for him here, why would the shooter? My treating Barnes wasn't an official part of the investigation. It was at the personal request of the director. Leaks or no leaks, it was under the task force radar. Off the books.

I drained my coffee without tasting it and rinsed the mug in the sink. Now the next thing to consider was how to approach treating the stubborn, arrogant bastard. As a stubborn, arrogant bastard myself, I suspected trying the conventional forms of treatment would prove fruitless.

For one thing, aside from medication—which Barnes had firmly ruled out—the usual treatment modalities ranged from ineffective to marginally useful. Since science wasn't sure what caused night terrors, developing approaches to dealing with it has been difficult.

Most experts believe the condition is caused by a sudden disruption in the central nervous system, usually triggered by stress, sleep deprivation, or substance abuse. With such a broad range of potential causes, treatment options are limited to—in addition to proper medication—hypnotherapy, stress management techniques, and good old talk therapy. That is, as long as you have something to talk *about*.

And there's the problem. Patients suffering from garden-variety nightmares can usually recount the content of their dreams, which perhaps can lead to interpretation. Often, once the meaning of a patient's dream becomes clear, the therapist can aid the patient in working through its various themes. The patient may find support in leavening the anxiety and dread left in the nightmare's wake.

Unfortunately, people with night terrors can't find the same solace, for the simple reason that, unlike nightmares, they don't occur during REM sleep. Typically, night terrors erupt during stage four of the sleep cycle. Which means the sufferer doesn't remember the dream images, giving both patient and therapist very little to work with.

I put the mug back up in the cupboard and looked out the bay window above the sink. The sun was brighter now, its rays sprinkling the sluggish river below with glitter.

Leaning over, I turned the tap and splashed cold water on my face, hoping to energize my own sluggish thoughts.

There were two ways to address Barnes' symptoms: I could urge him to explore with me the dynamics of his childhood, which, I suspected, was the source of his loner, crusader-against-evil persona. Perhaps here lay the seeds of the horrors that invaded his sleep. The problem with this approach was that it would take too long, under the present circumstances. Barnes was not in conventional, long-term therapy with me. I also was convinced he'd never agree to looking at early family material.

The other approach was to get him to open up about his years as a profiler. His thousands of hours of contact with the most heinous and notorius serial killers. Sociopaths who felt no remorse, no empathy. Who killed for reasons running the gamut from the deeply delusional to the coldly systematic. From the disturbed to the grandiose.

I returned to my seat at the table and looked at the files Barnes had so carefully arranged there. *His work.*

Yes, given who he was and what gave him meaning, the best way to address his nocturnal demons was to get him to open up about the real-life demons with whom he'd spent most of his career.

Assuming, of course, I could persuade him to do so.

◇◇◇

I heard Barnes leave the bathroom and pad down the hall to my bedroom. I could also hear him muttering aloud for my benefit as he shoved hangers around in my clothes closet. Since I outweighed him by about thirty pounds, and was slightly bigger in the chest, he'd probably have to hunt carefully for clothes that wouldn't be too loose. Luckily, we were both equally tall.

While he looked for something to wear, I went into the front room and hauled out my laptop. Sitting at the rolltop desk, I waited for it to boot up. I had planned to take a shower myself right after Barnes, but a sudden impulse made me want to look at the YouTube video that Mr. and Mrs. Greer had made about their missing daughter.

In moments, I'd loaded it and began to watch. It was as painful to view as Angie had described, yet was so blatantly prejudicial against Wes Currim that I was amazed it hadn't been taken down, disclaimer or not. When it ended, I glanced at the view counter below. Almost eighty thousand hits now.

Following that same inexplicable impulse, I reached for the landline phone and called information in Wheeling, West Virginia. I was directed to City Hall, then Records, then Passports. Ten minutes of my life I'd never get back.

When I finally got a clerk on the line, I identified myself as Sergeant Harry Polk, Pittsburgh PD, and gave the detective's badge number. Luckily, the clerk was too young, bored, and incompetent to question my authority.

"I'm lookin' to find out the status of Lily Greer's passport application," I said, making my voice as gruff as possible. "I understand she applied some years back."

"You got a date of birth, social security number, date of filing?"

"Listen, buddy, I got a shield and twelve years on the force. I also got a computer and can watch videos on YouTube. Maybe you can, too?"

I could practically hear him thinking on the other end of the line.

"Wait a minute…Lily Greer's that girl in the video, right? Went missing? Her parents cryin' and moanin' about it on YouTube?"

"Her *distraught* parents, you unfeeling moron, who have friends in high places. I happen to be one of 'em."

"Meanin' what?"

"Meanin' I think all of us involved in lookin' for Lily deserve some cooperation. For Christ's sake, she's a Wheeling girl."

"Yeah, I know. Buddy o' mine went to Montcliff High with her. We were just talkin' about it the other day."

"Okay, so here's what you do. I'll hold on the line and you call Montcliff High. Identify yourself and have them look up Lily Greer's DOB and social. Tell 'em you're transferring records to digital or something like that. They'll give you what you need if you tell 'em you're calling from City Hall. Then come back to me."

"And this is a police thing, right?"

"Do we gotta go through that again, or should I just call one o' my friends at Wheeling PD and make sure you get ticketed every time you drive your fuckin' car?"

"Okay, okay. Give me a minute."

The kid put me on hold, which was just as well, since my Harry Polk impersonation was making my throat hurt. Not that I really needed to sound like him for my little trick to work, but for some reason it added verisimilitude. Or at least I thought it did.

Five minutes later, the clerk came back on the line.

"All right, I got the stats on Lily Greer."

"Now use 'em to pull up her passport application."

Another minute went by, and then he was back.

"Well, I got what you wanted, Sergeant, but it don't make any sense."

"Don't strain your brain, junior. Just tell me what you got."

"Lily's application was approved, and her completed passport arrived here at the office. According to the records, when she didn't show up on the appointed date to collect the passport, somebody from the office called her. Left a message on her answering machine. But she never came by to pick it up."

"You mean, the passport's still there?"

"I'm sittin' here, lookin' at it. Damn, she takes a nice photo. Ain't easy to do for a passport picture."

"But why would someone go to the trouble of applying for a passport and then not come get it?"

"Don't ask me, man. You're the detective."

He was still chuckling at his own wit when I hung up.

At the same time, I heard Barnes coming down the hallway from the bedroom.

As I waited to greet him, I thought briefly about the phone call. Why hadn't Lily Greer picked up her passport?

When I'd learned she'd applied for one, I assumed that her lover, Jack Currim, already had his, and that she would need one too if they were to run away together.

Overseas, that is.

But what if they decided against that? Maggie Currim had decribed her husband as a conventional, small town, blue-collar guy. Hard to imagine he'd be that comfortable spending the rest of his life in some busy European metropolis, or even some isolated country village. Lily was also a Wheeling native, and, by all accounts, another typical small town type. Would she be willing to give up the country she knew, with its familiar habits and culture, to live in some foreign land?

Suddenly, I didn't think so. In fact, I was convinced otherwise.

Jack Currim and Lily Greer, I now felt with a strange, unaccountable certainty, were still here. In the USA.

But where?

Chapter Thirty-seven

Newly shaved and scrubbed, and somewhat swallowed up in a Pitt sweatshirt and jeans belted tight at the waist, Lyle Barnes came into the front room and sat opposite me on the sofa. With a pair of my thickest woolen socks completing the ensemble, he at least looked warm. If not happy.

"I couldn't find any *adult* clothes that even came close to fitting." He tugged at the sweatshirt's sleeve. "A man of your stature ought to have a closet full of dress suits. Christ, you wouldn't last two days in the bureau."

"I'd have to agree. But probably not because of my clothes."

He grunted sourly, then sat back against the sofa.

"Okay, Doc, you've had time to think while I was in the shower. Are you gonna turn me in to Alcott?"

"Nope. But that option's still open."

"Good man. Now, get me up to speed on where things stand. First of all, I assume the powers-that-be have had enough sense to shut down the tri-state Internet grid?"

"They just did. What made you assume that?"

"Logic. So far, the killer has been one step ahead of the task force. He knew where Claire Cobb was being held, and when she was being transferred. He knows when witnesses are about to be interviewed—"

"You mean, Vincent Beck? In Steubenville? His murder made the news, too."

"Yeah, but it didn't get the coverage Claire Cobb's death did. Probably because she was one of the killer's potential targets."

"Tell me. The media's having a field day guessing the names of those on the shooter's hitlist. Not to mention all the amateur crime junkies online."

Barnes frowned. "Forget about those rubes. *And* the goddam media. The point is, it's clear that the killer has access to task force intel. And if he's getting it from the tri-state interface, that means—"

"The killer is a cop. Or FBI."

"Not necessarily. Lotta people have access to the interface. Cops and agents, sure, but also administrative staff, communications, tech support, civil authorities. That's federal *and* local."

"Besides," I added, "there's a chance it's not even the killer himself. Maybe someone who has access to the grid is working *with* the killer, supplying him the intel."

Barnes scratched his chin, pink from being freshly shaved. "My gut says otherwise, Doc. The guy who wrote those letters—the guy methodically working down his hitlist—doesn't strike me as a team player. He's a loner."

Like you? I thought, but didn't say.

"Well, I'm no profiler," I did reply, "but I'm inclined to agree with you. We're looking for someone plugged into the grid himself. Or at least he *was*. It's probably been completely shut down by now."

"Which means he's working blind."

I nodded. "Plus, Alcott has all the potential targets in a bureau safe house somewhere in Ohio. I wasn't exactly sure what he meant, but I assume he's not talking about some hotel."

"No, we have a number of underground facilities across the country. More like bunkers than anything else. Way off the proverbial radar."

As if on cue, my cell rang. I gave Barnes a puzzled look, then picked it up. It was Neal Alcott.

"Thought you might like to know, all the potential targets are sequestered. Even your buddy Dave Parnelli."

He coughed roughly, clearing phlegm. Sounded like his cold had migrated to his chest.

"I'm betting Dave didn't go quietly."

"You got that right. And he's pretty unhappy with the acco-modations, too. He asked for you to send him a cake with a bottle of good whiskey hidden inside."

"Tell him I'm baking it as we speak."

He hesitated. "Look, Doc…over the past few days, I've… well, I sorta changed my mind about you. You're okay. So I don't want you to think this is personal."

"What are we talking about, Neal?"

"Well, now that the search for Lyle Barnes has been called off, your services won't be needed. You're out of this thing, as of now."

"What about the director? Isn't he still worried about his old Academy buddy?"

"Sure, but right now his feelings about Barnes are not a prior-ity. He's signed off on letting you go, Doc."

"Agent Barnes might still turn up some day, right?"

"We'll cross that bridge when we come to it. Since Ms. Cobb's murder, this thing has gone supernova. Every available local cop and federal agent not working some other major case has been added to the task force. The media is killing us on this, which means the pressure is coming down hard on the director and Pittsburgh PD. From the mayor, the governor. Not to mention *Ohio's* governor. Which means it's coming down hard on *me*. Hell, I may be gone before the end of today."

"Sorry about that, Neal. Really." And I meant it. "You've busted your ass."

He sniffed mightily, then coughed again. "Whatever. Anyway, thank your lucky stars that you're outta this shitstorm. Maybe I'll see ya someday on the other side."

We hung up. I could tell Barnes had heard enough of the conversation from my end to fill in the rest.

"And they still don't have squat, do they?" he said without preamble.

"My guess is, not much."

"Figures." He stretched out some kinks. "That's 'cause they rely too much on procedure and modern forensics."

"What do you mean?"

Instead of answering, Barnes got up and went into the kitchen. He returned a moment later with the files, now squared into a tidy stack once more.

"It's the files." He re-took his seat on the sofa. "All the new forensics on the letters Jessup received in prison, presumably from the shooter. The ones signed 'Your Biggest Fan.' No fin-gerprints, of course, but the tech guys have identified the make and weave of the paper, the color and make of the typewriter ink. What kinda typewriter was used. They've even done algo-rythmic studies of the writer's sentence structure, vocabulary, syntax. Then there are the standard psych evals of the shooter himself. Ya know, like trying to dope out someone who'd be both grandiose and sycophantic enough to call himself Jessup's 'biggest fan.' Plus reams of psychometrics and personality assessments."

"And…?"

"And it all adds up to nothing. Because they didn't make use of their most valuable asset."

"Which is…?"

"They forgot to show the letters to old, gray-beard profilers like myself. See, I recognize the style of the letters. I *remember*."

"Remember what?"

"The guy…the shooter…sending letters to a serial killer? Doc, he's done it before."

Chapter Thirty-eight

We'd exchanged places. Now I was on the sofa, while Lyle Barnes sat at the desk. Working at my laptop. To my surprise, he'd asked to use it to log onto the FBI data base at Quantico.

His lean frame bent over the keyboard, I had no choice but to speak to the back of his head.

"How are you going to get in? Won't they have locked out your password by now?"

"*I* wouldn't," he answered without turning. "They have to hope I'd be stupid enough to log on, so they can trace it. Which is what I'm being stupid enough to do right now. But I have to risk it."

He sat back and turned finally, rubbing his eyes.

"This could take a while, since I gotta figure out how to get past any new firewalls they installed. They probably know I can do it, but figure it'll take me enough time for them to start a trace. Maybe it will, maybe it won't."

He jerked his thumb toward the bathroom. "Meanwhile, the shower's free, and I didn't use up all the towels."

"Damned considerate." I got to my feet. "But I'm counting the silverware when I get back."

◇◇◇

I'd left my cell on the bathroom counter, and it was ringing as I stepped out of the shower. I snatched it up.

"Eleanor? What's up?"

"We just got out of the latest strategy meeting. We had both the director and Chief Logan on Skype and speaker, while junior G-men passed out FBI murder books on the case. Not like the department's murder books, Danny. These suckers were color-coded."

"Our tax dollars at work."

"Anyway, I'm sure you know the kinda heat this thing has now. Every piece of evidence is being re-examined and re-evaluated. Fresh boots are on the ground, canvassing all the crime scenes again. Cranshaw's neighborhood in Steubenville, the warehouse where Beck was killed, the Hilton where Judge Loftus was shot…"

"And, I'm sure, the Majestic Motel, where they'd had Claire Cobb before attempting a transfer out of town."

"Especially there. They're trying to run down and question anyone inside the task force who knew about the transfer. Who'd arranged the vehicles, booked the B&B in Sewickley. They're checking every call, every email."

"I hope they come up with something."

"Me, too. Seems like Claire's death has hit everyone particularly hard. Both in the media and here inside the investigation. God knows, I still feel like hell about it."

"Luckily, thanks to my years of clinical training, I tried to drown how badly *I* felt about it in alcohol."

A pained sigh. "I know, I was right there with you. I have the hangover to prove it."

I couldn't stop myself. "Any regrets, Eleanor? About last night?"

"Not yet. You?"

I smiled into the phone. "Not yet."

A mute moment between us. Then: "Okay, Danny, I gotta go help catch this prick. First, Biegler wants me to call Harry and make sure he understands that he's on the bench for now. Doctor's orders."

"Polk is back in town?"

"And home in bed. At least, that's the last report from the uniform who supposedly tucked him in. Biegler's worried that Harry will fly the coop the first chance he gets, and only injure himself worse."

"I'm surprised Biegler cares."

"He doesn't. But he doesn't want the department exposed to any liability claims if Harry gets hurt."

"Of course. What was I thinking?"

Though I could well imagine Harry's obscenity-laced response, I asked Eleanor to give him my best wishes anyway. Then we hung up.

A moment later, Barnes called in from the front room.

"Hey, Doc, finish jerkin' off in there and get out here. I found what I was lookin' for."

◇◇◇

I dressed quickly, but still gingerly, in jeans and a pullover sweater and joined Barnes at the rolltop desk. By now, the midmorning sun was streaming coldly through narrow openings in the broad window curtains.

"Told ya, Doc." He pointed proudly at the computer screen. "The techs didn't cross reference the Jessup letters with this batch because these were handwritten. I remember reading these six, seven years ago. Though they were transcribed and scanned into the data base, the originals were written in ink with a ballpoint pen on lined paper. That fact misdirected the software."

"Yeah, yeah. But what am I looking at?"

Barnes scrolled up some scanned transcripts of short, single-sentence-paragraph letters. My hand on the chair back, I leaned over his shoulder.

"These were sent to a felon named Gary Squires," he said, "in a prison in Ohio. Not Markham Correctional, where Jessup was, but a place called Hawkfield."

"Was this Squires guy a serial killer?"

"Sure was. He was convicted on multiple counts of rape and murder. Victims all prostitutes. Just like John Jessup. Only

Squires managed to kill seven women before he was caught. Jessup was believed to have killed just four."

"That we know about."

Barnes nodded grimly. "That's the way it always is, Doc. Most of the time, with serials, the real number of their victims isn't revealed until years later. If at all."

"So this Squires guy got letters like the ones sent to Jessup?"

"Yes. Here's an example." He squinted at the screen and read aloud. "'You don't belong in prison, you should be celebrated. It's the system that has failed. But I hope you know that you have a faithful fan in me.'"

"It's like an earlier version of the kind of language he would use with Jessup. I notice he doesn't even sign it 'Your Biggest Fan.'"

"That's right. Remember, these were written in block letters in ink, with a pen. More like notes than letters. As though he was just beginning to organize his thoughts, develop his concepts. He hadn't yet honed his message."

"What happened to Squires?"

"Died in prison some years ago. Heart attack."

"But I don't understand," I said. "After Squires died, why didn't the letter writer go after all the people who'd put *him* in prison? The prosecutor, or Squires' unsuccessful defense attorney?"

"Who knows?" Barnes wheeled himself back from the roll-top. "Maybe, at the point in time when he wrote to Squires, he was only fantasizing about it. Or maybe the idea of retribution came later, but he was still too afraid to act. Like I said, I saw those original handwritten letters, and from the depth of the ink marks on the page, and the uneven graph of the lines, I'd say the writer was on the young side. Or else, if older, quite regressed."

"Unless that's what he *wanted* people to think."

"Always a possibility, yes."

But I'd had another thought. I pointed to the screen.

"When did Squires die?"

"March 31, 2009."

"Okay, now look something up for me. When did John Jessup's first victim die? The first prostitute he raped and killed?"

Barnes wheeled back to the desk and scooped up the files Alcott had given me. He flipped quickly through some loose-leaf pages.

"The first vic was a woman in Ohio. According to the initial police report, the date of the crime was…" His voice quieted. "The date was June 13, 2009."

He looked up at me.

"Are you saying?.."

I nodded. "Shortly after Squires died, *another* serial took up the task of killing prostitutes. Our letter writer had a new champion."

"Jesus…" Barnes pulled at his lower lip.

"Don't you see? It's not the *killers* that obsess the letter writer, it's their victims. Prostitutes."

"I get it. Squires croaks, then the guy who's been writing to him learns of another hooker's murder. Maybe even a second one, not long afterwards. And realizes that someone else is now out there, continuing the mission."

I stepped back, sat on the sofa. Suddenly deflated.

"But how does he know about the murders? The seemingly random killing of a prostitute rarely makes the news."

"Yeah, but law enforcement types *would* know. Every cop in every police department in the country. So would every agent in the Bureau. *If* they were interested. You want me to find out whether any hookers were murdered last week in Stockton, California? Who the vics were, when they got killed, who's been arrested? Give me five minutes and I can tell you. There are multiple and overlapping data bases. Hell, VICAP alone gives you a perfect window into homicide here in the good ol' USA. I'm surprised there hasn't been a reality TV show built around it yet."

I let this all sink in.

"We're just guessing here, granted," I said, "but it looks like our letter writer shifted his hero worship from Gary Squires to John Jessup. He didn't know who Jessup was, of course, until his arrest and trial. But he'd learned *somebody* was out there killing prostitutes, and he was following his exploits. Like you might follow and root for your favorite athlete."

Barnes shook his head. "He's not just *following* the serial's exploits, Doc, he's *living* them. Vicariously. He's killing prostitutes by proxy."

Chapter Thirty-nine

"By proxy?"

I fell silent, slowly accepting the logic of Barnes' theory. "Then Neal Alcott was wrong when he said the shooter was just a garden-variety murderer with a hitlist. In a way, our guy *is* a serial killer. In his fantasies, anyway. He's just been having somebody else do it for him all these years."

"Exactly. My guess is, the same psychological dynamic is at work with our guy as it probably was for the serial killers he idolized." Barnes looked off, voice sober. "There's an internal pressure, insistent, all consuming. Like his head's gonna explode. The emotional need for catharsis, for release, builds and builds, until a predator like Gary Squires—and then John Jessup—rapes and kills a prostitute. Our guy reads about it, experiences the vicarious thrill, then his bottled-up tension is released. Drains away."

"A return to homeostasis," I suggested. "Until, over time, the cycle begins again…"

"That's right."

I paused, noting the reflective cast that veiled his pale eyes. Whether from extreme fatigue or the excitement of the chase, he seemed less guarded. Less armored against any incursions into his interior world. At ease discussing the particulars of his unique, difficult profession. I realized it might be the opportunity I'd been waiting for.

"Is that cycle typical of serial killers you've profiled?" I asked casually.

Barnes leaned back in the desk chair.

"For most, yeah, in some variation. But not all. I remember the Chris Wilder case. When we finally ID'd him, he led us on a cross-country chase for weeks, killing a new victim every other day. Swiftly, brutally."

"What happened to him?"

"Some cops spotted him at a gas station and Wilder shot himself. Just a killing machine, that prick. All in a day's work. No cycles involved. Like I say, some serials feel no more compulsive urges than it takes to order a cheeseburger. I interviewed one guy on death row who kidnapped and tortured adolescent girls because, in his opinion, they dressed immorally nowadays. You see, from his perspective, he had a *reason* to do what he did. Unconscious cycles are one thing, motive is something else."

"What do you mean?"

"The cold fact is, whether psychotic or sociopathic, a serial usually has his or her reasons. David Berkowitz, the Son of Sam, believed his neighbor was a demon ordering him to kill. Communicating instructions via his pet dog. Mary Martin Speck, a nurse who killed twenty-three patients, claimed to be doing the Lord's work. Dennis Rader, the BTK Killer, felt a profound need to prove his superiority over us lesser beings who were trying to catch him. Hell, I ought to know. After his arrest, we spent hours talking about it. Interesting guy."

He regarded me wearily. "As I say, the reasons may be irrational—based on delusional beliefs or unfounded grandiosity—but they're reasons nonetheless. At least in the killer's mind."

"Now you're talking about rationality. That it's no guarantee of sane behavior."

"Shit, no. In my experience, a perfect rationality is not incompatible with psychosis. If carried to the extreme. Hell, you could argue that it *leads* to it."

"What about men like Ted Bundy or Jeffrey Dalhmer?"

He stoked his chin. "Jesus, monsters like that…Reminds me of something Holderin wrote. 'It is now the night of the world.' Afraid he got *that* right."

"Another poet I never heard of?"

"Only a fucking genius. Son, your education is sorely lacking, ya know that?"

"If you say so."

"By the way, I interviewed Bundy. Twice. Charming son-of-a-bitch, I'll give him that. Not that it ever worked on me. His smile had too many teeth, if ya know what I mean. As for Dalhmer, you're better off asking a theologian, not me. There you're in the realm of the unimaginable. Real evil. With young boys. Necrophile, cannibal...Besides, he was killed by his fellow inmates before we had a chance to chew the fat." A wicked grin. "Sorry. Bad joke."

"*Christ*, Lyle! Anyway, don't some studies suggest an organic cause in these serials? Something neurological?"

"It's possible. Like maybe some kind of lesion in the limbic lobe. The site of unmediated aggression. Pure id, if you guys still use that quaint term."

Then, briefly, he yawned. I'd been carefully watching his body language. Gauging the depth and regularity of his breathing. Noting how his body had slumped in the chair, the tension leaving his arms and legs. As I'd hoped, he was lapsing into a presleep stage of relaxation.

I knew I had to continue the rhythmnic balance of our conversation. Maintain the cadence that was lulling him.

"So getting back to our guy," I said, "if we're right, *he* had his reasons too. For years now he's been using two successive serial killers to enact his fantasies of killing prostitutes. First Gary Squires, then John Jessup."

Barnes blinked lazily. "And then, after Jessup is sent to prison, the letter writer—older, more sophisticated now—starts sending his new idol fan mail. Signing it 'Your Biggest Fan.' Until Jessup is killed in a prison riot."

"Not only that, but the man responsible, the guard Earl Cranshaw, isn't punished for it. Not sufficiently, anyway. Not in the fan's mind. So he sends a final, posthumous letter to Jessup, assuring him that his death will be avenged. Two weeks later, Cranshaw is shot and killed. The first name on the avenger's list."

Neither one of us spoke for a full minute. During which, I watched as his eyes slowly closed…

Abruptly, to my chagrin, Barnes roused himself and awkwardly rose to his full height.

"Lyle, wait…"

"Sorry, I was starting to drift off…"

"That's the goddam idea."

Ignoring me, he went padding in stockinged feet into the kitchen. I followed, and found him opening the plastic lid to the coffee canister.

"Don't you think you've had enough caffeine, Lyle? Your hand tremors are getting worse."

"Bullshit. I'm fine."

"I watched while you typed on the keyboard. I saw the effort it took to keep hitting the right keys. How often you had to backspace, retype."

He turned from the counter, coffee scooper in hand.

"And your point is…?"

"My point is, you need to give it up. You need to let yourself sleep. Regardless of our theory about the shooter, for now it's just a theory. And it doesn't get us one inch closer to knowing who this guy is. Even if we're right, and it *is* a cop. Or an agent."

"*Or* ATF, or Homeland Security. They use VICAP and all the other data bases, too. They have as much interest in violent criminals as the cops and the bureau. Anybody in one of those agencies could also be our guy. Which means we got a helluva lot of work to do."

"Though we can't do much if our mental resources are strained to the max." I smiled. "By the way, I'm just saying 'we' to be polite. I really mean *you*. You've got to let yourself sleep. And I think I can help you do that."

"I'm not taking any fucking meds."

"No problem, I can't prescribe them. But what I *can* do is use hypnosis to relax you. Put you in a tranquil frame of mind.

With any luck, you might get some real sleep for a change. Even if only for a couple hours. I watched you in there, Lyle. Your body is *desperate* for sleep."

"Great. And when I wake up screaming—"

"I'll be here."

A beat. "Let me give it some thought. Over coffee."

"No way." I snapped the lid back on the coffee canister. "My house, my rules."

He stared, anger reddening his cheeks.

"Are you shittin' me?"

For a moment, I thought he was going to take a swing at me. If so, he never had the chance.

Because suddenly there was a loud, insistent pounding at my front door. Then an equally loud, insistent voice calling into the house.

"FBI, Dr. Rinaldi! Open up!"

Barnes froze where he stood. Then, abruptly, he ran out of the kitchen and down the hall. Toward the bedroom.

As the pounding at my front door grew louder. Afraid they might break it down, I hurried across the house and looked out the door's peephole.

The fish-eye lens distorted her features, but I could still make out Agent Gloria Reese's stern, dark-eyed face. Which threw me for a moment. It couldn't have been *her* voice I'd heard shouting. It had definitely been male.

Regardless, I turned the knob. I'd just opened the door a crack when it was violently pushed in, knocking me back. Surprised, I had to struggle to keep my balance.

As I'd guessed, Agent Reese wasn't alone. She was flanked on either side by Agents Green and Zarnicki, looking as adrenaline-pumped and formidable as linebackers. All three had their handguns drawn, at the ready.

"What the hell—?"

I'd barely gotten the words out when Agent Green grasped my elbow with his free hand. His fingers dug meaningfully into my flesh. A statement.

"Where's Lyle Barnes, Dr. Rinaldi?" His angry gaze lasered back at my own. "We know he's here."

Reese stepped up beside us, lowering her gun.

"He's been here all along, hasn't he?" Deliberately keeping her voice calm, quiet. "You've been hiding him."

Ignoring her, I kept my eyes riveted on my captor.

"You better remove that federally-funded hand, Agent Green, before I do it for you."

He smirked, as only the young and testosterone-fueled can, and merely squeezed harder.

"*You're* not callin' the shots, Rinaldi. We are."

"Hey!" Reese nudged him with her elbow. "Doc here's not the target. Don't go all caveman now, okay?"

She looked beseechingly at me, silently asking me to chill out and cooperate. I acquiesced, turning my attention from Green to her.

"What's going on, Agent Reese? Why do you people think Barnes is here?"

"A credible source gave us the address, okay? So now you need to be smart about this. You're in enough trouble already, you don't want to add aiding and abetting. Or worse, accessory after the fact."

I probably stared.

"What the hell are you talking about?"

Behind her, Agent Zarnicki gave a short laugh.

"She's talkin' about Lyle Barnes, Doc. We're here to arrest the son-of-a-bitch."

"What? Why?"

"You don't get it, do ya? *Lyle Barnes is the shooter!*"

Chapter Forty

Agent Green finally let go of my elbow, but only so that he could pull my arms behind my back and put me in handcuffs. I felt their sharp pinch on my wrists.

"Is that really necessary?" Reese asked him.

"Judgment call."

"Don't you think Alcott will question your judgment? I mean, the doc here's cooperating."

I felt rather than saw Green's body shift slightly behind me. Then I heard him slide a key into the cuffs' release and remove them.

I smiled at the female agent.

"Thanks, Agent Reese. I owe you one."

She knew better than to reply. Instead, she focused on Green as he swept the house with a gesture.

"Okay, let's find this prick. Reese, check out the basement. Zarnicki, the back rooms."

I shrugged. "Knowing Barnes, he's probably halfway down Grandview by now, thumbing a ride."

"Don't think so, buddy. We got another team out front, watching the house. And the street. He's still in here somewhere, bet on it."

"C'mon, you *can't* really think he's the shooter. That makes no sense and you know it. I mean, why would he—?"

"This ain't a debate, Rinaldi. So shut the hell up."

Meanwhile, Reese and Zarnicki had hurried off, two-handing their guns. From where I stood with Green, I could hear Reese moving carefully down the stairs to the basement, while Zarnicki padded along the carpeted hall. In my mind's eye, I saw him poking into closets, swinging his gun in a chest-high arc as he checked the bedroom and bath.

At a nudge from Green, I headed back into the kitchen, the agent right on my heels. Once there, he glanced about the sunlight-bathed room. Noting the two coffee mugs, he gave me a significant look. After which he pulled open the tall pantry door. Canned goods. Cereal boxes. Plastic bags.

"No retired profilers in there, Agent Green. Promise."

He frowned, then drew back the glass door that led out to the deck. This time, I followed him.

Green didn't acknowledge me as I came to stand beside him at the deck's wooden railng. Though the air was still frigid, the sun was noon high, and brighter than it had been in a week. You could see its wintry light skittering across the surface of the river below. Beyond, the cityscape shone, stormswept, glistening.

I leaned carefully over the rail. Looked down at the white-shouldered trees that dotted the steep slope falling away behind my house.

Green noted this and chuckled nervously.

"You're right up against the edge, eh, Doc? Aren't you worried the house is gonna go slidin' off some day?"

"Nope. 'Course, *I'm* not the one afraid of heights."

He flushed, embarrassed. Then stared down at his hands, as though seeing their white-knuckled grip on the railing for the first time. Grunting, he made a big show of releasing their grasp, though he took an imperceptible step back from the deck's edge.

Just then, coming out from the kitchen, Reese and Zarnicki joined us at the rail.

"He's been here, all right," Reese reported. "But he's gone now."

Zarnicki nodded. "Yeah, Barnes ain't in the house. Upstairs *or* down. But the bedroom window's open."

Jaw working, Green turned to me. "How big a drop from the window to the ground below us? The lip of the hill."

"About the same as from here. Ten, twelve feet."

"Shit," Reese said sharply. "He must've jumped."

At almost the same moment, Zarnicki shoved past her, pointing down at a sharp angle. Down at the gnarled, snow-draped trees hugging the slope.

"There he is!"

Following his line of sight, we all peered over the rail. Squinting in the sun, I could just make out the figure of a man flitting between the trees below. Slipping and sliding on the steep, ice-coated face of the hillside.

"Motherfucker!" Green yelled. "Get him!"

"How?" Zarnicki clapped my shoulder. "Is there some way to get down there?"

"You mean, other than jumping out the bedroom window?"

Reese tugged Zarnicki's sleeve.

"C'mon, let's go out the front and around the house to the back. He's not moving too fast. He *can't*."

Green nodded vigorously. "Yes, go! Go, goddammit! If he resists, *shoot* the son-of-a-bitch!"

Weapons drawn again, Reese and Zarnicki sped off the deck, through the kitchen, and toward the front room. Green watched them go, then turned and, shading his eyes against the sun, peered down again at the slanting tangle of trees.

I knew I'd never have a better chance.

Whirling, I stiff armed Agent Green, sending him sprawling to the deck floor. Before he even realized what was happening, I clamped both hands on the railing, took a deep breath, and vaulted over the side.

I might've been wrong about the length of the drop, because it sure felt farther than ten or twelve feet. I hit the icy ground hard, rolled completely over the rounded crest of the hill, and went tumbling down into the trees.

Gasping in pain, I grabbed awkwardly at branches with my bandaged hands to arrest my rolling fall. My feet twisted and turned beneath me, trying to find purchase in the days-old snow and frozen earth. But the physics were against me. The combination of gravity, the sharp angle of the sloping hill, and the velocity of my descent from the deck added up to a hurtling, remorseless momentum.

If I didn't stop myself soon, I'd crash through the tree line and go sprawling into empty space. Until I hit the pavement far below, at the foot of the mountain.

Luckily, I managed to reach out finally and wrap one arm around a thick, low-hanging branch. Though the sudden, agonizing halt nearly pulled my shoulder out of its socket. My feet still scraping on the slick ground, the branch trembled under my weight. Old snow, shaken loose from the impact, fell in chunks from the foliage above.

My arm wracked with pain, I managed to cling to the branch and right myself on the treacherous slope. Gulping mouthfuls of frigid air, I squinted back up through the trees and saw Reese and Zarnicki picking their way carefully along a ridge just below the lip of the hill. They'd each pocketed their weapons, freeing their hands to clutch at bushes and jutting rocks, trying to maintain their balance on the slanted hillside.

I let go of the branch. Though I feared I'd dislocated my shoulder, at least I had a big lead on them.

Gathering myself, I moved carefully in a more or less horizontal line through the trees. Based on what I'd seen from the deck, Lyle Barnes was traversing the slope at approximately this same level, and was about a hundred yards ahead of me. But I couldn't risk calling out to him. The last thing I wanted to do was pinpoint his location to the pursuing agents above me.

Especially since my only goal, once Barnes had been spotted in the trees, was to get to him first. He was sleep deprived, mentally and physically spent, and acting completely on instinct. Flight or fight. And now he wasn't just in hiding from the bureau, he was a murder suspect. A wanted fugitive, with armed, pissed-off agents on his tail.

I paused for a moment, catching my breath, and saw that a patch of dazzlng sunlight indicated a broad opening in the trees up ahead. From there, I thought, maybe I could get a bead on Barnes' location.

Scrambling along the hillside, pushing my way through spindly branches and dense foliage, stumbling over rocks half-buried in the snow, I made my slow, methodical way toward the sunlit clearing. It seemed to take forever, though it was probably more like ten minutes.

But finally, as though emerging from an enchanted forest in a fairy tale, I stepped onto a sloped, ice-covered patch of grass and crumbled rock over which the tree canopy had parted. Even the angle of the ground was less severe, more a gentle hillock stretching toward where the treeline resumed below.

I kept my feet wide apart to anchor myself and turned first one way, then the other. Not even daring to breathe, I strained to hear any nearby sounds. Any telltale sign that Barnes had passed this same way, and was still close.

Just then, I heard two things. The sharp crack of a tree branch snapping and the hoarse, whispered curse of the man who'd stepped on it. Lyle Barnes. Not thirty feet away, on the other side of the wintry knoll, in a thatch of foliage. I could make out his lean frame, twisting and turning as he disentangled himself from a web of branches.

Fearing that Reese and Zarnicki were soon to stumble into the clearing, I moved quickly, in a crouch, toward the far bank of trees. I reached it just as Barnes was pulling himself awkwardly from a slush-filled ditch. When he heard my own footsteps on the crinkling, frozen grass, he looked up at me with a pained expression.

Shoving aside a tangle of thin, ice-sheened branches, he hobbled over the few feet between us. His body bent, skin sickly pale, hair unkempt and mud-spattered.

"I think I sprained my ankle," he said matter-of-factly. He tried putting weight on it, and winced.

"Well, I think *I* dislocated my shoulder."

"From the way you're holding it, yeah. Maybe."

"Regardless, it's a good thing I found you."

"Oh, yeah? Why's that?"

"I wanted to stop you before you became a fugitive-at-large. And a target for itchy trigger fingers."

"What the hell are you talking about?"

"You're a wanted man, Lyle. The bureau thinks *you're* the shooter."

"They think *what?*…"

The exhausted, bruised, and disheveled agent, clothes torn and covered with damp earth, just stared at me. In wonderment. Disbelief. And then, finally, defeat.

"The Bard was right, Doc." Letting out a long, weary breath. "Life really *is* a tale told by an idiot…"

Then, to my surprise, he abruptly sat down on the frozen grass. Knees up, arms draped loosely across them. As casual as if sitting on a blanket in the park, waiting for the fireworks to start.

I regarded him. "How's your ankle?"

"Hurts like hell. How's your arm?"

"Ditto."

A long, thick beat of silence.

"So, Doc," he said at last. "Now that we have a moment, how would you say our therapy's going so far?"

"I'd have to consult my notes."

He managed a wan smile. "Yeah, well, if you really want to understand me, you oughtta look up a poem by Jack Gilbert. That guy I mentioned before? It's called 'The Abandoned Valley.'"

"I'll try to remember."

His eyes fell to the scuffed, smudged dress shoes on his feet. One of the pair was missing its tongue.

"By the way, I borrowed these shoes from your closet before I went out the bedroom window. They're pretty nice. Are they new?"

"Not anymore."

Another, broader smile. "I'm gonna miss you, Doc."

"Don't worry, Lyle. I'm not going anywhere." Wincing some-what myself, I gingerly took a seat beside him in the wet dirt. "At least, not for the moment."

He nodded, and we sat in an odd, companionable silence in the light of the cold afternoon sun.

Which is how, only a short time later, Agents Reese and Zarnicki, guns aimed with clear intent, found us.

Chapter Forty-one

Two hours later, Lyle Barnes and I were sitting side by side at a conference room table in the Federal Building.

Across from us, Special Agent Neal Alcott was arranging a pile of files, evidence envelopes, and sealed plastic bags.

Behind him, at the rear wall, a disgruntled Agent Zarnicki stood with his arms folded. Making the bulge of his shoulder holster even more obvious.

After being driven here through heavy midday traffic, Barnes and I were attended by a doctor and nurse summoned from nearby Pittsburgh Memorial. To my surprise, it was the same ER resident who'd treated me earlier. I have to admit, he seemed pretty surprised, too.

Our wounds were cleaned and tended, bruises wrapped in bandages. Thankfully, I hadn't dislocated my shoulder, though the deep scarlet gash under my armpit throbbed sharply. The resident also taped up my ribs.

Unfortunately, Barnes hadn't been as lucky. As he'd suspected, he'd suffered a severe ankle sprain, which required that his foot be strapped into an orthopedic boot.

Finally, we were whisked by elevator up to the top floor, and perp-walked down the corridor to the main conference room. Just as Zarnicki was taking his position against the back wall, Alcott strode in, carrying a small cardboard box. Without a word, he began unloading its contents on the table.

"Know why you're here, Agent Barnes?" he said finally, not looking up.

"You people are stupid enough to think I'm your guy." Barnes linked his fingers, stretched. "Right?"

"No, I mean why you're *here*, in a conference room, instead of a jail cell?"

I spoke up. "I think *I* know. He's here because you haven't informed Pittsburgh PD of his arrest. You're keeping Biegler and company out of the loop."

"That's right, Dr. Rinaldi. At the request of the director, we're withholding that information from the police. *And* the district attorney."

He turned to Barnes. "For the moment, at least."

"Probably a good move," Barnes said. "This way, once you realize you're wrong about me, nobody else has to know what fuck-ups you are. It'll be our little secret."

Alcott reddened. "Watch your goddam mouth, Barnes. If it weren't for the director, I'd…"

He let the words die in the air. Then he shifted his attention back to me.

"I wanted *you* here, too, so I could get corroboration on some of the facts. We figure you can help plug a few holes we're still having trouble with."

"Am I under arrest, too? If so, I want a lawyer."

He shook his head mournfully. "Shit, Doc. Just when I'd started to like you…But, no, you're not under arrest. For now, we just consider you a person of interest. So you don't need a lawyer."

"But you'll be sure to tell me when I do?"

"You'll be the first to hear about it."

I indicated Barnes. "What about Lyle? Shouldn't *he* have legal counsel?"

Alcott swiveled back to the older man. "You're under arrest, but no charges have been filed. And I want you to consider this more as an interview than an interrogation. Think we can play it that way?"

Barnes grinned. "I will if you will."

I stirred. "Mind if I ask a question, Neal? How did you find out Lyle was at my place?"

"That's kinda funny. An old buddy of Agent Barnes at Quantico, guy named Henderson, dropped the dime on him. Volunteered that Barnes had contacted him, asking him for your home address."

I gave Barnes a sidelong glance. "So much for having the goods on the guy to keep him quiet…"

Alcott chuckled. "Oh, that. Yeah, well, Henderson's wife found out about his regular trips up to Georgetown for a little S and M. Since his secret was out, he figured there was no reason to risk criminal action once Barnes was eventually found. As he knew he would be. So Henderson caved and told us everything. Including the fact that Barnes called him regularly—using your landline phone, Doc—getting updates on the task force investigation."

I glared at Barnes. "You used my landline to call this guy from the house? You never mentioned that!"

He shrugged. "C'mon, Doc. Nobody tells their therapist *everything*…"

"Damn it, Lyle…" Rubbing my forehead, at a loss.

"My bad, okay?" Giving me a mock-contrite look.

"Barnes picked up a lot of intel that way," Alcott went on, obviously enjoying the tension between Barnes and me. "Like where the shooter's potential victims were being held, when they were being moved…"

"Wait a minute, *that's* your evidence?" Barnes stared, fatigued eyes wide with disbelief. "*That's* the reason you like me for these shootings? Christ, I always knew you had shit for brains, Alcott, but this is just—"

That was too much for the other agent. Bristling with sudden anger, he slammed his palm on the table.

"Cut the crap, Barnes! I'm sick of your attitude, your disrespect, your insubordination. I'm sick of *you*, period. I don't care about how you and the goddam director go way back. We have more than enough to bury you, and if you'll just shut the fuck up for once in your life, I'll lay it all out for you!"

At first, Barnes looked taken aback by Alcott's outburst. Momentarily stunned. Then, with some effort, he squared his shoulders and straightened in his chair. Face unreadable. He'd given the younger agent all the emotional reaction he was going to get.

For his part, Alcott seemed visibly embarrassed by what he probably felt was a personal lapse. Not in keeping with the Bureau's storied professionalism, nor his own carefully-built reputation for grace under pressure, for a cool, self-assured demeanor. Eyes dropping to the table, he busied himself arranging papers and files.

"All right, Alcott," Barnes said quietly. "If, as you say, this is just an interview, let me see what you have."

Keeping his own voice equally reasonable, Alcott began: "First of all, there's the timeline. The murders of Earl Cranshaw and Judge Loftus occurred prior to our understanding that they were part of a pattern. Prior to our decision to provide protection for those we considered potential targets. In short, both men were already dead by the time we brought you down from Franklin Park and put you up in that motel in Braddock. So you'd certainly had the freedom of movement to carry out those two shootings."

He sniffed loudly—obviously still fighting that persistent cold—and withdrew another file from the array before him.

"Then, at the downtown Marriott, you go out the window and disappear. Apparently, the first thing you did was acquire Dr. Rinaldi's address and make your way there."

He raised skeptical eyes to find mine.

"Whether the doctor was aware or not that you were hiding there is open to question."

"I wasn't, Neal. I only found out a few hours before you did that Lyle had been secretly living in my house."

"Somehow, I find that hard to believe."

"That makes two of us, but it's the truth."

"Then why didn't you contact us the moment you found out about it? Why didn't you turn him in?"

I paused. "Good question. I'll let you know when I have an answer. All I can say is, it seemed like a good idea at the time."

"Hardly a satisfactory response, Doctor."

"Life is full of disappointments, Neal."

"Uh-huh. Ya know, you're not helping yourself much at the moment."

Barnes cleared his throat. "Listen, Alcott, the doc here's tellin' the truth. He never knew I was squattin' in his place till early this morning. He wasn't too happy about it, either, but—"

Alcott held up his hand. "Not my concern, Agent Barnes. What *is* relevant is that now you had use of Rinaldi's house as a base of operations. Which means you were free to continue carrying out your plan."

"My plan to kill all these people on the hitlist."

"Exactly. Because of your regular calls to your buddy Henderson at Quantico, you knew everything that the task force knew. For example, you knew that Sergeant Harry Polk was slated to interview an eyewitness to the Cranshaw killing. A man named Vincent Beck. So you got yourself to Beck's place of employment before Polk arrived, and, using a hunting rifle stolen from a gun store, you shot the witness and wounded the sergeant."

"And how did I get to Steubenville to do this?"

"Same M.O. as with Cranshaw and Loftus. You stole a car and later abandoned it."

"A car you haven't found yet, I'm guessing."

"Not yet, no. But we will. Just as we now have the stolen panel truck you used to drive up alongside the car Claire Cobb was in, when we left that motel in Wilkinsburg. You knew she was scheduled to be taken to Sewickley, you even knew when. So you acted quickly to prevent it."

The whole time Alcott was speaking, I was watching Lyle Barnes. The toll his long days and nights of sleeplessness was taking on him had grown even more obvious. His pale, sunken cheeks. Moist, half-closed eyes. The caffeine-fueled hand tremors, now markedly worse. Not to mention the battering his body took from the jump from my bedroom window and his slog through the woods.

Given how stiff and sore *I* felt, how difficult I found even the slightest movement, I couldn't begin to imagine the sheer physical pain he was in. I was amazed, noting the effort it was taking now to keep himself upright in his chair, that he hadn't already passed out.

"You realize," I said to Alcott, "that this so-called timeline would hold true for literally *everyone* who wasn't under FBI sequestration during the period involved. To say the evidence is circumstantial doesn't even begin to describe how ludicrous it is."

"Really, Dr. Rinaldi? So you're practicing law now?"

"No. But I know we haven't perfected cloning yet. Which is the only way Lyle Barnes could've taken a shot at Claire Cobb outside her office in Cleveland. Remember, when the shooter made his first attempt on her life, Lyle had already been put under FBI protection. In fact, when we first learned about it, he was standing in the same room with you and me."

I smiled at the retired profiler.

"I know he's a clever son-of-a-bitch, but even Agent Barnes can't be in two places at once."

Alcott looked unperturbed.

"Like I said, we still have holes to plug. Besides, he could be working with an accomplice."

"Nice reach, Alcott. But it doesn't stand up and you know it."

"Maybe not. But then there's this…"

I'd thought that Alcott had emptied his little cardboard box, but I was wrong. With a meaningful look at Barnes, he reached in and withdrew a plastic envelope. Placed it carefully on the table, almost exactly centered between himself and the older agent.

Inside the envelope was a gun. A revolver, squat and ugly within its transparent sheath.

"Recognize this, Agent Barnes?" Alcott folded his hands before him, as though in prayer. "It's a Taurus 44M Tracker."

"Same make as the shooter's."

"That's because it *is* the shooter's. It's the murder weapon, and it was found at your house."

Sitting next to me, I heard Barnes draw in a breath.

I stared down at the gun. "Are you serious, Alcott?"

A brisk nod. "It's the killer's gun, all right. No prints, of course, but ballistics matched it to the bullets that killed all three victims—Cranshaw, Loftus, and Claire. As you know, Steubenville PD recovered the rifle used to kill Vincent Beck. The one time the shooter was forced to improvise."

Barnes finally found his voice, though it was so frayed by sleeplessness and disbelief that it was barely recognizeable. Without its usual bravado and blunt disdain, it sounded as faded as the man himself looked.

"You say you found it at my place?"

"One of our agents did," Alcott said. "After we got the go-ahead to arrest you, we secured a search warrant for your home and surrounding premises. It didn't take long for our people to find the gun. It was in a toolbox on a shelf in the attached garage. Wrapped in some rags."

I regarded him. "Pretty convenient, if you ask me."

"Nobody did." Eyes now back on his suspect. "We also brought your home laptop in, had our tech guys go to work."

By now, through his haze of fatigue, physical pain, and incredulity, Barnes had recovered some of his grit.

"Let me guess. You found the names and contact info of the victims. In a file marked 'My Personal Hitlist.'"

"Actually, your computer was a dead end. Though I was surprised to hear you'd visited over a dozen websites about Tuscany. Is that where you planned to spend your declining years after your killing spree was finished?"

"Been there already. Great food, friendly people. But too hot for my delicate constitution."

I spoke up. "You find anything else, Neal?"

"There wasn't much to find. No Facebook page, Twitter account. Any social media at all. No porn site history. Just a bunch of sites devoted to serial killers, psychopathology. True crime cases. Cold cases."

"In other words, pretty much what you'd expect of a retired FBI profiler."

"Well, there *were* a couple of surprises. Regular visits to online poetry magazines, for example."

Barnes grunted. "I'm a man of many facets, Neal."

"We also found some instructional videos on fly fishing."

"I was thinking of taking it up. In my 'declining years.'" Barnes rubbed his lidded eyes. "So what do you deduce from all this poking around in my private life?"

"Well…other than being a mass murderer, Lyle, you're kind of a boring guy."

I leaned back and folded my arms. "So all you really have is the gun?"

"Found in *his* house. Then there's his special access, through Bob Henderson, to all task force intel. The whereabouts and movements of the potential victims on his hitlist. Plus his mysterious disappearance, damned unusual for a loyal bureau agent in the midst of an investigation."

"You left out one important thing: motive. Why the hell would Lyle want to kill these people?"

Alcott shrugged. "*You're* the headshrinker, you tell me. Maybe after the Jessup case, his last case, he went off his nut." A studied look at Barnes. "I don't know how much he told you about his retirement, Doc. But let's just say, he didn't go quietly. Maybe the stress of losing his job, the only real thing he had in his pathetic life, sent him over the edge."

"I see. Was this before or after he started sending fan mail to John Jessup in prison?"

"Obviously, we haven't connected all the dots. The letter writer *could* be somebody else. Maybe that accomplice I mentioned. But remember, those letters were written on an ancient electric typewriter. Just the kind of thing an old fart like Barnes would use."

I stroked my beard.

"You know, I have a feeling there's another reason you've kept Lyle's arrest a secret from the cops. And it isn't because of his relationship with the director."

"Yeah, why's that?"

Barnes hit the table with his fist. "Because all your evidence is bullshit! Even the doc here can see that, and he's just a civilian with a hero complex."

I winced. Almost the same thing Harry Polk had said.

But Barnes kept his eyes trained on Alcott. "Other than the gun, which was obviously planted, everything else you have is circumstantial. Hell, not even that. It's speculation. You arrested me to get me off the goddam street. You figure I'll never sit still for being stuck in some safehouse. But on the other hand, if I get myself killed, the bureau looks like shit. The press would eat you alive. The FBI unable even to protect one of its own."

He slumped back in his chair, winded. As if he'd gone fifteen rounds in the ring. Totally spent, physically and emotionally. Running pretty much on attitude alone.

I know what that's like. I've been there myself.

"Lyle's right," I said to Alcott. "I happen to know District Attorney Sinclair, and he's no fool. You come to him with evidence this lame and he'll laugh you out of his office. Besides, no guy with his political ambitions is gonna charge a decorated FBI agent with murder, only to later have to drop the charges."

Alcott took a long time before answering. Hands still clasped before him, he tapped his chin with his knuckles.

"I'm not authorized to say more than this: We have the murder weapon, Agent Barnes, found at your house. With everything else we have, circumstantial or not, that's enough to hold you. At least for further questioning. Let's call it protective custody."

I turned to Barnes.

"*Now* will you get a lawyer?"

Alcott groaned. "*Christ*, Rinaldi…"

Barnes looked from Alcott to me, then back again. His features grown pale, bloodless.

"Enough…" Voice strained, ragged in defeat. "You two can argue about it without me. I mean, I don't give a shit anymore. I gotta find a bed before I pass out. *Fuck* my night terrors. Let 'em come. I just gotta…I gotta sleep."

His head literally started to loll. I gripped his shoulders, at the same time staring across the table.

"Alcott—!"

"Don't worry, I figured he'd be on his last legs. We have rooms—"

"You mean, cells—"

"*Rooms.* Sometimes agents pull all nighters and need to crash for a few hours."

He turned in his seat and gestured to Agent Zarnicki.

"Take Agent Barnes here and find him a room on Six. With a bed. Lock it and post a guard."

Zarnicki nodded and came over to help me get Barnes to his feet. Supporting most of the older agent's weight, he guided his charge toward the door.

Barnes' eyes had almost completely closed, and his arms hung lifelessly at his sides. His gait was a slow shuffle, made more so by the heavy orthopedic boot. I suspected he was already half asleep.

As he was being led out of the room by Zarnicki, Alcott stood and called after the younger agent.

"And whatever room you put him in, make sure it doesn't have a goddam window!"

Chapter Forty-two

Alcott kept me a little longer, but couldn't get me to admit I'd known all along that Barnes had been hiding at my place. Because I hadn't. Sure is easier to stick to your story when it's true.

Finally, he gave up and arranged to have me driven home. But not before letting me know how disappointed he was with me.

"You're backing the wrong horse, Doc. Whether Barnes is our guy or not, he hasn't behaved according to normal bureau standards. Way I see it, it's conduct unbecoming."

"I can't help it, Neal. I like the guy. I mean, as much as he'll let me."

He shook his head sadly, as though reluctantly breaking up with his new best friend, but managed to hold out his hand. I took it.

"No matter what, Rinaldi, you're out of this. For good. Agent Barnes is no longer your concern."

"He still suffers from the same symptoms."

"Maybe. But I'm sure the director can find another therapist to treat him. The thing is, I just don't trust you anymore. Besides, given the events of the past week, I'd say your clinical effectiveness is compromised."

"Funny. I'd say the exact opposite."

An insincere smile. "Then I guess we'll just have to agree to disagree. You take care now, okay?"

◇◇◇

As soon as I got home, I pulled wide the curtains in the front room, bathing it in winter sunlight. Though it was already late afternoon, which meant it wouldn't be shining like that much longer.

Kicking off my shoes, I went into the kitchen and grabbed a Rolling Rock out of the fridge. Standing at the glass door, I took a long pull of the stuff, looking out on the rear deck.

Had I really, just hours before, vaulted over the wooden railing and rolled down the hill? In pursuit of a renegade FBI agent whose colleagues had come here to arrest him for murder?

Wincing from the memory as much as from physical pain, I carefully settled into my chair at the kitchen table. Held the cold glass of the bottle against my forehead.

Were my friends and colleagues right about me? After all, my ostensible job was to sit in my venerable office in my venerable building on Forbes Avenue, treating traumatized patients. Trying to alleviate their pain. Helping them make sense of seemingly senseless events—events marked by violence, loss, a sudden and inexplicable rent in the fabric of their lives.

In other words, as a clinician, my territory was the interior world of my patients. The subjective terrain through which I was hopefully a guide and support.

So what was I doing in this *outer* world, this world of criminals, gunplay, and murder? Was I, as Barnes said, just a civilian with a hero complex?

I considered this. The classic therapist trap is to see oneself as a rescuer, a savior. As the sympathetic and understanding hero in the shattered narrative of the patient's lived experience.

Had I, in recent years, taken this concept one step further? I mean, why the hell *had* I chased the shooter into that warehouse after he'd killed Vincent Beck? What made me follow Claire Cobb down that godforsaken alley after she'd jumped from the car?

And yet, as I'd told Eleanor, I couldn't imagine having done anything else. Even now, sitting alone in my kitchen—and after everything that had happened—I still couldn't.

I finished my beer, then got up and tossed it in the trash can under the sink. Which brought my thoughts back to Lyle Barnes.

It seemed incredible, almost surrealistic, now that he was gone, to realize he'd actually lived here, under my roof. Especially since he'd been so careful to keep himself hidden that there wasn't an observable trace of his presence. No indication he'd ever been here at all.

Instead, he seemed like a spirit who'd briefly haunted this house, until he'd been chased out. Exorcised.

No, I thought. He hadn't haunted the house. He *himself* was haunted. By his past, the emotional toll of his work, the countless stories of torture and murder that crowded his sleep-starved head. As he was equally haunted, I felt sure, by the death of his wife and estrangement of his son.

And, finally, by the loss of his job, the only thing left in his life that gave it meaning.

I remembered then his telling me that to understand him, I'd have to look up a poem by Jack Gilbert. What was its title again?…"The Abandoned Valley."

I returned to the front room and got online, and, within moments, found the poem. Short, simple, vivid:

> *Can you understand being alone so long*
> *you would go out in the middle of the night*
> *and put a bucket in the well*
> *so you could feel something down there*
> *tug at the other end of the rope?*

◇◇◇

An hour later, stretched out on my sofa and nursing my second Rock, I clicked on the TV remote. The evening's first newscast had already begun.

The lead story, unsurprisingly, concerned the still unknown shooter and his deadly rampage of the past weeks. After a quick summation of the acknowledged facts of the case, including the dispiriting and by now familiar photos of the victims, the station cut to a live press conference from City Hall, just getting underway.

I carefully levered myself up on my elbows. Standing at a podium emblazoned with the seal of the City of Pittsburgh, District Attorney Leland Sinclair addressed an array of upraised mikes with his trademark strong, clear voice. Answering the barrage of questions from reporters with just the right combination of calm self-assurance and barely-suppressed outrage.

Sinclair appeared a bit more careworn than the last time I'd seen him, though, as always, he retained his patrician good looks and Ivy League demeanor. Tailored suit and burgandy tie setting off his focused blue eyes and trimmed, silver-gray hair.

I smiled to myself, recalling the many verbal jousts the ambitious DA and I had fought, pretty much to a draw, over the years. Especially last summer, during his charged, abortive campaign for governor. And while pundits predicted he'd probably make another run for the office, at the moment he seemed solidly engaged in his role as the city's no-nonsense district attorney.

Right behind him, on either side, Chief Logan and Special Agent Alcott stood like sentinels, grim-faced and determined. Neither man offered a single word in answer to the reporters' shouted questions, apparently content to let Sinclair speak now on behalf of the investigation.

I also guessed that Alcott and his superiors at the Bureau were still keeping their suspicions about Lyle Barnes—including the fact that they had him in protective custody—under wraps.

I became convinced of this as the press conference wound down. Overall, Sinclair's responses to the reporters' questions had done nothing more than restate the known facts of the case. Though he did announce that all the presumed potential targets on the killer's hitlist had been sequestered in a secured, undisclosed location.

This brought a boisterous murmur from his crowd of listeners, one of whom called out a final question.

"Does that mean you don't expect the killer to strike again?"

Sinclair smiled. "As a veteran in this office, I've learned not to put much faith in expectations. All I will say is that we're confident the most likely targets of this murderer's reign of terror are safely out of his reach."

With that, Sinclair showed the room the palm of his hand and stepped away from the podium. As he walked briskly out of camera range, followed by Chief Logan and Agent Alcott, a few determined reporters shouted follow-up questions. Which were studiously ignored.

Careful of my bruises, I pulled myself up to a sitting position and clicked off the TV.

Was Sinclair right? Now that his likely victims were—at least for the present—hidden away, would the killer have no choice but to stop? Would he now just go to ground, disappear?

And coldly, patiently…wait?

Chapter Forty-three

"How often are you supposed to change dressings?"

Eleanor Lowrey gave me a pointed look as she carefully peeled a blood-darkened bandage from my ribs. I was sitting, shirtless, next to her on the sofa in her living room. She'd thrown another log on the fire right after I showed up, and put two snifters of brandy on the coffee table.

"To take the chill off," she'd said, though clearly she was the one who was cold. When she answered my knock on her door, twenty minutes before, she was bundled in a thick sweater and loose-fitting yoga pants. And her hair was wet.

After the press conference had ended, I'd called Eleanor to see if she was free to grab a drink somewhere. To my surprise, she was at home when she answered her cell.

She explained that she'd just come from checking in on Harry Polk at his apartment, and had gone home for a quick shower and to feed her dog.

"No reason I can't feed *you*, too," she'd added, that familiar wry smile in her voice. "Why don'tcha come over?"

Now, removing a second bandage with decidedly more force, she said, "Well? What did the doctor say about changing these?"

"I didn't ask. And by the way—Ouch!"

"Ooh, tough guy…" She bent and peered at my bruises.

"Any more of these anywhere?"

"Lots, Detective. All over. I may require a full-body examination."

She raised her brandy to her lips. "I'll take your word for it."

I smiled and took a sip of my own drink. Breathing deeply and easily for the first time that day.

Outside, the night had begun gathering itself like a winter coat about the city's steel and concrete shoulders. Though the weather forecast I heard on the drive over promised a continued break from the snow, the temperature was expected to plummet.

I finished my drink and reached for Eleanor, drawing her close. And visibly winced, as the weave of her sweater abraded my exposed bruises.

"You're really banged up, aren't you?" She gently kissed me on the cheek. "And you *do* need fresh bandages. I'll get you some."

Before I could protest, she rolled the used dressings in a ball and rose to her feet. All business.

"Meanwhile, you better take a shower and give those war wounds another good cleaning."

"Yes, ma'am."

Reluctantly, I got up from the sofa and padded to the bathroom. On the way, I passed her bedroom, Luther's threatening growl coming through the closed door. Closed and *locked*, I hoped.

Once inside the bathroom, I undressed and peeled off the remaining bandages. Standing in front of the mirror, I surveyed the many black-and-blue marks tattooing my body. Especially the raised, tender-to-the-touch skin above my ribs. Either a deep bruise or hairline fracture. Terrific.

All of which reminded me that I wasn't a kid anymore. Nor a ranked amateur boxer. But just a forty-year-old psychologist who probably should no longer be left off his leash.

Something about that image made me smile at myself in the mirror. Which lifted my spirits somewhat. Despite recent events, at least I hadn't lost any teeth.

I stepped into the shower. The hot, steaming water stung at all the places I expected it to, but I slowly soaped them up anyway. Finally, I put my head under the nozzle and, gratefully closing my eyes, let the cascading water douse me. Obliterate my thoughts.

Then, suddenly, I heard the click of the shower door opening. Through slitted eyes, I saw Eleanor standing there, her smooth, naked body half-obscured by steam.

"Want some company?"

I did indeed, though that meant my shower lasted a bit longer than I'd planned.

◇◇◇

"Glad you changed your mind about that full-body exam, Detective."

Eleanor playfully punched my arm, then instantly said "Sorry!" and gave it a kiss. I smiled manfully, not letting on how much it had hurt.

We were back on the sofa again, under a big blanket she'd brought from her bedroom. The room was suffused with a palpable warmth from the fireplace.

She stirred.

"Don't go." I nuzzled her wet hair. "I'm just starting to come back to life."

She nodded toward the bathroom.

"You had plenty of life in there."

"Hell, I was just trying not to pass out. Damn near everything hurts."

We kissed, softly, and then she wriggled out from under the blanket. Reached for the fresh roll of bandages and surgical tape she'd put on the coffee table.

"I'm no medic, but I'll do my best."

She shoved aside the blanket and quickly scanned my bruises, scrubbed clean though uglier still against my freshly-showered skin.

I watched as she tentatively applied the bandages, her face hidden beneath her curled tangle of wet hair.

"I *do* have some news." Her voice seemed strangely subdued now, reluctant.

"About the case?"

"No, about my brother Ted. I was on the phone with my mother right before you got here. Teddy snuck out of rehab last night and took off."

"Oh, hell. What happened?"

"What usually happens. He scored, got loaded, and crashed in some hell hole on the North Side. The local blues recognized him, knew he had a sister on the job, and brought him home. My mother was in hysterics on the phone."

"I'm so sorry, El."

I pushed aside her hair and saw that her hands were trembling as she unrolled another strip of surgical tape.

"That's enough. Thanks."

I took hold of her wrists. She brought her eyes up. Blurred with tears.

"I can finish this, Danny."

"It's fine. Really."

She sighed her assent, put the roll of tape aside and sat back on the sofa. Pressed her fingertips to her brow.

"Look," I said. "Why don't you ask Biegler for some time off? Surely the investigation can spare one detective—even if it *is* their best one."

I offered her an encouraging smile, which she didn't return. Instead, she gave me a sad, frank look.

"I…Well, the truth is, I'm thinking of taking an extended leave of absence. At least two or three months."

"A leave?"

"Mom can't handle Ted's kids by herself. Let alone having to deal with *him*. Not that she complains. Shit, I'd like to strangle my brother sometimes, but he'll always be my mother's little boy. No matter what."

Her words reminded me of something I'd thought about earlier. About mothers and their sons. That sudden, almost painfully intense connection from the moment of childbirth. The primal, unbreakable bond. Like that between Maggie Currim and her youngest son, Wes.

Then I had another thought. "I guess you're heading over to your mom's place later?"

"After I feed you, like I promised. I have some steaks in the fridge."

"But given what's happened with Ted, you didn't have to invite me over at all."

She hesitated. "I—I wanted to see you before—"

"Before *we* took a leave of absence, too. Right? Because of Ted and…"

I watched something shift in her eyes. Like a hand passing across a light. A flicker.

"Look, Danny…"

She didn't need to finish the sentence. Stung, I spoke without thinking.

"So what *was* that in there? A farewell fuck?"

Her jaw tightened. "Very nice. Very classy."

I ran my hand through my hair. "Jesus, I'm sorry. I—"

"No, maybe you're right. Things are so…I'm pretty confused about everything right now, okay? Including us."

She gently stroked my arm.

"But I admit I wanted to see what it felt like to be with you again…"

"And?.."

"I don't know. I *like* you, Danny. A lot. It's just…"

Shivering suddenly, she moved farther from me on the sofa. Wrapped her arms across her naked breasts. Her eyes averted.

"I guess…I guess, right now, I don't know *what* I want. Or if I want anything. With any*one*."

I debated closing the distance between us again, but didn't. Instead, I took a long, deep breath.

"Look, if you really need to—"

"I do, Danny. I'm sorry, but I do."

Still not looking at me.

Another measured silence. Then: "If it's okay with you, El, I think I'll take a raincheck on those steaks."

She nodded dumbly.

I dressed quickly and headed for the door. When I glanced back, I saw that she'd wrapped herself once more in the blanket. Staring evenly at the hissing, dying fire.

I closed the door behind me.

Chapter Forty-four

It was just past nine when I got home from Eleanor's. The last thing I remember thinking, before collapsing into bed, was that the next morning was Saturday. Which meant that, since my involvement with the FBI had ended, I was free to go back to work on Monday. Recovered from my bout with the "flu." Able to see patients again.

I probably thought about Eleanor and me as well, but an urgent need for sleep overtook me so quickly I don't recall what conclusions I came to. If any.

I must've slept over ten hours, until the insistent buzz of my cell on the nightstand woke me. I gasped as I reached for it, feeling the full effects of the physical punishment I'd taken recently. Everything ached, pinched.

The display on my cell read 7:15 a.m.

"Dr. Rinaldi?" A young, hearty voice I struggled to recognize. "This is Sergeant Harve Randall, Wheeling PD. Remember me?"

"Of course, Sergeant." Still half asleep.

"Chief Block gave me your number and asked that I call you. We got us a little situation here and he thought you could help."

I rubbed my eyes into wakefulness. Sat up in the bed.

"What kind of situation?"

"Well, I don't know all the details, exactly, but Wes Currim got himself arraigned yesterday, so we're moving him to county jail. General population."

"I didn't know…"

"No reason you should, I guess. Anyway, when Wes' mother learned about it, she kinda freaked out."

"What do you mean, Sergeant?"

"Mrs. Currim came down here to the station and started cussin' out the chief. Throwin' stuff, too."

"That doesn't sound like Maggie Currim."

"I know. She always seemed real ladylike to me, too. But she said she was afraid of what's gonna happen to Wes when he goes to county. Threatened to go on a sit-down strike right there in the chief's office. We had to have some uniforms remove her bodily."

"You're kidding me." By now, I was desperate for some black coffee and a fistful of aspirin. "Where is she now?"

"In lockup. Remember where I took you to see Wes? Same building. Different cell, though."

"That seems wise, Sergeant. And Chief Block wanted you to call me—?"

"He hopes you can get down here ASAP and talk some sense into the lady. We got enough to deal with today—movin' Wes, dodging reporters. That whole circus again."

I considered my response, but only for a moment. The image of Maggie Currim sitting in a jail cell, hands demurely folded on her lap, made the decision for me.

"On my way, Sergeant."

◇◇◇

Thankfully, the weatherman had gotten it right and no new snow had fallen during the night. And the highway to Wheeling, now both plowed *and* salted, presented no problem, either. Though my rental was equipped with snow tires.

I pulled into the precinct parking lot and stepped out into a cold but sunlit day. There were no TV news vans in sight, which probably meant that Wes Currim had already been relocated to county jail.

Entering the precinct's lobby, I found Sergeant Randall talking with that same desk officer I'd seen the last time I was here.

Randall was taking a jacket from a rack of hanging coats whose hooks were deer antlers.

"Hey, Doc." He reached to shake hands, then noticed the bandages. "You okay?"

"I'm fine. Little accident."

He absorbed this. "You made good time."

"Roads were fine. Is Chief Block in his office? I'd like to speak to him before I talk to Mrs. Currim."

Randall buttoned his jacket. "Ya just missed him. He went with the wagon takin' Wes to County. A couple news vans were waitin' across the street, plannin' to follow 'em. The Chief wanted to be there when they made the delivery. Wes' lawyer—what the hell's his name?…"

"Willard Hansen."

"Right. Hansen's gonna be there. Givin' Wes moral support or whatever. Chief Block wants to make sure they don't turn this into a media event."

"Lotsa luck."

"Tell me about it." He turned to the desk officer. "See ya later, Stan. And don't forget to put ten bucks down on the Browns for me. I got a feelin' about this one."

As Randall led me across the parking lot to the lockup, he jerked his thumb back toward the precinct.

"Stan runs a little action on the side. Chief Block don't mind and it puts a few extra bucks in Stan's pocket. He's got an autistic kid."

"I'm glad the chief sees it that way."

"It's a small town, Doc. Makes us a pretty tight-knit group, know what I mean? Like a family."

When we stepped into the building, we followed the same procedure as before. Randall handed me off to a guard, who walked me down to the visitor's room. The guard left me there for a minute, and then returned with Maggie Currim. Without a word, he went out and took his place in the corridor beyond. Eyes staring flatly into the room through the rectangular window.

Maggie was equally silent as she took a seat opposite mine at the pinewood table. Sitting in the same chair her son Wes had used when I questioned him.

I went first. "It's good to see you again, Maggie."

"I wish I could say the same, Dr. Rinaldi. Oh, dear, did you burn yourself?"

My goddam hands again. "It's nothing."

Wearing a beaded blouse and black slacks, her coat wrapped about her shoulders, she presented the same picture of dignified poise as when we spoke in my office. Though her face was pale and drawn, and her fingers, interlaced and resting on the table, twitched noticeably.

"I think I understand why you came here to see Chief Block," I said. "Why you were so upset."

"Upset? I behaved like a harpy. Using foul language. Throwing things in the chief's office. I swear, I'll never forgive myself."

"None of that matters, Maggie. You have every right to be concerned. Given the crime Wes is charged with, and his media notoriety, I can see his having trouble with other inmates in County. That's why I came down. I wanted to see *you*, of course. But I also want to talk to the DA. Maybe I can persuade her to put Wes in a protected cell block. Out of the general population."

"Good luck with that one, Doctor. Our lawyer, Mr. Hansen, already approached her with the same request. She denied it." Her voice broke. "Something's going to happen to my Wesley in that place, I know it. Something bad."

I covered her clasped hands with mine.

"Look, Maggie. This DA owes me a favor. I helped out when Wes took the police to where Ed Meachem's body was found. I'm hoping I can call in that favor now."

Blinking back tears, she managed to look squarely at me. That familiar mix of pride and vulnerability.

"But why would you help us? I know you think Wesley is guilty. Even though *I* know he isn't."

"The truth is, I don't know whether Wes is guilty or not. I *do* know that justice wouldn't be served if something happened to him in prison before his trial. *Or after.*"

"I…Thank you, Doctor. You're a good man."

Then, hesitating, she spoke again. "I also…I've been think-ing about our conversation in your office, and—well, I wasn't exactly honest with you about something."

"About what?"

"My husband Jack. I told you I didn't care about him any-more. Since he ran away with that girl…"

"Lily Greer."

She nodded sadly. "I mean, I know I said she could have him and all that…But it isn't true. No matter how badly he treated me, I always loved Jack. And I still do."

"I'm surprised to hear that."

A thin smile. "I'm surprised myself, Doctor. I guess I'm not as proud as I like to think. Even though he cheated on me, I'd take him back. In a heartbeat. Wesley can't understand it, of course. He never could. But love is…" She paused. "Love is God's gift to us, I suppose. Whether we deserve it or not. Most people would probably say that Jack doesn't deserve it. But I love him just the same. If he came back from Fiji or wherever tomorrow, I'd want to be with him again. And I'd hope he felt the same about me."

She searched my face. "Does that make me a fool, Dr. Rinaldi?"

"Not in my book. Besides, Jack isn't—"

I silently cursed myself, instantly regretting my words. I felt my face flush.

Maggie slipped her hands out from beneath mine.

"Do you know something? About Jack?"

"Not really. I probably shouldn't have said anything. It's just that…well, the truth is, I think Jack and Lily are still here. In the United States."

"How do you know?"

"Like I said, I don't. But I have a strong hunch. Lily Greer never picked up her passport, which she would need to travel overseas. Plus I don't get the impression that either one of them would be that comfortable living abroad. Not indefinitely, anyway."

She sighed heavily. "I used to think the same thing. I even consulted a private detective once, hoping he might be able to locate them. But he said that, by now, the trail has probably gone cold."

"Doesn't sound like much of a detective."

"I think he was just trying to spare my feelings. I imagine, if people really don't *want* to be found…"

Maggie let the words die on her lips.

I cleared my throat and slowly got to my feet. Her eyes, strangely unfocused, didn't follow me.

"Let's concentrate on what we *can* do," I said. "First thing, I'll talk to Chief Block about getting you out of here. Then I'll call the DA about Wes."

She didn't stir. Spoke to the air.

"I don't care about me, Dr. Rinaldi. It's my son I'm worried about."

"I understand. And I promise I'll do my best."

I motioned to the guard through the viewing window.

◇◇◇

Walking back through the midmorning chill to the precinct, I caught sight of Sergeant Randall. He'd changed into a thicker winter coat and ear muffs, and was climbing behind the wheel of his police cruiser.

I trotted over to where he sat waiting, with the car door open. He started up the engine and revved it. A milk-white cloud of exhaust rose against the clear sky.

"Needs a tune-up, I think." He gave me a toothy grin. "How'd things go with Mrs. Currim?"

"Fine, Sergeant. But I do need to speak with the chief now. Is he back from county jail yet?"

Randall clucked his tongue. "I just got off the phone with him. Sounded like he'd had enough o' police business for the day. Hell, he don't usually work Saturdays anyway."

"Then where is he?"

"He said he was goin' home. You can call him there if you want."

"I'd rather talk to him in person. Can you give me his address?"

Randall hesitated for a moment, then grinned again.

"I guess that'd be okay. But if he gives me hell about it later, I'm puttin' the blame on you."

"Seems only fair."

He wrote the address on the back of his business card and handed it to me.

"See ya around, Doc." Shutting his car door.

I watched as he pulled out of the lot, trailing a thinning plume of exhaust smoke. Then I got into my car and turned the key.

Unfortunately, the rental wasn't equipped with a GPS. So I dutifully pulled out the map of the area I'd picked up at a gas station on the way down here and looked for Chief Block's place.

It wasn't easy to find. When I finally did, I groaned audibly.

Great, I thought. *In the middle of fucking nowhere.*

Chapter Forty-five

I realized, soon after turning off the main highway and venturing into the stark January woods outside of town, that I'd neglected to get Chief Block's number from Sgt. Randall. Which meant I'd be showing up unannounced.

The only route to Block's house was a series of bumpy, poorly-marked dirt roads. None of which had seen a snowplow in weeks, if ever. To make any headway, even with snow tires, I had to keep my wheels positioned in the deep furrows carved by the few vehicles that had preceded me. One of which, I presumed, had been the chief's.

Finally, I made a sharp right onto what looked to be a fire road. There was only one set of tire tracks—some kind of four-wheel-drive vehicle, from the look of the tread marks—and I again let my own tires slip into the deep, soot-spackled grooves.

After a hundred yards or so, I turned again, this time onto a narrow gravel driveway. Passing slowly through a tree-ribbed tunnel of icy branches and window-high snow banks, I approached a modest though well-kept ranch house. Front walk and porch recently shoveled clear, it was a brick and redwood structure boasting an impressively peaked, snow-collared roof. A Ford SUV I took to be the chief's was parked in an attached covered car port.

I'd just pulled next to it when I heard the gunshot. Then its echo, fluting off the surrounding woods.

About to bolt out of the car, I thought better of it and carefully opened the door. Looked left and right. And listened. Hard.

It took me a moment to get a fix on where the shot had come from. Then I had it. Behind the house. Before I could decide my next move, there was a second shot. Again, its booming echo, this time accompanied by the outraged cry of a crow.

Followed by the harsh, throaty growl of a man, hurling a volley of curses into the trees.

A voice I recognized. Chief Avery Block.

My senses tightened like coiled wire, I hazarded a slow, careful walk around the near side of the house.

Rounding the corner, I came upon a broad, snow-dotted yard, overhung with thin black branches that reached down like gnarled fingers.

Chief Block stood in the middle of the yard, beside a picnic table incongrously buried inches up its legs in snow. Though the table itself had been swept clean in curved swatches, as though by a gloved palm. Two empty beer cans lay crumpled atop it.

The Chief turned and peered with open irritation at my approach. He was bareheaded, and his winter coat was unbuttoned. In his left hand was another beer can, from which he casually took a swig.

In his right hand was a gun.

A Taurus 44M Tracker. It was easy to recognize, since I'd seen one fairly recently. In an evidence bag at the Federal Building in Pittsburgh.

"Chief Block. Sorry to drop in uninvited, but—"

Block threw back the rest of his beer, crumpled the can, and tossed it on the tabletop with its breathren.

"How'd you know where I live, Doc?"

"Sergeant Randall gave me your address."

"Figures."

"Look, it was my fault. I pressed him for it."

He tugged at his red-veined nose. "Goddam, I can't catch any kinda break. Ever since I became chief, I can't grab me a moment's peace. A moment to myself."

By now, I'd crossed the distance between us. Without making too much of it, I glanced at the gun in his hand.

"I heard a couple shots."

A crooked, self-satisfied grin.

"That was me. Target practice."

He pointed the revolver's muzzle out toward a clutch of leafless trees. From one sturdy branch hung a broad sheet of tin, pockmarked with bullet holes. A crude target had been painted in red on its battered skin.

"Wanna give it a try?" Block swiveled the gun around and, with a puzzled look at my hands, offered its butt to me. "If you can still work your fingers, that is."

"No thanks. But I did want to speak with you. I'll just need a minute of your time."

"That's what people always say. Next thing I know, my whole fuckin' life's gone by."

I paused. "Could we sit somewhere and talk, Chief?"

He considered this. Then, without answering, he turned and headed toward the rear of the house. I followed.

We approached an oak-framed back door, flanked on either side by weathered Adirondack chairs. They too had been hand-swept of recent snow, and looked damp and uncomfortable. Turned out I was right on both counts.

Chief Block sank heavily into the other chair. "I'd invite you inside, but the place is a mess. Besides, like you say, you ain't stayin' long."

Grunting, he lay the revolver on his lap and reached into his coat pocket for some beef jerky. Offered me a stick. I shook my head.

"Suit yourself." He took a sizeable bite, chewing noisily. "It's this shit or that goddam nicotine gum. But I always gotta have somethin' in my mouth. Guess that's what you people call bein' oral, right, Doc?"

I didn't reply, keeping my eyes trained on the gun.

Again, that easy, challenging smile. "I know you're dyin' to ask me about this revolver, ain'tcha?"

"It's a Taurus 44M Tracker, Chief. You know that's the same make as the shooter used."

"Of course I know. It was on the tri-state interface, before the feds shut it down. Now I don't know what the fuck's goin' on with their investigation. Not that I'm real interested. Not my case. More like professional curiosity. Hell, I got enough on my plate."

"Maybe. But I have to wonder what you're doing with the same kind of gun. Using it for target practice."

"I happen to like the Tracker, not that it's any o' your goddam concern. Though not *this* one. Not as much as I liked the other one."

"What other one?"

"The other Taurus revolver. I have a pair of 'em. Or at least I *did*, until the mate to this one was stolen."

"Stolen? When?"

"Beats me. Musta been a while back. I hadn't taken 'em out of the gun cabinet for the longest time. But then I went to get 'em, use 'em for some shootin' out back here, and I saw that one of the pair was missin'."

I sat forward in my chair.

"Who has access to your gun cabinet? Where is it?"

"In the house, where else? In the den. Since my wife left me, I can keep stuff wherever I want to. In the den, in the crapper. Wherever the fuck I want."

"Do you keep the cabinet locked?"

He was enjoying my look of consternation.

"What can I say? Now and again, I forget to lock it. And I got all kinda people comin' in and outta here. Like the mayor, my squad. My weekly poker game. And then there's the gun club. We rotate meetings, now that the Moose Hall's burned down, and I've had the boys here a bunch o' times. I guess just 'bout anyone coulda taken the damn gun."

"But that missing revolver...Don't you see? It could be the murder weapon. I happen to know the FBI has the shooter's gun. If it still has its serial number, and we can match it to the one that was stolen—"

He held up a rough, nail-bitten forefinger.

"Whoa, sonny. First of all, there are thousands of Taurus 44M's out there. Second, both this baby and its twin got their serial numbers filed off."

"I don't understand."

"That's 'cause you ain't on the job. My two revolvers were recovered in a raid at a meth lab years ago, along with a dozen others. After the trials, they weren't needed as evidence no more. So me and a couple o' other cops sorta kept them. As souvenirs. I always hate to see a fine piece o' armament go to waste."

I was probably staring at him, for he started to laugh, a sound laced with years of casual disregard for the finer points of the law. A small-town cop with an equally small-town view of how the world worked. Or, rather, with only too *clear* a view of how *his* particular world worked.

Keeping the revolver on his lap, Block bent and withdrew another beer from a small cooler at his feet.

"All this yakkin' is makin' me thirsty. Ya want one?"

"Bit early in the day for me."

"Spoken like a true city boy. Hell, beer's like mother's milk to me."

As if for emphasis, he took a healthy swig.

I was still uneasy about his gun, and whether or not it might be the mate of the shooter's. Though, as Block pointed out, it was unlikely. On the other hand, maybe I ought to alert the FBI about it anyway. Let *them* come down and look into it.

Regardless, I figured I'd better get to what I'd actually come to see Chief Block about.

"I *did* want to talk to you about Maggie Currim. I just spoke to her in lockup."

"Good. I appreciate you comin' down. She okay now?"

"I think so. She told me she's sorry for the way she acted in your office."

"Stupid cow *should* be sorry. So now you're here to ask me to let her outta her cage, right?"

"She's no danger to anyone, Chief. Not really. She's just worried about Wes."

"Yeah, I know." Another swallow of beer. "I guess she learned her lesson. When you get back to town, you can tell Sergeant Randall I said to let Mrs. Currim go home."

"Randall's not at the precinct. At least, I doubt it. He drove off right before I came up here to see you."

Block grimaced. "Again? Damn, the guy asks me for some personal time, and 'cause I'm soft in the head I give it to him." He grew thoughtful. "No, wait a minute…today's Saturday, ain't it? He's got that class."

"What do you mean, personal time?"

"Last couple weeks, he's been takin' time off—without pay— to visit his mother. Sometimes days, sometimes nights. Looks like she's dyin'."

"I'm sorry to hear that. Must be hard on Randall…"

Block squinted in the noon light. "If it is, it makes a nice change. 'Cause Harve's hated her guts his whole life. When she took sick a couple years back, she got put in the county hospital for the indigent. Real shithole. This whole time, he's never even visited her. Not till recently. I guess I nagged him about it so much he figured it'd be easier to go check in on the old bag. At least a couple times before she croaks."

"Why'd he hate her so much?"

"Hey, I don't blame the guy. *I'd* hate her, too."

He finished his beer in one long, noisy gulp. Wiped his mouth with the back of his hand. Crumpling the empty can, he looked awkwardly about for a place to put it.

Finally he tossed it, underhanded, toward the picnic table. It missed. At the same time, the sudden movement made the revolver slip from his lap and fall to the ground. Luckily, it didn't go off.

I scooped it up and handed it over to Block, who checked the safety and pocketed it. Then shook his head.

"Christ, listen to me airin' out poor Harve's dirty laundry. I probably shouldn't be tellin' you all this."

"You don't have to tell me anything, Chief."

"Damned right, I don't. If Harve wants to tell ya the story of his life, that's his business…"

"I agree."

But I made a point of edging my chair a bit closer to his. I had no idea what was on the chief's mind, but I could tell he wanted to get it out.

"Not that there's any big secret. Most folks in town know about Harve. How 'Randall' ain't even his real name. He just picked it outta the phone book when he was a kid."

Block scratched his chin stubble.

"And let me tell you, given where he came from, he's done real well for himself. Worked his way up to detective sergeant. Yessir, *real* goddam well."

"Given where he came from..?"

"Poor bastard grew up in low rent foster care, all kinds of abuse, neglect, that shit. Abandoned by his no-good mother, Doreen Somethin', when he was just a baby. Real piece o' work, that broad. Drugs. Livin' on the street. The whole nine yards."

"What about his father?"

"He never even knew who the hell his father *was*. The lousy prick abandoned Harve, too. Just knocked up his mother and took off. No big surprise there, I guess."

"What do you mean?"

"I *mean*, what did the bitch expect? He was one of her johns and she got careless. It was her own stupid fault."

My stomach twisted. "Her johns?"

Block's eyes narrowed.

"That's why Harve *hated* her so much. All his life. His mother was a goddam whore."

Chapter Forty-six

After getting Chief Block's promise to call the precinct and order Maggie Currim's release, I climbed in my car and sped back along those same treacherous roads toward town. Unmindful of the deep ruts and patches of frozen mud.

Driving with one hand, I used the other to smooth out the map on the passenger seat. Glancing at it as much as I dared. Looking for the address I'd also been given by the chief.

The county hospital for the indigent.

My mind was a jumble of thoughts, a tangle of ideas being pulled into a pattern. One that I was beginning to comprehend. Or, at least, believed I did.

I hadn't shared my suspicions with Chief Block, nor was I ready to call Agent Alcott or Pittsburgh PD. After all, I had no proof. Not one shred of solid evidence.

But I knew. My every instinct told me I was right.

Sergeant Harve Randall was the shooter.

The way I saw it, he'd spent his whole life marinating in shame and self-loathing. His mother was a prostitute who'd been impregnated by one of her johns. Instead of raising Harve, she'd abandoned him to his fate, drifting back into her drug-addled life on the streets.

Growing up in a series of abusive foster homes, shuttled from one horrific environment to another, I believed Harve developed an obsessive, murderous hatred for his mother. But from a distance. Never seeking her out.

Because though he nursed an overwhelming, psychotic desire to kill her, he couldn't bring himself to do it. He'd probably fantasized about doing it since childhood, and certainly even more so as he became an adult.

But he couldn't make himself kill her, no matter how virulent his hatred. No matter how fervently, desperately he wanted her dead.

She was his mother.

So Harve Randall satisfied himself with the murders of *other* prostitutes. Women who were surrogate victims of his homicidal rage. Whose brutal deaths he could read about, over and over. And whose killers he could idolize. Experiencing their crimes vicariously…

By now, I'd reached the main highway. Making the turn toward downtown Wheeling, I found myself weaving in and out of weekend traffic. And speeding. Exhaling deeply, I made the conscious effort to slow down. Drive more cautiously. Follow the train of my thoughts in a calmer fashion.

Not an easy task, given the adrenaline surging through my system. But I had to try. There was still so much I didn't know or understand.

I assumed, once Randall had become a cop, he was able to use the network of law enforcement databases to learn about any new murders of prostitutes. To recognize patterns that indicated a serial killer might be on the prowl. Someone whose exploits he could follow. Whose horrific actions provided him the excitement and gratification of the kill, and then the catharsis of release.

But what I didn't know was what first prompted him to write fan letters to Gary Squires. Then, after Squires died, to John Jessup. Moreover, after Jessup was killed in prison, what triggered Randall's desire to avenge his death? To methodically work his way down a hitlist of those whom he held responsible? Maybe I'd never know.

However, other pieces of the puzzle were easier to fit together. For one thing, all the "personal time" Randall took—ostensibly to visit his dying mother—gave him plenty of opportunity to make the short trips across state lines necessary to attack his victims.

Just as important, once the joint FBI-police task force was up and running, Harve Randall—as a member of the Wheeling PD—would have access to the tri-state interface. Which meant access to all case intel: Knowledge of the investigation's progress, the whereabouts and movements of potential targets on the hitlist, advanced word when a suspect or witness was to be interviewed. That's how he knew about Harry Polk's trip to Steubenville to question Vincent Beck. How he knew where Claire Cobb was being hidden, and when she was being transferred out of town.

Until the task force brass shut down the Internet grid, and Randall lost his window into the investigation. Now, in the words of Lyle Barnes, he was working blind.

I could just imagine Randall's growing frustration and outrage. My guess was, with the remaining potential victims sequestered in some unknown FBI safehouse, the only option that occurred to him was to frame Barnes. At least it was one way to punish the man who'd initially identified and tracked down Randall's hero, John Jessup. And the easiest way to do *that* was to plant the revolver he'd used, the Taurus 44M, in Barnes' Franklin Park home. A revolver that Randall had undoubtably stolen some time ago from Chief Block's gun cabinet.

Suddenly, my thoughts were interrupted by the sight of the hospital turnoff the chief had described. I made a sharp left and found myself on a cracked asphalt road that curved around some kind of deserted, long-abandoned park. A sad array of rusting playground equipment. Broad swaths of broken earth, tufts of unruly grass glistening with ice.

I followed the road past a row of apartment complexes that had seen better days, until I came to a small, paved driveway. This led me to the front gates of the Marshall County Public Hospital. Five stories of government-funded, lowest-bidder construction. A forlorn, ugly building of chipped red bricks and barred, cracked windows. Heavy steel doors and a weather-beaten, black-shingled roof.

After I parked in the gravel lot, I sat thinking about what I was doing here. And why I was doing it. Despite the fact that all my theories about Harve Randall were just that—theories—maybe I ought to just call the authorities and step away. Leave things to the *real* detectives.

But I knew I wouldn't. Couldn't. Because there was one thing left I needed to know. One question to which I had to have the answer.

And only one person who could give it to me.

◇◇◇

The ward nurse was a small, middle-aged woman with a placid, almost serene face. Filipino, I guessed, with the merest trace of an accent. As she led me down the dreary, paint-flecked corridor, past a row of rooms whose bedridden occupants looked more like cadavers than patients, she made a point of smiling brightly into each opened door.

"I'm often the only other soul they see all day," she explained, flipping through patient files attached to a clipboard. "The least I can do is give them each a smile."

After I'd been directed to this wing of the hospital from the front lobby, I showed the ward nurse my ID and explained I was a friend of the family, paying a condolence call. I felt badly lying to her, but had no choice.

"I'm so glad Doreen has a visitor," she was saying now. "You're the first one she's had in weeks. Months."

"But what about her son Harve? I understand he's been here many times to see her."

"A young man claiming to be her son *did* visit, but only once. And only for a few minutes. Then he stormed out of the room, cursing out loud. I was so concerned, I went into Doreen's room to see if she was okay."

"Was she?"

Her shoulders dropped. "Truthfully, sir, it's hard to tell. Body riddled with cancer. She can't even raise her head. Nor barely talk, except in a whisper."

We'd arrived at the door to Doreen's room. Unlike the others, hers was closed.

The nurse leaned toward me, conspiratorily. "Some of the people we get here…like Doreen…Well, in my view, this place is more hospice than hospital. Such a shame, to end your life that way. Alone, and in a place like this."

I smiled at her open face.

"Not totally alone," I said. "They have you."

She flushed under her burnished-gold skin and hurried away, heels clicking on the linoleum, clipboard tucked smartly under her arm.

I opened the door and went into Doreen's room. It was unlit, gray walled and sparely furnished, with one window whose blinds were closed against the midday sun. As I stepped softly to her bedside, I was aware of the faint though unmistakeable smell of imminent death.

I paused at the bed rails, looking down at her pale, wrinkled face. Eyes half-closed. Breathing a slow hiss.

Her body seemed as small and frail as a child's under the threadbare blankets, and the skin of her exposed forearm, punctured by an IV drip, was as thin as rice paper.

"Doreen?" My voice calm, measured. "Are you awake?"

Her eyelids fluttered. It took an effort for her lips to part, to form words.

"Who are you?" A soft, hoarse croak.

"A friend."

"Don't have no friends."

"I'm a friend of Harve's. Your son."

"He don't have no friends, neither. He…"

Her mouth tightened, as though pulled closed by hidden strings. A thin, milky crust coated her lips.

I leaned slightly over the bed rails, my face hovering above hers. I hoped my smile was reassuring.

"Doreen, I just need—"

"Go away." Barely audible, mostly air. "Please…"

"I will. I promise. But if I could just ask you one question…"

Eyes still lidded, she managed a slow nod.

I straightened then, hands gripping the bed rails. Drew in a long, uneasy breath.

"Doreen…that one time, when Harve came to visit… Did you tell him who his father was?"

Her eyes opened.

◇◇◇

A half-hour later, I went into the Wheeling precinct and walked across the lobby. Stan, the desk officer, was still on duty.

"Has Sergeant Randall come back yet, Officer?"

"Not yet, Dr. Rinaldi. But he should be headin' back soon. He teaches a class to rookies on Saturdays, ya know, over at the Academy. We're all real proud."

"I can imagine."

"By the way, I figure you'd want to know that Wes Currim's mom was released. Chief Block called me from home, told me to cut her loose."

"Thanks, Officer. That's good news."

He shrugged, clearly uninterested. Then the landline on his desk rang and he swiveled in his chair to snatch it up. With his back turned, I was free to do two things.

First, I leaned over and lifted an empty envelope from a tray on his desk.

Then I stepped quickly to the rack of coats on the wall. And had my first piece of real luck in a long time.

Putting what I found in the empty envelope, I called a quick goodbye to Stan as I went out the door. Still facing away from me, phone to his ear, he absently waved his hand in reply.

Chapter Forty-seven

Five minutes later, I was back in the rental, going as fast as I dared on I-70 West to Pittsburgh. Barely conscious of the now-cleared roads, passing cars and trucks, and frost-tipped rural landscape. Instead, I drove with a mixture of excitement and dread feeding my senses.

It was time, I knew, to call in the cavalry.

With my cell on speaker, I made the first call to Stu Biegler, Pittsburgh PD, and was pointedly told that the lieutenant was unavailable. I hesitated only a moment. There was no way I was going to speak to some junior detective or the departmental clearing desk about Harve Randall. Not when all I had was a theory. So I hung up.

Next I tried Special Agent Neal Alcott at the Federal Building. After a series of maddening delays and transfers, I was finally directed—to my chagrin—to Agent Green.

I told him I needed to speak to Alcott urgently.

"Sorry, Doc." He didn't sound sorry. "My understanding from Agent Alcott is that you're not involved anymore. Tell ya what, how 'bout I take a message?"

"Okay. Tell him I know who the shooter is. And that if he wants the Bureau to make the collar instead of the cops, he better call me back before Stu Biegler does."

"Right." A terse chuckle. "Give it up, will ya, Doc?"

He was still chuckling as he hung up.

So much for trying official channels, I thought.

Next I called Eleanor's cell, but got her answering message. My fingers thumping the steering wheel, I waited impatiently for the beep.

"El, it's Danny. It's about the shooter. I think he's a cop. Sergeant Harve Randall, Wheeling PD. Call me back ASAP. Or try to get a hold of Biegler. Or both."

I clicked off, almost howling aloud in frustration. It didn't help that traffic ahead of me had begun to slow. Leaning up in my seat, I saw that a huge semi was riding its brakes around a long, down-sloping curve of highway.

Calming myself, I realized what I needed to do. *Of course.* Get Agent Green back on the phone and tell him about Harve Randall. Or try to contact Agent Reese. Make *somebody* I knew at the Bureau listen.

Before I could do so, my own cell rang. Lyle Barnes.

"Lyle? Aren't you in protective custody?"

"Ancient history, Doc. Soon as they locked me up, I had a long heart-to-heart on the phone with the director. He knows damned well I'm not the guy. So I told him, out of deference to our friendship, I'd give him ten minutes to get me released or I leak my arrest to the media."

"From inside a guarded room in the Federal Building?"

"I was on the phone with *him*, wasn't I?"

"Good point. How'd you manage that, by the way?"

"I pick-pocketed Agent Zarnicki's cell on the way out of that meeting with Alcott."

"Amazing. You looked dead on your feet to me."

"I *was*—and still am. I'm ridin' on fumes here, son. Hell, maybe I'm asleep right now."

"You still using Zarnicki's phone?"

"Nah. The director came through, and I got my personal effects back, including my phone. Though I'm still in the building, in the cafeteria. But don't worry. Soon as Zarnicki let me out of the room, I gave him back his cell. Somehow he failed to see the humor in the situation."

"I'll bet. Listen, Lyle, I'm glad you called. I think you're gonna wanna get back to your old buddy the director. 'Cause I know who the shooter is."

"*What?*"

"Guy's name is Harve Randall. A detective sergeant in the Wheeling PD."

"A Wheeling cop? Holy shit! Are you sure?"

As quickly and cogently as I could, I explained my reasoning. "I realize it's all just theory, but—"

"No, it makes sense. All of it. Now I think—"

Suddenly, another call clicked in. I checked the display. Neal Alcott.

"Hang on, Lyle. It's Alcott."

I clicked over and heard the Special Agent's weary, suspicious voice.

"You better not be jerkin' my chain, Rinaldi—"

For the second time in less than a minute, I detailed my thoughts about Harve Randall. Alcott listened without interrupting me, and kept silent for another long moment after I'd finished. Finally, he spoke.

"You've gotta be kiddin' me. Not one tangible piece of evidence in anything you just laid out. All a bunch of psychobabble, if you don't mind my sayin'."

Still, I heard a rare hesitancy in his tone.

"But you're desperate enough to consider it, right?"

"I wouldn't say the bureau's desperate," he replied carefully, "but I admit your idea's worth following up."

"Glad to hear it."

"First thing, I'll put in a call to Wheeling PD. Talk to that Chief Block you mentioned. I'll want to verify the exact dates and logged hours of that personal time Sergeant Randall took these last few weeks. See if they line up with when the victims were killed."

"Good idea. Though the chief's at home at the moment."

I could almost see his smirk. "Is that a fact? Not once I have them give me his home number. I guarantee the chief will be back at work in short order."

Alcott cleared his throat. "I just have one more question, Doc. You tell all this to the Pittsburgh PD?"

"I tried to, but haven't heard back yet."

A dry laugh. "Sweet."

He hung up. Which was when I remembered that I still had Lyle Barnes on the other line, on hold. I clicked over.

And just got a dial tone.

◇◇◇

As I pulled into midtown, the winter sun's rays were like pale yellow spokes fanned out behind Pittsburgh's multi-tiered skyline. It would be dusk in less than an hour, and with the roads cleared and no fresh snow in the forecast, the Saturday night crowd would soon pour into the city's trendy, newly-gentrified havens. The Point. Shadyside. The South Side. The Riverfront.

But I had a different destination. Two blocks past City Hall, I turned into a parking lot behind a low-roofed, nondescript building that was long overdue for a paint job. It was a privately-owned forensics lab that frequently contracted with the Pittsburgh Police. Moreover, the guy who ran the place had been in grad school with me at Pitt.

Though it was the weekend, I wasn't surprised to find the facility open. Henry Stiles had been a workaholic even as a student, and his precise, indefatigable personality had only solidified with age.

It had been years since I'd last seen him, however, so I needed the receptionist to direct me to Henry's office. Still, when I knocked at his opened door and he came from behind his desk greet me, I was vaguely unsettled to see how much older he looked than I'd remembered. Heavy-set, with greying hair and veined eyes behind wire-rim glasses.

"Dan Rinaldi!" He gave me a hearty, collegial hug. "Good Lord, it must be—"

"Far too long, Henry. Unforgiveable, on my part. So naturally, I need a favor."

"Naturally. What are old friends for?"

Folding his arms, he sat back on the edge of his desk.

"Though you must have a portrait mysteriously growing old up in your attic, Danny. You look the same as always. Or else it's those damned Italian genes."

I smiled. "That's the other good thing about old friends, Henry. They know how and when to lie."

He gave a short laugh, then, almost reluctantly, sighed. "Okay, we've done the obligatory old-school-chums bullshit. You'll also note I haven't even asked about those bandages. So what do you want?"

I handed him the envelope I'd lifted from the Wheeling police station.

"I need you to analyze what's inside. And Henry—"

"Yeah, I know. You need it yesterday."

"If not sooner."

"Right. Now tell me what's in here and what I'm looking for. And why."

So I did.

◇◇◇

The temperature must have dropped ten degrees by the time I came back outside. Night was coming.

I got behind the wheel of the rental and turned the key. Then, gunning it, I pulled out onto the street.

I hadn't gone three city blocks when the car died.

Chapter Forty-eight

Putting it in neutral, I climbed out into the cold and, leaning in to steer through the open window, pushed the car to the curb. Some side street, off Fifth.

Sighing, I popped the hood and peered inside, though I didn't know what I was looking for. Dead battery? Faulty fuel pump?

It didn't matter. The truth was, I didn't want to deal with it. Not now, when it seemed as though things were suddenly coming to a head.

I shut the hood and locked the car. I'd let the rental company handle it later. Right now, all I cared about was getting new transport. Buttoning my coat against the wind and the chill, I trudged up to the corner. Where the traffic was.

I was still curbside, looking up and down Fifth Avenue for a passing cab, when my cell rang again. It was Eleanor Lowrey, her voice high, breathless.

"I just got your message. Jesus, Danny, are you *sure* about the shooter? 'Cause before I go to Biegler with this, I need—"

"That's okay, I've already talked to Neal Alcott and he's on it. Makes sense anyway, since he heads up the task force. Probably deserves the collar."

I heard her grateful—and obvious—sigh of relief.

"Thank God. I was afraid you'd do something stupid again—like go after this Randall guy yourself."

"Nope, I'm being a good boy this time. Letting you real law enforcement types earn your salaries."

"But what tipped you to Randall in the first place?"

"Long story, and I'm outside, freezing my ass off. Soon as I grab a cab—"

"Like hell. Where are you? I'll come pick you up."

◇◇◇

We were in Eleanor's unmarked, heading along surface streets toward the Liberty Tubes. I could tell she was driving with no particular destination in mind. Just moving cautiously through the urban maze, violet eyes focused on the thickening traffic, listening to my theory about Harve Randall.

"Ya know," she said at last, "if you're right, it helps explain something that's always bothered me."

"And that is?..."

"The night our eyewitness, Vincent Beck, was killed. We never found any abandoned vehicle, which was a real break from the shooter's typical M.O. Just like his using that hunting rifle instead of his usual revolver."

"I see where you're going, El. We assumed—correctly, I think—that the shooter broke with his standard pattern because he was forced to. Which means that Randall was away from his home base, either his residence or the Wheeling precinct, when he learned that Harry Polk was on his way to interview Beck. Randall was probably in his patrol car."

She nodded excitedly.

"Sure. Maybe he heard about it from some dispatcher. Or maybe Randall's patrol car is equipped with an onboard computer, linked into the tri-state interface. So he could monitor the task force investigation even if on the road."

"Whichever. The thing is, once he hears about the Beck interview, he has to get to Steubenville before Harry does. He can't take the chance that Beck hadn't seen something that could expose him. But there wasn't time to get his usual gun—which, by the way, I'm beginning to believe has some kind of totemic meaning for him. It's too specific a weapon of choice, if you get my drift."

She offered me an indulgent half-smile. "If you say so, Doc... *Anyway*, if there wasn't time to get his usual gun, there sure as hell wasn't time to steal a car."

"Right. He had no option other than to risk driving to Steubenville in his patrol car. *And* breaking into that gun shop to get hold of a weapon. He couldn't use his own service piece. Ballistics could match it."

I gave this more thought. "Wheeling, West Virginia, to Steubenville, Ohio. That's roughly twenty-five or thirty miles. Then, after he escapes from the warehouse, another thirty miles back to Wheeling. It's tight, but doable."

I suddenly remembered hearing the approaching sirens as the Steubenville police sped to the crime scene.

"Funny. Randall must've been barreling out from behind the warehouse just as the local cops were pulling up to the front."

"The guy's got brass balls, all right." She stopped at a light and looked over at me. "I just hope nothing spooks him before the bureau closes in."

"I was thinking the same thing. In fact, I figured I'd have heard something from Alcott by now."

The light changed and Eleanor turned onto a narrow side street. She kept going until she found an open space, pulled to the curb and cut the engine.

"You giving Biegler a call now?" I asked.

She shook her head. Sat back in her seat.

"Before I call him...before it all cranks up again...I just wanted to explain. I mean, about last night."

I turned her chin gently toward me.

"Nothing to explain, El. It's *her*, isn't it?..."

Her eyes lowered. "I...I just can't stop thinking about her... wishing things were different..."

I knew what she was talking about, of course. The woman she'd once called the love of her life. Who'd come back into that life last summer, if only briefly...

"I *do* understand, Eleanor. More than you could know."

Her hand found mine. We sat like that for a long, unbroken moment. As the windshield began to fog. From the heat of our bodies, the twinned breath from our lungs.

Finally, she said, "Don't worry. I'm not gonna screw up the moment by saying we'll always be friends."

"Thanks. I appreciate that."

Still clutching her hand, I leaned over and kissed her on the cheek. Drank in, for one last time, the sweet aroma of her. The silken touch of her skin to my lips.

Then, jarringly, my cell rang. Eleanor and I both started, as though jostled from a dream.

"Christ!" I grabbed up the phone.

"It's Barnes again, Doc."

"Lyle? Where are you now?"

"On the road. I boosted a car from the Bureau motor pool. Look, I only got a minute, so shut up and listen. I figure I owe ya."

"Owe me? What are you talking about?"

Eleanor was staring at me in confusion, but I held up a warning hand. Something in Barnes' voice, some mix of urgency and manic excitement, worried me. I was right.

"Let's face it, Danny. *My* gut agrees with yours about Harve Randall. But guts aren't evidence, and our guy is too smart to stick around once he knows somebody's checking out his time logs."

"Shit, Lyle, what did you do?"

"Now don't get all pissed off, but I called Wheeling PD and asked for Randall. Identified myself as FBI. Desk guy told me Randall was on his way back to the precinct, so I asked him to patch me into his patrol car."

"You *what*?!…"

"I got Randall on the phone and told him we knew he was the shooter. *That* sure got his attention."

I couldn't even find words to speak.

"C'mon, Danny. I had no choice. A guy like Randall finds out we're circling his ass, he doesn't just take the collar and hire a lawyer. He's gone. In the wind."

"Sure, Lyle, now that you've *warned* him—"

"But here's the beauty part. I offered him the one sure bait he couldn't resist. The one thing he'd *have* to do before taking off for parts unknown."

I took a breath. "You told him where to find *you*."

"And he bit! No way a determined, methodical, anal guy like that leaves town before crossing *my* name off his list. You know it's true, Doc. I'm his ultimate prize. The guy who first ID'd and bagged his idol, John Jessup."

Phone still at my ear, I gestured to Eleanor with my free hand to start the engine. We needed to get back on the road. Fast.

"Where are you meeting him, Lyle?"

He hesitated. "Ya gotta understand, I was makin' it up as I went along. Thinkin' fast, just tryin' to keep him talking. On the line."

"*Where*, Lyle?…"

"Look, I just said the first thing that popped in my head. Remember Braddock, where the Bureau had me stashed in that shitty Motel 6?"

"Yeah."

"When they brought me there, I noticed a big building just outside town. Some kind of abandoned steel mill."

"I saw it, too. Is that—?"

"I'm meetin' Randall at the main gate, east side of the building. The place looks like it's been deserted for years. Like on the edge of nowhere. I gave him an hour to get there. No cops, no Feds. Just him and me, *mano a mano*."

"My God, you're out of your fucking mind!"

"I guess *you'd* know, Doc. Anyway, I gotta go. Almost there. I just called because…"

I heard a rasping, exhausted intake of breath on the line. And wondered, for the hundredth time, how he was managing to stay upright.

"Look, Danny," he said quietly, "in case this thing goes sideways, do me a favor? Call up my son in Chicago and tell him… shit, just tell him his old man's sorry. About everything. Okay?"

I shouted into the phone. *"Lyle, don't! Please—"*

But the line had gone dead.

Chapter Forty-nine

I'd looked over at Eleanor, but hadn't had to say a word. She put her unmarked in gear, did a squealing U-turn and sped up the street, back the way we'd come. By the time we were driving up the highway on-ramp, she'd reached out her open window, put the mobile warning light on the roof, and hit the siren.

As we headed east, toward Braddock, I gave her a brief recap of what Barnes had said. And was on his way to do.

"Lunatic," was her only comment, before grabbing up her dashboard mike and calling for backup. From both the Pittsburgh PD and the Braddock local blues.

"Have them alert the FBI, too," I said. "If they can get past all the bullshit gatekeepers. Alcott and his people know the location."

As she explained the situation to the dispatcher in her clear, unhurried voice, I replayed my conversation with Barnes. Something else had finally become clear.

I'd always been troubled by the illogical pattern of the shootings. The geographic inefficiency of the order of the murders. First, Earl Cranshaw in Steubenville, Ohio. Then Judge Ralph Loftus here in Pittsburgh. Then back to Ohio—Cleveland, this time—for the initial failed attempt on ADA Claire Cobb.

I realized now that Harve Randall hadn't been interested in efficiency. He was killing those he held responsible for John Jessup's death *in ascending order of their importance*. At least, how *he* saw it in his supremely rational, deeply disturbed mind.

Cranshaw, the prison guard, may have been Jessup's actual assailant—the serial killer had died at *his* hands during that riot—but he hadn't been the one who put Jessup in prison. Cranshaw was merely a blunt instrument, as far as Randall was concerned. The smallest cog in the complex legal machinery that had victimized Jessup.

More important to Randall was Judge Loftus, the man who'd sentenced Jessup to prison. Then, one step higher up, Claire Cobb, the ambitious assistant district attorney who'd prosecuted him. Dave Parnelli, Jessup's ineffective defense attorney, was most likely to be next. Or else maybe the jury foreman. Regardless, there was no doubt who Harve Randall would want to save for last: Lyle Barnes, the famed FBI profiler who'd started that legal machinery going. The one most responsible for Jessup's ultimate fate.

Eleanor's terse voice interrupted my thoughts.

"Ya know, Danny, that call from Barnes doesn't make sense. He knows what he's doing with Randall is dangerous. Hell, it's *crazy*. So why call and tell you about it? Unless he wants you to *stop* him…"

I concentrated my gaze on the night-shrouded highway.

"I doubt it. Or else he wouldn't have waited till he was practically there to tell me. No, I'm afraid it's something else. Think about it. Barnes has nothing left in his life. No job, no family. In *his* view, anyway."

"Are you saying…?"

"Look, he knows there's a good chance he's not going to survive this encounter with Randall, and he—I think he intends to go out in a blaze of glory. And he wants *me* to bear witness to it." I paused. "He wants to feel at least one tug on the other end of the rope."

"What?"

"Nevermind."

Her hands tightened on the wheel. "Well, even if you're right, he's not gonna get his wish. You hearin' me, Danny? When we get to this old deserted mill or whatever, we stay in the car, wait for backup…"

"By that time, it may be too late. And you know it."

"Okay. Then *you* stay in the car, and I'll—"

"Not gonna happen, El. And you know *that*, too."

"For God's sake, *look* at you! You're the walking wounded. Remember, I *saw* how messed up you are—!"

I jabbed my forefinger toward the windshield.

"Here come the Braddock exits. Take the second one and hang a left."

Still fuming, she peered ahead, smoothly changing lanes and angling onto the correct off-ramp. Slowing just enough to keep us from going through the guardrail as we curved around, then speeding up again on the surface road.

"We're not through talkin' about this, Danny." As she wove in and out of traffic, oncoming vehicles moving to the curb before our wailing siren and flashing light.

"Maybe *you're* not, Detective, but *I* am. I'm going in after Barnes, with or without you. Feel free to arrest me afterwards."

Too focused on her driving to argue further, at least at the moment, she grudgingly followed my directions. Which I silently hoped, given my unfamiliarity with the town, would prove correct.

We'd gone a dozen blocks down the main steet when I spotted the abandoned steel mill I'd seen that time before, from the back seat of Alcott's town car. Its long, saw-toothed silhouette loomed black against the blacker night, the knobbed buildings and spindly towers like the bleak, skeletal remains of some huge prehistoric creature.

Eleanor had seen it too, and turned onto the next side street we came to. This led to an unlit, winding dirt road, at whose end was a corrugated metal sign that rose up suddenly from the darkness, ablaze in the glow of our headlights. Extruded block letters, stained and paint-flecked, indicated the twin entrances to the mill, east and west. We followed the arrow pointing east, and were soon rumbling along ice-encrusted gravel toward the sagging wire-mesh fence that formed a wide oval around the plant.

When we reached the east entrance, we passed through a tall, rusted gate which had recently been forced open. Its lower struts had gouged a curved groove in the frozen earth, and a chain dangled from the gate's broken lock.

A hundred yards ahead, two empty vehicles were parked at sharp angles to the massive steel doors of the east entrance. One was an unmarked sedan, presumably the car Barnes had stolen from the FBI motor pool. The other was a police cruiser, bearing the insignia of the Wheeling PD.

No other cars were in sight. Nor did I hear the sound of approaching sirens. Or FBI choppers.

I glanced over at Eleanor, who was slowly bringing her car to a stop behind the other two vehicles.

"Backup's not on-scene yet," she murmured, as much to herself as to me.

Almost at the same time, we peered up through the windshield at the shadowy expanse of buildings that stood, silent and implacable, before us. And whose length receded back into the maw of night, as though swallowed by it.

"Damned thing must be a mile long, all told." I squinted at the ribbed, elongated shapes and uneven array of smoke stacks. The windowless, black-bricked walls and slanted roofs.

I turned to Eleanor's profile.

"They're in there. Both of them." My voice an awed whisper, as though the dark, somber buildings themselves could hear. "Somewhere."

She nodded, lips pursed. Then she cut the engine, unholstered her service weapon, and opened her door. The ceiling light came on, bright, ghostly white.

I readied myself for another round of protests from Eleanor, but instead she merely looked at me. A kind of sad, knowing resignation in her eyes.

"C'mon, then."

Before I could respond, she'd unclipped a sturdy, department-issue flashlight from below the dashboard and tossed it to me.

Without another word, we got out of the car.

Chapter Fifty

There was no lock on the massive entrance doors, so I was able to carefully shove one of them open, its rusted hinges creaking, and we were inside.

I aimed my flashlight beam at the floor and spotted a thick industrial lock whose hasp had been twisted awry, as though by a crowbar. Or, more likely, a tire iron.

Eleanor read my mind. "Randall's armed with more than a gun."

She was right behind me, having withdrawn a small but powerful flashlight of her own from her belt. In her other hand was her service piece, a 9 mm Glock.

I took a few measured steps forward, the soles of my shoes scraping on the steel sheets that served as flooring. I shone my light ahead. The thin metal squares had been laid atop a concrete foundation like poorly-spaced tiles, their edges overlapping, creating a treacherous, uneven path beneath us. Combined with the freezing, unremitting darkness, they forced us to move excruciatingly slowly and carefully across the mill's expanse.

Fine with me, since my every movement brought a stab of pain. My ribs ached, and my shoulders were stiff, as though cased in cement. Plus I could barely turn my head.

All of which I did my best to hide from Eleanor.

Meanwhile, swinging my light in small, discrete arcs as we crept into its cavernous mouth, I slowly formed some kind of mental picture of the desolate structure. Huge machinery webbed with dust and grime, great coils of steel resting in shadowed corners. Piles of two-by-fours. Rusted trash bins. A row of foremen's cubicles lining one side, their Plexiglas walls cracked and smoke-stained.

From every corner came the hushed, skittering sounds of the mill's current inhabitants. Rats, mice. Raising the hairs on the back of my neck. Once, as I trained my flashlight beam across wire cables hanging haphazardly from the ceiling, a pair of bats flew out from some unseen perch. Startled, I reeled back. I also heard, right at my heels, Eleanor's muffled gasp of surprise.

But neither of us said a word. Not daring to speak, in case Randall was somewhere near enough to hear, Eleanor and I had been communicating with a series of shoulder taps. *Move left here, watch your step there.*

Turning, I looked into her violet eyes, shining in the glow of her upraised light. A kind of silent reassurance passed between us, then she lowered her flashlight again.

I exhaled slowly and went another few feet into the frigid, musty gloom, ears pricked for any telltale sound. Any fix on where either Randall or Barnes might be.

Suddenly, I heard something. Or *thought* I did. A panicked voice, crying out—?

Which made me careless. I hastened my steps and—

Collided with a thick, hanging chain. Rattling noisily in the dark, its cold, intertwined links raked my face. I stumbled backwards, then righted myself and traced its length with my flashlight. Attached to its end was a huge clawed hook that twisted and swayed from the impact.

Eleanor's fingers rested on my shoulder.

"You okay?" she whispered.

I nodded. Taking a breath, I trained my light upwards and caught sight, far above us, of a large overhead crane. Its glass-enclosed operator's cab hung like a dark cocoon from beneath twin wheeled tracks embedded in the ceiling. Two sets of those massive, twined chains—one of which I'd walked into—dangled from the floor of the cab.

Frustrated, I wiped my brow with my forearm. Risked the words. "At this rate, we'll never—"

We both heard it at the same time.

A gunshot. Echoing sharply. A metallic reverberation that shattered the opaque silence of the long-dead mill.

Eleanor pointed with her light. "This way!"

She took off at a run, heedless of the darkness and the maze of unseen obstacles. With effort, I caught up with her and grabbed her arm. She whirled, eyes wide.

I jerked my thumb to my right, and she immediately saw what I'd noticed. A long, raised conveyor belt that ran along the wall for half the length of the building. Its cracked, ribbed loading band stretched atop great, rivet-encircled wheels that hadn't turned in many, many years.

I gingerly climbed up on top of the belt, pulling her behind me. Ignoring the jolts of pain shooting up my injured arm. We'd just gotten to our feet on the broad, uneven band when a second shot rang out.

"Hurry!"

Eleanor raised her gun hand and started running again, down the length of the conveyor belt. I did the best I could to match her stride.

Then, abruptly, we reached the end of the belt's thick rubber tongue. It extended into a wide slot that fed a three-story-high array of machinery, all hinged struts and massive, time-frozen gears. Another opening to the right of the structure led to a cracked, sloping concrete ramp. Swinging my light wildly about, I soon found out why.

I nudged Eleanor and we both came to stand at the conveyor's edge. Below us, matching nearly the length of the belt, was what looked like an open subway tunnel. Twin locomotive tracks were embedded in its floor, at the end of which stood a flatbed train car. Steel wheels locked. Silent, dust-draped and long-stilled.

Along the tunnel's far side was a series of garage-sized, vertical-hanging iron doors. Something tugged at my memory, and I suddenly recalled hearing about them from a fellow undergrad at college, who'd spent summers working in a steel mill. Behind these doors, I realized, were vast brick ovens, fed by the adjacent blast furnace, in which new rolled steel was "cooked." Prepared to be shaped into car fenders, battleship plating, girders…

"Danny!" Eleanor's voice an urgent whisper. "Look!"

She played her flashlight beam across the width of the tunnel and aimed it at one of the iron doors. Though, at this distance, it was barely visible in the feeble light, I saw what she had seen. The door to the massive oven hung halfway down. Probably rusted in place a long time ago.

I knew instantly what she was thinking. From what we'd heard, the gunshots must've come from there.

Not taking time to think about it, I launched myself off the edge of the belt into the tunnel. Landing with bone-rattling impact between the set of train tracks, feet buried up to the calves in sand. I glanced back up at Eleanor. Then she too leapt from the belt.

I pointed my flashlight beam before us and we started moving awkwardly through caked, clumped sand that hadn't been disturbed in years. Using our outstretched arms for balance, we stumbled across the width of the tunnel to the far wall, then sidled quickly along its length till we came to the half-opened oven.

Though I said nothing to Eleanor as we clambered under the two-ton iron door, I would have welcomed the sound of another gunshot. Or any sound at all. It was the ominous silence that was worrying me.

Had Harve Randall finally done what he'd long planned? Was Lyle Barnes already dead?

I pushed such thoughts from my mind as I led Eleanor through the ink-black interior of the cold, dead oven. Our flashlight beams guiding our steps through charred rubble buried inches deep in coal dust. Finally, a crude opening—little more than a wide crack in the brickwork—was revealed by my light in the back wall. I went first, squeezing sideways through the jagged opening, dislodging small, crumbling bits of masonry. Eleanor followed.

There was a narrow brick-walled corridor on the other side, as dark and soul-chilling as every other part of the place. Not knowing which direction to go, I went left for ten or fifteen yards, until I came to an iron door blocked by boulder-sized rubble. So I reversed direction, leading Eleanor far down the passage to the other end.

Where we found another iron door. Opened.

Just as we were stepping through it—

Another gun shot. Loud. *Closer.*

Before I could react, Eleanor had crossed the door's threshold and begun running at full speed down another passage. I awkwardly gave chase, and almost collided with her when she abruptly stopped.

I peered past her shoulder and saw, through this second door, a narrow catwalk extending above and across a shadowed cluster of huge generators, multileveled ramps, and steam pumps. Racks of pressure valves. All silent, frozen in place, shrouded with coal dust. A graveyard of industrial debris. The unbeating heart of the old mill.

The catwalk's corroded, wire-mesh floor and sagging railings didn't inspire much confidence. But the shot had clearly come from the opened door at its far end.

I whirled to face her.

"We *have* to, El. *I* have to—"

She merely nodded. Turning back again, I made my way unsteadily across the catwalk, Eleanor on my heels. The thin wire mesh swayed and rolled under our combined weight, and I grabbed the metal railing to maintain balance.

Halfway across, the door at the other end drawing closer with every step, I felt that familiar surge of adrenaline. My heart thumped wildly in my chest. I knew we had to hurry, but I also knew we were going to make it—

Suddenly, behind me, I heard Eleanor cry out.

Startled, I almost dropped my flashlight. Clutching it hard in my fist, I turned—

Too late.

Her leg had broken through a part of the catwalk's mesh, and she was falling. Arms flailing, her gun flying from her grasp, she struggled to right herself. Grab hold of the railing.

I threw myself down on the wire flooring and stretched out my hand. Reaching for hers.

And clutched empty air.

I could only watch as Eleanor tumbled to a narrow ramp about a dozen feet below. She landed hard, on her knees, and then rolled to her side.

"El! El, are you all right?"

I looked frantically about me, swinging the flashlight beam, in search of a way down. All I saw was a clutch of coiled tubes, dusty motor casements, rows of blank dials.

"Danny!"

I aimed the light down and saw her waving feebly up at me. Her legs curled beneath her, her face etched with pain.

"El! Are you okay?"

She shifted position, testing her arms and legs.

"Yeah. Everything hurts, but I think I'm okay. I just gotta find my gun. It fell somewhere near here…"

"Soon as I find a way down—"

"No!" She raised her chin, so that her eyes leapt into view in my light. "Keep going! You've gotta find Barnes!"

"But—"

"Goddammit, Rinaldi! I'm fine! *Go!*"

I hesitated only a moment, then awkwardly got to my feet. I knew she was right, but…

Gulping air, I gripped the railing again and strode as quickly as I dared to the other end of the catwalk.

Once there, I shone my light through the door, which opened onto another small passage. Revealing a web-draped, iron-runged ladder. Leading up.

I grabbed either side of the ladder with both hands.

By now, blood had begun seeping through the bandages. My neck and shoulders screamed in protest at the smallest movement. Every muscle in my body ached. Every nerve was frayed.

I was done. Finished. Useless. To myself or anyone else. I knew this. In my mind and in my heart.

Then I thought about Clare Cobb.

And put my foot on the first rung...

I'd only climbed halfway up the ladder when I heard the voices. Hard, angry voices. Threaded with fear, panic.

I started climbing faster.

Chapter Fifty-one

The ladder reached up to some kind of wooden trap door. I pushed it open and cautiously crawled out into a frigid, starless night.

I was on the flat, tarred roof of the building, whose stark expanse was intermittently broken by towering smokestacks and huge, brick-backed chimneys.

I'd only a moment to register my new surroundings when another volley of shouts and frenzied cries pierced the darkness. I turned, bringing my flashlight up.

And saw them, maybe fifty feet away. Randall and Barnes, their bodies contorted in struggle. On their feet, arms locked. Faces obscured, gasping, cursing, they clashed like savage creatures in a dream. A nightmare.

I hurried toward the base of the nearest smokestack, as big around as a redwood, and crouched behind it. Now close enough to see that the two men were fighting over something in Randall's hands. Hard, black. A tire iron.

I stepped from behind the curved concrete tower, shining my light in their direction.

"Randall!"

Startled, Harve Randall turned toward me. Momentarily distracted, he lessened his grip on the tire iron. Giving Barnes the opportunity to wrest it from his opponent and swing mightily at Randall's head.

The younger man managed to duck at the last moment, and then threw himself out of my light's reach. Swallowed instantly by the cold, engulfing darkness.

Almost simultaneously, Lyle Barnes himself half ran, half stumbled out of the light. I swung the beam around and just caught sight of him, still gripping the tire iron, as he scrambled for the safety of another smokestack. Maybe a dozen yards from my own.

He didn't make it.

From out of the night came the roar and muzzle flash of a gun. Randall. Firing wildly at Barnes in the dark.

A strangled gasp not too far from me told me the FBI agent had been hit. I heard his staggering footsteps, and then the muffled rattle of the tire iron skittering across the roof.

"Lyle!"

Not a sound from Barnes. Nor another gunshot.

I had no idea what kind of gun Randall had now, so there was no way to know how many bullets he had left. Maybe the abrupt silence meant he was out of ammo. Or maybe it just meant he was reloading.

Casting my light about, I searched for some sign of the injured agent. Then, with barely a whisper of movement, Lyle Barnes was suddenly crouching at my side. Somehow he'd spotted me in the dark and made his way over.

"Jesus, Lyle!" My voice a soft, strained rasp.

"Good seein' *you* again, too, Doc."

I turned my light. His pale, fatigue-ravaged face was bruised, spotted with dirt and grime. Eyes a sickly yellow.

"Where are you hit?"

He raised his arm slightly. "Flesh wound, that's all. I've had worse, plenty o' times."

Regardless, I trained the light up and down his body. And noticed immediately that his orthopedic boot was gone.

"What's that wrapped around your ankle? Duct tape?"

He nodded. "Couldn't move in that goddam boot."

Suddenly, I heard a sharp, crackling sound. I craned my neck around and saw that something was sailing through the air, thrown from behind a squat, brick-walled chimney. Glowing orange, sizzling, trailing a ribbon of smoke.

I recognized it as soon as it fell to the roof and rolled to a stop. Harve Randall, hidden behind that chimney, had lit a roadside flare. Its bright, flickering light pulsed against the surrounding darkness.

Emboldened by its illumination, Randall leaned out from behind his hiding place and fired, twice. I ducked back as the bullets flew past us, one slug taking a small chunk out of the concrete inches from my face.

But I'd had my first good look, if only briefly, at Randall. He was wearing the same winter coat I'd last seen, when he'd driven off the precinct lot. I also recognized the gun he'd two-handed to shoot at us. A standard-issue police weapon, like Eleanor's. A 9 mm Glock.

I leaned back against the smokestack's unyielding concrete. Peered over at Barnes. He didn't look too good. Blood-soaked sleeve, skin lacerations, hand tremors. His glance back at me a strange, blasted stare.

"He's got us pinned down, son."

At a loss. "Hang in there, Lyle."

He offered me a wan smile, then stirred. Before I could stop him, he'd hoisted himself to his feet.

"Hey, Randall! Harve! You gonna kill *both* of us? I mean, hell, the doc here ain't done you any harm."

I rose, too. Gripped his shoulder.

"Dammit, Lyle—"

He shrugged me off. Called out again.

"I bet you think that means you're a *real* man at last. No more piggy-backing off the crimes of others. No more letting other killers do your dirty work."

I leaned hard against him. Got in his face.

"What the hell are you doing?"

"Situation like this, it never hurts to rattle 'em a little. They lose focus."

"But—"

Ignoring me, Barnes raised his voice even louder.

"Hey, Harve! I guess, once you shot Cranshaw, your first kill, shootin' the rest got easier. That's what the *other* whack-jobs like you tell me, anyway. Am I right?"

For the first time, Randall shouted back.

"You don't know what the fuck you're talkin' about, old man."

Barnes started to reply, but I covered his mouth.

"You're right, Harve," I called out. "He *doesn't* know what he's talking about. But *I* do. And so do you."

"You don't know shit, Rinaldi."

Barnes peeled my hand from his mouth, gave me an angry, puzzled look. But kept quiet.

"I know more than you think, Harve. For one thing, I know Earl Cranshaw *wasn't* your first kill."

Randall suddenly fell silent.

Steeling myself, I went on. "I'm right, aren't I, Harve? Your first kill happened *before* Cranshaw. It was when you killed a Wheeling businessman named Ed Meachem. Your father."

Another deep silence. Then: "You're crazy, Rinaldi, I don't—"

"Meachem was your father, all right. I can prove it!"

And I could. Before I left the Wheeling precinct, I'd taken a strand of Randall's hair from his other jacket, hanging on the coat rack. As soon as Henry Stiles isolated its DNA, and it was matched to that taken from Meachem's remains, the police could establish paternity.

"You can't prove nothin'!"

I knew I had to keep going. Keep him riveted, stunned and angry, where he was. Keep him from storming across that roof toward us, gun blazing.

"You just found out yourself, eh, Harve? That one and only time you visited your mother in the hospital."

"Goddam you, shut up!"

"Poor Doreen. In *your* eyes, nothing but a hooker who abandoned you as a child. Who you refused to acknowledge your whole life. Until she was dying, and you went to see her. And made her tell you the truth about your father."

"I said, *shut the fuck up!*—"

For the first time, his voice had cracked. His level of agitation rising.

No surprise. I could only imagine what he felt. Raised in brutal foster homes, while his actual father went on with his privileged life. Playing the loving family man to the hilt. Rich, well-regarded. A pillar of the community. No one suspecting that he'd once fathered a child with a prostitute and then abandoned them both.

"That's why you killed him," I shouted. "And then got Wes Currim to take the fall for it. You knew all about him. You also knew how devoted he was to his mother. So you threatened to kill Maggie Currim unless Wes confessed to a crime he didn't commit."

"You think you're so fucking smart…"

No, I thought, just smart enough to finally believe Maggie. Wes was so willing to protect her, he even accused her of lying when she claimed he'd been with *her* the night of Meachem's murder. Which was where he'd actually been.

"That's why you tried to kill me when I came to Wheeling to talk with Wes." I kept pressing him. "It was *you* that ran me off the road. You were afraid I might somehow get Wes to change his story, tell the truth about who really killed Ed Meachem."

Suddenly, I was aware of Barnes moving away from me. Slowly, cautiously. His back to the smokestack, inching around its curve toward the other side.

I turned, caught his eye.

He smiled at my quizzical look. "Good job, Danny. Keep him talkin'…"

Then he pointed toward a patch of roof just beyond, and something barely visible in the flare's sputtering light. Glinting dully. The tire iron.

"No, Lyle!" I whispered. "Don't—"

"Piece o' cake."

"NO!…"

He bent and pushed off, moving as quickly as he could toward the makeshift weapon. His hobbling figure suddenly backlit by the road flare. In the open. Exposed.

Harve Randall stepped easily from behind the chimney, aimed and fired. With an agonized cry, Barnes went down.

I leapt from behind the smokestack, flashlight held like a cudgel, and lurched forward into that same light. Randall turned and pointed his gun at me.

I stopped dead, staring into the muzzle of his gun.

Not ten feet away from where Lyle Barnes writhed on the hard, cinder-strewn surface of the roof. Bathed in a sickening, dying light.

Harve Randall motioned with his gun for me to step back. Then he indicated the heavy flashlight still gripped in my blood-smeared hand.

"*Lose* that sucker. Now!"

I hesitated, torn. But didn't see much choice. Letting my arm drop, I wearily tossed the flashlight into the darkness surrounding us. Heard it roll noisily to a stop.

Randall smirked, then calmly approached Barnes, who was clutching his stomach with both hands.

"Gut shot, eh?" Randall leaned over him, smiling. "Jesus, Barnes, that's gotta hurt like hell."

I stood frozen, impotent, mind racing. I couldn't let it happen again. Like with Claire Cobb. I *couldn't…*

Meanwhile, Randall kept swiveling his head, looking down at Barnes, then over to me, and back again. As though unsure who to kill first.

It was then that I heard it. The wail of police sirens, approaching fast.

I risked a glance over the lip of the roof, and could see three police cruisers, lights flashing, barreling down that same access road. On their way here.

"That's it, Randall," I called to him. "It's over."

His laugh was bitter, mirthless. Resigned.

"It's over when I say so, Rinaldi. Which will be when I've killed this son-of-a-bitch here, and put any leftover slugs in *your* skull. *Then* it'll be over."

"Maybe. But *you'll* be done, too."

Randall shrugged. "Like I give a fuck. I did what I wanted to do. Needed to do. Especially since my whore of a mother is gonna die any minute now."

He looked off, reflectve. "Though I *would* like to stick around long enough to see that. Watch the life go outta that fuckin' cunt. *That'd* be sweet."

The sirens grew louder, closer.

Randall straightened his shoulders. "Guess we'll just have to see how it all plays out. Meanwhile, I got me a G-man to kill..."

He took hold of his gun with both hands and aimed at Barnes' head. The agent lay silent, curled in a fetal position, and I realized he'd probably lost consciousness.

I swallowed hard. Muscles tensed, I tried to gauge the distance between Randall and me. Could I even make it?...

Suddenly, a clear, commanding voice pierced the night air.

"Police, Randall! Drop your weapon!"

I turned at the same time Randall did, both of us staring mutely at Eleanor Lowrey, two-handing her Glock. Leaning against a smokestack's support strut, obviously in pain, she had her gun leveled directly at the killer.

"I mean it, asshole. Drop the fucking gun!"

Randall hesitated only a moment, then whirled, bringing his own weapon up. He never had the chance to shoot.

Eleanor fired, twice. Randall cried out, staggering backwards, and then his knees gave out. He fell, clutching his chest, blood seeping between his fingers.

I stared at Eleanor. "But how—?"

"Found my gun. Found you."

As Eleanor came limping over, her gun still trained on Randall, I hurried to where Barnes lay. Blood oozed slowly from his gut, spreading in rivulets.

"El!" I called to her. "Get an ambulance!"

"I'm on it." She was already hitting buttons on her cell phone.

Meanwhile, I could hear the sounds of police cruisers squealing to a stop down below in the lot. Could see the angled reflection of the turning lights flicker against the opaque, untroubled sky.

Then, to my surprise, I heard Randall's voice. Hoarse, choked. The rasp of a dying man.

"Doc…"

I exchanged puzzled looks with Eleanor, but, for some reason, got to my feet. Went over to where Randall lay.

As I bent over him, he grabbed my coat collar with a feeble hand. Though there was no mistaking the urgency in his eyes.

"Doc…" His voice already weaker. Fading.

With a supreme effort, he pulled me down closer to him. Positioned my ear to his thin, parched lips.

He had perhaps a minute more to live. Maybe not even that. But it was enough time for him to whisper something in my ear.

Chapter Fifty-two

As I'd expected, Harve Randall died at the scene from his wounds. As I'd hoped, Lyle Barnes didn't.

Though he remained unconscious throughout the entire ambulance ride to Pittsburgh Memorial. Secured in a gurney, his face ashen, he didn't respond as the stoic EMT worked on him.

"How bad?"

I sat opposite in the cramped compartment, hanging on to a ceiling strap as the ambulance raced west to town. Eleanor sat next to me.

"Bad enough." The EMT had finished bandaging Barnes' wounds and was running an IV drip. "But his vitals are good. I think he'll make it."

Eleanor exhaled deeply. "Thank God. Sure looked bad."

I turned to her. "How about you?"

"Just sore. All over."

I put my arm around her. "I can relate to that. But it's best to let them check you out, too. You took a helluva fall in that place."

She held a Styrofoam cup of hot coffee in both hands. Put it to her lips.

"The *real* pain comes later," she said. "The IA review. Officer-involved shooting."

"You kidding? They'll probably give you a medal."

Which, in fact, they did.

◇◇◇

From the moment Randall died, his fist still clutching my coat, everything seemed to happen at once. Cops from two different jurisdictions swarmed the rooftop, guns drawn, flashlights like miniature suns threading the darkness.

Eleanor and I stood together, off to one side, as she made her initial report to the detective in charge. Then came the EMT team, attending first to Barnes, then to Eleanor and me. Then the medical examiner, pronouncing on Randall. And the crime scene unit. A cacophony of hard voices, boots scraping the cindered tar, equipment bags snapping open and then shut. The controlled, practiced chaos of veteran police personnel working a crime scene.

The last thing I remember, as Eleanor and I followed behind Barnes on his stretcher, was the sight of Harve Randall being zipped into a body bag.

Now, in the sudden stillness of the ambulance, as Eleanor rested her head on my shoulder and the EMT busily wrote in his chart, I found myself staring down at Lyle Barnes. FBI, retired. Features hidden behind an oxygen mask. Except for those steely, knowing eyes, now closed in slumber. For the first time, I realized, in too many days to count.

◇◇◇

Sunday brought a welcomed rise in temperature, along with what I imagined was a collective sigh of relief from the entire city. One I was happy to share.

I'd spent the morning giving my statement about the previous night's events to the cops, then been driven home.

After a long shower, I somewhat clumsily retaped my ribs and rebandaged my hands. Then threw on some sweats, made a huge pot of coffee, and settled down in front of the tube. Ready for the media circus to begin. I wasn't disappointed.

Randall's death at the hands of a Pittsburgh PD detective led every newscast and, I presumed, every online report. District Attorney Leland Sinclair and Chief Logan held a joint press conference at noon, taking turns congratulating each other on the successful conclusion to the case. Not surprisingly, no representative of the FBI shared the podium.

"Harve Randall's reign of terror has ended," Sinclair pronounced. "Justice has been done."

Chief Logan then expressed his sincere admiration for Detective Eleanor Lowrey, whose brave actions would undoubtably earn her a special commendation.

Follow-up news stories presented details of Harve Randall's life, at least what little was known so far. As well as biographical recaps of his murdered victims, including their unusual mutual connection to a little-known serial killer named John Jessup.

The final story featured video of the FBI's Deputy Director, announcing that the remaining people presumed to have been on Randall's hitlist were being released from the bureau's safehouse. And that all concerned were relieved to be out of danger, and looking forward to returning to their regular routines.

Especially ADA Dave Parnelli, I thought. I bet he couldn't wait to get back to town and make his way to the nearest bar.

Notable for its absence was any mention of Randall's *first* victim, Wheeling businessman Ed Meachem. My guess was, in response to what I'd told Lieutenant Biegler this morning, that crime was still being investigated, in cooperation with Wheeling PD. Perhaps nothing would move forward until Henry Stiles isolated Randall's DNA, and it was compared to that of Meachem.

Meanwhile, tomorrow was Monday, and I was looking forward to getting back to work. Practicing therapy. Living my real life.

I smiled at the comforting image, even though I knew damned well that this wasn't likely to happen. Not yet, anyway.

Not once I'd made the lone call I'd been dreading since I first got home.

◇◇◇

I made myself a ham and swiss on rye and sat at the kitchen table. Coffee and a sandwich. My old man's favorite meal, any time of the day. Until the sun went down and the Jim Beam came out.

Jesus, my dad the beat cop. What he'd make of me, of how I'd turned out, I couldn't begin to guess.

Thankfully, my cell rang just then, preventing my thoughts from following their customary slide into melancholy. At least where my late father was concerned.

I checked the phone display. Noah Frye.

"Hey, Danny, I see you took my advice and got back into the crime-bustin' business."

"Not this time, Noah. I was more the innocent bystander. Detective Lowrey took Randall down."

"Whatever. You were there and the crazy bastard is dead. Good enough for me. Next time you come in, drinks are on the house."

"Thanks, man."

"But stay away from Charlene, okay? She's really pissed that you risked your life again, playin' hero. I mean, hell, she's givin' *me* all kinds o' shit about it, and I wasn't even there."

"Things are tough all over, Noah."

He snorted. "*That* the kinda stuff you say to your patients? If so, dude, you're stealin' their money."

My cell beeped as another call came in.

"Gotta go." I clicked over to the other line. Eleanor.

"They just released me from the hospital, Danny. I'm fine. Just like I thought."

"That's great, El."

"And guess who came by to check on me? Chief Logan. They're giving me a commendation."

"You've earned it."

"Maybe. Though, to be fair, I oughtta share it with you."

"Bullshit. I'm really happy for you."

Her voice grew quiet, pensive. "Listen, Danny…I figured, since the chief was there, it was a good time to ask for a leave of absence. Logan signed off on it right away. He said I definitely deserved some R and R."

"How long?"

"I asked for six months. And I got it."

I paused, feeling an odd tightness in my chest.

"My mom needs my help, Danny. You know that. With my brother Teddy and his kids. This is a rough time."

"I know."

"But I'll stay in touch. I promise."

We shared a long, awkward beat of silence.

"Take care of yourself, Eleanor."

"You, too, Danny."

We hung up.

◇◇◇

I spent the rest of the afternoon fielding more phone calls. The first was from Stu Biegler, asking me to come down to the Old County Building the next morning for more questions.

"Better figure on being available another day or two," the lieutenant said importantly. "I know Alcott wants a follow-up, too."

"You mean I get to hang out with both you *and* Agent Alcott? Gee, that sounds like fun."

He grunted. "Just make sure you're here early."

"Right. By the way, how's Harry Polk?"

"Doing fine, last I heard. Should be back at work in a couple weeks."

"Tell him I send my best."

"Screw you, Rinaldi. Tell him yourself." *Click.*

The next dozen calls came from various news outlets. Local, national. Print, radio, TV. My landline here as well as my office phone. I let the answering machine and my voice mail take them all.

Then, finally, as I nursed a beer out on the deck and watched the sunlight fade over the Three Rivers, my cell rang. Angie Villanova. The call I'd been waiting for.

"Danny, you watchin' the news?"

"Kinda burned out on it. What's up?"

"They just reported that Harve Randall was also responsible for Ed Meachem's death. The Wheeling DA confirmed the DNA match with Meachem. They're father and son. You were right, Danny!"

"Still, that doesn't prove Randall killed him."

"Maybe not, but I just heard from Maggie Currim. She says the DA dropped the charges against her son Wes."

"You mean they finally believed Maggie about Wes being with her that night?"

"Not only that, but when Wes was told about Randall's death, he broke down and admitted everything. That it was Randall who'd really killed Meachem, and that he'd forced Wes to take the fall for it. Maggie says Wes was actually weeping with relief."

"I'll bet he was."

"One last thing. They're releasing Wes from prison tomorrow afternoon. Takes that long to process out a county prisoner down there, I guess. Anyway, Maggie's so grateful, she wants you to be there when it happens. So what do ya say? I figure you owe her for doubtin' her story."

"Only at first."

"Big deal. What do ya want, a parade? I *told* ya I had a good feelin' about her."

"And you were right. Tell Maggie I'll be there. That I wouldn't miss it for the world."

Chapter Fifty-three

"Why is it taking so long?"

Maggie Currim, wearing a new winter coat and with more color in her cheeks than I'd seen before, tapped her foot.

"I'm sure there's a ton of paperwork, Maggie."

We were sitting side by side in the waiting area of the Marshall County Prison, whose walls glowed a pale green under the hanging fluorescents. We occupied the only sofa in the sterile room. A bland-looking prison official sat on one of the three folding chairs, while an equally bland desk officer manned a cluttered cubicle.

Wes Currim's two older brothers were conspicuous by their absence.

"They're both so busy with the business," Maggie had explained earlier. "It's a Monday, after all."

She'd also explained that she wanted to greet Wes herself, privately, when he came through the cell block door. Before they went out to the front of the prison, where his attorney, Willard Hansen—along with a crowd of reporters and TV news crews—waited. Apparently, Hansen had orchestrated Wes' release into a pretty impressive media event.

I'd spent my day somewhat differently, giving repeated accounts of the past two weeks to both Pittsburgh PD and the FBI. Though I spoke with a Bureau agent I'd never met before. When I asked about Neal Alcott, I was told he'd been called suddenly to Quantico. I figured his superiors weren't too happy that it was a lowly Pittsburgh cop, and not the bureau, that had taken down Harve Randall.

After giving my statements, I drove a second rental car down here to Wheeling. But not before checking in with the auto repair place. The service manager told me on the phone that he didn't have an estimate yet for my Mustang, but assured me he'd do everything possible to keep costs down. Which didn't sound good.

Yet now, sitting next to Maggie Currim, aware of her palpable anxiety, I realized how little such things mattered. Not when compared to what was about to happen in this room.

I'd no sooner had that thought when the door to the cell block swung open. Wes Currim, in street clothes once more, was escorted out by a guard.

"Mom!"

Wes was halfway across the floor by the time Maggie got to her feet. Both bursting into tears, mother and son hugged each other fiercely. Even the desk officer's eyebrows went up. Their impassioned embrace was probably not an everyday occurrence around here.

I stood as well, but stayed where I was. Waiting.

Maggie Currim and her son finally stepped apart, though she did so reluctantly. Keeping her hands still on her son's slender arms. Rubbing them up and down, as though to confirm the evidence of her own eyes. That he was really here, really free.

It was then that the outer door, on the far side of the room, opened. Chief Avery Block, Wheeling PD, his face a grim mask, strode in. Followed by two uniforms, each with his hand on his holstered gun.

Maggie blinked over at the Chief, surprised. Arms dropping to her sides.

Block ignored her and approached Wes.

"Chief Block..." Wes tried on a grin. "You came by to see me outta here?"

Block's voice was as cold as the deep winter's chill.

"We *know*, Wes. We found the bodies."

"What?" Wes Currim blanched.

His mother struggled to find words.

"Bodies…? What do you mean—?"

I came over then, gently took her hands in mine.

"I'm so sorry, Maggie. I didn't know for sure till Chief Block came through that door. It meant he'd found them. Right where Harve Randall said they'd be."

"I…I don't understand…"

Wes Currim shrank back against the cell block door.

"Don't listen to him, Mom! He don't know nothin'—"

But Maggie kept her gaze on mine. "*What* bodies…?"

I took a breath.

"Your husband Jack. And the girl he ran away with. Lily Greer. Wes killed them, and buried them in the yard behind his uncle's house. That's why they were never found. Why no one knew where they'd gone."

Her mouth sagged open. She aged a decade in the space of a moment, right before my eyes.

"No…that *can't* be…"

"Mom!" Wes spit out the word, half cry, half rage. Then looked wildly about, suddenly trapped. Desperate for a way out. But there wasn't any.

"Mom, *please!*" he shouted again, as the two Wheeling officers closed in on him. In moments, his hands had been cuffed behind his back.

Maggie Currim could hardly stand, weaving as though about to faint. I glanced quickly at Chief Block, who stepped over and helped me get her to the sofa.

Block gave her a brief, pitying look, then turned his somber eyes on me.

"I couldn't believe it when you called me, Doc. But Jack and the Greer girl were right where you said they'd be. In the back yard, near the south fence post. Five, six feet down."

"Just like Randall told me. When he was dying. He said I was wrong about how he got Wes to take the blame for Meachem.

He didn't threaten to kill Maggie. He threatened to tell her that Wes had killed her husband."

"But how did Randall know?"

"He said he'd been tailing Wes in his truck a couple years back, figuring he was on a drug run. Instead, Wes drove out to the old farmhouse, where Randall saw him take two bodies from the back of the truck. Randall knew who they were, of course. Everybody in town knew that Jack Currim had run off with his secretary. But Randall didn't do a thing. Just watched Wes get a shovel and bury them near the fence post."

Block scratched his bulbous nose.

"But why?"

"Randall died before he could say any more. I'd guess he wanted to have something on Wes. Something he could use if he ever needed a fall guy."

I turned to Wes Currim, who'd slumped a bit in the firm grip of his two captors. "Am I right?"

He nodded miserably.

"Harve Randall…that prick…one day last month, outta the blue, he pulls up in that piece o' shit pickup of his…"

I knew it well, having seen it in my rear view mirror when Randall had run me off the road.

"Anyway, Harve says he got some guy in the back, guy named Meachem he snatched from a parking lot and knocked out. Says he needs my help. I tell him to go fuck himself, but then he says he knows what I did. Where I planted the bodies. And that he'd tell my mother everything."

At this, Maggie Currim roused herself. Looked up from her seat at her youngest son. Staring in wonderment, as though she'd never seen him before.

"But, Wesley…how *could* you? Jack was your father…"

"*He was a fucking shit, Mom*! And you *know* it! Look how he treated you all those years. Then he takes off with that skanky bitch…" His voice trailed off.

"How'd it go down, Wes?" Chief Block asked.

"I overheard my old man tell Mom about him and Lily. Though I suspected he'd been cheatin' on her for weeks. Anyway, it was just dumb luck that I spotted the two of 'em the next day. Comin' outta City Hall…"

"Where Lily had just applied for a passport," I said. "I assume Jack already had one."

Wes threw me a surly glance. "Yeah. From when he took that one business trip to Tokyo, years ago. Got some deal on auto parts and hadda go himself."

The chief spoke again. "Is that when you grabbed them, Wes? Outside City Hall?"

"Nah. I followed 'em to some shitty motel, way outta town. Place was practically empty, that time o' day. I got my rifle outta my truck, knocked on the door of their room. Marched 'em outside, around back. Bang-bang, they're dead. Nobody hears nothin'. Then I load 'em in the truck and head out to my uncle's place. Who the fuck figures Randall sees me, follows me?…I mean, *fuck*, right?"

I collected my thoughts. This explained why Lily Greer had never returned to collect her passport. She was dead. Funny, I'd been wrong about Jack and Lily. They *had* decided to go abroad, maybe permanently. The awful irony was what I'd been *right* about. The two had indeed never left US soil. They'd been buried beneath it.

Maggie had said nothing during Wes' entire narrative. She merely sat, as I'd seen her do before, with her hands on her lap, fingers twisting convulsively.

Her son, caught up in telling his story, seemed not to have noticed. Until then. Restrained by officers on either side, he leaned toward her.

"Don't you see, Mom? I *couldn't* let 'em get away with it. I couldn't let him *do* that to you!"

"But I *loved* your father, with all my heart. Despite everything, I loved him…You *knew* that!"

"Yeah…just like I knew you'd never forgive me if you found out what I did. Harve knew it, too. Knew I'd do *anything* to keep you from findin' out. Even go to prison for a crime I didn't commit. Even *that*…" Voice choked.

Fresh tears welling in his eyes. "As long as it meant you still loved me…that you'd never have a reason to hate me instead…"

He bent lower, face near to hers. And wept.

His mother took a long time before answering. "I…I *couldn't* hate you, Wesley. But I'm afraid you may be right. I don't know if I can ever forgive you…"

Maggie averted her eyes, as though to hide from him her own agony. Her nameless grief.

For his part, Wes drew himself up, face gone flat, expressionless. Seemingly oblivious now to the officers guarding him. Even of the cuffs binding his arms behind his back.

The leaden silence was broken by Chief Block, who noisily cleared his throat.

"Who cut up Ed Meachem, Wes? That was one goddam nasty piece o' work. Was that you?"

"No." His voice now strangely calm, sure. "Harve did that. Up at the house, in the kitchen. Just as Meachem was comin' to, Harve took a big ol' carving knife and hacked him to pieces. Looked like he was enjoyin' himself, too."

A shrug. "Then he stuck the knife in his belt and we hightailed it back to town. And then I drove over to my mom's to help her clean out the attic. Just like I promised. I'm a *good* son, Chief. Ask anybody."

Block merely stared at him. "Jesus Christ."

Sighing, he took a stick of nicotine gum from his coat pocket and slowly unwrapped it. Popped it in his mouth. Then he nodded to his officers, and they began leading Wes Currim out of the room.

I stopped them, my hand gripping Wes' shoulder. I had to ask.

"What about Meachem's head, Wes? Whose idea was it to put it on the snowman?"

Something flickered in his eyes. Something strange, unsettling. Then his face broke into a grotesque grin.

"It was *mine*, Doc. Like I told ya before. Not even the Handyman ever did shit like that. The thing with the head… *That was all mine.*"

Wes was still smiling about it as they led him away.

Chapter Fifty-four

Lyle Barnes was looking better. He'd been moved from ICU, and now had a private room at Pittsburgh Memorial.

"The bureau has a great health plan," he'd explained soon after I showed up. It was midafternoon, three days later, and a blinding sun bathed the spacious room with cool, unstained light.

Though hampered by a tangle of wires and tubes, he animatedly discussed his prognosis, which, he assured me, was good, despite the incompetence of his doctors.

"When I get outta here, I'm gonna research surgical protocols. No way my gut should still hurt this bad."

"Lyle, as your therapist, I have to tell you: You're an idiot. You took a bullet at close range, the surgery was a success, and you're lucky to be alive. Deal with it."

He frowned, shifting position under the bedsheets. He moved with obvious discomfort, but his face had resumed a reasonably human pallor. And his eyes were clear.

"I heard about that kid in Wheeling. Wes Currim. Some weird stuff you get yourself mixed up in, son."

"Not by choice, I assure you."

He looked skeptical. "I don't know...I'm stickin' with my initial interpretation. Civilian with a hero complex."

"Gimme a break."

"Speakin' of heroics, I got a call from the director yesterday. He says he's recommending me for some kinda medal. 'Retired Agent of the Year,' or some shit."

"Great. I think both you *and* Detective Lowrey deserve credit for Randall."

"Maybe. But the thing is, I gotta sign something that forbids me to discuss the case, or my unsanctioned actions, with anyone. Especially the media. Total nondisclosure. Can you believe that crap?"

"Nothing about the bureau surprises me. Not anymore."

He smiled. "I've taught you well, Grasshopper."

We chatted a few more minutes, until I noticed his voice faltering.

"Look, Lyle, I better go. You should rest."

"Hey, that reminds me. I didn't have any night terrors the whole time I was out of it. Not even during surgery. Think I got cured?"

"I think you got shot. We've still got a lot of work ahead of us. And someday, if you're a good patient, I'll explain the difference between sleeping and sedation."

"And I'll teach *you* the difference between a Hallmark card and classic poetry."

He shakily offered me his hand. I took it.

"Deal."

◇◇◇

I crossed town in my new rental beneath a crystalline, cloudless sky, heading for Mt. Washington. And home. According to the auto shop in Wheeling, it would take at least another week to repair my Mustang. And, as I'd guessed, it wasn't going to be cheap.

I headed toward the bridge, traffic already clogging the on-ramp. The improving weather had obviously prompted more people to get out and about.

I tapped my fingers on the wheel. After all that'd happened, my thoughts kept returning to Eleanor Lowrey. And what the future would bring. If anything.

Until I realized I was too tired to think about it. Or much else. And too beat up. Though I'd removed the bandages from my hands, my ribs were still taped and my neck still hurt like hell.

All I wanted to do now was get home, pour myself a tall drink, and watch the setting sun give the Three Rivers its nightly coat of many colors.

Tomorrow, it was back to work. Seeing my patients, especially those traumatized by physical violence and emotional pain, victimized by the brutality of crime and its aftermath. These included—as soon as he was well enough—retired FBI agent Lyle Barnes. I truly hoped to someday rid him of his night terrors.

Regardless, given the events of the past weeks, I knew one thing for certain. There were enough terrors in *waking* life to occupy me for a long time to come.

To receive a free catalog of Poisoned Pen Press titles, please contact us in one of the following ways:

Phone: 1-800-421-3976
Facsimile: 1-480-949-1707
Email: info@poisonedpenpress.com
Website: www.poisonedpenpress.com

Poisoned Pen Press
6962 E. First Ave. Ste 103
Scottsdale, AZ 85251